HOHAs *in* LOVE

a novel

Laurence Graham

FIRST 49 PRESS

NEW YORK

First 49 Press
www.first49press.com

HOHAs in Love is a work of fiction. The persons, places, and particulars that it portrays are the products of the author's fantasy and are used fictitiously. Any resemblance to actual persons, places, and particulars is completely coincidental.

Publisher's Cataloging-in-Publication

Graham, Laurence.
   HOHAs in love / Laurence Graham.
      p. cm.
   LCCN 2010920545
   ISBN-13: 978-0-9826258-0-4
   ISBN-10: 0-9826258-0-4

   1. Long-distance runners--Fiction. 2. Running--Fiction. 3. Hoboken (N.J.)--Fiction. 4. Love stories. I. Title.

PS3607.R342H64 2010   813'.6
                  QBI10–600021

When we walk,
one foot is always on the ground;
but when we run, there is a moment,
as brief as it may be,
when both feet are in the air,
and we can truly say we fly.

COACH

Falling in love
is like climbing a tree:
it is easy to get up
and hard to get down.

GLORIA

Go in your own direction,
and go at your own speed.
Now look around.
The place you see is your home.
The people you see are your friends.

BISCUIT

Running isn't just some sport, Grandma.
Running is a way of life.

ANDY

We don't win when others fail.
We only win when we don't fail our self.

MOSES

Death: it is nothing;
it just finish Chuck off.
But love: Oh my God!
It play with Chuck first.

CHUCK

If you need a hand,
I have two:
one for me
and one for you.

JUNE

Time is a master magician.
It distracts us with one hand,
while playing its trick with the other.
It holds out the future,
while stealing our past.

UNCLE BILL

for

Paul F. Peacock

for

Olivia Graham

and for

runners everywhere

HOHAs in LOVE

CONTENTS

DESIRES   109

DREAMS 227

1. On Your Mark

EMMITT F. BEAN, the founder, first president, and coach of the Hoboken Harriers Running Club—or the HOHAs, as the club affectionately came to be known—was a visionary, a goofball, and the luckiest man alive. Coach was one of those young men—rare, yet belonging to every generation—who believe that anything is possible and that by thinking positively enough and working hard enough we can overcome any obstacle, vanquish any opponent, and achieve success on our own terms. Young men like Coach apply their can-do philosophy to endeavors as varied as science, business, politics, art, and even sports. Indeed, Coach's love was for sports, and he believed that running was the purest of sports and therefore most worthy of his passion and energies.

Running is pure, Coach believed, because it exists only in space and time. There is no ball, puck, bat, net, or even a field. There is just a starting line, a finishing line, and the time that separates them. It is nothing less than birth, death, and the valiant struggle in between. The start is innocence, the finish exhaustion, but oh how our blood rages and struggles on its course. Coach believed that the purity of this struggle is the meaning of success, and purity means giving all one's mind, body, and heart to the practice of running.

None of this was unique to Coach or to the runners he attracted and trained. Wise men before him had taught that if we truly know one small thing through and through, we know all things. But Coach didn't care for wise men before him, or for anything other than running. His passion itself was pure, and that passion was his blessing and his lesson and his gift to all he met.

In the spring of 1990, events unfolded and destiny swung its doors wide to bring young Coach to the little city of Hoboken, New Jersey. Hoboken is a square-mile patch of land tucked cozy between palisades and the Hudson River, across from the heart of Manhattan. From Hoboken, looking across the wide expanse of the Hudson, Manhattan looks like a castle rising above its moat. When the wind blows hard from the north, as it often does, the passing clouds make the castle even grander and more imposing in its granite stillness, and each day when the sun appears, the shadow of its central tower—the symbol of the Empire State—falls across the moat and wakes its humble neighbor with its shadowy spire.

It's tough for a little city to be in the shadow of a big one. It becomes a Cinderella in a way, doing a portion of the dirty work for the big sister. And Hoboken, with its factories and railroads and shipyards, did a lot of that dirty work over the years. But of all the hardworking cities and boroughs in the shadow of Manhattan, the Mile Square City was able to shine some stars of its own. Magic can happen beyond the spotlight, and the Gods often work their wonders in the wings.

When one enters Hoboken from the North, on the road that winds from the town of Weehawken, there is a sign—as there is at the limits of many proud, plucky places—that welcomes visitors and announces its claim to fame. Hoboken's sign, painted a clean white with cheerful blue lettering, says "Welcome to Hoboken—Birthplace of Baseball & Frank Sinatra."

Hoboken is not just Beantown, the Halibut Capital or the Cucumber King. It's the birthplace of America's game, a game played without a clock, under a summer sky, a sky big enough to hold any dream. And Hoboken is the birthplace of one of America's great dreamers, a boy with teenage sass, adult bravado, and old-age charm, who out of a modern cynicism in the wake of war still sang of love, of endless hope, and of even bigger dreams.

There's more to any town than what is printed on a sign, of course, just as there is more to a man's life than he can proclaim on a bumper sticker. Compared with Manhattan—the birthplace of much of America's history and of many great men—Hoboken's hard work and accomplishments may not seem like much. But for a scrappy little mile-square city, that sign said a lot.

When Coach arrived, he saw rising up—as if newborn—rows of brownstone apartments, bustling businesses, and busy streets. He did not see Hoboken's scrappy past. How could it have even existed before he arrived? Nor did he know then of its small claims to fame. What did any of that have to do with him? Coach had come to Hoboken to found a running club, and found a running club he would.

This is the story of Coach, of his club, of the runners who came to join it, and of the seemingly disparate events that led to what Coach would then view as their ultimate downfall. Children are beset with measles and mumps, the elderly with arthritis and gout, but it is our life in between—when our blood surges and we are pummeled by storms of passion—that is most dangerous. No man, and no plan of man—small successes notwithstanding—can hold strong against life and all its mystical forces—forces that can drive us from our own minds and lay waste to all our plans. Through the calmness, in the gentle turning of the seasons, there came rains of hope and snows of despair. Out of the quiet, through the darkness, there came phone calls in the night. From distant places, from times forgotten, they came with fears and dreams. Really, what chance did Coach have? Despite all of Coach's talent, hard work, and meticulous planning, his beloved Hoboken Harriers, and Coach himself, were finally undone, or so it seemed, by the trickiest, the most befuddling, and the most powerful life force of them all. This is the story of HOHAs in love.

HOHAs *in* LOVE

VISIONS

Coach saw not what Hoboken had been—he didn't
care—or even what it was—that mattered just as
little—but only what he would make it to be.

HOHAs *in* LOVE

2. Ninety Miles

RIDGEWOOD, NEW JERSEY, 2047—"On a journey of one hundred miles, consider ninety miles half way." That was the ancient wisdom, and the lesson, Bill knew, was to stay focused at the end, where with victory almost yours, all could still be lost.

On suburban streets shaded with old elms in Northern New Jersey, Bill had mapped out a short training course. This particular morning was relatively dry and cool, a respite from the muggy heat typical of the Northeast in summer, and Bill had decided to take advantage of the weather and run his training course as a time trial. It had been a while since he had tested his speed, and he was running well that day, but now, only a block from the finish, exhaustion was overcoming him. His legs were on fire and his lungs were ready to explode. Every cell in his body was screaming for relief.

"Pain is your friend; you can always count on it." Bill remembered Coach's words and told himself to remain focused, keep himself in the present, and hold his form. "You don't think of the hurt; you think of the things that you can control: your breathing, your form. The speed and the pain and any competition will take care of itself. Keep your upper body, your hands, and your face relaxed, don't overstride, don't flail or grasp. There is only perfect form, with each stride, right now."

Splotches of sun and shade flashed by him in wild ecstasy, and Bill reached the tree that marked the finish of the course. He grabbed at his watch to record the time and then jogged to a stop and put his hands to his knees to catch his breath. Only then did he look down to check the time: fifteen minutes, twenty-three seconds and seventy-four one-hundredths. Then, over his heavy breathing, his face spread into a smile that was a mixture of surprise and triumph. Fifteen twenty-three! A new personal record.

Bill could hardly believe it. When he had got out of bed that morning, he felt tired and sore from his workout the day before. He would not have thought that he'd set a new PR today, and yet he'd just shattered his previous record by a solid three seconds. He looked at his watch again, just to enjoy those marvelous numbers—15:23. He looked up from the sidewalk at the dappled sunlight through the trees and could feel the sweat on his forehead and the warmth of the light across his face. He felt blessed and thankful. He raised his arms toward the sun and let out a wild whoop of victory.

"You're getting over-excited again, Mr. Bill." The voice belonged to Louise, one of the attendants at the home. She had come out onto the front lawn to shake out a throw rug.

Bill smiled at her. "You'd be excited too, Louise, if you'd just set a personal record."

"How many times I tell you, Mr. Bill. You eighty years old. You gotta stop running around like a kid."

"Eighty is just a number, Louise."

"Uh-huh," Louise agreed. "And it's a *big* number too."

Bill laughed. He liked Louise and her humorous skepticism, and he liked to tease her about her chubbiness, her love of chocolate, and her lazy boyfriend, Hector. "I've gotta stay in shape if I'm gonna catch you," he said. "Got to outrun Hector."

"Don't you get teasing me, Mr. Bill." Louise gave the rug a final shake, as if to make her point. "I've got work to do, and you'll be busy too. Jeanie just called. She's coming over later for a visit."

Jeanie was Bill's great-niece, his sister's granddaughter. She would be a senior in high school in the fall, and she ran on the school's cross-country team. She often dropped by to tell Bill about the team's practices and meets and to ask Bill for running advice. She loved his stories about the old days, too.

"She said that she's bringing a friend," Louise added.

"Thanks, Louise. I'll cool down and be right in."

Louise returned to the house, and Bill walked once around the block and then lay down on the lawn to stretch. The grass of the home's manicured lawn was luxurious and warm, and Bill stretched out his thin arms and legs and allowed himself to sink into it. As he gazed without focus at the paleness of the sky, he imagined that he could feel the curve of the earth under his back, that he could feel the roundness of it. He watched puffy clouds pass overhead and imagined he was dizzy with the Earth revolving on its axis, and dizzier still with its orbiting of the sun, and with the eighty times he himself had completed that journey.

He knew that the world itself was alive, not just a place, a stage, but a being that included man, and he wondered if the world was young or old. Or maybe it was beyond the realm of time, he thought, beyond evolutions and orbits, or at least the counting of them. Bill had watched the world in its storms of youthful energy and in its stillness like old age. It was young and old at the same time, and he smiled at himself, because he had learned long ago that the world baffles little concepts and their silly words. It was simply glorious in its all-encompassing presence and silence, refusing to acknowledge the slightest trace of what had been or to provide the slightest hint of what was to be.

He closed his eyes and breathed in deeply. He had been around eighty times and didn't care if that was old or not. He had lived through good times, and through bad times too, but now he just felt joy. The white clouds were blowing high overhead. The earth was spinning under them. "Jeanie's bringing a friend," he said to the sky. To a cloud he added, "They'll want me to tell a story." A hawk circled into view—drifting, floating—and Bill spoke to it, too. "They'll want a love story," he said. "We'll all have to think about that."

How does a chance meeting become a lasting bond? How does a stranger become a friend? Where do those friends go when our time together is gone? How do we find our way after them? The warmth of the day and the exertion of Bill's run played on him. He began to drift, and a soft smile crossed his features like a cloud passing in the sky. "Hold on," he said. He turned his hands in the grass and held tightly to fistfuls of the green blades, so that the speed of the Earth's spinning, the kaleidoscope of his life, wouldn't send him flying.

3. The Holy Ones

NEWARK, NEW JERSEY, 1992—Moses had something he needed to tell Buddy, but he didn't know how to get it started. The two old men were sitting on their haunches, huddled together next to a barrier they had against the wind. It was extra cold that morning, and they could see the cold on their breath. They were stirring at their coffee with those little wooden sticks you get when you buy it to go. On Sunday morning they treated themselves to coffee from Dunkin Donuts. It was twenty cents more than the coffee they got from the bodega, but they liked it better and thought that once a week they could splurge. They didn't drink it there though, because they disliked the looks they got. Moses, the more presentable and outgoing of the two, would go get it and bring it back to the underpass where they lived.

They lived in the elevated space, tucked in up under the road. Buddy had lived there first in an old cardboard box that a bathtub had come in. He considered this box a great find, because it had an interior wooden frame that lent it a comforting sturdiness, and he had cut out a small hole for a window and taped up part of a T-shirt for a curtain. Buddy had met up with Moses later on the streets and had taken him in. Moses had lived in a refrigerator box to start with, but had later added two stove boxes onto it. A "three-bedroom unit," Buddy called it. On the wicked nights of winter, when the newspapers and tarps they used to insulate their sleeping quarters just couldn't fight off the cold, they went to the shelter, taking turns sleeping through the night to protect themselves from the crazies there. They had been living together for years now.

Moses was tall and thin, lanky yet graceful, with movements quicker than one would expect in an older man. It was that quickness, and a lightness he had, that made one think of a bird. It was only then, when one thought that he could take flight, that one would notice the gentle curve of his nose and the fineness of his frame.

Buddy was short, with a round, oversized head. His hair had been red, but now it was rusty brown. His complexion was ruddy and aged, but there were still the freckles of his youth. He had a goofy grin and crooked teeth that made him look like a jack-o-lantern, and a glow came from him too, as if his candle burned hot and bright.

Both old men were unshaven and their whiskers were gray, some of Buddy's still tinged with rusty red. They only shaved on Sunday. There was a Mobil gas station nearby that had a men's room off the back, and the part-timer who worked Sundays didn't care when they went back there. It was dirty, and Buddy said it smelled like an outhouse he had used once in Mexico, but the water was good and hot out of the sink, and they could wash and take their shave.

Life had hammered hard on both of them. Its hardness had made Moses as calm and quiet as it had made Buddy agitated and intense. Moses accepted things the way they came, and didn't see the need for a lot of talk. He would much rather listen to Buddy, who used words to work out his thoughts and enjoyed having Moses there to listen. But Moses knew he had to do the talking today, or at least get it started. Something had happened that had unsettled even him, and he needed to tell Buddy about it, so they could work it out.

It was quiet still. The sunrise sky was pumpkin, black and blue. They almost had their coffee ready now. It would soon be time to speak, but Moses didn't want to tell Buddy what he knew he had to tell him. Buddy liked to talk about his dreams and analyze them and such, and Moses knew that the dreams he'd had meant something, and Buddy would surely confirm that.

Stirring the morning coffee was one of the rituals of their day, and they were silent when they did it. Buddy stirred his in quick, hard strokes against the side of the cup, as if he were kicking away a dog. Moses stirred his in slow, elliptical orbits, each revolution a lifetime of thought. Now Buddy had kicked the dog free and was bringing his coffee to his lips. After he took the first sip, he would start thinking and start the talking that was its form. But Moses knew that he had to speak first today. If he let Buddy start, and then came in with his news, it would be like letting someone go on and on about their ingrown toenail before telling them that you had a broken leg.

Buddy had just swallowed and was feeling that first pleasure of taste and warmth and energy. Moses could see the thoughts start to percolate in Buddy's eyes, and heard himself speak with slightly more urgency than he had intended to reveal. "Buddy," he said, "I've been working hard in my dreams lately."

Buddy believed in dreams bad. He believed that in the dreamworld, we work out the plans for our waking days. He would sometimes wake up and say, "I'm just exhausted. I worked a ten-hour shift last night." He thought that a real hard night of dreaming meant that things were stirring, that there would follow actions and events of importance.

Buddy looked over at Moses across the top of his coffee, the way Moses had known that he would. Buddy had often asked Moses about his dreams, and Moses had said that he hadn't dreamt or that he couldn't remember, so for Moses to talk about dreaming hard—without even being asked—meant a lot in itself. Moses was relieved that he had gotten in first, but he was still nervous and hesitant, because he knew that he had just got started, and had even more startling news to share.

"And I've had the same dream three nights in a row," he added.

That was another thing. Buddy believed in numbers. Things could be counted, and Buddy was always counting. If one shoelace broke, that was just tough; if both shoelaces broke, that was a sign. There weren't just crows sitting on a telephone wire; there were three crows. Spirits travelled in threes. Death came in threes too. When anyone famous died, Buddy was on watch, scanning the tabloids for the second death, and the inevitable third. Three was completion, fruition. Even numbers were balanced. Seven was lucky, and twelve was bountiful, like a pair of boxcars, Buddy said.

Moses waited while Buddy worked it through. The same dream. Three nights in a row. "There's one more thing," Moses said. He paused again. This was the part that unsettled him, and he knew would unsettle Buddy too. He waited until Buddy looked up. "In all three dreams, I saw my own grave."

Moses watched Buddy, but still there was silence. What Buddy had just heard had sent a buzz through his brain, like a short circuit, and had covered his skin with goose bumps. He placed his coffee on the ground and rubbed his arms to keep from shivering, then stirred his coffee again. He never did that. It was as if he wanted to move back in time a few minutes and start all over, having not heard what he had just heard.

He caught himself staring at the ground and snapped himself back. This wasn't about him. He needed to be there for Moses, who wouldn't have brought the subject up, knowing how Buddy felt about it, if he didn't need help. This wasn't a time to panic. It was the time—if ever there was a time—to stay calm. "Moses," he said calmly. "Let's just see what we got." Buddy wouldn't really know what he thought himself until he'd talked it over. "And let's not sugar it," he said. "We both know that three dreams about your grave is serious. You wouldn't've told me if it wasn't. But what we gotta remember now is that dreams have symbols that stand for other stuff." Buddy felt warmer as he began to understand what he knew. "A grave means bodily death normally, but in a dream it could mean death of another kind. Like death to a certain way of life or thought. Or the end of a period in time for you. It could be a sign that something is coming to an end for you, gonna change."

"But it felt real, Buddy. It felt like the real thing. I woke up in a sweat all three nights. I couldn't sleep." Moses had told Buddy the worst of it, and he felt relieved. Now he just wanted to pour it all out to his friend. "I got up and started walking on the streets. You know how I like to walk things off, and the more worried I am, the faster I walk. On that last night, Buddy, after the third dream, I started out walking, but I ended up running. I was running down the middle of Newark Avenue in the middle of the night. I was moving fast, too. I didn't know I could still run that fast. A police car stopped me, and the officer asked me what I was doing, and I just looked at him and said, 'Officer, I'm running away from my grave.' He must've thought I was loony. He looked over at his partner, and she talked me down. She said, 'Honey, nobody can run that fast or that far. You just go on home now and go to bed.'"

"She was right," Buddy said. "There's no problem we can run away from. We gotta face everything that comes our way. Now tell me everything you can about the dreams themselves."

"Gladys was there. In the first one. There was junk all over my grave and Gladys was pushing it away."

"What kind of junk?"

"Some chairs and an old sofa bed. Gladys couldn't budge it. And there was a table and piles of clothes and boxes all around. But it was foggy. Things were mixed up."

Gladys had been Moses' wife. She was dead now. Buddy thought it made it worse that she was there, a dead person herself, in that dream. "Was Gladys in the other dreams?"

"No. Just that first one. In the other two I could fly, and I could see my grave down below."

"That's good," Buddy said. "You were above your grave. It was in the distance. You see? And that part about flying, that's good. Flying means freedom in the dreamworld."

"I feel like I'm being called to another place, or another life. I feel like I'm kinda only dreamin' this life now, like I'm only half here."

Buddy reached over and punched Moses in the arm. "You feel that?"

Buddy was small, but he could throw a punch, and Moses more than felt it. "Yeah," he said.

"Then you're here all right."

"Yeah, I guess."

Buddy might have acted tough, but he knew what Moses meant, and had felt the same. "Then don't talk stupid," he said.

Moses was doubtful, and still uneasy. "I don't know, Buddy. It felt creepy to me, real, and it came three times."

"Three times means you should pay attention, but it doesn't mean it's bad or that it's going to be just that way. Do you remember that time I dreamt about Gina Lollobrigida three nights in a row?"

"Remember? You didn't talk about nothing else for a month."

"Exactly. I was all worked up about nothin', wasn't I? Because I sure didn't meet Gina Lollobrigida, did I?"

"No," Moses said, seeing the logic. Then he suddenly smiled. "But you did meet that grocery clerk named Geena Stoll."

"That's right. Remember? You called her Geena Stollobrigida."

"And she gave you that free pineapple." Moses laughed now. "You dreamed about Gina Lollobrigida three nights running, and you only got a free pineapple." Moses had kidded Buddy about this before, and now, as worried and as tense as he had been, he suddenly thought it the funniest thing ever. He rolled over on his side and laughed.

Buddy was happy that he had made Moses laugh, even if it was at his own expense. It was true about Geena, but Buddy hadn't told Moses the whole story. She had given him the pineapple because somebody had torn off the top to make it weigh less and had then decided not to buy it. The grocery couldn't sell it without its top, so Geena had given it to him, but the real reason she'd done it was because she was sweet on him. Whenever he'd gone into the store, she'd given him the sweet eye.

Geena—buck-toothed, cross-eyed, and covered in moles—was the homeliest woman in Newark, if not in all New Jersey, and that was saying a lot. Moses had seen her first, and when he told Buddy about her, he said, "Whatever you do, Buddy, don't look in her ears." Of course, that's like telling somebody not to think of a monkey, and the first time Buddy saw Geena, he looked her right in the ears and saw all that hair. Buddy couldn't figure why Moses had singled out her ears, though; Geena's face alone made a man want to run away. At the same time, she had a shirt full of titties that were saying, "Come on home." A man wanted to run away from her and get caught by her at the same time. Buddy thought that was what they called mixed signals. He had read about it once in an old Cosmo. Because of Geena's homeliness, Buddy hadn't told Moses that the pineapple had only been flirtatious foreplay and that he and Geena had consummated their friendship out back by the grocery dumpster, and then every evening for a week after that at Geena's apartment. Those weren't his proudest moments, but if the truth be told, Geena Stoll, if you took her in a dark enough light, was as pleasing as any movie starlet would have been, and she would lick ya and smooch ya like a lonely dog.

Buddy's dreams of Gina Lollobrigida had been dreams of desire, and that passion had followed, and that the object of that passion was named Geena— even if spelled with two e's—validated the truth of the dreams, or at least the heart of that truth, as far as Buddy was concerned. That the details of the dream were off was beside the point—that was just the fuzziness that makes a dream what it is.

Now Moses' dreams, according to Buddy's interpretation, didn't mean death necessarily, but they meant change for sure, and they would have to keep an eye out for that change and for the further signs that would precede it. As for now, it was no good just sitting around dwelling on what might be. Now, more than ever, they would have to hold a steady course, Buddy thought, and keep up with their routines.

One of the ways that Moses and Buddy made money was to scavenge for recyclable bottles and cans and newspaper, and they had shopping carts and trash bags that they used for this purpose. One of their regular routes was through Branch Brook Park on Sunday morning, when they could loot the lucrative trash from the Saturday picnics, and they started right after their morning coffee.

"C'mon," Buddy said suddenly. "Let's go."

"Where?" Moses said. He was shocked by Buddy's sudden command, and still surprised by the silence that had followed his revelation.

"Where we always go on Sunday morning," Buddy said, as if there could be no doubt. "To the park."

"We're still going?"

"It's Sunday, isn't it?" Buddy said.

"Sure. Sure. I'll go get the carts."

"Well, hurry up then."

"Sure, Buddy," but Moses still hesitated. "But what about tomorrow, Buddy? What about Monday?"

"Tomorrow's tomorrow," Buddy said. "We'll see what tomorrow brings."

Buddy, with deep concern, watched his old friend walk away. His coffee was already cold, but he took the wooden stick and kicked at it some more. It was early and the day still silent, but Buddy listened. He knew that there are many sounds to silence, just as there are many shades to white. When you listen to silence, you hear it by how you feel, so Buddy didn't listen with his ears—that's why most people thought they heard nothing. He listened with his whole body. He felt for the beat of his heart, the rhythm of his breathing, the tension in his muscles, the sensations on his skin. His body would know and tell him things that his skittish mind would only confuse, or lie about.

Out of the silence the wind flowed around the embankment, and Buddy felt the hair on the back of his neck stand on end. He listened to the voice of the wind, the howling hum of it. Messages vital and mortal come without words. Woooooooo-WOOOOoooooooo. The wind was restless, moody, and strong. His shoulders stiffened, and he felt the goose bumps on his arms. "God bless us," Buddy said, as much to God as to break the fearful spell. Woooooooo-WOOOOoooooooo, the wind said again. Buddy swallowed, looked toward heaven, and closed his eyes. Then he crossed himself—first once, and then twice, and then a third time.

4. My Sweet Angel

GREEN BAY, WISCONSIN, 1969—Brenda's husband was sleeping now, and the four boys had been put down an hour ago. It was quiet in the house. This was a time that Brenda looked forward to all day long: the time before bed when she could be alone for a while in peace. The only sounds now were the occasional creak of a floorboard and the clicking from the grandfather clock in the living room, and even its slow beat only accentuated the deep silence of the night.

Brenda listened to the clock and to her own breathing in time with it. In six years of marriage she had delivered four sons. Her husband had been a defensive lineman on the football team at the University of Wisconsin where they'd met, and all four of their boys had weighed in at over ten pounds. They were good boys but, like her husband, they were all boy. Sometimes their size and rambunctiousness just wore her down. Even the youngest one, only a year old, could destroy anything he got his hands on. They couldn't have a knickknack even, let alone anything of value, within four feet of the floor, and that floor was always covered with trucks and army men and sporting goods. She felt more like the equipment manager at a training camp than a wife and mother. Just that day she'd spent a half hour dislodging a Wiffle ball from the toilet bowl. She just couldn't buy or cook enough food, and had come home from the store that day to find the formula she had left set aside and her husband feeding the baby from his own biscuits and gravy.

Now she was pregnant for a fifth time, and felt a need to pray. Her husband didn't stir from his sleep as she slipped to her knees beside the bed. She didn't pray often, and she felt guilty to be asking for something now. She started by giving thanks; she thanked God for her husband, and for her sons, and for the home and life they had together. It was all a blessing, but at the same time it wasn't enough. She was ashamed of that last thought, but God knew everything, so she might as well just get to what she wanted. "Dear God," she prayed, "we all want healthy babies, and when you give us one, we thank you with all our heart, but if you could just make this next one of ours not only healthy, but also a girl, then I'll know you have mercy on me and hold me dear. Amen."

That was all Brenda asked, and she didn't ask again. She had made her desire known, she thought, and now it was in the hands of God. She and her husband had agreed that it would be nice to have a girl this time around, but she didn't tell him that she had actually pleaded to God for one. She felt that prayer was a private thing, between a person and God alone, and talking about it would just bring bad luck. When it came time for the sonograms, she told her doctor that she didn't want to look at the pictures or to know the sex of the baby, and the doctor honored that request, telling her only that everything looked fine.

In the spiritual world, our mind is felt. Our thoughts are wind, our tears are rain, our cries are thunder, and our heavy questions are echoed with light answers. Where shall I go? Look where you're going. What shall I be? Mind who you are. How shall I manage? See what you have.

Brenda's prayer was desperate of voice and received a soothing reply. Before the baby even arrived, Brenda felt the calm of her. Her heartbeat paced her own. Her movement gave her pause. Her silence made her listen. She thought of how, together, they would balance the family. She would be not just a daughter, but a friend and ally. She secretly named her Amy, and spoke to her through the quiet time at each day's end.

All births are miracles, and all babies are beautiful, but Brenda knew as soon as she saw her that Amy was special. She could see that others saw it too. Even the doctors and nurses, who brought babies into the world every day, couldn't take their eyes off her. They huddled around and called others to come and see her. Amy glowed like a bride on her wedding day, and she accepted all the attention as if it were her due. She had a regal composure and presence that belied her tiny size. Brenda's husband could hold her in one of his burly hands.

Before she came home from the hospital, Brenda prepared presents for the boys from Amy, and they were still too young themselves to wonder how she could have bought them. They accepted her in wonder, and understood the power and place she held. Brenda told the boys that they had to wash their hands before they could touch her, and afterwards she would hear them in the bathroom with the water running, fighting over the soap of all things. Then they would appear in the kitchen, side by side and still wet, and ask if they could touch her now. She sat with them and watched as they each caressed their sister with gentle fingers and talked to her in hushed tones. Brenda saw the calmness in them when they were near Amy, who continued to have that effect on them through the years. From the beginning, there was a quiet space around Amy, a halo, which hushed people and brought out their best. All who came into that halo felt her peace and shared in it, sensing without knowing that she was heaven's soothing answer to someone's secret prayer.

5. Coe vs. Ovett

BROOKLYN, NEW YORK, 1990—When Emmitt F. Bean first came from Ireland to work in the States, he lived for a short while in Brooklyn Heights with an Englishman named Harry Horton. Emmitt had needed a place to stay, Harry had a room to let, and a mutual acquaintance had introduced them. This acquaintance had thought that Emmitt and Harry would get on, because both worked in the software industry and both were avid runners. The same logic would have made roommates of Roosevelt and Hitler, because both were politicians and both enjoyed a good cup of tea. As it turned out, Emmitt and Harry disliked nothing more than talking about work, and had little else in common other than their running. Their talks about running—laced with personal anecdotes about the runners they knew, full of theories on training, and knee-deep in racing results and statistics—kept them on the same page at first, but as time passed, and the honeymoon of their cohabitation passed with it, their differences emerged.

Both had fallen in love with running at an early age, but there the similarity ended. Emmitt had been introduced to the sport by his older brother, and ran with him in a local amateur club while growing up. He then went on to run for the cross-country team at college. After college, Emmitt was once lucky enough to win a small race when the lead pack of runners, far in front and out of sight of Emmitt himself, made a wrong turn and got lost on the course. There was prize money for the race, and Emmitt declared that money on his taxes and felt justified then—since he had been paid for his effort—in calling himself a professional. Although Emmitt worked as a computer analyst, on every form he was obliged to fill out, he proudly listed his occupation as "Runner."

Emmitt lacked any running talent, but he had hung on to the fringes of his club and college teams with his determination, hard work, and self-taught knowledge of the sport. He read all the books on training and nutrition, and as his understanding increased, he began advising other runners and then devising workouts and successful training programs for them. When Emmitt finally came to realize that he would never distinguish himself as a runner, he still held to his passion for the sport and transformed his dream of being a great runner into the dream of being a great coach.

It is well known in sports that a great athlete rarely becomes a great coach. A great athlete performs naturally, and doesn't have to think about how he does it. He doesn't analyze his shot; he just shoots. He doesn't analyze his stroke; he just swings. And a great athlete, if he tries to coach, often lacks patience with athletes of lesser talent. A lesser athlete, on the other hand, if he wants to succeed, has to learn every trick and technique that will give him even the slightest advantage and, having painstakingly learned the way himself, has not only the knowledge, but also the patience to impart that knowledge to others. In general, one could say that the less-talented an athlete is, the better chance he has of becoming a great coach. Let's just say that Emmitt was a great coach.

Emmitt augmented his daily experience with coaching by attending clinics and by continuing his voracious reading. He subscribed to not just commonplace periodicals like *Runner's World* and *Running Times*, but to *US Track and Field*, *Track and Field News* and several European journals. He came to have an encyclopedic knowledge of the sport, and knew the names and records of all the top runners in the world. Emmitt had posters of them throughout his rooms, their pictures stuck to the refrigerator door with magnets and to the bathroom mirror with tape.

Emmitt also read the biographies of the great track coaches, men like Arthur Lydiard and Bill Bowerman, and knew that the great coaches were not just teachers but innovators in the sport. Lydiard had pioneered new training methods that were still followed today, and Bowerman, the co-founder of Nike, had invented the waffle-soled running shoe. Emmitt felt that besides coaching, his contribution to the world of running would be a new and improved sports drink. He was dissatisfied with the drinks that were on the market then—Gatorade, PowerAde, and the others—and was experimenting with a new drink, to be called Coach-Aid, that would deliver the ultimate solution of electrolytes and carbohydrates to the runner's system.

Emmitt's experiments with Coach-Aid were his first source of conflict with Harry. Within twenty-four hours of moving in to the apartment, Emmitt had turned the kitchen into a laboratory. Every pot, pan, and bowl was filled with a different colored concoction, and every surface was covered with the ingredients—apple cider, cranberry juice, sugar, barley malt, honey, fruits, and vitamins and nutritional supplements of every kind—that Emmitt was analyzing and testing for the drink. Pots boiled over and there were spills and smoke. The smells coming from the kitchen were horrible, and when Emmitt left the flame too high on one experimental batch, the steam set off alarms throughout the building and prompted the neighbors to call the fire department.

Aside from his work on Coach-Aid, Emmitt was in truth a slob, and his messes were not confined to the kitchen. He aired his running shoes on the window sills, dried his socks on lampshades, and left a trail of running books and magazines wherever he went. Harry complained, and Emmitt made halfhearted attempts to pick up after himself, but for his part, Emmitt resented Harry's neatness, and was annoyed by what he thought of as Harry's "pretty-boy" ways. Harry was habitually well-groomed, with never a hair out of place. His prissy gels and lotions neatly lined the bathroom cabinet and were a daily affront to Emmitt's own sloppy ways.

These were just the banal differences between roommates, but the underlying competition between Emmitt and Harry was the root of their problem. As a runner, Harry was everything that Emmitt was not: fast and graceful and a beauty to watch. Running had come easy to Harry. He won his first race in grade school and enjoyed the attention it brought him, and he went on to run for the track team in college and enjoyed success there too. Now, in the States, he had established his own running club, not because he wanted to lead a team, but because he liked to be the center of attention. What was the use of being good at something if you didn't have other people around to admire you?

It was Harry's pride and vanity that pricked Emmitt the most. Harry had a tone that suggested, "And why would my opinion mean anything on the subject? Well, I was just the best runner in Northampton, and I now preside over a top running club here in the States. And you are ...?" Insult stings the most when it contains the salt of truth, and the recognition of that truth inflamed Emmitt. Yes, who was he? A mediocre runner who had just hung precariously on the fringe of his own clubs, and who here in the States did not even belong to a club, much less preside over one.

Harry, for his part, was galled by Emmitt's obstinate refusal to recognize and acknowledge Harry's own talent and superiority. Emmitt had even had the nerve to analyze Harry's running stride and to recommend drills to correct the defects. After one such critique, Emmitt had suggested that Harry call him "Coach." In response to that suggestion, Emmitt received from Harry only a supercilious and infuriating smirk.

Their differences came to a head one fateful evening at their neighborhood pub. Emmitt had offered an opinion about a runner they both knew, and Harry responded by saying, "Oh, come on, Emmitt." It was not the outright dismissal that rankled him, but the way Harry had emphasized his name. In that emphasis, Emmitt detected a note of disdain, and a pointed reminder of Harry's recent refusal to call him "Coach." Emmitt stiffened and, fuelled by the pints of beer in his belly and his fill of Harry's nonsense, decided to have it out with Harry Horton then and there.

With a feigned calm, he introduced one of the few running topics they had yet to discuss. Emmitt asked Harry who he thought had been the greater middle-distance runner, Sebastian Coe or Steve Ovett. Both had been great runners, indeed, but in Emmitt's mind a connoisseur's distinction had to be made. To the pedestrian observer, this may have seemed like a harmless enough subject for discussion, but to a Chariot of Fire like Emmitt Bean, the stakes couldn't have been higher, or the emotions more engaged, if he and Harry were to debate the moral issues of abortion or the pros and cons of capital punishment. For Emmitt, this question was the litmus test for Harry's value as a runner and even as a human being. With this question, Emmitt would discover once and for all the true character of one Harry Horton, and Harry's answer would mark him unmistakably as friend or bloody foe.

Before Harry could answer, Emmitt laid out his own position and described, in lap-by-lap detail, Coe's defeat of Ovett in the 1500 meters at the Moscow Olympics. Then he added sententiously, "There is no greatness without obstacle. And when talent is bestowed, life provides a challenge to it, and when this challenge is in the form of another person, and their talents are closely matched, the dual is truly perfect, because surely then the victory goes to the competitor with the greatest heart."

Emmitt had, by then, consumed three pints of Fuller's, his favorite brew. Fuller's is an extraordinary potion that fuels a warmth in the belly, rises to the heart and then to the throat, whence one's words come forth with an emotion that defies in its sincerity alone any contradiction. In that all-encompassing warmth, Emmitt then threw down the gauntlet. "The race may not go to the swiftest," he said, "but that was a day when the best man surely won."

Harry was on his third pint of Fuller's himself, and Emmitt's words cut at an emotional, beer-sotted vein. "Am I hearing right?" Harry said. "Surely you're not suggesting that Coe was a better runner than Ovett? Surely you're not suggesting that Ovett was only the nemesis to Coe's greatness?"

Emmitt could feel the wind blowing from the ocean, and he didn't like the smell. He took another swig from his pint and rose to meet this pungent air head on. "Oh, you picked up on that, did you? How bloody clever. But I'm not *suggesting* anything. I'm *saying* that not only was Coe a better runner than Ovett, he was the best British middle-distance runner to ever live."

"Couldn't carry Ovett's jockstrap," Harry countered.

"Why should he?" Emmitt answered back. "Ovett doesn't need a jockstrap."

"Are you saying that Steve Ovett doesn't have any balls?"

"No, Harry." Emmitt smiled sarcastically. "I'm *suggesting* it."

It was inane, like two Beatles fans arguing over the superiority of Lennon or McCartney, but such were the passions of Bean and Horton that the situation deteriorated from there. Harry pushed Emmitt, although Harry would later maintain that Emmitt had slipped from his bar stool, and then Emmitt gave Harry a push of his own. There was more pushing and shoving, and the other patrons cleared a circle around them.

Emmitt was bleeding from the lip. "You bloody arse," he said. "You hit me."

"You hit yourself with your own pint," Harry countered.

"I say you hit me," Emmitt shouted.

"If I had meant to hit you," Harry said, "that goofy head of yours wouldn't be parked on your shoulders now."

"Bloody hell," Emmitt said. "When I get through with you, Horton, you'll have to pee sitting down."

Emmitt lunged toward Harry then, but Harry stepped aside, and Emmitt fell to the floor.

"You Ovett-loving piece of crap," Emmitt said, getting up and squaring off at Harry.

That's when Harry did take a swing at Emmitt. It was an awkward, off-balance punch, and Emmitt dodged it. Harry's fist flew over Emmitt's shoulder, and his momentum carried him into Emmitt, sending them both crashing to the floor, where the fight continued, with Harry and Emmitt rolling around and flailing at each other like a couple of schoolboys.

The bartender came around the bar and pulled them apart. "That's enough, Emmitt," he said. "You too, Harry. I've had enough out of the both of ya's." The bartender grabbed Emmitt by the shoulders and turned him toward the door. "Go home," he said. "And you stay here until you cool down," he said to Harry.

Emmitt left in a huff of curses and, full of drunken and righteous indignation, marched straight to a Brooklyn real estate agency to find an apartment of his own, whereupon he found himself shocked to sobriety by the rental prices in Brooklyn Heights. "I can't afford any of these," he said to the agent.

"Where do you work?" the agent asked.

"Manhattan."

"Well, then you could try Hoboken."

"What's that?" Emmitt said.

"It's a city, in New Jersey."

"What's that?"

"It's one of the States," the agent said. "You know? The United States?"

"Different from New York?"

"Well, yes." She was wondering by then if Emmitt knew what planet he was on. "There are trains from Hoboken into Manhattan. You could commute from there."

Emmitt liked the idea. He was still worked up, and he didn't want to be in the same city, or even the same state, with that wanker Harry Horton. He would go to a virgin land, far from the prissy sight and perfumed stink of Harry, and establish his own running club, and there his obvious running expertise would mold a great team of runners, and might even produce—or if not produce, at least nurture—another Sebastian Coe, or if not a Coe, then at least a bloody Ovett.

The trains from New York come into Hoboken at the old Port Authority terminal on the south side of town, and there is a covered stairwell from the station up to the street. Emmitt believed in life's significant moments, and as he came up that stairwell he prepared himself for this first glimpse of his new home. Emmitt saw the brightness at the top of the stairs and lowered his eyes. When he saw the place for the first time, he wanted to take it all in at once. He took the steps slowly and one at a time, and he kept his eyes lowered as he reached the landing and took his first steps out of the tunnel and into the light. It was late March, and there was a cold wind from the north and a glaring sun. To Emmitt, still hot from his argument with Harry and filled with determination, the wind was a pleasant breeze and the sun a bright welcome. He felt the wind in his hair and the sun on his shoulders, but still didn't look up. He lowered his bags to the ground, took two more steps forward, as if leaving the past and all that belonged to it behind, and then put his hands on his hips. Only then did he raise his eyes to gaze into his future.

6. A Terrified Smile

PITTSBURGH, PENNSYLVANIA, 1998—The results of her tests were in, and Dr. Spencer would like to see her. Gloria knew it was bad news. She couldn't read anything from the nurse's voice, and maybe the nurse didn't even know, but why would Dr. Spencer call her in if it were nothing? Wouldn't he just have the nurse tell her that all the tests were negative?

She had decided to go alone; she would have to get herself together first before Coconut could know. Coco was her daughter, and Gloria often called her by the pet name that she had given her as a child, "Coconut"—hard and tough on the outside, but soft and mushy underneath. That was how she thought of herself too, and worried that if she cracked now, she would not get through this.

When she arrived, the nurse said that the doctor would see her in his private office, rather than in one of the examining rooms. The shades were drawn, the desk lamp was on, and the office was in sunset hue. Dr. Spencer rose from his work to greet her when she entered. As soon as she was seated, he started in with the test results. As tempting as it was for Dr. Spencer to delay, it would be unkind to precede with small talk the news he had to deliver.

She listened calmly as he spoke. When he had told her all that he could, he stopped suddenly, or at least it seemed sudden to her. She had been mesmerized by his words, as if they were a strange music in the air. And she had been startled at first by how much weight words could carry—they were loaded like freight trains—and by how much damage they could do—she was glad that she was sitting down. Perhaps she had closed herself off somehow, in self-defense, and was only half listening, and that was why the sudden silence surprised her. Dr. Spencer waited for her to respond.

"How long do I have, Doctor?" was what she said. It was such a cliché. Gloria listened as each word came from her mouth, but it was hard for her to believe that she had said it. But then, what else would one say, she thought, when told what she had just been told. Doctor Spencer paused. He wouldn't speak in clichés, Gloria thought. He was thinking of something fitting, just for her. He was thoughtful, and he took his time. This was what she liked about him best, and was why she had left her old doctor to come to him. She waited, but was not in a hurry. She thought how already each second was more precious to her.

"Mrs. Matushky, each patient is different, and I've seen it go both ways. I've seen patients in extremely poor health live longer than I could have imagined, and I've seen patients succumb to illness when I had thought that they could live for years. I don't like to make predictions. A patient's life often depends on how much they want to live and on how hard they are willing to fight."

"I am a fighter, Doctor, and I need to know whether I have five rounds to beat this or fifteen."

"Again, that depends a lot on you."

"Doctor, I know you have seen cases like mine. I know you have seen how the illness progresses." She paused, looked at him squarely, and spoke now in a forceful staccato, stressing each word. "Tell me how long you think I have."

"If you don't get a donor, perhaps a year, and the last three months could be difficult. If it comes to that, we'll do the best we can to make you comfortable."

"Thank you, Doctor. Thank you for being honest with me. I'll do my best to make a liar out of you." Gloria smiled, but Doctor Spencer did not smile back. She didn't blame him; he had probably seen many smiles like hers before: brave and terrified.

Despite her fears, Gloria thought she had handled things well. Again, she worried about how Coco would take the news. In the waiting room, when she bent down to get her umbrella from the rack, she noticed that while her shoes were both brown, they were from two different pairs. She suddenly realized her deep state of distraction, and as she rose she was overwhelmed with fear. She stood wavering for a moment, and then started to faint. The nurse had been watching her and was already rushing from behind the desk. She popped an ammonia capsule under Gloria's nose, and the acrid explosion brought Gloria soaring back to consciousness. "Mrs. Matushky," she heard the nurse say. "Let's sit you down."

The nurse helped Gloria to a chair. Gloria was in shock, and said absently, "Where do you go?"

"What do you mean, sweetheart?" the nurse said.

"Where do you go?" Gloria repeated. She looked at the nurse as if she might actually have the answer. "Where do you go when you go to pieces?"

7. Just Plain Ridiculous

LONG BEACH, CALIFORNIA, 1997—When Andy saw the green Studebaker parked way up the driveway next to his Grandma June's kitchen door, he stopped in the middle of the street and wished he could turn around. This cartoon of a car belonged to Gen, his grandma's long-time friend. His grandma couldn't drive any more, but Gen was still loose on the roads. When she drove, only her head appeared in view, held steadfastly forward, straining to see through the steering wheel what she could of the road. She was afraid to make a left-hand turn now, so she would circle her destination until some combination of rights and petrified pedestrians suddenly called upon for directions would eventually get her there. The previous month she had come to a series of traffic cones where she needed to make a left, and she'd turned to the wrong side of the cones, knocking several of them over, ignoring or not hearing the frantic whistles of a policeman and the laughing shouts of onlookers, and ended up in the middle of the annual Filipino Day parade. She was driving down the center of Bellflower Boulevard between a float and a high school band and wondering why there was a crowd waving at her. "They were such friendly people," Gen recounted later, "so I just waved back."

Gen and June had met years ago at church, and now Gen came over to pray with June at a shrine that June had in her living room. They prayed not just for world peace and an end to hunger, but also for personal friends and interests of their own. Above the votive candles and statues of saints, June had a corkboard upon which they pinned the obituaries, names, or pictures of those who needed special prayer. A picture of Andy was always there, along with a picture of Andy's father, and Gen and June's late husbands. These pictures had been joined at various times with those of Lady Di, Pee-wee Herman, Billy Carter, and others. When the two ladies weren't praying, they had lunch and watched the children at recess in the schoolyard across the street, or they played cards or Yahtzee, or made jigsaw puzzles.

Andy loved his grandma, and he loved Gen too, but the two of them together were most times more than he could take. They teased him endlessly, meddled in his life, and sooner or later got on his case about his hair or his clothes or his friends until they had succeeded in putting a big bug up his butt. Why should he stand the aggravation? And if Gen was coming over, why couldn't she have brought the brandy? Andy stared at the Studebaker. Maybe they just wanted a third for 500 Rummy, he hoped, but he knew better, and had a sinking suspicion that he was heading into a trap.

Andy was correct in that suspicion. When his grandmother had called him to bring her the brandy, she already knew that Gen would be there, and that they would be discussing Andy and his future, and that they would agree on a plan to help him, and she wanted the brandy to toast their plan and to seal her pledge to bring that plan to fruition. They were already warm on the subject by the time Andy was on his way.

"I raised him alone after his mother left and his dad died," June said. "I'm old now, almost as old as I look, and it's time a younger woman carried the bucket."

June believed that men were a lifetime job for women, that women had to work on a man in tag-team fashion. The mother, or whoever did the mothering, builds the foundation; then she hands the man off to a wife to finish off the structure; and if the wife can't outlive her husband and finish the job, a daughter or niece has to step up and maintain the man through to his end.

"And you did a good job raising him, June," Gen said. "He's a good boy."

"Boy?" June said. "He's twenty-five years old. When I was his age, I was raising three children, milking a dozen cows, and breaking a mule. What's he got on his plate? He's got his part-time job at that computer store, and his running, and those guys he drinks beer with. It's not enough. He's just drifting, and he knows it too inside. That's why he's frustrated, and short-tempered, and just plain ridiculous."

"We'll keep praying for him, June. We'll say a rosary."

"The boy's beyond prayer, Gen. The Pope couldn't help him if he said a rosary with beads blessed by the Holy Virgin herself."

"Then what are we going to do?"

"We need to take matters into our own hands. We need to get him a girl. Why can't we be like those Indian families and just match the young people up whether they like it or not and by God that's all there is to it?"

"Well, nobody can say we haven't tried, June. Look at all the nice girls we've introduced him to, and not one of them good enough, according to him."

The hurtful tone with which Gen colored that last phrase was meant to remind June that two of those girls had been Gen's own great-nieces, and although Gen hadn't really been put out by their rejection, she never missed a chance to force June to smooth it over.

"Of course they were all lovely girls, Gen, especially your two. It's not the girls; it's him. He doesn't give them a chance. He doesn't trust them, and he's afraid to open up."

"I guess you can't blame the boy for that," Gen said, "not after the way his mother left and broke his father's heart."

"That's it," June said. "We know that. He's scared, and why should he take a chance when he's got all his comfortable routines. We take care of him, and he's got his lazy friends and all the running he does. He's in a cozy rut, and we need to goose him out of it."

"What are we going to do?"

"I've already done something," June said. "You know that professor that

Andy liked at UCLA?"

"Professor Hubble?"

"Yes. He's teaching back East now."

"Back East? Oh, fancy."

"I called him this week, and the professor said Andy has great promise. He said he can get him into the school there. That will be just the challenge and the change of scenery that Andy needs. If your destiny doesn't come to you, then you've got to go to it."

"He'll never go for it, June."

"Just leave it to me, Gen," June said. "Just follow my lead."

"OK," Gen said with solemnity and resolve. "Don't worry, June; I've got your back."

June and Gen were playing cards when Andy came in the kitchen door. Andy was tall and lean, and he stooped slightly as he passed through the doorway, as if he might hit his head. His hair was uncombed and he had a stubble of beard. His rumpled T-shirt and cargo pants hung off his frame.

"Look what the cat dragged in," his grandma said.

"Did you bring the hooch, boy?" Gen said.

Andy put the bottle on the table and gave both of them a kiss.

"Sit down, Andy," his grandma said.

Andy found her tone alarmingly casual.

"Yes, and play some cards with us, boy," Gen said. "We haven't got all your money yet."

Andy sat down tentatively on the edge of a chair. "I can't really stay long," he said. "I'm meeting some guys this afternoon for a run." He put his hands on the kitchen table and tapped his fingers nervously.

"You've got strong hands, boy," Gen said. "Your father's hands were like that."

Gen was on to her favorite subject now. She loved discussing people's physical attributes and their genealogy. She always had a picture album with her, and she brought out a small one then from her purse. Her late husband's name had been Joseph, and although he had passed five years before, she referred to him so often that one thought he could walk into the room at any moment. She would point to the picture of one of their children and say that she had Joseph's eyes, and then to the picture of another and say that he had Joseph's chin. Finally she pointed to a picture of their eldest daughter. "And look at that big hind end on Edith," she said. "*That*, she got from her mother."

Gen was not entirely consumed with the attributes of her own family. With equal interest and enthusiasm she turned the topic toward Andy again and asked June, with some animation, where, she thought, Andy had got his nose.

Andy winced. At one time or another Gen had gone over the source of most of his anatomy, but he knew that wouldn't stop her from giving him a thorough going-over again.

"Well, it's not a Bell nose, that's for sure," June said. "You see how it turns down there a bit at the end." Gen joined June in looking at Andy's nose, and there was nothing poor Andy could do but cross his eyes and look down at it himself. "The Bell nose is as straight as an arrow," she continued. "Andy must have got that nose from his mother's side, the Thompsons. That crookedness is the Thompson influence."

"But the boy looks like he has your eyes, June."

"Yes," June agreed, "he's got the Bell eyes. You see how they squint up like a Chinaman's when he frowns. That's just how my father's eyes would do."

They talked about Andy openly and frankly, the way adults will talk about a two-year-old in his presence, as if he couldn't hear or understand what they were saying, and as if they had the parental right of ownership.

"The boy's got good color," Gen commented. "His complexion's close to yours, June."

"Yes, he's got the Bell color too, but look at his lips, a shade on the pale side. Those are Thompson lips."

June attributed all Andy's weak qualities to the Thompsons and his good qualities to the Bells. "Just look at those broad shoulders," she said. "They remind me of my Uncle Don. His would hunch down like that too when he was beat."

Andy straightened his shoulders and shifted in his seat. He had delivered the brandy and stayed for a polite amount of time. Now he was going to make his escape. "I really need to get going," he said. "I'm meeting the guys over at Signal Hill."

"So you're still hard at your running," June said. "I'd have thought you'd have given that up after college."

"Running is a sport, Grandma. It's not a class that you finish taking."

"And what about your classes, Andy? You were going to go for your doctorate in computers. Whatever happened to that?"

They'd been over this before, and Andy wished that he hadn't sat down. "I've gotta go, Grandma," he said.

"I know," June said. "But before you go, why don't you get off your computer and go get us a couple of glasses."

Andy went to the cupboard to get the glasses, and June made a face toward Gen. It was a face that said she intended to start in on Andy right now, and when Andy came back with the glasses, June said, "Andy, I have a problem."

"What problem could you have, Grandma?" Andy said. "You've got everything you need, and you've got a young man waiting on you like a servant." He poured them both a tumbler of brandy.

"Thank you, boy," Gen said.

"I'm getting old," his grandmother said.

Andy laughed. Despite his unease with the subject that he was sure would follow, he was amused now by his grandma's difficulty and clumsiness at broaching it.

"I'm getting old, and I haven't fulfilled my vow."

"What vow?"

"The one I made to myself when your father died."

There was a heavy silence then, and all three instinctively looked toward a painting at the far end of the dining room. It was a painting by Andy's father of a reclining woman. The painting was beautiful, yet it was essentially a mockery of the woman and of all women. Parts of the woman were distorted, the feet and hands abnormally large.

"Why did he do the hands that way?" Gen said. "How would anyone ever get hands like that?"

"It's not meant to be realistic," Andy said. "It's impressionistic. That's his *impression* of her hands and how she uses them."

"You been taking drugs, boy?" Gen said.

"It's true about hands though," June said. "They're an expressive part of a person's body. A person may lie with his eyes and still reveal the truth with his hands. Look at your own hands, Andy, clenched together as if praying for your life. I don't care about that silly grin of yours either. I can take one look at those hands and tell that you need help."

"Oh, Grandma," Andy said. "Please don't start."

"I remember your father when he came back from the war. I remember the way he smoked a cigarette. He held it with his thumb and forefinger, right at the tip, and he smoked it all the way down, as if that cigarette was his last link with life." June looked with concern at Andy. "I worry about you," she said.

"I'm doing fine, Grandma."

"When your father died, I vowed to make sure you got on the right track in life."

"I'm doing fine, I said. You can just leave me alone."

"I'm not going to leave you alone, Andy, and I'm not going to argue with you either. I've called Professor Hubble and made arrangements for you to start school back East."

"You what?"

"He's going to call you tonight. You listen to what he has to say."

"You can't run my life like that."

"When Professor Hubble calls, you listen to what he has to say. The money part of it is already taken care of."

"I've got a life here. I've got a job."

"I thought of that too. I told Professor Hubble that you'd need spending money, and he says he can get you a part-time job at the school's computer lab."

"Unbelievable!"

"Just listen to him and keep an open mind."

"Keeping an open mind," Gen said, "that's a good policy."

"I've got to go," Andy said, and rose to leave.

June would cement her work now by speaking of it as a done deal and by bringing the talk back to the mundane. "I'll get your father's suitcase down out of the closet," she said. "After your run, you come back here and have dinner with us, Andy. I've got a roast in the Crock-Pot."

Andy was speechless. His grandmother had just made plans to commandeer his life and send him all the way across the country, and now she was talking about the Crock-Pot.

"Before you leave, will you go out to the curb and bring in those trash cans for your old granny? Little Johnny next door has Little League practice and won't be home till dark."

"Oh sure, Grandma," Andy said sarcastically. "I'll take care of them."

Andy left without a good-bye and stalked toward his car in the driveway, mumbling to himself, "Will they ever mind their own goddamn business?" He threw the car in reverse and put his arm over the back of the seat, while June and Gen watched from the window. Andy spotted the trash cans at the curb and veered toward them, clipping them both into the gutter like a couple of bowling pins. The two old ladies laughed with delight.

"Well, that takes care of that," June said.

"Andy's kinda moody today, don't you think, June? I think he got that moodiness from his father."

"Yeah, he's in a bit of a mood."

"But he's a good boy," Gen said. "He's just stubborn. *Stubborn*," she repeated. "That's the word I'd use."

June picked up her glass and laughed again, and then raised it in a toast toward Gen. "Oh sure, he's stubborn all right," said June. She clinked their glasses together, took in the fragrant aroma of the brandy, and broke into a smile. "But he got *that* from somewhere too."

8. Wedding Cake

HOBOKEN, NEW JERSEY, 1989—Hoboken was known for its Italian bakeries with their brick ovens and tasty breads, and one of the finest of these was "Marie's" on Second Street. It was a family business, with the younger generations manning the ovens while the grandfather, who didn't speak a word of English, handled the customers. The customers pointed to items in the display cases, and the old man rang them up and pointed to the total on the register.

Howie Mooch, a young man who lived in the neighborhood, was a regular at Marie's and was fluent with the hand signals needed to communicate with the old man, while the old man, for his part, when he saw Howie come in the door, knew to reach for the largest bag he had to package Howie's order. Howie came from a family that loved to eat. His father was big, and his mother was even bigger. They'd had their wedding bands inscribed, and the engraver, assuming that the larger band must belong to the husband, had mixed up the inscriptions, so that Howie's father wore a ring that said, "Love always, Albert," and Howie's mother wore a ring that said, "Forever yours, Regina."

All of Albert and Regina's children had inherited their love of food, but even in a family that bought ice cream by the gallon and donuts by the dozen, Howie's own appetite was prodigious and his knowledge of food precocious. Even as a young boy he was exchanging recipes with ladies in the neighborhood and subscribing to magazines devoted to cooking. When other kids were playing baseball and hide-and-seek, Howie was growing basil in the backyard garden and creating the ultimate omelet.

Howie was the connoisseur of the family. His taste became so refined over the years that with a single bite he could not only judge the quality of a dish but could also detect from its taste, smell, and appearance its exact method of preparation and storage. "This lasagna was cooked in a gas stove, placed in a metal container, covered with Saran Wrap, and frozen for two days. It was then defrosted—not thawed—and reheated in a microwave oven." A critique of this type was accepted as fact, not speculation, and would culminate with a resigned sigh and a raised eyebrow on Howie's pudgy and disapproving face.

Family and friends thought that Howie would become a chef or restaurant critic, but Howie didn't want to sully his love of food by making work of it. His life revolved around eating, and it surprised no one that he met his girlfriend, Donna, at an all-you-can-eat buffet. They were both back for thirds and discussed their favorite dishes: Howie found the baby-back ribs in duck sauce interesting, if slightly overdone, and Donna favored the mash potatoes covered with bacon and garnished with cheddar cheese. Howie offered to give Donna his recipe for that very dish, and their love grew from there. They had been eating happily together for over a year when Howie was caught completely off guard by the first sign of trouble in their relationship.

Marie's always had fine displays in the window, and on this day they had a beautiful three-tier wedding cake. Howie and Donna stopped to admire it.

The cake had yellow frosting and white trim, and on top were the traditional figurines of bride and groom. "Look, how beautiful," Donna said.

"Yes," Howie said, in appreciative agreement shaded with slight disappointment. The cookies they had just purchased suddenly seemed inadequate. "The layers are lofted nicely, and the frosting is of pure butter."

"No, silly," Donna said. "I meant the bride and groom." The groom was in black tux and tails and the bride in a white wedding gown and veil. They looked like the Ken and Barbie dolls that one of his sisters had, and Howie was about to mention that when he noticed that Donna was crying.

"What's wrong?"

They could see their reflections in the bakery window, double exposed upon the cake. "Can you imagine figures of us, Howie, on top of that cake? We'd squash it flat."

Howie knew that he was heavy. He didn't worry about it, but would occasionally cut back on his eating to keep from getting huge. Alcoholics take it one day at a time without a drink, and during his diet days, Howie took it one day at a time without a cookie. As far as Donna's weight was concerned, he thought that there was just that much more of her to love.

"Just look at us," Donna said. "When people see us together, I bet they think, 'Oh, look at that fat young man and his fat girlfriend. That's too bad, but at least they have each other.' As if our relationship is a consolation prize."

The elegant bride and groom stood between Howie and Donna's reflections in the window, as if Howie and Donna were a distorted mirroring of their slim ideal. Donna had taken a tissue from her purse and was dabbing at her eyes. She was crying silently in that heartbreaking way women have, as if they are feeling something so sad that they have no energy to even cry aloud or to make any motion other than to gently erase each tear rising from the bottomless sorrow within.

Other signs of trouble soon followed. Donna started a diet and enrolled in Jazzercise and step classes, and she began choosing the restaurants that they frequented, which now tended to be the trendier and more health-conscious ones. There were small portions where the buffets had once been, and there were steamed vegetables and tofu to replace the meats. Then Donna began ordering just salads, and suggested that Howie might like to do the same. He would often oblige her and then sneak out later for a second meal. Donna lost weight, and along with these weight loses came new outfits in ever-smaller sizes and fashionable designs. Howie looked even heavier in comparison, and she mentioned lightly that he might like to lose a few pounds himself.

Donna was changing before his eyes, and despite the disregard for his own preferences, he was happy for her, because he could see how excited she was about her new tastes and appearance, but besides an occasional salad, Howie had no intention of changing himself. As time went on, however, Howie grew concerned over the increasing gap that was opening up between them and realized that if he continued to drag his heels, he'd be left behind.

One day she said to him, "You should see a doctor, Howie. If you don't start taking care of yourself, you're going to have a heart attack, and I love you too much to stand by and watch that happen." After she said that, she stood up defiantly and walked away. He felt scared and sick as she went. Their relationship had started with their common love of eating, but over time Howie had come to love Donna more than he loved food itself. Now she was giving him a taste of what was to come. If he didn't change, one day she would walk away for good.

Howie went to his doctor, and the doctor lectured him again about the correlation between obesity and heart disease. When he spoke of the risks of death, Howie's first thought was of the buffet his mother would have at his wake—the cold cuts, macaroni salads, and desserts—but his second thought was that he wouldn't be there to enjoy it. "I don't want to die," he said abruptly and blankly, as if he had just awakened from a bad dream. Then he came to and said flatly, "But I can't stop eating."

"You don't need to stop eating," the doctor said, "but you need to diet, and you need to exercise."

"What do you mean, *exercise*?" Howie said. Of course he had heard the word, but the concept was completely foreign to him, and he could do with a clarification.

"Bicycling, running, swimming, any aerobic activity that will raise your heart rate and will keep it up for at least twenty minutes continuously, for starters."

"For starters?"

"Yes, until you adjust and you can take it a bit longer. For someone like you, just starting out, I would suggest a vigorous twenty-minute walk, three times a week, and then you can take it from there."

Howie was deeply troubled by this dilemma: a twenty-minute walk or a heart attack. He wasn't able to walk five minutes without stopping to catch his breath or have a snack, so he knew how painful, and perhaps deadly, twenty minutes of non-stop walking could be. On the other hand, he knew heart attacks were usually quick. As Howie left the doctor's office, he was still weighing the options: exercise or a heart attack. He wasn't at all sure which would be worse.

9. Pony Express

MISSOURI, 1905—Dexter Wheeler's Grandpa Clyde had ridden for the Pony Express. He had gone west in the gold rush when little more than a boy and, like thousands of others, had come up shy of panning any strike. He'd worked as a ranch hand until his real destiny appeared in this ad in a California newspaper.

"Wanted. Young, wiry, skinny fellas. Must be expert horsemen. Willing to risk death daily. Orphans preferred."

Clyde told his sidekick, "They might as well draw my face right there next to those words, 'cause they're talking about me."

Clyde Wheeler did ride for the Pony Express through its short existence, covering stretches from California all the way to Missouri. The mission was speed, and the rides were difficult and dangerous. He rode tough terrain, battled blizzards, and fought off Indians. He would later tell his son, Lloyd, about his exploits and about the luscious land flowing to the horizons of Colorado, Kansas, and Nebraska. Lloyd, in turn, told those stories to his own son, Dexter, exaggerating and embellishing them until Grandpa Clyde was more of a lightning bolt than he was a man, and the land he struck with each horse-drawn stride and later remembered with fire-lit awe was more nuggets of gold than it was clumps of dirt.

The stories of Grandpa Clyde were Wheeler family legend and were told at every family gathering. Dexter grew up on them. He was a lovable boy with straw-colored hair and sky-blue eyes, but he was earnest and impressionable, and early on had earned his own family reputation as a well-meaning screw-up. He never lived down the time when, as a young boy, he wanted to help his pa with the chores and tried to milk a horse, or the time he hitched up the wagon with the mules facing the wrong way, so nobody was too surprised when at one family gathering, after the stories of Grandpa Clyde were told, including the one about how he had answered the newspaper ad, Dexter announced, "I'm going to ride for the Pony Express too when I grow up."

Lloyd and all the family had a good laugh. "Well, you better grow up backward then," his father said.

"That horse is long out of the barn," one of his uncles added.

Young Dexter didn't understand that expression and got his back up. "Why not?" he said to his uncle, with his father and mother standing right there. "Grandpa Clyde was an orphan, and I'm an orphan too."

Everybody laughed again, and Dexter's blood rose in defiance. "You wait," he said. "You just wait and see."

NEBRASKA, 1924—The early settlers to the prairie lands of Nebraska often had no lumber for homes, so they would build a dugout as a temporary shelter. A dugout was a cave of sorts carved into the side of a hillock, with the roof and front made from poles and sod. It was a primitive dwelling, but it provided protection from the wind, the summer heat, and the winter cold. The sod of the roofs continued to grow grass, blending with the hillside, and grazing horses and oxen would sometimes wander over the roof of a dugout and fall through into the living quarters of a startled prairie family.

In the spring of 1924, a pioneer named Mike Dugan built himself and his family such a dugout in the southeast corner of Nebraska on a square mile of fertile land that they had purchased to farm. Dugan built the dugout first, then had to dig a well, get a crop in the ground, and put up fencing for the few head of livestock they had. The chores were without end, and he had to do the heavy work alone, having only a wife and two daughters for support.

The days were long, and life was hard, and Mike Dugan had his problems, not the least of which was finding husbands for the girls. Eve was a fiery redhead, taking after his wife, and Emma was a hay-haired blonde, taking after his own side of the family. Both girls were comely and strong and would make good wives, and they were sure ripe for the picking. Eve was sixteen already and Emma fifteen, three-months turned and, well, there was just no use denying it, they weren't getting any younger.

Every night, exhausted from his day's labors, Mike Dugan, a God-fearing man, would kneel down next to his bed and pray. He would turn his head up toward the thin layer of thatch and sod that formed the roof of his humble dwelling as if he were looking straight through it to the rich blackness of the far-reaching night, to its distant stars, all the way to the eternal home of Sweet Jesus above. "Sweet Jesus, give me your strength," he would say, "and help me to prevail over all the bountiful trials with which, in your ever-lovin' wisdom, you have deigned to beset me.

"Sweet Jesus, I know you had it tough when you were down here in your own day, you being born in a manger, and what with all those Romans and Pharisees troubling you at every turn, and you not even having a rifle or a two-axle wagon or any of the other present-day luxuries we enjoy. And I know it didn't end any too pretty for you either, what with that cross and you dying to save all of sinful mankind. You sure set a fearsome example in the way of trials but, Sweet Jesus, I just ask you to consider that, all in all, maybe you have blessed me with more trials than a solitary man can take. If you'll recollect, you had those twelve apostles, all able-bodied men, to lend you a hand, and you only had the one womanfolk, your blessed virgin mother, God bless her, to look after.

"As for myself, I don't have a single hired hand, let alone an apostle, and I got three women to look after too. So, Sweet Jesus, what I'm getting at is if you could just help me find husbands for the girls, that would be a big load off my wagon, and I won't be botherin' you for any other assistance until the crop comes in. If you can't spare two husbands, at least send one for my Emma, because I got to tell you, Sweet Jesus, when the moon comes up for her, even the coyotes get out of the way." Mike concluded fervently, "Sweet merciful Jesus, I thank you ahead of time, and leave it up to you, in your all-knowing wisdom, to handle in the best way you see fit." Mike lowered his eyes from the ceiling of the dugout and the star-studded sky above to his humble quilted bed and said, "Amen."

Dexter Wheeler hunched over his campfire and stirred at his coffee with a twig to cool it down, and he took that same twig and poked absentmindedly at the coals. The sun was just a red glow on the horizon, and a breeze was whistling over the grasses of the plain. The land stretched forever in every direction, just like Grandpa Clyde had said it did. Dexter could hardly believe he was finally here. He had started in Missouri, tracing the route of the Pony Express to Nebraska, and it was here that he had decided to lay claim to one of those sweet pieces of farmland that his grandpa and his own pa had described for him and that in his own mind was already partly his. Dexter had his horse saddled and ready to ride, and he wished that his Grandpa Clyde could see him now.

Dexter took one last swig of coffee and kicked out the embers of his fire. Then he mounted his horse and sat high and proud in the saddle. He looked out now over an expanse of land wondrous not only in its breadth and beauty but in its moon-like solitude. He had ridden all the day before without seeing a soul and had made camp only when it was too dark to ride any more. Now in the morning light he got his first look at the land he would call his home. He peered out from under the brim of his hat at the restless shadows across the waving grass. In the far distance he saw what appeared to be a wagon and a few head of cattle. If there was a farmer there, he could ask him about any land for sale. He imagined the farmer pointing toward the horizon and saying, "Land? Right there. Right there's all the land a man can want that's got the smarts and the gumption to claim it and to work it."

Dexter thought of his uncles and how they had teased him about his dream. "Dexter wouldn't know good farmland if he was knee-deep in it," one had said. Another had said, "Farmland? Dexter wouldn't identify bullshit if it were up to his nose." Oh, they'd had a good laugh all right, Dexter thought, but I'll be the one laughing soon. Dexter adjusted his hold on the reigns. Oh, how Dexter wished all of his uncles could see him now.

Just this side of the wagon and cattle, the morning light now revealed a small hillock. I'll just ride up onto that hillock, Dexter thought, and get a better view. That would be the smart thing to do. Dexter smiled with pride and satisfaction and took one last look at the panorama and one last second to savor the sweet moment. This is the start of my future, he thought, and I, Dexter Wheeler, am here to claim it. Dexter raised his hat and bowed in tribute to himself and his accomplishment. Then he slapped gently at the flank of his horse, looked toward the hillock in the near distance, and said, "Giddyup."

10. Wake Up, Mr. Bill

"WAKE UP, MR. BILL." Louise's voice came to Bill as if across a great distance, and he couldn't place it at first. It was just a strange song. "Wake up, Mr. Bill." Bill opened his eyes and saw once more the placeless, eternal sky. He could be anywhere, any time. Clouds were still passing, shading the sun, creating the coolness that had helped him that morning. He remembered then, with a pleasant relief, his run and his stretching on the lawn. He looked to his sides and saw his hands still clutching at clumps of grass. He was still here. "What you been doin'?" Louise said. "Dreamin' again?"

"I don't remember, Louise."

"Uh-huh," she said. "I guess that's my job: remembering. Remembering to wake you up. Remembering to feed you. Remembering to get you to bed. If it wasn't for me, you'd all just float away."

"I love you, Louise."

"You stop that now."

"Will you marry me?"

"I gotta help get lunch together."

"After lunch, then," Bill persisted. "On a full stomach."

"Once you're fed, you'll forget all about me."

"How could I ever forget you, Louise?"

"The same way you forget everything else would be my guess. Jeanie's coming after lunch with a friend. Do you remember that?"

"Bridesmaids," Bill said.

"You'd better get in and wash up."

"I'll give you a head start," Bill said.

"You go on now."

A breeze had come up, and Louise had turned her back to Bill as she shook out another rug. Bill looked at her in her white uniform dress and stockings. The sun came through her skirt, revealing her plump legs.

"I love you, Louise."

"You stop that now."

"Here I come, Louise," Bill shouted.

Louise looked over her shoulder and saw that Bill had risen and was making a few quick steps in her direction. "You go on now," she said again, but she was laughing and hurrying back into the home.

Bill had been living for the last several years in a small home for the elderly called Elysian Fields. There were only twelve residents—senile citizens, Bill called them—and one live-in aid, and Louise, who came on weekdays. The home was an original neighborhood house that had been renovated to create a central living and dining area, and had additional bedrooms built off the back. Bill had not wanted to move into a group home, but his niece had insisted on it when Bill had started to "space out," as she called it. A couple of times he had neglected to pay his bills, and his electricity and telephone had been shut down, but the clincher was when he started a fire by forgetting a frying pan on the stove. Bill didn't think he was forgetful. The only problem was that he had too many things to remember, and couldn't keep them all straight sometimes.

Bill simply refused to move into one of those large old-age facilities, and he was too independent-minded to move to Florida. "As if when you get older, some sunshine and a leisure suit are going to solve all your problems," he'd said. So his niece had found him a spot in this little home, and once he got used to it, he liked it fine and was glad he'd come. It was comfortable, the neighborhood had good roads, and even some good trails, for his running, and he had to admit that he liked having people to talk to during the day.

Elysian Fields was distinguished by what it wasn't as much as by what it was. It wasn't stainless steel and white walls and the smell of industrial cleanser. It was orderly and clean all right—Louise saw to that—but it was the orderliness and cleanliness of a stay-at-home mom with Ivory soap, Lemon Pledge, and lavender air freshener. Elysian Fields wasn't the cold of air-conditioning, but the coolness of a ceiling fan, moving slowly enough that you could count its orbits, and a breeze coming through the front windows, teasing dainty curtains, and continuing through the home and out the open doors of the shaded patio. Elysian Fields wasn't a row of patients in wheelchairs, but oldsters—as Louise called them—plumped on overstuffed chairs and couches throughout the home's common rooms. It wasn't schedules and rigid routine, but a day-by-day adjustment to everybody's wants and needs. "We're having peach cobbler for dessert today," Louise would announce. "That's Mrs. Dunn's favorite, and she reminded me this morning that we haven't had it for a while." So peach cobbler it was.

The home was just that, a home, not a nursing hospital. The residents were allowed to bring some of their own furniture and belongings with them, and the dayroom had become an eclectic and comfortable collection of couches and chairs and lamps, with pillows and coffee tables and end tables, where the oldsters were free to build their nests of necessities: reading glasses, tissues, medications, coupons, TV guides, word puzzles, magnifying glasses, honey, rubber bands, and the small calendars that helped them remember the day, the month, and even the year—calendars that on this day reminded them that it was Wednesday, July 23, 2047.

Bill had showered and had dressed neatly. He had chosen one of his brighter shirts, a cobalt blue, to offset the grayness of his hair and to give himself a younger, fresher look for the visit of his great-niece.

He had the chicken broth and sandwich that was served for lunch and then went to his favorite spot in the dayroom—the big, overstuffed chair that he had brought from his own home and that now sat in the corner nearest the kitchen. His chair was one of several chairs, along with two couches, that circled a coffee table in that corner of the room. Sitting across from Bill that morning were Bert and Mabel. Bert was wearing a shirt with red polka dots, suspenders, and a bow tie. He was holding a cane between his legs. Mabel was wearing a flower-print housedress. Both of them were sleeping.

Bill turned on his reading lamp and took a newspaper from the end table. He was reading when his great-niece Jeanie arrived. Louise had a view of the street from the kitchen window, and she was the first to see Jeanie drive up. She came into the day room to tell Bill. "Jeanie's here, Mr. Bill, with her friend."

Elysian Fields was cheerful enough, but when the girls came in, it was as if all the doors and windows had been opened to fresh air and rainbow colors. Jeanie's hair was dyed red—new since Bill had last seen her—and her friend's hair was jet-black with golden streaks. Their clothes were neon, Jeanie's purple and her friend's pink. They had been joking about something and were still laughing delightedly as they entered the room.

Jeanie gave Bill a kiss.

"Uncle Bill, this is my friend Britney from school."

"Good to meet you, sir."

"Please. Call me Uncle Bill." Bill motioned them toward the couch next to his chair. "Sit down, girls; it don't cost more." The girls sat, and Bill returned to his chair. "I'll just sit next to you," he said, "like a thorn among roses."

Jeanie reached into her handbag, a large netted and buckled affair, brought out a pastry box and handed it to Bill. "Mom sent you over this cake," she said.

"She's a doll," Bill said.

"We were hoping you would tell us a story."

"What kind?"

"A love story."

"No. I meant what kind of cake."

"Your favorite: chocolate with chocolate frosting."

"Ooooh, tell your mom thanks."

Bert woke up from his slumber on the couch and saw the girls. "Hi, girls," he said. "Do you go to high school?"

"Yes," Jeanie said.

"That's nice," Bert said. He got up and ambled off toward the kitchen. Mabel remained sleeping.

"That was Bert," Bill said to Britney. "And the lady he was sleeping with is Mabel. They just got married two weeks ago, and they spent their wedding night playing pinochle with Bert's sister. They're a couple of lovebirds. Bert's probably going for a cookie, and he'll bring one back for Mabel too."

"They're so sweet," Jeanie said.

"Do you see that eyeliner on Mabel's eyelids?" Bill said.

Britney nodded.

"It's not really eyeliner. She had it tattooed on. When she was young, she got tired of putting it on every day, so she had a brainstorm and got the tattoos. She was an exotic dancer who sunlighted as a beautician. She teased men at night and hair during the day. Now she's an old lady napping on the couch, and she looks like she's ready for a cocktail party."

Bert came back from the kitchen with a couple of cookies, and sat back down next to Mabel. "You girls go to high school?" he said.

"No, Bert," Bill said. "They're in college now."

"That's nice."

Bert nudged Mabel and handed her a cookie, and they both nibbled on them.

Bill said to Jeanie, "How are the workouts going?"

"I did thirty miles last week, and I did that hill workout you suggested. It was hard."

"It's supposed to be. You do one workout like that a week for the rest of the summer, and you'll see the improvement right away when the cross-country season starts."

"My legs were sore the next day."

"That's good. It means you were working some new muscles."

"Should I take an off-day after the hills?"

"No, don't take a day off after a hard training run. You need to go out to stretch those muscles, get them loose. Just do some easy miles the following day."

"OK."

"Excuse us, Britney," Bill said. "We have to get our running talk out of the way.

"That's OK," Britney said.

"Uncle Bill," Jeanie said sweetly, "We didn't come over to talk just about running."

"Of course you didn't," Bill smiled. "What *do* you want to talk about?"

"We want you to tell us one of your love stories."

"Which one?"

"*HOHAs in Love.*"

"But I've told you that one at least a half-dozen times."

"I know. But Britney hasn't heard it, and it's the greatest love story ever."

"Well, there were a couple of kids named Romeo and Juliet, but that *was* before my time."

"Please, Uncle Bill."

"Yes, please," Britney said. "Jeanie told me about Biscuit, and I want to hear more."

"Jeanie, did you tell Britney part of the story?"

"No, Uncle Bill, just a couple of things about Biscuit. That's all I told. I promise."

"I've been having trouble with my boyfriend," Britney said, "and Jeanie told me that if I heard your story I'd know what to do."

Bill looked at Britney seriously and pretended to be reading her mind. "Your boyfriend is inconsiderate and takes you for granted. He doesn't understand the meaning of true love. He's not always there for you and says that he needs to spend time with his friends."

"That's amazing," Britney said. "How did you know?"

"Lucky guess."

"He's such a rap-head," Britney said. "And you were right: he does want to be with his friends more than with me. That's how the whole fight started."

"What happened?"

"I asked if he'd go to my cousin's wedding with me, and he wouldn't, because it was the same day he was going to a baseball game with his friends."

"Couldn't he go to another game?"

"Exactly. That's what I said. But no. They already had their tickets, and one of the visiting players is this nod-wad that everybody hates, so they're all going to paint their bodies Met blue and paint the letters for "Igno sucks" on their chests. My boyfriend is going to be the first 's' of 'sucks.'"

"I see."

"I don't know what to do," Britney said. "I don't know if I should even stay with him."

"Jeanie told you a little about Biscuit, and Biscuit would say, 'The answer to a question is who you are. If you know yourself, you'll have your answer.'"

"I don't understand."

"Britney, if I could tell you in so many words, I would, but that's why we live our lives, and that's why we have stories."

"So will you tell the story, Uncle Bill?"

A cuckoo sounded from a bedroom down the hall.

"What was that?" Britney said.

"A cuckoo clock," Bill said. He saw the blank expression on Britney's face and explained, "That's a clock that has a little bird that pops out of a house and cuckoos once for every hour." Bill laughed. "Isn't it wonderful the oddball things that the human race comes up with?"

Bill reached into his pocket and took out some change and tossed the coins onto the floor.

"What are you doing, Uncle Bill?"

"It's one o'clock now. Stan will be getting up from his nap. He has breakfast at 7:00, lunch at 11:00, and then takes a nap until 1:00. He'll have dinner at 5:30 and be in bed at 8:00. You could set your watch to him. I don't understand why we need another cuckoo around here." Bill tossed a couple more coins out onto the floor. "Just sit tight," he said, "and watch."

Only a few seconds passed before there was a shuffling down the hall and Stan appeared, looking grumpy after his nap. He spotted some of the coins right away and went for them faster than a five-year-old goes for eggs on Easter.

"Stan, what ya doin'?" Bill said.

"Somebody dropped some change," he said.

"What? Quarters and dimes and nickels and the like?"

"What other change is there?" Stan said.

"Well, I'm missing some quarters and dimes and nickels. I got a hole in my pocket. That change must be mine." Bill had raised his voice slightly, indignantly. He winked at the girls.

"Well, I got two words for you, Bill."

"And what would they be, Stan?"

Stan stopped his search and looked squarely at Bill. "Finders keepers," he said.

"Damn it!" Bill shouted, in mock vexation.

"Ha Ha!" Stan shook his head from side to side in wouldn't-you-know-it disappointment in Bill. "Losers weepers."

"I don't know if I like your attitude, Stan Nolan."

"Well, if you don't like it, then I got two more words for you, Bill."

"And what would they be, Stan?"

"If you don't like it," Stan said, pointing a finger at Bill, "you can just LUMP IT!"

"Ahhhhhh," Bill groaned.

Stan picked up the last coin, shook his head grumpily at Bill, and shuffled back toward his bedroom.

"Don't get lost," Bill called after him.

"You don't get lost yourself, Bill." Stan made an obscene arm gesture in Bill's direction before he continued on his way.

"Wasn't that fun?" Bill said to the girls, laughing. "It was worth every penny. He'll go back to his room now and count the money, and roll it up, if he's got enough for a roll, and hide it in his secret hiding place." Bill whispered, "It's in a coffee can on the bottom shelf of his bureau, next to his bedpan." Bill laughed again. "It'll take him a while. That will give us more time to talk."

"Is he always that grumpy, Uncle Bill?"

"No. Stan's a good guy if you don't bump into him after his nap. Before his wife passed, he lived down at the shore. He was one of those old duffers who would scan the sand with a metal detector looking for change. His wife would go out with him every evening in the summer. He gets a tear in his eye when he talks about it. I like to drop some change every once in a while for him, for old time's sake. It makes his day. I don't usually tease him about it though."

"That's sweet of you," Britney said.

"Stan and I play cards most afternoons. He'll have forgotten all about our squabble by the next time we play, and I'll win my coins back. It's a little ecosystem we got going," Bill laughed. "It's fun being old," he concluded. "You two girls got something to look forward to."

Jeanie got up and kissed Bill on the cheek.

Bert awoke from another snooze and noticed the girls again. "Hi, girls," he said. "Do you go to high school?"

"No, Bert," Bill said. "They're shuttle pilots. They just brought back a payload of tourists from the moon."

Bert turned to Mabel and kissed her on the cheek. "Did you hear that Mabel? The girls just landed from the moon."

"Now," Bill said, "where were we?"

"The love story," Britney said.

"*HOHAs in Love*," Jeanie said.

Mabel, in a delayed response to Bert's voice, reached over and took Bert's hand, and Bert, with dreamy admiration, placed his other hand on top of hers.

"Oh yes," Bill said. "Love."

11. A Love Story

"I'LL BE HAPPY to tell you that story, but before we get started, I want you to know that I have a couple of rules. Jeanie knows them, Britney, and I want you to hear them too. First, no cell phones. I want you to turn them off now and keep them off until we're finished. Nothing bothers me more than to be telling a story and get interrupted by a phone call. Go ahead, turn them off now."

Both girls turned off their phones.

"And the second rule, and this is the most important," Bill smiled broadly at both Britney and Jeanie in turn, "I like to start a story with a cup of tea. Jeanie, will you ask Louise if she'll bring us some? Tell her I have a piece of cake for her if she will."

Jeanie started to get up, but just then Louise came into the room pushing a man in a wheelchair. The man was wearing pajamas and slippers and a light bathrobe. His face held no expression, and his eyes were half closed. "I thought Mr. Dizzy could use a change of scenery," Louise said. "Do you mind if he joins you?"

Bill exchanged a look with Jeanie. "Well, I was about to tell a story," Bill said to Louise, "but Dizzy can stay, as long as he doesn't talk too much." Bill was teasing Louise again, because Dizzy hadn't said a word in over a year.

Louise repeated the instructions to Dizzy. "You can join the party, Mr. Dizzy, but you'll have to keep it down."

"We were just about to have a piece of our cake, Louise. Would you mind bringing us some tea to go with it? The cake's chocolate, and there's a big piece for you."

"I'll be happy to bring your tea, Mr. Bill, but I'll have to leave my cake for later. I have too much work to do right now." Louise parked Dizzy next to Bert and Mabel and put the brakes on his wheelchair. "I'll be right back with the tea."

Jeanie went to help Louise, and Bill got up and took a small throw blanket from the couch. He went over to Dizzy and spread it carefully over his lap, then explained to Britney, "Dizzy's been off in his own world for a while now, but before that, we had some great times." He touched Dizzy gently on the hand. "Take it easy, Diz," he said to him. "I'm going to tell us your favorite story now."

Louise and Jeanie returned with the tea just then, and Louise said, "Oh, are you telling the HOHAs story? I wish I had time to listen."

"Don't worry, Louise; it's Jeanie's favorite too." He winked at Jeanie. "I'm sure I'll be telling it again."

Louise left then, and while Jeanie served the cake, Bill said to Britney, "A lot of this story is about running. Are you a runner too?"

"I've been to a couple of Jeanie's cross-country meets," Britney said, "but I'm not a runner myself."

"That's fine," Bill said. "Running isn't for everybody, and it isn't the only thing, but, as I said, I'm going to be talking about running during this story, and I need you to understand some things from the start."

"OK."

Bill sat back in his chair and composed himself. Then he looked thoughtfully at Jeanie and Britney before he began. "Wiser people than I have said that if we can understand one single small thing in our life through and through, then we will have come to an understanding of everything." Bill looked at both the girls and then extended his arms as if to embrace the world. "We look out at the universe with a telescope, and it is more than we can comprehend, and we look at a single cell with a microscope, and we see that there is an entire universe there too. The immensity of the world is frightening, and we feel small and alone, and we don't know where to turn, so we settle our energies on something small, something simple, something we can get our arms around and control, like a job, a hobby, or maybe a person, and on the surface that small thing looks simple enough.

"Take running, for example. You'd think you just need to put on a pair of sneakers and go at it. Ha! And I guess you could look at life and think the same thing. But of course it isn't that simple. You go at it and quickly learn—often the hard way—that there are all kinds of obstacles, and you need to learn ways to get around them or over them. With running, for example, you need to learn about the right shoes for you, the right clothes for all weather, when to eat and what to eat, how much rest you need, how to stretch before a run. You need to learn about fatigue, injuries, pain, perseverance, constancy, training methods and techniques, racing tactics, how to handle victory, how to handle defeat, and how to get along with your fellow runners, to whom you will inevitably turn. And little by little, over years, if you've learned and mastered all these small lessons of this *simple* pursuit, you come to realize that by becoming a good runner, you've learned all you need to know to live the rest of your life too, and that even the universe—which looked imposing from the start—is really only a beautiful road, if you will, that, of course, you will take one breath and one stride and one problem at a time."

Britney looked over at Jeanie and smiled, as if to share the silliness of what Bill had said, but Jeanie didn't return the smile. Instead, she closed her eyes and nodded in confirmation of her uncle's words.

"Every moment of our life has meaning," Bill continued, "whether we can see it or not, whether we want to believe it or not. Things happen, seemingly inconsequential things. We don't see how they're connected, but every moment is a miracle of consequence. That seems silly, and fools laugh at it, but it's true.

"Who can pull one story apart from the next? There is no beginning and no end to any of them, big or small. The seeds of one story are planted in the time of another story, and the fruits of that story blossom in the midst of another story still. Everything is connected and continuous in ways that go on and on beyond our imagination, but when we want to tell a piece of that big story, we need to make a decision, and that decision can only be based on feeling, a feeling that a person, or time, or series of events stand out from the whole, by creating even the slightest perceptible pause or shift in the course of things, so that we feel it is important and stands apart from all the rest.

"That's the feeling I have about the small town of Hoboken in the 1990s when I was a young man there, and the story I'm going to tell takes place there during that time. It was the time of the Bill Clinton administration, and let me tell you, from the White House on down throughout the entire land, there was hanky-panky in the air. Maybe this was just the party before the harder times we sensed would follow, and the bulk of this story happened in the late nineties when things were craziest, and all the seemingly inconsequential events of that decade in that place came together and revealed the marvelous connection that was always there.

"There are some who even say that time itself doesn't exist, that everything that did happen, or will happen, is all happening all at once, right now. I don't know about that, and even if it's true, it's too much for me. I gotta start somewhere. Some storytellers like to plop you down right in the middle and then work their way out, or jump ahead and then work their way back, but that's not my way. I like to start at the beginning. A young man came into Hoboken in 1990 to found and preside over a running club. And for me, the way I see it, the story can only start with the name of that young man: Emmitt F. Bean."

Britney giggled and looked at Jeanie again.

"Listen!" Bill said this sharply and loudly. Britney, who was unaccustomed to Uncle Bill's narrative devices, sat straighter in startled attention, which was just the effect Bill had wanted. Bill leaned forward in his chair, motioning the girls toward him, and they leaned forward too. Then he looked from one to the other and whispered, "Listen closely."

12. Coach

EMMITT F. BEAN was the founder, first president, and coach—as he preferred to be called, and we shall call him—of the Hoboken Harriers Running Club. Coach had an Irish father and a British mother and was cursed, or blessed, depending on how you looked at it, with a combination of determination and eccentricity that was both flabbergasting and charming. Some thought he was just plain nuts. It was rumored that he had fallen from a tricycle as a child and landed on his head. This hadn't damaged his brain so much as altered it in a peculiar way, but it was the exact nature of that alteration that no one could quite comprehend.

Coach didn't say a word until he was four years old. His poor mother took him to doctors and therapists and worried herself sick over him. Then, one day he just started talking in complete sentences and didn't stop. It was as if he had spent the first four years formulating his opinions and was now determined to spend the rest of his life blabbering about them. His mother went from praying for him to speak to paying him to shut up. "I'll give you a quid, Emmitt," she'd say, "if for God's sake you'll just be quiet for one single precious holy hour." His Irish relatives said he had the "gift of gab," and one of his runners later quipped, "Scientists want to know if there is life on Mars. They should just shoot Coach up there, because if there's anything to talk to, Coach will find it."

Throughout his childhood and adolescence, Coach was also much smaller than normal, which in itself could have accounted for much of his talk. Then, at age sixteen, he had an amazing growth spurt and grew almost a foot in just over a year. Again, his poor mother was challenged, this time to keep him in trousers. But even though he topped out at six-foot-one, he retained the feisty attitude, hummingbird energy, and fierce competitiveness that he'd needed to survive as a boy of diminutive stature. A person's appearance isn't always important, but with Coach it was part of the package. Think of a big nerd. He had black horn-rimmed glasses, with lenses like coke bottles that magnified his eyes and, like a resourceful third-grader, he wasn't above repairing them when needed with tape or a Band Aid. His hair was light brown, thinning on top, and often disheveled, standing up in cowlicks that were beyond prediction, let alone taming. Members of his running club would sometimes bet on which direction they would be pointing on any given day. As a kid, he always had a shoe untied, his fly unzipped, or a shirttail out, often all three, and as an adult he didn't fare much better. His movements were awkward, and yet his manner and expressions conveyed a singleness of purpose that was at the same time comical and profound. Along with this nerdiness came a muscular body. He had worked with weights since grade school to compensate for his lack of height, and to increase his power for middle-distance running, and had built a sturdy strength onto his lanky frame. His nerdy intellectuality was at odds with his physical appearance, and created in those meeting him for the first time an initial confusion and puzzlement, until they inevitably gave up trying to place him in one category or the other and came to realize that Coach was beyond any categorization, a creature all his own.

But all of this aside, it was Coach's passion for running that was quickly noticed and that set him apart. There are people for whom a central interest is the core of their personality: for example, a person who believes that everything—the weather, politics, the price of a loaf of bread—is the work of aliens and that the entire government is united in conspiracy to keep that knowledge from us. That one idea is the person's fixed center, and everything is eventually sucked into its gravitational pull. With Coach, that fixed idea, that core belief, was the beauty and value of running, and his passion for it and his dedication to it. Just when you thought you were having a normal conversation with him, and that perhaps he wasn't as nuts as everybody thought he was, he would slip in some reference to heart rate or stride length or a Kenyan marathoner, and you'd think, "My God, it's true. He's completely odd."

Coach was also a mathematical whiz, and he had come to the States fresh from college to find work in the computer field. At first he stayed with a friend of a friend named Harry Horton who had a running club in Brooklyn.

The Brooklyn Striders were one of the best amateur clubs in the region, consistently fielding competitive teams, with the occasional brilliant runner. I'll give Harry that.

Coach had been introduced to Harry because of their mutual love of running, and they got along well enough for a few weeks. Then their egos collided, and Coach moved to Hoboken, cursing Harry and vowing to start a running club of his own.

13. Building a Club

COACH DECIDED that the first thing his new running club needed, of course, was a name. He had been a member of a club in Britain called the Manchester Harriers. "Harrier" was a term that the British, for whatever reason, used to describe runners.

The term "harrier" dates back to the old English sport of "Hares and Hounds." In this sport a runner, or group of runners, the hares, set out and leave a trail of paper scrapes. The other runners, the

*hounds, follow the trail until they've run down—harried—the hares.
The early running clubs, initially established for this sport, called
themselves "Hares and Hounds" or simply "Harriers."*

Anyway, Coach thought that the name Hoboken Harriers had an alliterative
ring. It was in fashion back then to abbreviate everything, and Coach, being
new to the USA, had had to learn the meaning of KFC, TGIF, IHOP, and many
others, and he soon hit upon the abbreviation HOHAs, by which the Hoboken
Harriers came to be commonly known.

The next order of business was the club's running schedule. Regular group
runs are the foundation of any club, and Coach would have these runs on
weekdays, so they were part of the membership's regular work-week schedule.
There would be other runs—long runs on the weekends, and track and hill
workouts, of course—but the weekday runs would be the cornerstone of the
club's running schedule. Mondays and Fridays were no good, because of their
proximity to the weekend. Mondays were for recuperating and getting into
the groove, and Fridays were for partying and winding down. So he settled on
Tuesdays and Thursdays, with a rest day in between.

Within days of arriving in Hoboken, Coach had run all its streets looking
for suitable courses, and he decided upon courses along the river that would
take advantage of the views of New York. The Tuesday run would start at
Washington and Thirteenth Street in front of the YMCA at 8:00 PM, and the
Thursday run would start at Washington and Fourth Street at 7:30 PM.

This was a simple enough arrangement on the surface, but even this was
based upon Coach's thoughtful logic. There would be two runs, not just one,
because a serious running club needed more than one, and this arrangement
would provide for choice. One run started in upper Hoboken and the other
in lower Hoboken, to make at least one of the runs convenient to all club
members, and the Tuesday run started a half-hour later for those who couldn't
get home from work and ready for a run at the earlier time. Both runs started on
Washington Street, the main drag of Hoboken. Washington Street was busy and
well lit and therefore a safe place to meet. Coach knew this would be important
to the female club members, especially in the winter months when both runs
would begin after dark. So Tuesdays and Thursdays it was. Coach marked the

days, times, and meeting places of the runs prominently on the flyer he was designing to promote the club.

Hoboken had a small printing business on Park Avenue called Counter-Fit Printing, and Coach went there to get the flyers done. A man was standing behind the counter when Coach walked in, and Coach introduced himself. "I'm Emmitt F. Bean, the founder, first president, and coach of the Hoboken Harriers Running Club," he said, "but you can just call me Coach."

The man behind the counter had his head angled slightly to the side, struggling to understand the unusual person standing before him and the odd statement he had just uttered. Then he said simply, "I'm Ben." As an afterthought, he added with a smile, "Benjamin T. Abrams, the founder, sole owner, and manager of Counter-Fit Printing."

"Glad to meet you, Ben."

"I didn't know we had a running club in town."

"I just founded it," Coach said. "In fact, that's why I'm here. I need some flyers to advertise." Coach handed Ben the paper on which he had scribbled the words for the flyer, and Ben looked it over.

"The HOHAs," Ben read aloud. "The premier running club of the East Coast."

"It will be," Coach said.

"No problem," Ben said. "How many do you need?"

"A hundred."

"It would be cheaper by unit if you ordered more. I'll have to charge you twelve dollars just to set this up."

Coach wanted the club to pay for itself, and he had a plan for the flyers. "I was hoping you would do it for free," he said.

Ben's whole head twitched, his mouth dropped slightly open, and he looked back at Coach blankly in disbelief. Coach often got looks like that, as if he were from another planet and had committed a breach of the established and absolute rules of etiquette or conduct. It was the same look he'd once got at the doctor's office when he told the administrator that his car was going to be at the mechanics, so for his next appointment, would the doctor please make a house call. The dumbfounded look brought on by statements like these was immediately followed by, depending upon the person's temperament, either laughter or disdain.

Ben laughed. "Now, Coach, why would I do that?"

"Because, Ben, I'm looking for sponsors for the club," Coach explained, "and I was thinking that some free printing could cover your sponsorship fee. We could put "Sponsored by Counter-Fit Printing" on each flyer. I'm going to post the flyers all over town. It will be free printing for me and free advertising for you. That sounds like win-win to me. What d'ya think, Ben?"

"I don't know."

"There'll be other opportunities for you too," Coach continued. "The HOHAs will need business cards, a monthly newsletter, and club T-shirts. Imagine "Counter-Fit Printing" on the back of every runner in town. Hundreds of them. Running up and down every street in Hoboken."

Coach paused to picture it, and Ben was picturing it too. Their heads were moving, following the dizzying parade of Counter-Fit runners.

"So, do we have a deal?"

"Let's start with the flyers," Ben said. "I'll print you up two hundred, and if you need more, come back and let me know."

"Congratulations," Coach said.

"For what?"

"For being the first Official Sponsor of the HOHAs."

When Coach left, Ben returned to his work, still shaking his head. "Emmitt F. Bean," he said. He shook his head again and chuckled. "The HOHAs."

Coach got the flyers from Ben that afternoon and posted them on light poles and bulletin boards all over town, and he spoke with every business owner along his way.

"I'm Emmitt F. Bean, the founder, first president, and coach of the Hoboken Harriers Running Club."

"I didn't even know that Hoboken had a running club."

"It does now."

"Well, I never heard of them."

"You will."

Coach would then ask to put a flyer in their storefront window, and he'd hit them up for sponsorship. He solicited sponsorships from the Hoboken

Farmboy health-food store, Marie's Bakery, the Antique Bakery, the Baja and East L.A. restaurants, and the Malibu Diner, but he garnered the highest-paid sponsorships—Coach's Club Sponsorships, he called them—from the Hoboken bars. Coach had a natural rapport with bar owners, and over a beer he easily convinced them of the benefits of a financial relationship with his club. Not only would the name of the bar appear on HOHAs T-shirts, but the HOHAs would frequent the bar after the weekly club runs, and Coach, taking a long swig from his beer and smacking his lips in appreciation, emphasized just how thirsty runners could get.

From establishment to establishment he went, and within days of his arrival in Hoboken, scores of Hobokeners had met him or heard his name, knew that there was a strange new character in town, and had a nodding recognition of his energy and obsession, and the news of Coach's upstart running club—the premier running club of the East Coast—was plastered all over town.

14. Magic Shoes

FROM BENEATH THE BRIDGE, Moses could hear voices on the sidewalk above. There was a high school nearby, and the schoolboys were particularly loud when they crossed over. Moses didn't mind them; he enjoyed their energy and their joking banter. The evening before, he'd heard two of them teasing another. They had something of his that he wanted back, and Moses could tell from their voices that they were throwing it back and forth to keep it from him. "Give them back." "Over here, Doug, quick." "Come on, guys." "Jim, this way." "Stop it." "Throw them over." Then there was silence. "Oh shit, they're in the wires." There was laughter then, followed by the sound of the boys running away and laughing some more. The one boy called after them, "My dad is going to kill me," and then he ran after the others.

The next morning, Moses saw a pair of sneakers hanging from the telephone wires that ran adjacent the bridge. The morning sky was blue and orange, and the silver sneakers shone like stars in the rising sun. The laces were tangled in the wires, near the place where he had heard the boys. They weren't far from the bridge, but there was no way to get at them. They hung there for three days, until a telephone crew arrived to do some work and the guy in the cherry picker untangled the laces and brought them down in the bucket. "I'd like those shoes, sir," Moses said to the man, "if you don't need them."

It only took a glance for the man to peg Moses as a bum. His eyes rolled down from Moses' unkempt hair to the ragged boots on his feet. "They're all yours, Pops," he said. The man bowed slightly and held the shoes out to Moses in the palm of his hand as if he were a waiter serving hors d'oeuvres at a dinner party. Moses took them gently and examined them intently. They were new and high-tech, with a red streak down the side, and with air cushions that you could see through windows in the heels. Moses marveled at the luxury of windows as clear as glass in the heels of shoes. The laces were white and starchy and long enough to tie up two times. They were the latest thing. "Cool," is what Moses would call them, but he didn't know what word the kids used now.

Moses listened for the boys for a couple of days, thinking he could return the sneakers to the boy who'd lost them, but the boys didn't return, as far as Moses knew, and on the third day he gave in to the temptation to try on the shoes. He put on his best socks before he did, holding his breath as he slipped on the first sneaker, praying that it would fit, and it did. He put on the other one, laced them up carefully, and then rolled up his pants so he could get a good look. Then, feeling proud and self-conscious, he walked a block to the pawn shop that had that dark reflective window that he could use as a mirror. The shoes looked as good as he thought they would, even though they made the rest of him look rundown, but what he liked best was how they felt. They were cushiony in the front and in the heel, and they gave his step a little spring and his feet a little bounce. He remembered the pogo stick he'd had when he was a kid. He remembered the time he got to jump on a trampoline, and he remembered the race he had won in school that had made him the fifth-grade champ. Moses walked back toward the bridge, enjoying each soft step, as if the shoes were taking him back in time.

Moses thought a lot about the shoes, examining them and occasionally putting them on. He could tell that they weren't basketball shoes, or cross-training shoes, or shoes just for walking. The heels were high to support the Achilles tendon, and the sides of the heels were stiff to keep the foot and ankle from rolling over. The shoes were built for forward motion only; they were meant for running. Moses had run cross-country in high school, but they hadn't had shoes like these back then. He wondered if he would have been able to run faster in them. Just wearing them made him feel fast now. He thought of running in them, but then thought better of it; if the police saw him running down the street, dressed as he was, they'd think that he'd stolen something. Maybe they would think he'd stolen the shoes themselves.

Not far from the bridge was Branch Brook Park, just on the outskirts of downtown Newark. The park was known for its cherry trees and for the brook that meandered through its center. There was a paved road that ran the length of the park, winding and rolling along the brook and over the park's gentle hills. It was a beautiful place for running, and that afternoon Moses walked over there to test his new shoes.

All his clothes were from the Salvation Army: a blue, short-sleeved sport shirt—35 cents; a pair of green khakis—75 cents; and a brown leather belt with covered wagons etched into it—25 cents. He had a canary-yellow baseball cap, which said "Arnold's Trucking" on the front, and which he had found in a trash can—free, and now he was sporting the new sneakers—probably worth a hundred dollars. He tightened the circle of covered wagons to keep his pants from falling down, and rolled up his pants to free his legs. He thought about stretching, but had forgotten how, so, with no further preparation, he started to run.

He remembered enough to go slow at first, and the running felt good. Moses had been self-conscious just wearing the shoes, and now running in them he couldn't help glancing around to see if anyone was watching. He knew that he must look a sight, an old street bum in grungy clothes, pretending to have the luxury of exercise. Two mothers with strollers passed him going the other way, and he tipped his cap to them. One of the women gave him a smile, and that made Moses smile too.

After a few minutes, he picked up the pace, and remembered—not in his mind, but in the muscles of his calves and thighs—that he had been a natural. After all these years, his body had not forgotten, his legs still had the memory of the warmth and the rhythm of running, and after a few minutes more, his heart and breath got in sync too, and he felt the joy of everything working together. Oh, he was out of shape all right, and his legs soon tired and his breathing got heavy, but he'd had a glimpse of what he had been and, more surprising yet, a glimpse of what he could be again. He stopped while he was ahead. The first day should be just a howdy-do, he knew. He tried not to get excited, wiped the sweet sweat from his forehead, and enjoyed the tired looseness of his body and the casual softness of the walk back to the bridge.

Moses started running in the park every day, and his friend Buddy soon noticed the pleasure he was taking in it. "I never saw you so happy," Buddy said, "since you found those shoes."

"It's OK to keep them, isn't it, Buddy?"

"Of course it is." Buddy had been looking for a sign ever since Moses had had those bad dreams, and now, seeing the transformation the shoes had brought to Moses, Buddy declared that the shoes were it. "Those shoes are a good sign," he said. "They're magic."

"What do you mean, Buddy?"

"Shoes mean you have a mission, somewhere to go, and those shoes are the magic carpet. They're gonna take you wherever that is."

"But I don't need to go anywhere, Buddy."

"That's where you're wrong," Buddy said. "You wouldn't have been sent shoes if you didn't have somewhere you're supposed to go."

"But they weren't sent to me. I just found them."

"You just found them, huh? Let me ask you this. How many boys did you say crossed the bridge and lost those shoes?"

"Three."

"And how many days did those shoes hang up in those wires?"

"Three."

"Three. And haven't we seen shoes that hung in wires for years on end? But with these shoes, a city crew appeared and handed them right to you. Tell me, Moses, how many fellas were in that telephone crew that just chanced to come along and hand those shoes to you on a silver platter?"

"Three."

"And what size are those shoes?"

"Twelve."

"And what size do you wear?"

"Twelve."

"Damn it, Moses. Do I have to connect the dots for you? Do I have to draw you a picture and color it in too? Those shoes were sent to you special, and they're gonna take you somewhere."

"But where is that, Buddy?"

"We can't know that yet. That's why they're magic." Buddy looked up at the sky. Then he put his hand on Moses' shoulder. "We gotta be on the lookout though," he said. "We gotta look for further signs."

"And what do I do, Buddy?"

"All you gotta do is what you been doing, Moses," Buddy said. "Just keep wearing those shoes, and we'll see where they take you."

15. A Second Calling

AMY WAITED until the evening of the annual dinner dance to tell her sorority sisters that she would be taking a job in New York City. She thought that the gaiety of the evening would cushion the blow. Her sorority sisters had been hoping she would accept the fellowship she had been offered and stay another year with them. Amy was the most popular girl at the sorority and was the unspoken leader. She organized most of the sorority's charity events, and the annual 5K run that she'd founded as a freshman was now the biggest fund-raiser of the year.

The girls loved her because they felt at peace around her. She had a way of softening the mood and knowing what each of them needed, and more often than not they needed to forget their difficulties with school and with boys and to have some fun. Amy was good at finding the humor in the smallest things and helping everyone else share in it.

Once, one of the girls had returned from a family visit with a ceramic statue of a Cheshire cat that her grandmother had given her for her room. The cat was a foot in height, a gaudy pink, and had a lascivious grin. "God, have you ever seen anything uglier?" the girl lamented. "But I can't throw it away. Grandma painted it herself, and she calls it Pussy."

That night, Amy took the statue and had a Polaroid taken of it in front of a McDonald's. When the girls awoke in the morning, the picture was on the bulletin board. Amy had written below it: "Hungry Pussy." The next night, one of the other girls took the statue to the library and the following morning there was another picture. This one was captioned "Studious Pussy." After that, it became a running joke to get pictures of Pussy in different places. Amy was the first to take Pussy on vacation, and sent back a picture of "Grand Canyon Pussy." Over the years, the bulletin board became covered with pictures of Pussy from all over the country and all over the world: "Pussy at Niagara Falls," and "Pussy Does the Pyramids."

The girls did other silly things like that, and Amy was usually in the middle of the action. She made the girls feel like real sisters, and all the games and pranks brought them closer. She often reminded them that they hadn't come together by accident, for Amy believed that people met for a reason and were linked somehow in a common purpose, and she believed that even apparently chance encounters were not chance at all.

Occasionally she would bring a homeless person back to the house for dinner. The latest was a shopping-bag lady named Mildred, who ate two full plates of angel-hair spaghetti and an entire loaf of garlic bread while she told the girls of her own younger days in New York City. She had been a dancer there, and between plates of spaghetti she did a few steps to prove it. She said New York was the greatest city in the world, and that if it weren't for her bunions, she'd be dancing there still. The next day, Amy got her job offer in New York, and she took Mildred's words as a sign.

Why are we where we are? Why are some of us attached to a place, as if our feet were rooted in the ground? Why are others footloose and scattered by the wind? Amy believed that we all have a place to be, and that if it is no longer the place where we were born, then we find our way there. How else could one explain the affinity that some have to the place they call home? How else could one explain the restlessness that others feel, their urge to move on? Or the unhappiness of others who feel homeless, who have reached a dead end, or who can't find their way?

Amy loved the stories of family pets who, when lost far from home, somehow found their way back, sometimes across hundreds and even thousands of miles. How did they do it? What could be the explanation, other than their having a tremendous need and a guiding light? Amy believed that people too are guided by some mysterious sense, not back to the place from which we have come, but forward, following our inexplicable dreams and our restless hearts to what we are supposed to be.

But how do we know the way? Amy believed that often others are sent to guide us, but that sometimes we are given signs. How do we read the signs? Amy believed that the only way was to pay attention to everything and everyone around us and to understand how those things and people made us feel. Amy believed that answers are never far from their questions, just as parents are never far from their child, and that the smaller the question, the closer the answer has to be, so she simply asked small questions of herself. She asked how things made her feel, and she listened closely to those feelings. When she heard of the job in New York City, she felt excitement. She trusted that feeling as an inner direction, and said to those who asked, "And that is why I have to go."

Amy's sorority sisters bowed not to their understanding of Amy's feeling, but to Amy's unspeakable confidence in it. Only the pledges, and even then only the ones who knew her least, second-guessed her. "It's expensive in New York," they argued.

"I'll be staying in Hoboken with my cousin," she said.

"The winters are tough there," they tried.

"I'm from Wisconsin," she replied.

"We'll miss you, and you'll miss us," they argued.

"You'll be in my heart."

When we know that it's time to move on, we climb on the bus, we walk to the back and press our nose to the window, and we watch all we thought we were fade into the past. Then we turn in our seat and wonder what the next stop for us will be, and we wonder if it will be the last, because more than all else, we long to be home.

In the spring of 1998, Amy, by way of Wisconsin, arrived in Hoboken, New Jersey. She looked in awe across the river to New York City, where her friend Mildred had danced. She took a deep breath, and to steady herself in the face of her future, and all its possibilities, she laced up her sneakers and went for a run.

16. First Rule of HOHA

THE HOHAs were to be about running, first and foremost. That is why Coach established the first rule of HOHA: "You can only join the HOHAs by coming to a club run." That made sense, Coach thought. If you don't want to run, or if you're not ready to run, don't join. The rule would deter those who thought that the HOHAs were just another social group, where you could pay your dues and then only go to the meetings and parties.

> *You can't approach running through the mind. You can talk about it and read about it all you want, and you will know next to nothing. You must learn running through your bones, your blood, your muscles, and even the pores of your skin. Every cell must learn and know. Get out of your mind, lace up your shoes, and run those first few steps, and you will already know more than any scholar or sports writer ever will. And your learning will have just begun.*

Coach believed that the club would be properly founded only when it had its first run, because how could you found a club that didn't have a single member. By the Tuesday evening of the first run publicized on the flyers, Coach had received no inquiries about the club, but he thought that at least a few runners would show up. Coach got to the meeting place outside the YMCA fifteen minutes before the specified eight o'clock start. It was a nice evening for running, still chilly for shorts, but some leggings and a couple of layers on top would do you fine. Coach was wearing one of those belts with a pouch on it—fanny packs, they were called—and in the pouch he had an optimistic number of membership applications and pens. He was ready for the onslaught of new members.

Coach had had one of the graphic artists at his work design a logo for the club and he had talked Ben into printing up an initial run of two dozen T-shirts with "Counter-Fit Printing" across the back and the new logo on the front. The logo was the acronym for Hoboken Harriers, HO on top, HA on the bottom, and below that the current year, 1990. The T-shirt was white, and the lettering was a royal blue, and Coach was wearing it proudly that night.

Coach stood conspicuously in the middle of the sidewalk and did an occasional stretch. People came and went from the Y in the evenings dressed to work out, and Coach was disappointed a few times when someone he thought was coming for the run continued on by him. He waited until ten past eight—a fair grace period he thought for anyone running late—but still no one appeared. He dismissed a brief feeling of disappointment and resolutely took an application from his fanny pack and filled it out with his own name and address.

Coach then decided to make the short speech that he had practiced at home in front of the mirror. "Welcome to the first meeting of the Hoboken Harriers Running Club, known in short as the HOHAs. I am Emmitt F. Bean, the founder, first president, and coach of the club. Please feel free to call me Coach. If you haven't already filled out an application form, please see me after the run, at which time you may do so. The Tuesday night course is a 2.5 mile loop beginning and ending right here. I will lead the way until the course is known. After the run we will gather here until all runners have completed the course, and then we will adjourn to Maxwell's bar and restaurant, one of our fine sponsors, for refreshments. Are there any questions?"

There were no questions.

"Excellent. Let's start."

Coach, undaunted and with his humor intact, then ran the course alone, and after the run he went to Maxwell's and had a beer to celebrate. That night, he wrote in his running log:

"May 8, 1990. Ran the Tuesday night run alone and finished in first place, establishing a club record of 19 minutes, 18 seconds for the course! The Hoboken Harriers Running Club is officially founded. Membership: Me. Long live the HOHAs!!!"

17. To Your Health

THE BEDDING in the hospital room was cool and crisp and glaringly white. The winter sun poured through the blinds and flooded the room with a bright light, and Coco sat in the chair next to the bed and looked at her mother's pale face.

"I'm not going to make it, baby," Gloria said.

"Mom, don't talk like that. It's just a setback. You'll be OK."

"Listen to me. I don't want you to make the mistakes I made."

"Mom."

"No, listen. We're going to have this talk. I need to have it with you. Then I'll have some peace."

"Please, Mom, don't be like this."

"I made a lot of mistakes, but I learned from them, and I have some advice for you. Three pieces of advice actually. That sounds terrible, doesn't it? It sounds as if I'm going to give you a lecture." Gloria laughed at herself and then gently patted the bedding next to her. "Come sit by me here." Coco sat on the bed next to her mother, and Gloria took her hand. "Do you remember that Chinese restaurant downtown that we liked when you were a little girl?"

"Of course."

"Do you remember how you loved water chestnuts and I'd give you every one I found in the dish?"

"Yes."

"I was in that restaurant last week, and I saw a mother with her daughter. The girl was the same age as you were when we used to go there. I realized how much I missed you at that age, and I cried. Isn't that silly? You're still here, and I love the young woman you've become, but my little girl is gone. Where did you go? I cried, because I realized that I couldn't get that time back, and I missed it so."

"Oh, Mom."

"I realized that we lose each other every day. It made me see that every moment is precious."

Gloria rubbed Coco's hand. "That's why I need to have this talk. I'll give you my advice now, and I'll tell you in the way I would have when you were a little girl. Are you ready for a story?"

"Mom, you know I'm always ready for a story."

"I know. And this one is your favorite kind. It's about three wishes."

"Did someone find a lantern?"

"Yes. Someone found a lantern, and this time it was me. I found a lantern, and I rubbed it with the hem of my dress, and a genie appeared. He was big and strong and kinda cute." Gloria smiled impishly at Coco and reached over and rubbed her arm. "And he said, 'Gloria Matushky, close your eyes and make three wishes and they shall be granted you.'

"'Thank you, genie,' I said. 'I have three wishes for my daughter.'

"'And what is your first wish for her?' the genie said.

"'The first wish is simple,' I said, 'but most important. I wish my daughter lifelong health.'

"I wish you health, Coconut, because I've made such a mess of mine. Maybe I couldn't have prevented this illness. I don't know. But I know that my smoking and drinking and laziness sure didn't help. I started smoking when I met your dad and haven't stopped since. We didn't know any better back then, and once you start on those things, God help you. And I drank more than was good for me, especially when your dad and stepdad left, but the worst thing was how I just let my body go. I had a desk job, and at home I sat on the couch with a remote. Look at me now, an overweight woman in a moo-moo. I don't want this to happen to you.

"When you were five I started you in ballet. Do you remember? The fives wore pink leotards and white tights. You were sweet, like a pop tart. You danced until you were twelve, and that's where you got your grace and poise. Your teacher said you were good enough to continue too, but you lost interest. That's when you got serious about school."

"I was at an awkward stage."

"I've come to think that every stage of our lives is an awkward stage. We're not sure what we're doing, and every time we look back, we say, 'What was I thinking?' You were just realizing how smart you are.

"You're a brain. You didn't get that from me, and you sure as tootin' didn't get it from your dad. Maybe it skipped a generation. Scientists say some things skip like that. Or is that just diseases and bald heads? Anyway, your Aunt Eve was a smart woman; maybe you got your brain from her.

"Anyway, what I'm getting at is that after you quit ballet, you stopped exercising. That's not good, Coconut. Brain or no brain, you can't ignore your body. If you do, it will come back to haunt you later. I want you to promise me that you'll take up some activity that will keep you healthy. Do you promise?"

Coco thought that this was unnecessary, but she would deny nothing to her mother now. "Yes, Mom," she said. Her voice was acquiescent, but her words were sincere. "I promise you."

"What are you going to do?" Gloria persisted. "I've heard hiking is good."

"I don't know yet, Mom."

"Or Rollerblading. That looks like fun. I'd try that myself if I weren't old."

"Maybe."

"Or bicycling," Gloria continued. "Or even running."

"I don't know, Mom, but I promise I'll do something."

"Good," Gloria said, satisfied now. Then she added, as if she were putting a check mark to a list, "That's one."

18. The Terminator

ON THE EVENING of the first Thursday night run, Coach again ran alone, but the weather had been cold and windy, and Coach reasoned that it was the weather alone that kept the runners away. On the following Tuesday, it was fifty degrees, almost perfect running weather, and Coach was hopeful that on this night there would be some runners already waiting to join the club. As Coach approached the meeting place at the Y, he saw one young guy standing awkwardly near the bus bench. He was dressed in a full sweat suit of heavy gray cotton, and he had the sleeves all the way down and the hood all the way up over his head. The sweat suit was brand new, and there were still creases where it had been folded in the store.

There are many things that give away a novice runner, but the most noticeable is their attire. Beginners tend to overdress, not realizing how much heat their body will generate during a run. The rule of thumb is to dress for a run as if it were twenty degrees warmer than it actually is. In fifty degree weather, for example, you should dress in shorts and T-shirt, as if it were a pleasant seventy degrees. You may feel cold at the start, and then later when you've finished, but you'll feel just right for the main part of the run, and that's what Coach would say: "Dress for the middle of the run."

The guy wearing the sweat suit was short and heavy, with bulges of fat pushing at every seam. A second indication of a runner's experience is his weight. Not all thin people are good runners, but all good runners are thin. If a runner is doing the requisite training to increase endurance and hone speed, and has adapted his diet to his training regimen, then any excess weight simply burns away. There are other, more subtle indicators of experience and skill, but the runner's attire and weight can be seen at a glance, and form an unmistakable first impression.

Coach had sized up the guy in front of the Y and knew that if he was a runner at all, he was a beginner at best. The guy looked nervous, and he looked as if he were waiting for someone. Coach approached him. "Excuse me," he said, "are you here for the running club?"

"I want to be a runner," the guy said. He said it not so much in answer to Coach's question, but as if it were a line he had rehearsed. "I want to join the club."

"I'm Emmitt F. Bean, the founder, first president, and coach of the club," Coach said. "What's your name?"

"My name is Howie Mooch."

"Have you ever run before, Howie?" Coach asked.

"No."

"Why do you want to run now?"

"I'm in love."

"What?" Coach knew that people ran for many different reasons, but he had never once considered love.

Howie saw Coach's surprise and realized how ridiculous his answer had sounded, and he reached for a more logical response. "I need to look good on a wedding cake," he said.

Coach took that in and then realized Howie's state of nervousness and agitation. "Now just take a deep breath," he said, "and tell me what's wrong."

"My girlfriend saw this wedding cake with a perfect couple on it, and she's going to leave me if I don't get in shape. She's taking Jazzercise to lose weight, and I can't dance. I need to exercise, and with other sports you need equipment, balls and such. And I'm not good with balls, catching them or throwing them, I mean."

"OK. OK. Take it easy," Coach said. "What's your girlfriend's name?"

"Donna."

"Is she pretty?"

"She has pretty eyes. They're green. Like the inside of a kiwi."

"That's great. And you want to get in shape to make Donna happy."

"Yes."

"Well, you've come to the right place, because running is a great way to get in shape."

"That's what my doctor told me."

"Did your doctor tell you it was all right for you to start an exercise program?"

"Yes, he said I had to. He said running was good."

"Do you know anything about running?"

"I've read a couple of books about it," Howie said hopefully.

"Which ones?"

"*The Complete Runner's Cookbook* and *Eat to Win*."

"Any books on training?"

"No." Howie looked uncomfortable, as if he had enrolled for a class and just realized he hadn't taken the prerequisites. There were perfect beads of sweat on his forehead and upper lip.

"That's OK," Coach assured him. "We'll work on that. That's what I'm here for."

I never turned a boy away. They'd come to me not big enough to play football, not tall enough to play basketball, and sure not athletic enough to play anything else, these skinny and chubby freshman boys, all pimples and braces and elbows and knees, odd collections of skin and bones with small tender fires burning inside. They wanted to be men and knew that they'd have to prove that they were, and sometime soon, even if it were only to themselves. They'd come to me as their only chance, and I could see the desperation in their eyes. They'd be huddled in a group that first day and their eyes would say, "Please don't tell me that I can't even do this." They didn't know yet how tough running is and how much there is to learn. All they knew was that it was the only thing left to them. I'd take every one of them, even if he had a wooden leg. I'd let them know right off that they were on the team as long as they'd do the work. Then I set to work myself, making them into the men they had to be.

The Tuesday course was only two-and-a-half miles, but Coach knew that there was no way that Howie could make it. Coach started the run in the slowest of jogs, and even at that pace Howie had to stop after thirty seconds. Coach walked with him a while and then devised a shortcut of the course that Howie could walk alone. Coach completed the run on his own, and several minutes later Howie came struggling to the finish. Howie was out of breath, and the light gray of his new outfit was dark with sweat.

"Running is even harder than I thought it would be," Howie panted.

"Running is tough in the beginning," Coach said. "There's a difficult initiation period. Every cell in your body has to adjust to the demands of running before you start feeling the rewards. But it does get easier after six months to a year."

"A year?" Howie said. "I didn't think I was going to make it through today."

Coach sensed Howie's discouragement, and his inclination to give up. "But you did make it," he said instinctively. "Even though it was tough, you wouldn't quit. Have you ever run a marathon, Howie?"

"Have you ever walked on the moon?" is what Howie heard, but Howie was flattered that Coach would even think it possible that he had, and planting that seed of possibility was just Coach's point.

"No," Howie said, "I haven't."

"The marathon is 26.2 miles, and that is a long way to run, no matter how good a runner you are, no matter how strong. After 20 miles, you're exhausted, and the finish line is a world away. To make it, you have to dig deeper into yourself, fighting your desire to give up, and searching for strength that you're not sure you have. Experienced runners say that the marathon begins at Mile 20, because that's where you begin to learn who you are." Coach paused and looked purposefully at Howie. "Do you know who you are?"

"I'm Howie Mooch."

"I know you're Howie Mooch, but who *are* you?"

Howie looked at Coach with alarm. "I don't know what you're talking about."

"I'm talking about who you are deep down inside. I'm talking about your character. I'm talking about what you are going to do when things get tough."

"I don't know what I'll do," Howie said.

"I think you do know," Coach said. "You're doing it tonight. You had a setback in your life, and instead of feeling sorry for yourself, you came out here to get in shape, even though that's not easy for you. And even though you just started your exercise program, and even though you were ready to drop, you kept fighting to the end. I can tell you're the type who doesn't give up. I can tell that you're a finisher."

Howie's shoulders straightened. "You think so?" he said.

"I know so," Coach said. "And because of that, I'm going to give you a special running name." Coach paused for effect.

"What are you going to call me?" Howie said.

There was a series of movies out then about this robot called the Terminator, played by this actor named Arnold Schwarzenegger, who had once been Mr. Universe, and later went on to become the governor of California. Anyway, the Terminator was this magnificent hunk of computerized testosterone, a killing machine that just couldn't be stopped. Coach said, "I'm going to call you 'The Terminator.'"

Howie fought an urge to look over his chubby shoulder, to look for Schwarzenegger, who surely must be walking up behind him right now, and to whom Coach must obviously be referring, but Coach was looking right at him, right into his eyes, with a conviction and fervor meant to make the words not just a name but the incarnate truth. Then Howie heard himself confirming that truth with the simple words of acceptance, "Thanks, Emmitt."

"Don't call me Emmitt. Call me Coach."

Coach then explained to Howie the importance of stretching after a run, and showed him the stretch where you stand back a few feet from a wall, put your palms against the wall, and then lean forward to stretch the hamstrings. Howie leaned forward against the bricks of the YMCA and grunted. "Don't strain," Coach said. "We're not trying to push the building over; we're just stretching our hamstrings."

When they'd finished their stretching, Coach told Howie that he would devise a special training program just for him, and that Howie should be at the Thursday run that week to get started. "I'll chart out a new diet for you too," Coach said.

"A diet?" Howie questioned. Howie was already dreaming ahead to the milk shake he was going to suck down as soon as he could escape from Coach. "I don't know."

"An exercise program and a diet go hand in hand," Coach explained. Coach saw Howie's reluctance, looked straight into his eyes, and drove the point home. "Hand in hand," he said, "like a couple on a wedding cake."

Again, Howie was mesmerized by Coach's conviction, and he was still absorbing the strangeness of it all. Not only was he now considered a runner, but he had his own coach, his own running name, and would soon have his own training program. How could he do anything but go along? "Yes, Emmitt," he said.

"Yes, what?" Coach said.

"Yes, Coach."

Howie, aka the Terminator, limped away from his first workout that evening exhausted and dazed, feeling not only that he had abused his body in ways beyond his imagination but also that he had exposed his mind to a new reality, a reality—as hard as it was for him to believe—that was even odder and more delusional than his own.

That night, Coach would write in his running log:

"This evening's run was a tremendous success. The first HOHA joined the club. A young runner named Howie Mooch, "The

Terminator." I will put Howie on a special training program to foster his innate potential. Every great venture has humble beginnings, and if tonight's run is any indication, then the HOHAs will be a great running club indeed!"

19. Snail's Pace

THE HOHAs were to become a great running club in their own time, but that time did not come nearly as quickly as Coach would have liked. In the first months of its existence, the club comprised only Coach and Howie and a handful of other occasional and lackluster runners. Some decent runners did come along, but they soon saw that there was no one in the club at their level, and despite Coach's fawning and attention, they quickly dropped out or slowly drifted away. In the fall of that first year, Coach would write in his running log:

"Here's a scary thought: the HOHAs are a half-year old already, and I am still the club's fastest runner."

But all that was about to change. One evening on his way home from work, Coach saw a "COMING SOON" sign in a storefront on Washington Avenue near Eleventh Street, and he stopped in his tracks when he saw what was coming: it was to be a running store called "Snail's Pace." Coach had been thinking that a running store was just what Hoboken and the HOHAs needed, and he had even toyed with the idea of opening one himself. A store would not only provide for runners and their endless need for re-shoeing, but he could use it to recruit runners, publicize club activities, and serve as a central meeting place. Now, it appeared, the store Coach wanted was soon to be.

Coach kept a close eye on that storefront over the next week, and the first time he saw someone inside, he went in to introduce himself. A young man just a few years older than Coach himself was setting up a shoe display, and he saw Coach enter the store. "May I help you?" he said.

"I'm Emmitt F. Bean, the founder, first president, and coach of the Hoboken Harriers Running Club," Coach said. "Is this your store?"

"Yes it is," the man said. "My name is Edsel."

Edsel was short, but he had an athletic body and the lean look of a runner. "Do you run, Edsel?" Coach said.

"I ran track and cross-country in high school," Edsel said, "and I fell in love with the sport. That's why I'm opening the store."

"What's your 5K PR?" Coach asked. This was a blunt and straightforward question, but Edsel wasn't surprised by it. Runners often ask each other their racing times, sometimes before they even exchange names.

"15:44," Edsel said, without hesitation. This was an excellent time, and Coach was impressed. It is one of the beauties of the sport that a simple number can tell so much. "15:44" was like a long conversation, and Coach already knew a lot about Edsel's talent and training and commitment to running. "What's yours?" Edsel said.

"17:52," Coach said, and quickly added, "but I'm more into coaching. That's why I established the club."

Edsel's eyes were clear and intelligent, and he looked squarely and shrewdly at Coach. "I was thinking of starting a running club myself," he said, "to support my store."

Coach eyed Edsel suspiciously, sizing him up, and he decided to meet Edsel's provocative statement head on. "Hoboken only has room for one running club," he said, "and I already founded it." Edsel didn't blink, and Coach went on. "But it's funny you should say that, because I was thinking of opening a running store myself, to support my club."

Now it was Edsel who eyed Coach suspiciously. "There's only room in Hoboken for one running store," he said. Coach didn't blink either, and continued staring stubbornly at Edsel. They were like two gunfighters squaring off on Main Street at noon. It was Edsel who saw the humor in the situation first and smiled. "Well, I won't start a club if you won't open a store," he said. "Maybe we can work together."

Edsel also understood the mutual benefits of an affiliation between a running store and a running club, and it turned out that he had a passion for running and knowledge of the sport every bit as great as Coach's. As they talked, they quickly overcame their initial suspicions of each other and warmed to the possibilities and particulars of their cooperation. One of the first things they agreed upon was that the HOHAs would meet for their Saturday and Sunday morning runs, and for any carpooling to weekend races, right in front of Edsel's store. This would give Edsel the exposure to runners that he needed. In turn, Edsel would give the HOHAs a ten-percent discount on all purchases, and the club would display its flyers and membership applications in the store. "Snail's Pace" would be an official club sponsor, and in turn would receive free advertising in the club newsletter.

"How did you come up with the name 'Snail's Pace?'" Coach asked at one point.

"From my high school coach. Whenever he was getting on us for running too slow, he'd say, 'Come on, girls. That's a snail's pace.' I remembered that. He was the best coach I ever had."

Coach helped Edsel with the shoe display and they continued talking about their coaches and teammates and running history. At one point, Edsel told Coach that his favorite race distance was five miles, because it was a classic combination of the speed of the 5K and the endurance of the 10K, and then he told Coach that he was going to organize a five-mile race in Hoboken to be called the Hoboken Classic.

Coach thought this was a great idea, and he offered the help of the HOHAs with the event. He and Edsel talked for another hour about the layout of the course and the promotion of the race, and they agreed to meet the next day to continue their planning. Coach was excited, but as he was leaving, he had the troubling thought that Edsel was just too good to be true. He stopped in the doorway and then reluctantly turned. He had to ask a question, the answer to which he was afraid to hear. He squared off at Edsel once again. "By the way, Edsel," he said, masking his seriousness with nonchalance, "Who do you think was a better runner, Sebastian Coe or Steve Ovett?"

Edsel looked at Coach as if he were daft. "Coe, of course," he said. "And if you say any differently, I'll have to kick your butt across all of Hoboken."

Coach was not a sentimental man, and could not remember ever crying, but as he left Snail's Pace that day, convinced that the gods of running were finally smiling upon him, in his throat was a lump of gratitude and in his eyes were tears of pure joy.

Coach and Edsel's agreement worked out just as both had hoped. Edsel's store did good business, and Coach's club found new members through the store, and found, in the store itself, the center it needed. Edsel kept a watercooler at the front of the store and welcomed runners to stop in any time for a drink, and he encouraged runners to try new running shoes by taking them for a spin around the block. HOHAs met there regularly and even helped out when needed. One Saturday after a club run, Edsel got swamped with customers, and Coach helped with selling shoes. He was great at it. Customers got caught up in his friendly banter and his enthusiasm for running, and he asked them about their training and made recommendations. Those who had come in for one pair of shoes often left with two and, more often than not, they were also loaded down with the latest running accessories and clothing. That first day, after the rush subsided, Edsel offered Coach a part-time job. Coach accepted, and worked at the store almost every Saturday afternoon after that.

Edsel's appearance in Hoboken shortly after Coach's arrival was a coincidence so fortuitous that one suspected it was no coincidence at all. Somehow, it was destined to be. Through that first winter, Edsel and Coach plotted and planned what they considered to be the most important event in Hoboken and HOHAs history: the running that coming spring of the first annual Hoboken Classic.

20. An Omen

THE RUNNING made Moses sore at first, but it was a pleasant soreness. It was the soreness that comes to muscles awakened from their lack of use. Moses knew that it wasn't old age, because he remembered the same soreness in high school at the beginning of the season or after the coach introduced a particularly tough workout into their training. It was the soreness of progress, and Moses appreciated it as such.

Moses ran at different times of the day, and found that he enjoyed the evenings the best. It was cooler, and there was a calmness in the transition from day to night. There were more people in the park then too, and Moses enjoyed that, enjoyed being part of the activity. There were runners and cyclists and Rollerbladers, kids playing ball and parents with small children, and Moses was among them, sharing the evening with all of them. He felt a special affinity to the runners though, and waved to other runners passing by. They usually responded in some way, acknowledging their bond in the sport they shared, and Moses was proud that he belonged.

As days passed, he recognized the regulars and they recognized him. Moses' speed was improving and he gauged his progress against the other runners. One runner in particular became his focus. He was a man about Moses' age, thin and fit and dressed in the latest running gear. He was a good runner too, with a fluid stride and a fast pace. At first he had run by as if Moses were standing still, but as Moses improved, the gap between them lessened. When he passed, Moses would increase his own pace to stay with the man for as long as he could. After a while he could shadow him for a quarter mile or more.

One day, the man sensed Moses running behind him, and looked over his shoulder and slowed until Moses caught up. He then introduced himself as Duane Elmquist. Moses and Duane ran together for a while that day and talked mostly about their running careers in high school. Moses saw Duane regularly in the park, and they ran together more and more. Duane did most of the talking, because Moses needed most of his breath just to keep up. Duane talked about running mostly, about books he had read and races he had run. Moses learned a lot from Duane, and his running steadily improved. Soon, he no longer had any problem keeping up with Duane, and sometimes he even thought that he was holding back so that Duane could keep up with him.

One day, Duane told Moses that he wouldn't be at the park the following week because he had to go on a business trip. He also said that he wouldn't be able to run a race in Hoboken for which he had already registered, and offered Moses his race number. It was a Wednesday, and the race was that Saturday afternoon. The prospect of racing was a shock to Moses. "I don't know, Duane," he said. "I'm just a beginner."

"Malarkey," Duane said. "You're doing great." Duane didn't know the full story of Moses' life, but he understood that Moses didn't have much money. "Besides," he added, "I already paid for the race. It would be a waste if you didn't go."

The next day when they met at the park, Duane had a large manila envelope with him. "This is your race packet," he said. "I've already registered, so all you have to do is show up." Moses reached inside the envelope and pulled out a T-shirt. The front of the shirt said "The Hoboken Classic—Five Miler," and on the back were the logos of the race sponsors. "That's the race T-shirt," Duane said. "We're about the same size, so it should fit you."

"Gee, thanks, Duane. Are you sure you don't want it?"

"No. I wouldn't wear a shirt from a race I didn't run in."

"Do I wear this shirt for the race?"

"No, it's just a souvenir. Only beginners wear the shirt during the race." Duane saw Moses' disappointment, and then remembered the meagerness of Moses' wardrobe. "But sure, you can wear it if you want to."

"I think I might," Moses said. "It's real nice."

"The directions to the race are in the envelope too, but all you have to do is catch the PATH train into Hoboken. When you get off the train, you'll see all the other runners, and the start of the race will be right there.

"And your bib number is in there too," Duane said. Moses extracted a square of paper with a number on it. "You pin that onto the front of your shirt with those safety pins there. At the end of the race, they'll mark your time, and then at the end of the finishing chute, they'll tear that tag off the bottom to score your finishing place."

"I don't have to do anything?"

"All you have to do is run," Duane said. "And don't forget to run fast." Duane smiled. "Remember, you're running in my name."

"I'll run as fast as I can, Duane," Moses said earnestly.

"Good. I'll see you when I get back, and you can tell me how you did."

Moses admired the runners he saw on the streets and in the park. They had a purpose, some place to go, and now, just like that, Moses found himself part of a scheduled event, with a place to be and a time to be there. As he thought more about this, he grew nervous. He wasn't used to being in the mainstream of things. He and Buddy lived on the fringe of events like this, picking up the aluminum cans and perhaps some leftover food. When he got back to the bridge, he told Buddy about the race.

"I've got Duane's number," Moses said.

"You mean you have his number like you've figured him out?"

"No, I have his number to wear in the race." Moses showed Buddy the T-shirt and the race number and explained how it was used. "I don't know if I should do it though, Buddy," he said. "I never did anything like this before."

Buddy looked at the T-shirt, but he was more interested in the number. Ever since Moses had had those dreams, and then had received the shoes, Buddy had been watching for another sign, an indication of where the shoes would take him, and now Buddy thought that he had the answer. He held the number up to Moses and said, "This is your ticket."

"Duane called it a bib number."

"I don't care what Duane called it," Buddy said.

"But that's what it is," Moses argued.

"I don't care what he said it was," Buddy said. "Duane himself isn't even what he appears to be. You think he's just some guy you ran into in the park?" Moses had no idea what Buddy was getting at, and he just waited, knowing that Buddy would tell him soon enough. "He's a messenger."

"A messenger?"

"Yes. Someone sent to give you information that you need. Look at it. Those shoes took you right to the park, didn't they? And who was the first person you met in the park?"

"Duane."

"Uh-uh. And what did this Duane just hand to you?"

"A ticket?"

"That's right, but the more I think about it, the more I think it's more than an ordinary ticket. It's what they call an omen, a sign of something bigger to come."

"Then you think I should go?"

"God almighty, what would you do without me?" Buddy said. "Of course you should go. Don't you remember your dreams? How death was waiting for you here. Do you remember how I told you we had to wait for a further sign?"

"Yeah,"

"Well this is it. You've been sent a ticket. A ticket to the place you're supposed to be."

"Hoboken?"

"Well, for starters. And who knows who or what's waiting for you when you get there. Another messenger, probably. Maybe God's got a job for you."

"You think so, Buddy?"

Buddy reached out and held the bib number against Moses' chest. "I don't know," Buddy said, "but I know there's only one way to find out."

21. The Classic

ON A SATURDAY MORNING in May of 1993, Coach and Edsel were hustling with the last-minute preparations for their third annual Hoboken Classic five-mile race, and the race scene mirrored their nervous energy as more than four hundred runners worked through their pre-race routines. In every direction, in seeming chaos, runners warmed up and stretched and readied themselves for the start.

Moses had arrived early at the race site, but he didn't have a pre-race routine himself, or even know that he should have one. He just watched, and when there was an announcement over a megaphone and the runners moved toward the starting line, Moses followed, and then after the speeches, when the air horn sounded and everyone started running, Moses ran too. Duane had told him that he should run fast, and that's what he did. He followed the runners in front of him and kept running, and passing people too, until he reached the finish. It was only when he finished that he felt how tired he was. He walked off his heavy breathing and then sat down on a curb and watched the other runners come in. There was music from a stage they had set up, and Moses just listened and took in the scene.

Moses was still sitting on the curb, enjoying the sun and the tiredness of his body, when Edsel took the stage and took up the microphone. He thanked the race sponsors again, and everyone else for coming out, and then started the award presentations. Moses had no idea that he had won anything, and when Edsel got to the age-group awards for Men 60-69, Moses paid no special attention, although he recognized the third-place winner as someone he had passed during the race. He recognized the man's bald head. When the second-place winner got his award, Moses recognized him too, having passed him near the end, just before the last turn. "And in first place," Edsel then said, "with an excellent time of 31:21, from Newark, age 60, Duane Elmquist."

Moses heard the name. Duane's not here. He's on a business trip, he thought, before it struck him that he was Duane today, and that he had evidently won first prize.

Edsel waited and then said, "Duane? Are you out there?"

Moses shot to his feet, raised his arm in the air, and shouted, "I'm Duane Elmquist!"

The crowd laughed at Moses' excitement over his own identity, and through the laughter Moses somehow got himself to the stage. When Edsel handed him the trophy, Moses shook his hand, and then turned to the crowd and bowed. The crowd laughed again at Moses' formality and amusing manner. It was all a blur to Moses, and when he got down from the stage, he just stood staring in fascination at the small plastic trophy of a runner, as if it were an artifact from another realm.

When Coach went to races, he saw the award ceremony as an excellent recruiting opportunity. He knew all the top-notch runners in the area, and he knew their club affiliations, but occasionally a new runner would appear. He would talk with them and see if they were interested in running with the HOHAs. Coach had his eye on Duane now and approached him through the crowd. Although the name Duane Elmquist sounded familiar, he was sure he hadn't seen this man before.

"Duane," he said to Moses, but Moses was still focused on the trophy. He hadn't won a trophy since high school. "Duane," Coach repeated. I won it, Moses was thinking. Isn't it nice? Coach decided that the old man must be hard of hearing. "Duane Elmquist!" he almost shouted.

Moses turned his attention from the trophy to Coach. "Oh, I'm not Duane," he said.

"But you just accepted his award."

"Duane's my friend. I ran the race for him today, because he couldn't make it."

"But you are in the same age group, aren't you?"

"What's an age group?"

"The award was for the best male runner between 60 and 69 years old. Are you between 60 and 69?"

"I'm 63, and Duane, my friend, he's 60," Moses said. "Do I get to keep the trophy?"

"Sure you do," Coach said. "Wow, you're 63 and you ran a 31:21. That's great. How long have you been running?"

"About three months now," Moses said. "I run with Duane almost every day."

"That's a fantastic time, especially if you've only been training three months." Coach realized that they'd been talking for a while without introducing themselves. "I'm Emmitt F. Bean," he said, "the founder, first president, and coach of the Hoboken Harriers Running Club."

"Moses."

"Good to meet you, Moses."

"You're a president?" Moses said in awe.

"Of a running club," Coach said, "not a country."

"But still. That's something."

"It's the runners who make a club," Coach said. "Would you like to join ours?"

"You want me? To join your club?"

"Sure, we'd love to have a great runner like you, and if you trained with us, you'd get even faster."

"But I don't live here."

"Where you from?"

"Newark."

"That's no problem," Coach said. "It's only a short train ride. Even if you only came over once a week, that would be great. Let me give you our card. All our group runs, the times and places, are on the back. We'd love to have you run with us."

"You'd love to have me?"

"Are you kidding? A great master runner like you. Sure we would."

Moses could feel Coach's sincerity, and he felt flattered and choked up by the welcome. He couldn't remember the last time he had felt wanted, and on the train back, he couldn't stop looking at the trophy and at the card Coach had given him. When he got home, he moved some stuff out of the corner of his refrigerator box to create a place of honor for his trophy. Before he fell asleep that night, he turned on his flashlight and shone it one more time on the plastic figure of the runner. He read the inscription once again: "The Hoboken Classic 1993—First Place—Men 60-69." And he read the card that Coach had given him: "The Hoboken Harriers Running Club."

After Duane's return, Moses headed over to Branch Brook Park for his run with him. He was feeling proud of himself and couldn't wait to tell Duane about the race, so he was surprised when Duane yelled out "Congratulations!" before he could say a word.

"For what?" Moses said.

"What do you mean, 'For what?' For winning the race, of course."

"How did you know about that?"

"I read about it in the newspaper. It was great seeing my name in the headline: DUANE ELMQUIST TOP MASTER IN CLASSIC. I was pleased with my time, too. Great job, Moses."

Moses was shocked that it had all been in the newspaper. He had thought of his run as a personal experience, not a public event.

"How do you feel?"

"I feel sore."

"Did you cool down after the race?"

"What do you mean, 'cool down?'"

"After an intense workout or a race, you should run a mile or two at an easy pace to loosen up and clear the lactic acid out of your muscles. You'll recover quicker and feel much better the next day."

"I should?"

"My God, you've still got a lot to learn about running, and you're already racing great. What were your split times?"

"What are split times?"

"Did you notice that there were volunteers calling out times along the course? They were at the mile markers, and the times were your splits at that point in the race."

"I heard some numbers," Moses said, "but I didn't know what that was about. I was just running as hard as I could."

"You did great," Duane said. "You'll pick up on the other stuff along the way."

"A young man from Hoboken wants me to run with his club."

"Why don't you do it then?" Duane said. "You'll learn a lot that way."

Later that day, Moses found a copy of the newspaper in a trash can and saw the article about the race in the sports section. And there was his name—or rather Duane's name—in the headline.

He lived under a bridge, and he scavenged a newspaper from the trash, and sitting on the curb, in the light from a street lamp, he read about his victory.

Moses thought about what Duane had said. Why shouldn't he run with that club? He had enjoyed the race, and he thought he could do better, and maybe Coach's club could help him with that. Buddy was all for it too. He said that Coach was another messenger.

Moses propped up the newspaper article and the HOHAs card next to his trophy and read them again that night by flashlight before he fell asleep.

22. Puzzle Pieces

JUNE LIVED across the street from an elementary school, and only a chain-link fence stood between the school's playground and June's kitchen window.

She and Gen often watched the children during their recesses and lunch periods. Andy had gone to the school through eighth grade, and June and Gen had watched him play. There were hundreds of children, and spotting Andy had been difficult. It had been Gen's idea to dress Andy in bright colors so that it would be easier. Oranges and reds soon became neon and DayGlo, until Andy could be spotted not just from the kitchen across the street but from satellites in space.

This had worked well through the second grade, but then Andy's classmates had started teasing him about his clothing, and he'd insisted on dressing the same way as the other kids. He was much harder to spot then, and that's where the binoculars came in. First, there was just the one pair that June salvaged from her late husband's things in the garage, but the ladies argued over whose turn it was to use them, until one day Gen bought her own. Both sets of binoculars still sat on the cupboard near the window, long after Andy had graduated from the school, and June and Gen still used them occasionally to track the comings and goings and antics of their favorite neighborhood kids.

"There's Jimmy from down the street," Gen would say. "I wonder if he'll fall from the monkey bars again today."

"He will if he tries to do that backflip again with his finger up his nose."

"Andy was good on the monkey bars," Gen said. "Remember, June?"

"He was one of the best ever."

"Have you heard anything?" Gen said. "How he's getting on in Hoboken?"

"I called him yesterday. He started his classes and his work in the computer lab. Of course, he's still running up a storm. He's doing fine, but that doesn't stop him from complaining though."

"'Hell, heaven, or Hoboken,' Joseph used to say during the war."

"That's right, Gen." June laughed. "It's not heaven, but it could be worse."

"I guess we'll just have to wait and see. Right, June?"

June and Gen liked to work on jigsaw puzzles while they watched the kids. For no particular reason, they made the puzzles the way one would play cards, each player taking a turn. If one of them took too long, the other would grab her binoculars and scan the schoolyard. This was their MO until they neared the end of the puzzle, and then there was a free-for-all to put in the last piece. With the puzzles, they favored the smaller, 100-piece pictures that they could complete in a sitting. These were pictures of Big Ben or of furry kittens playing with a ball of twine. June had a stack of the puzzles in the corner near the kitchen table, along with an old breadboard on which they put them together. Gen had glued Popsicle sticks around the edge of the board to keep the pieces from falling off, but the unused pieces lined up around the edge of the table would sometimes get knocked to the floor by someone's sleeve, or by the loose skin hanging from June's arms.

"Who's supposed to keep track of all the pieces if you keep knocking them off the table?" Gen would say. "And who's supposed to bend down and pick them up when we both have bad backs?"

"Who's supposed to do this and who's supposed to do that," June mimicked. "Who, who, who. What are you? A hoot owl?"

Gen was suspicious of June's tricks. On more than one occasion, June had snuck a puzzle piece into her lap and didn't "find" it until it was the last piece needed to complete the puzzle. "I'm just saying, June."

"Gripe, groan, grumble, and grouch."

"What's that?"

"It's a club," June said. "And you're the president."

"I just want to make sure no pieces get lost," Gen said pointedly. "That's all."

"You're getting dopey," June said. "I think you've been hitting those new pills too hard."

"They're only ten percent milligrams," Gen said. June smiled at that, and Gen realized her mistake. "Ten milligrams, I mean."

June raised her binoculars to the window and scanned the schoolyard. "Oh, look," she said. "Jimmy's on the monkey bars. He's about to try that backflip of his."

Gen raised her own binoculars and took a look. While Gen was looking, June surreptitiously slid a puzzle piece from the table and placed it in the fold of her lap.

"That was a good one," Gen said. She turned her attention back to the board. "Whose turn is it?"

"It's my turn."

"Well then, hurry up."

"What's the rush?" June said. "All we got is time."

23. The Oldest HOHA

MOSES CONTINUED to think about the HOHAs and Coach, who was so nice to him, and whenever he looked at his trophy and the HOHAs card next to it, he thought he'd like to go over and run with that HOHAs bunch. It cost a dollar then to take the PATH train from Newark to Hoboken, and it would cost another dollar to get back. That was a luxury, especially when he could just walk over to Branch Brook Park and run for free, which was what he did, running with Duane most evenings. Then Duane had to go on a two-week business trip, and Moses, used to having him as a running partner, got lonely. That's when he finally decided to give the HOHAs a try.

He knew that their regular group runs were Tuesday and Thursday—he had memorized that from the card—so late the Thursday afternoon of the second week of Duane's absence, about the time he would normally have headed over to the park, he went instead to the PATH station and took a train into Hoboken. He was dressed in his street clothes, with his running clothes on underneath, and he had a canvas bag in which he carried his running shoes. He got into Hoboken by 6:30 according to the train-station clock, and so had a whole hour to wait before the run started.

In the train-station bathroom, he stuffed his street clothes into the bag and changed into his running shoes. Then he found a safe spot to hide the bag. He jogged over to Washington and Fourth Streets where, according to the card, the club met before the run. No one was there, but Moses knew it was early yet. He ran down Washington Street one way and then ran back. Then he ran the other direction and back again. Each time, he looked for other runners gathering. Washington is Main Street in Hoboken, and there were lots of people coming home from work or going out for dinner. Some of them stared at him, for even with his running clothes on he still looked like a bum, a skinny old bum running down the street. He wondered what he was doing himself, but he just kept running—warming up, as Duane would call it—and waiting for the club to gather. By 7:30 there were eight or nine runners at the meeting place, but Moses wouldn't join them until he saw Coach. When Coach arrived, Moses walked over to blend in with the group.

Coach turned and saw Moses and came over to shake his hand. "Moses. You made it. Great!" He turned to the group. "Everybody," he said with excitement, "I'd like you to meet Moses. Moses won his age group at the Classic." The HOHAs nodded appreciatively, and Coach introduced them one by one.

Everybody seemed friendly, Moses thought. They didn't mind his odd clothes and old age. They were all much younger, of course, kids in their twenties, some maybe in their thirties. They were in small groups of three or four, speaking casually. Coach told Moses about the five-mile course and said that everybody ran at their own speed. He said that he'd be happy to run with Moses, if Moses would let him keep up, that is.

There was a ten-minute grace period, so the run didn't really start until 7:40. Coach said that people often arrived late, and called this grace period "HOHA time." When the grace period was over, Coach started the run, and Moses liked the way that he did it. He yelled out, "Are we ready to run?" Then when he looked around and was somehow satisfied with the number of nods that he received, he raised one arm and lowered it forward while yelling "Ho," as if he were starting a wagon train. Everyone started in a slow shuffle that gradually gained speed. "I'm running with them," Moses thought. "I'm really running with a club."

Moses, afraid at first that he wouldn't be able to keep up, soon saw that several other runners were falling behind. He kept an eye on Coach, the only person he really knew, and was determined to stay with him. Coach looked over his shoulder, saw Moses trailing him, and fell back by his side. "How you doing, Moses?" he said.

"Good."

"Is this pace OK for you?"

"Yes. This is the speed me and Duane run."

"Good. We're going to stay on this street for about a mile till we get to Fourteenth. Then we'll go right and over to Hudson. This is the toughest running on the course."

It was dark on Bloomfield, and Moses thought that was one reason Coach called it tough. It was a one-way street too, and cars were parked on both sides.

There was only one lane, and the HOHAs were running in the same direction as the traffic. Some of the runners braved the street, staying close to the parked cars as traffic passed. Other runners kept to the sidewalk, dodging pedestrians and trash cans. Coach preferred the street, and that suited Moses too. The street lamps lit the roadway better than they did the sidewalks, and Moses' eyes weren't as good as they used to be in the dark.

The HOHAs were strung out, running at different paces and forming smaller groups of two, three, and four. Coach and Moses were running alone, with one group just ahead and another just behind. Moses liked the pace, and he liked having other runners around. He remembered that from the race.

When they got to Fourteenth Street, the HOHAs turned right and ran two blocks to Hudson, then turned right and headed back south toward the center of town. They stayed on Hudson until they got to Fourth and then turned left to go the two blocks down to the river. They then followed a short bend to the left that brought them to the back road leading up to the Stevens Institute of Technology. Coach explained to Moses that the college had been founded by Colonel John Stevens, the inventor of America's first steam locomotive. Stevens Institute is built on a promontory that rises a hundred feet above the Hudson, and Coach had designed both the HOHAs weekly runs to go through Stevens because of the steep hill up to the main area of the campus. He felt that the hill, which wound and rose for a quarter mile, added a good strengthening element to the HOHAs training.

"I remember this hill from the Hoboken Classic," Moses said, struggling with his breathing. "It's steep."

"That's why we run it," Coach said. "If you get used to this, no hill will bother you in a race."

Coach examined Moses' form. "You need to shorten your stride on hills, and you need to use your arms. Lean forward slightly and make your arms help with the work. Pump them like pistons. Think of Stevens' locomotive."

Moses did as Coach said, and he could feel the difference. When they started back down, Coach said, "On the downhills, let your stride lengthen and keep your knees slightly bent. Don't be braking with each step; let yourself go." Both Coach and Moses did just that, and they flew down the slope that led out of Stevens and back onto Hudson. They took Hudson back north, looped around one block to Fourteenth Street, and then returned south on Hudson again. Four blocks down, at Frank Sinatra Drive, they bore left and followed Sinatra Drive on its one-mile dogleg down along the river. The Hudson was to their left, and the city lights on the far side were beautiful that night. Moses stared in awe at the bedazzling sight of Manhattan. "It looks like a castle," he said, "with a moat around it."

"Not bad, huh," Coach said. Coach wasn't referring to the city, however, but to his HOHAs running route that afforded such a view.

Moses thought it was a beautiful run, better than any in Newark or Branch Brook Park, and Coach's comments and observations made Moses feel special, and made the run interesting. "Do you see that tower there, Moses?" Coach pointed to an ugly green tower of corrugated steel just ahead of them on the Jersey side. It was seven stories high and had a metal staircase running up the outside of it. "That tower was built by Stevens Institute," Coach said. "They wanted to test the dynamics of simultaneous toilet flushing in a high-rise building, so they built that tower and installed fourteen toilets on each floor. That made ninety-eight, so they put two more toilets on the roof to make it an even hundred. That's a hundred-seat crapper, Moses."

"Wow," Moses said. He was impressed, and he thought that there was just no end to Coach's knowledge.

"They call the tower Old John. It's gotta be the biggest crapper in the world. When they finished it, the students got inside, and the professor set off a signal, and the students flushed all the toilets at the exact same second."

"Did it work?"

"You bet it did," Coach said. "They had to experiment with the water pressure and the piping, and make adjustments, but when they were done, it worked just fine."

When the HOHAs passed Old John, they were within a half mile of the finish of the run. They just had a short climb to the right, where they continued south on Sinatra for three blocks to Second Street, took Second for one block to River and turned right to finish at River and Third. As Moses and Coach approached the finish, Moses counted six runners who were already there, but as long as he had managed to finish with the president, Moses figured he had run well enough. When they came in, one of the runners said, "38:45," and when they stopped, Coach gave Moses a high five. "Good job, Moses," he said. A couple of the other runners also nodded their approval. When he realized that more runners were coming in after them, he knew that he had done all right. A good dozen runners followed, and the last of them—a runner named Howie, who came in walking—was a good ten minutes behind Coach and himself.

The runners milled about, stretching and chatting. Coach shook Moses' hand. "You completed one of our runs, Moses. It's official: you're a HOHA now." He patted Moses on the back. "I usually have membership forms with me. The next time you come, you can fill one out. The dues are only five dollars a year, and that includes the HOHAs newsletter and a HOHAs T-shirt."

"OK, sure," Moses said, but he didn't know where he was going to get the five dollars, and he didn't know what he was going to put on a membership form. He didn't even have an address.

"How do you feel?"

"I feel good."

"You looked good," Coach said. "We go to Moran's after the run and have a beer. Do you want to join us?"

"Thank you. No," said Moses. "I'd better be gettin' home."

Coach shook Moses' hand again, and others waved good-bye. While most of the group headed for the bar to have a beer, Moses headed for the PATH station to reclaim his clothes from their hiding place under a dumpster.

24. Healthy Heart

MOSES RAN with the HOHAs for a couple of months, attending every one of the Thursday night runs and the Tuesday night runs as well. He fit right in, taking pride in his membership and showing joy in belonging. Coach thought everything was fine, until he went to a 5K race called Healthy Heart out in Morristown. This race used an age-graded scoring system that allowed older runners to compete evenly with the younger ones, and it offered good prize money to the top finishers. For those reasons, the race attracted the best master runners in New Jersey.

After the race, Coach stayed for the award ceremony on the chance that he might be able to recruit another good master runner for the club. When Duane Elmquist won an award, Coach recognized the name and went over to talk to him. "Are you the real Duane Elmquist," he said, "or are you just another imposter going by that name?"

Duane laughed. "Do I know you?"

"I'm Emmitt F. Bean, the founder, first president, and coach of the Hoboken Harriers Running Club." Coach then explained that he had met Moses the day Moses had run under Duane's name and number at the Hoboken Classic.

"So, you're Coach?" Duane said. "Glad to meet you finally. Moses is always talking about you. Coach said this, Coach did that. He thinks highly of you."

"I think highly of him too."

"He's a great runner, isn't he?" Duane said. Then he added, "Considering."

"Considering what?" Coach said. "His age?"

"No, I meant considering that he's homeless," Duane said.

"What are you talking about?" Coach said. He couldn't believe what he'd just heard.

"Exactly that," Duane said. "He lives on the street. He doesn't have a home."

Coach remembered something. "But when he filled out his club membership, he included an address."

"That's my address," Duane said. "Moses asked me if he could use it. I get those newsletters you send, and I pass them on to him."

"I guess that explains about his clothes."

"Yeah, it all falls together, doesn't it?" Duane said. "I suspected he was down-and-out, but I didn't know he was living on the street until one day I was driving near the park where we run together, and I saw him climbing up under a bridge."

"What bridge?"

"He lives with his friend, Buddy, under a bridge near downtown Newark."

"Good God!"

"I know. I've talked to him, and I've tried to help him out, but he's proud. He won't accept any help."

Coach realized just how little he knew about Moses. That he was a great runner and was running for the HOHAs was all he had cared about. He thought now of Moses' old clothes and ragged looks, and about how he appeared out of nowhere before the runs and then slipped away afterwards.

"How does he get by?"

"Taking cans and bottles to the recycling center. Finding junk to sell. And I think he has some odd jobs. There's a soup kitchen nearby, and I imagine he goes to the shelter when it's really cold."

"I've got to do something," Coach said. "I know people in Hoboken. I'll check around and see if I can get him some help."

"You can't let him know that you're helping him," Duane cautioned, "or he won't accept it."

"Don't tell Moses that you talked to me then," Coach said. "He might become suspicious. I'm going to see what I can do."

A good coach takes interest in every aspect of his athletes' lives, not only because he cares for them, but because he knows that if they are having problems at home, at work, or in love, it will affect their performance, so a good coach keeps an eye out for problems and tries to help if he can. Coach could see now that Moses needed a lot of help, and he thought that finding him a job and a place to live would be the way to start.

When Coach had founded the club and sought out club sponsors, he'd visited most of the businesses in town. Now he thought about all those visits again, hoping to remember one business that might have a job for someone like Moses. The most likely, he thought, was the Hoboken Car Wash.

Hoboken, like most towns, had a seedy side, and the Hoboken Car Wash had its place there. On the southwest corner of town, a mile from the Hudson River, it sat across from the railroad tracks that separated Hoboken from Jersey City. The car wash, its sign painted in red and blue—"Hoboken" in red, "Car Wash" in blue—straddled an otherwise useless diagonal of land between intersecting streets. On busier days—the ones with sun or the promise of it—customers lined up their cars on the trash-strewn shoulder of Observer Highway, were pulled through the brushes and sprays of the car wash's dingy, wet tunnel, and exited onto Newark Street, where the workers gave the cars a cursory wipe with damp, dirty towels and waited for the drivers to cough up a tip.

The owner was Ed McDougal, a surly and petty tyrant who smoked green cigars. His smoke-filled pit of an office was off the side of the car wash, with a dirty hole of a window looking onto the clank and grind of the conveyor and the slush of the brushes. The office walls were papered with pictures of bulbous tits and proffered asses, centerfolds torn from the scummier porn magazines. In the center of the room was McDougal's desk, which was the gray metal of government surplus now turned a moldy green, piled high with the Styrofoam and paper wrappers of the fast food he ate. The ashtrays were full, and gave off a stench of stale cigar butts. McDougal sat at this desk belching and farting while he used a blunt, stubby pencil to keep his corrupt accounts.

McDougal employed high-school dropouts, down-and-out transients, and elderly bums: in other words, those who had nowhere else to go. He understood … no, understood is too intellectual a word to use … he smelled their plight, and liked what he smelled. He reigned over his puny realm, bullying his workers, sharing the pain of his hangovers and constipation and gas. If tearing them a new asshole didn't give him enough satisfaction, he'd fire them from the jobs that even they had thought were too lowly to lose.

When a person has to deal in any way with a bottom dweller like McDougal, he realizes at some level of consciousness—perhaps only from a cold sweat on the palms or a slight shiver up the spine—that he has made a mistake in this life, or in some life past, and that just the sight and smell of McDougal himself, or of the dark and dank interior of the car wash he runs, is a part of the price—or maybe the price in full—he is being forced to pay.

When Coach had met McDougal the first time and solicited his sponsorship for the club, he'd said, "Can you imagine 'Hoboken Car Wash' printed on the shirts of every runner in town, running up and down every street in Hoboken?" to which McDougal had responded, "Can you imagine 'Fuck You' tattooed on your forehead?"

When Coach went to see McDougal about a job for Moses, he brought Howie along for moral support. They both stood uneasily in front of McDougal's desk.

"I'm Emmitt F. Bean, the founder, first president, and coach of the Hoboken Harriers Running Club," Coach said to McDougal. "Just call me Coach."

"Crotch?"

"No, Coach," Coach said. "We met once before."

McDougal didn't remember the meeting, and he looked over at Howie. "And who is this," he said sarcastically, "one of your vice-presidents?"

"Hey!" Howie said, taking a half step forward.

Coach put the back of his hand to Howie's chest, as if there were some danger that Howie would attack. "We didn't come here to start trouble," Coach said. "This is Howie Mooch, the first member of the club, and we came here to ask you a favor, sir."

"What's this *sir* shit?" McDougal said. "I'm no *sir*; I work for a living."

"And that's what we came to talk to you about; work for one of our friends."

Coach then told him about Moses, and was relieved when McDougal showed interest. "I've had it with the teenage turds I got now," McDougal said. "They work for a few bucks for weed or beer, get shit-faced, and then don't show the fuck up." He hacked up some snot and spit it on the floor. "The old farts are more reliable," he continued. "Send your old man around, and I'll put him to work."

"Just one more thing," Coach said. "My friend doesn't know that I'm getting him this job. I'm gonna tell him that he'll be taking the job as a favor to you."

"That's no sweat off my balls," McDougal said.

That was an image on which Coach didn't want to dwell. "Thanks," Coach said. "I'm going to make you an honorary club sponsor. I'll put the name of your car wash on the back of some of our T-shirts."

McDougal was giving Coach that look that Coach sometimes got, that look that wondered if Coach was from another planet.

"And you know what?" Coach continued. "For just a hundred bucks, you can become a full-fledged, Platinum Premier Club Sponsor."

"Here's some advice for you, Crotch," McDougal said, and then spat again. "Don't press your fucking luck."

Getting Moses a job had been easy enough, but finding him a place to live, Coach knew, would be a problem. The rents in Hoboken were high, and the money Moses would make at the car wash would cover little more than food and other necessities. Coach knew the realtors would have nothing cheap, so he figured all he could do was check around. At the HOHAs runs that week, Coach asked if anyone knew of an inexpensive apartment in Hoboken. Everyone smiled, trying to discern if Coach was serious, and then, when they saw that he was, they laughed out loud. He might as well have been in Honolulu inquiring about an igloo. He tried once more before the Saturday morning run that week and got the same reaction from the group of HOHAs there, but after they had started the run, Vinnie, a high-school runner who joined them occasionally, told Coach that his dad had a cheap place he might rent. Vinnie's dad was Augusto "Augie" DelVecchio, the owner of the salvage yard on the west side of town. Coach had met him while seeking sponsors for the club, and Mr. DelVecchio had become a sponsor, partly, Coach liked to think, because he and Augie had hit it off, but mostly because his son Vinnie was so into running then. Many of the HOHAs T-shirts still had "Augie's Salvage" printed across the back.

After that Saturday run, Coach went with Vinnie to the salvage yard to talk with Augie. The yard was next to the railroad tracks that ran along the palisades on the far west side of town, an area left to old warehouses and vacant lots. The yard was protected by a fence of corrugated steel, topped with a helix of barbed wire. Inside were stacks of cars and appliances and other metal objects that were sorted and fed into a crusher and sold as scrap. As they approached, Vinnie pointed to the building in one corner of the yard. "That's my dad's office on the ground floor," he said. "Up above is the vacant apartment. It's got its own entrance on the side."

Vinnie had to go somewhere, and he left Coach and Augie alone to talk. Coach felt free then to speak openly about Moses' troubles and his own desire to help. Augie was a barrel-chested bear of a man, and he had a softness about him that only big men can afford. He listened intently, and when Coach was finished, Augie summed up the situation with a succinctness that made Coach feel like a Chatty Cathy doll. "Sounds like a good man hitting on hard times," he said.

"So you'll help?"

"That place upstairs is a dump," he said. "I got boxes of paperwork thrown around, and it hasn't been painted in years. But it's got a small kitchen and a working toilet. I never rented it though; nobody wants to live in this part of town."

"Moses has been living under a bridge," Coach said.

Augie whistled. "I guess one man's shack is another man's palace, isn't it?"

"How much rent would you want?"

"Money's not the matter," he said. "I get people breaking into the yard at night to steal parts. I had a couple of watch dogs, but some mutts threw them poison meat. I don't like coming over here every night checking on things. If I had somebody living upstairs who'd let me know if they saw anything wrong, that'd be all I'd ask."

"Moses is proud and won't take charity" Coach said. "I'll need to tell him that he'd be moving in as a favor to you."

"That's fine," Augie said. "If he stays home most nights and keeps an eye out for the place, he *will* be doing me a favor. A big one, too."

Coach's plan was falling into place. All he had to do now was propose the move to Moses in a way that wouldn't hurt his pride, and he thought that shouldn't be too difficult. He knew that Moses thought the world of him and the club, and he intended to use that affection to his advantage.

At the next club run, Coach positioned himself so that Moses would run next to him. When Moses did come alongside, Coach looked lost in thought, and he waited for Moses to have the first word. Moses, for his part, was surprised by Coach's glumness and silence. "How you doin', Coach?" Moses started. "Feeling OK?"

"Oh, Moses, hey," Coach said. "I didn't see you there. I guess I'm preoccupied tonight."

"What's wrong?"

"Well, I went to visit the club sponsors this week, and a couple of them are in a fix. Mr. McDougal can't find dependable workers for his car wash business, and Mr. DelVecchio is pestered with thieves and needs a watchman to live in a place he's got at his salvage yard." Coach shook his head. "I just wish there was something that I could do."

"Is there any way I could be of help?" Moses said.

"Thanks, Moses," Coach said. "But I doubt it. You live in Newark and have a job and home there." Then Coach cocked his head to the side, as if something had just occurred to him. "But come to think of it, if you were willing to move to Hoboken, you'd be perfect in both spots, and it would be great having you here in Hoboken too, where you could run more with us."

Having a home and steady job again was a dream on which Moses had all but given up. Now Moses worked over the possibility. "There's only one problem," he said.

"What's that?"

"I'd have to leave my friend, Buddy."

"Buddy could visit you."

"He wouldn't do that," Moses said. "Buddy doesn't like to go too far from home."

"Well, then you could visit him."

"I could?"

"Of course. You'd just be taking a job and an apartment."

"I don't know, Coach."

"Moses, it would be a big favor to two of our club sponsors, and it would be a great relief to me."

They ran on in silence. Coach continued to look glum, and he even accentuated his woe with a few audible sighs. Moses felt bad for Coach, and he thought about all that Coach had done for him, and he thought about how much the HOHAs meant to Coach and to himself. And Coach was right: he could still visit Buddy any time. He thought mostly about Buddy, and he remembered Buddy's feeling about him, that he had somewhere else he was meant to be. He looked down at his own feet, and at the shoes that Buddy declared were meant to take him there. They were running through Stevens then, on that exhilarating downhill that Moses loved. That's when Moses said, "I'll do it, Coach. I'll do it for you and for the club." Coach let out a whoop, and Moses watched with relief and joy as the familiar delight and enthusiasm returned to Coach's face.

Moses' membership of the club and move to Hoboken proved to be a boon for the HOHAs. His mere presence brought legitimacy to the club, and an old-school example of loyalty and hard work. For the younger runners, who made up the bulk of the club at the time, the HOHAs had been just another activity between their working day and their social night, but for Moses, the club was nothing less than his home and salvation. He attended every club run, every meeting, and every event, and despite being almost forty years Coach's senior, he looked up to Coach as a leader and mentor. He hung on every word of advice that Coach had about running, and he brought Coach the trophies he won in the same way a grateful cat deposits a caught bird on the doorstep of his master. For his part, Coach bragged about Moses' victories and saw in Moses' talent the foundation of the club he had always envisioned. The other HOHAs saw the respect that Moses and Coach had for each other and the dedication they both had to running, and those attitudes rubbed off on them.

But that was later. Right then, Coach and Moses were shoulder to shoulder, with all the hope of new beginnings, smiling like kids on a lark, and flying faster and faster down Stevens hill and back into the heart of Hoboken.

DESIRES

Coach wanted to establish a great running club
more than he wanted anything else in this life,
but life rarely gives us what we want from it—
it always gives us much, much more.

HOHAs *in* Love

25. Birds of a Feather

THE MID-1990s were golden years in the history of the HOHAs. The club was well established by then, and the HOHAs had settled nicely into a mellow, albeit mediocre, groove. There was a comforting sameness and timelessness to HOHAs life—the weekly runs, the monthly meetings, the annual social events— and there was a sweetness to the HOHAs contentment with the way things were. This is not to say that the HOHAs were by any definition impressive or had become in any way a successful competitive club. Despite Coach's intentions and unflagging efforts, the HOHAs remained throughout those years the oddest ragbag collection of characters and back-of-the-pack runners imaginable.

Coach was fond of nicknames, and some of the names he came up with in the early days served best to describe the HOHAs then. He often picked a nickname in order to motivate or instruct a runner. For example, there was one HOHA who was too meek to be a good competitor, so Coach called him Bulldog to toughen him up, and there was one whom Coach called Slow-Mo because of the inefficient arm and leg movements that made him seem to run in slow motion. Coach called another runner Tums, because he got nervous before races and complained about his stomach, but most of the nicknames that Coach came up with were just for fun. One HOHA was a journalist who often helped Coach with the HOHAs newsletter. He was prematurely bald, and Coach called him Ballpoint. Compared with Moses, most of the HOHAs were young. The notable exceptions were Icky, a runner in his early 40s who didn't wash his running gear, and Boston, a veteran in his 50s who was always trying, and failing, to qualify for the Boston Marathon. There was a stocky runner named Sherman, whom Coach called The Tank, a cute girl named Quentin Thompson was Q-T, and Jim Eckersley was The Eck. There was EverReady and Kozy, Pinky and Barker, Animal, and many more. Not all of Coach's nicknames stuck, however. Howie Mooch, whom Coach still called Terminator, was just Howie to everybody else, and Coach tried to tag Edsel as Boss, but the HOHAs, and Coach himself, preferred his real name and eventually returned to it in the end.

In the early years, the HOHAs were modest in number, but Coach said that he'd rather have thirty runners dedicated to the sport and running together every week than a hundred runners who rarely showed up for a run or only came to the parties. That said, Coach persistently tried to grow the club. He had Ben at Counter-Fit print up HOHAs business cards with the times and locations of HOHAs runs on the back, and he had the HOHAs pass out the cards to other runners they saw in Hoboken. New runners came, and the ones who didn't fit in left. The others stayed, and over time there was a small but steady increase in club membership. Coach, with his mathematical mind, tracked the attendance at HOHAs runs and club events, and one could get a feel for the state of the club by the pronouncements he'd make at meetings or in the newsletter. "Thirty-three HOHAs attended the Tuesday run on August 14," he'd say, "shattering the old record of twenty-seven," or "Forty-one HOHAs ran the Hoboken Classic this year, eight more than last year."

There was a tongue-in-cheek megalomania in Coach's pride in the club. The New York Road Runners, just across the river, had thirty thousand members and directed the annual New York City Marathon, one of the great running events in the world, but Coach saw the HOHAs as the David to their Goliath and resented the success they had, as if it were the HOHAs' due. When one early HOHA joined the Peace Corps and moved to Thailand, Coach declared the HOHAs to be now international in scope and Hoboken to be the HOHAs' World Headquarters. Coach envisioned the club as nothing less than a fledgling empire, perhaps no less important than the Roman Empire itself, and even created a Latin motto for the HOHAs: "Honestas, Constantia, Celeritas," to wit, "Honor, Consistency, Speed." Coach had these altruistic words printed on the back of the club T-shirts, where they resided incongruently alongside the advertisements of club sponsors: "Get Your Buns Warm at Marie's Bakery" and "Hoboken Podiatry: We Care for the Athlete's Foot."

Coach said that the second best thing in life, after running itself, was talking about running, and the HOHAs met after the weekly runs to do just that. They met at Maxwell's on Tuesdays and at Moran's on Thursdays. These were informal gatherings for talking and drinking beer, "liquid carbo-loading," Coach called it. Runners are birds of a feather, and anytime the HOHAs got together, the conversations were mostly about running, but for more formal discussion of the art of running, Coach established the monthly club meetings, which were held on the third Wednesday of every month in the various back rooms of the restaurants and bars that were club sponsors.

Coach was holistic in his approach to running, and invited guest speakers to the meetings to talk on a wide range of subjects that were often only loosely related to running. Besides the running shoe and clothing reps, there were podiatrists, chiropractors, aromatherapists, acupuncturists, and even psychologists and astrologers. To their credit, the more esoteric speakers found a way to relate their subject—if only in some mind-body-spirit sense— to the sport of running. If the speaker needed a volunteer from the audience, Coach jumped in. He was always getting his shoulders massaged, his spine straightened, his future read, and even his aura adjusted.

Coach, as the president of a prominent Hoboken organization, was occasionally asked to speak himself at the meetings of other local groups. He was an untiring proponent of the importance of exercise for good health and longevity, and he would usually lecture on the benefits of regular exercise and good nutrition.

> *I once gave a speech at the Hoboken convalescent hospital. I was supposed to talk about diet and daily stretching, but I got carried away with talk about carbohydrates, and lactic acid, and aerobic threshold, and by the time I'd finished my speech, with all its technical jargon, the old folk thought I was a doctor. When I opened up the floor to questions, one little old lady asked, "Dr. Bean, can I eat horseradish with a heart condition?"*

Coach had a voluminous collection of books and magazines on running and fitness, and he would bring a selection of them to the meetings to share with club members. He proudly claimed that the HOHAs were the only running club in the world with its own lending library. Coach had plenty of photographs too.

He took pictures at races and club events, and the club meetings often included a slide show. Coach narrated these shows, and he used the photos of runners in action to provide tips on running form and racing tactics, more often than not using the photos of HOHAs runners as examples of what *not* to do.

To break up the routine of Tuesday and Thursday runs and the club meetings, Coach spiced things up with seasonal events. In January, he forecasted the coldest Sunday of the month and held a Polar Bear Run. It was the HOHAs version of a New Year's Day dip in the ocean. The heartiest HOHAs, dressed in only shorts and HOHAs singlet, ran the length of Washington Street, and then dashed back to Coach's apartment for hot chocolate. On April Fools' Day, Coach held the Backward Mile on Sinatra Drive. He divided the HOHAs into four-person relay teams, with each team member running backwards for a quarter mile. Then there was a party at Moran's afterward, and the losing teams had to buy the winning team all the beer they could drink. In the summer, there was a potluck picnic in a local park, where the HOHAs women were pitted against the HOHAs men in the annual HOs vs. HAs softball game. In the fall, Coach hosted a marathon party to honor all the HOHAs who had completed the New York City Marathon that day. And in December, Coach organized a run in Santa hats and the annual HOHAs Holiday dinner-dance for local charities, held at the Elks Lodge on Washington Street.

Forever ruling over this landscape of running and running-related events was Coach, the HOHAs president. "President" is a title normally associated with democratic elections, but Coach, like the Pope, held the title for life, or at least for as long as he was in town. He once described the duration of his presidential term as "eternal."

Coach's presidency was a benevolent dictatorship, not that there was any threat to his command. Nobody else wanted the job, but like a good dictator, Coach secured his reign with his complete control of the media. Every month, he published a HOHAs newsletter in which he touted the club's vision, growth, and accomplishments. "A HOHAs run has never been cancelled because of inclement weather!" Coach also used the newsletter as another forum for his odes to the beauty and importance of running, and for his lessons on training, diet, and safety. "Wear light-colored clothing and reflective vests during the dark winter months. If you don't have a vest, stop by Edsel's store and we'll fix you up." And, of course, he used the newsletter to remind members of all the upcoming club events and races.

HOHAs life under the reign of Coach was comforting repetition punctuated with invigorating zaniness. That was Coach himself, and through all the years of the HOHAs, he was the constant. You could depend on his obsession, his dedication to the sport, and even his stubbornness, but you could also depend on him to throw you off guard, to awaken you to possibilities, and to make you see the miracle in anything you were taking for granted. He wore on some people, and even those who loved him sometimes found his personality and energy to be more than they could take, but then, just when you were ready to give up on the whacked-out goofball, he'd pull something unexpected and, well, just poetic, and you'd be back in his camp again and thinking you were the luckiest person in the world just to know him.

There was the time he signed up the HOHAs for a 24-hour charity relay and cajoled and coerced a dozen HOHAs to attend. They pitched a tent on the infield of the high-school track and each ran for twenty minutes at a time, taking turns all through the day and night. They couldn't get much sleep in between their turns, and everyone complained, but when it was over, everyone was left with a warm feeling of togetherness and accomplishment.

And there were his occasional kidnappings. Coach had a 1967 Rogue Rambler—the RORA, he called it—on which he had installed one of Moses' running trophies as a hood ornament. He would drive the RORA to the apartments of selected HOHAs and declare that they were being kidnapped and had to come with him immediately, dressed just as they were. Usually he would just take the victims to a movie he wanted to see, or to the Malibu Diner for a late-night snack, but wherever it was, his unspoken message was that it's fun to do things together, to break from one's routine, and to find pleasure in the unexpected.

Coach created memorable moments, but it was the seemingly ordinary events, looking back, that made those times special. Through it all, throughout the nineties, the Tuesday and Thursday runs went on. The HOHAs met to run week after week, season after season, year after year. "First and foremost," Coach said, "we run, and we run together." Coach's obsessions, statistics, and pronouncements, along with the sightings of Howie eating pastries and of Moses running in the middle of the night, became part of HOHAs legend. Even these oddities, in their own repetition, became just part of the wallpaper of HOHAs life. It was mesmerizing really, hypnotizing, almost like a drug, this repetition. Nothing seemed to happen, because the same things happened over and over again.

Even this repetition provided—for those sensitive enough to be attuned to it—an excitement of sorts. The excitement was in the knowledge that things change—grass grows, rust forms, sidewalks crack—even if we can't see it happening. Even Manhattan, standing across the river like a castle built of eternal stone, if filmed in a series of stills taken over the years, would be seen to rise from nothing, undulate with motion, and fall again. Everyone feels this in their own way, the persistence of change and its inevitability. It is the relentlessness of time that amazes us most, and the way it has of sneaking up on us. There are periods when nothing seems to change, and we are lulled into thinking that everything will stay the same. Then there is a shift—a meeting, a marriage, a departure, a death—that startles us from our daydream and reminds us that time has continued working, without a vacation, a weekend, a lunch hour, or even a coffee break. It has been tirelessly and slowly pulling everything into its past. Startled by this sudden realization, we search for recent moments, as if we had just misplaced a set of keys. They were just here; we just had them; where could they be? But the search for the past, even just yesterday, is a fruitless one, and we quickly tire and give up on it. We realize that not only can we not find the past, it is no longer there, but the present moment is the consolation, and surely it will always be ours.

All times are eventually forgotten, but some are long remembered. The mid-1990s may have seemed like low years for the HOHAs, because the club failed to improve and nothing seemed to happen, but looking back, those years may have been the best. It was a time of apparent timelessness. Coach's vision nurtured a gentle seed of beauty and hope, and there was a peacefulness and togetherness before the glorious flowering, and all the changes to come.

26. Lucky in Love

AT FIRST GLANCE, it would be easy to consider Coach unlucky. All he'd ever wanted from life was to be a great runner, and yet he didn't have the speed to herd a turtle. His backup plan was to be a great running coach, and yet his HOHAs were known only for their last-place finishes and funny name. But running aside, in other areas of his life—areas about which he seemed not even to care—Coach was the luckiest guy around.

With Coach's mathematical brain and genius for computers, he always had well-paid consulting jobs. HOHAs marveled at the ease and boredom with which he moved in and out of the plum positions that came his way. They also marveled at his luck in love. As difficult as it was to keep track of his ever-changing jobs, it was just as difficult to keep track of his various girlfriends.

He met all of the girls through the running club. They were attracted by his nerdy good looks, his passion, and his goofy charm. Maybe they were attracted by his power, too. As humble as the title was, he was, after all, the HOHAs president, and there is a sexiness associated with leadership of any kind, but for whatever reasons, from Coach's founding of the club in the spring of 1990 through the spring of 1997, he had an uninterrupted string of thirteen HOHAs girlfriends.

There was Emily, Tracy, Suzanne, Quentin, Sue, Tricia, Trudy, Kathleen, Patti (with an "i"), Sheila, Anne, Diane, and Marilyn. Of all of them, Patti was the finest runner.

All of these romances developed in what would become a predictable pattern. The young woman would join the club; Coach would observe her running form and proffer some casual advice; she would be flattered by his presidential attention; Coach would offer a personal training session to develop what he referred to as her obvious running potential; after the session, Coach would suggest going for a drink; as one drink led to another, Coach's praise for her running would be followed by an appreciation of her beautiful eyes/hair/legs (choose one); and the rest, as the HOHAs would say, would be HOHAs history. Coach, to his credit, did improve each of the women as a runner. No one could dispute that. Even in his romantic adventures, Coach took his coaching seriously. Each affair included not only training schedules and sessions but running advice that Coach would offer day and night throughout their relationship. The relationships were the oddest mixture of running clinic and torrid affair. Only in Coach's mind did running and passion make such natural bedfellows, and the odd thing was that the romances continued only up to the point where his coaching was complete. Then, Coach had a way of proclaiming that he had nothing more to teach, and the lady of the moment had nothing more to learn. The young woman felt almost graduated, and was left thinking that all the dating and lovemaking had somehow been just a pleasant part of the overall curriculum. They would actually thank Coach when he broke up with them, and the rest of the HOHAs would shake their heads in disbelief and wonder how he managed it. These "graduations" would inevitably coincide with the appearance of the next attractive young woman on the HOHAs scene who, of course, required Coach's personal athletic touch.

Coach's affairs were another part of HOHAs legend, and the HOHAs took comfort in the regularity of the romances and in the streak itself; thirteen straight HOHAs girlfriends without a break. Maybe it wasn't as great as Lou Gehrig's streak of consecutive games played (2019), or Joe DiMaggio's streak of consecutive games with a hit (56), but it was impressive in its own right, and was the greatest streak the HOHAs had. People enjoy watching a streak, not only for its innate beauty and historical meaning, but because they want to see when it will come to an end, as all streaks eventually must.

Coach's streak ended on April 8, 1997, at 8:05 in the evening, at the start of what appeared to be just another Tuesday-night run. That was when Coach met Biscuit, although it would be more accurate to say when Coach met Amy, because she wasn't known as Biscuit yet. Until that moment, the HOHAs had considered Coach lucky in love, but they hadn't really known just how lucky he was, because what appeared to be the end of his luck would turn out to be his greatest luck of all.

From the moment of Biscuit's arrival, everything changed, not just for Coach himself, but for his HOHAs as well. The HOHAs noted the change at the time, but it wasn't until later that they recognized its significance. Then the HOHAs searched back in their memories to recreate the catalytic event, but the perceptions and memories of that evening are foggy, and the accounts are at odds.

There would be many different accounts of what happened and many interpretations of what it all meant, and each account and interpretation came to have its faithful adherents over time, but all accounts shared some common elements, and it's best to start with those. All agree that it was a regular HOHAs Tuesday-night run, and all agree it was one of those magical evenings of spring, so suddenly warm and beautiful that everyone had to be outside, basking in it. The evening was like one of those songs at a party that lifts everyone off their seats to dance, and everyone felt that there was something special about it. Ballpoint said there was a muted quality to the sounds, as when a car travels across snow. Slow-Mo described it as electricity and said that when Coach and Amy met, there was an actual spark between them. Edsel just said the whole evening was strange, in a way he couldn't explain, and that he just knew that "something major was going down."

At least thirty HOHAs turned out for that run, some say more. All agree that Coach made his usual announcements before the run, and that Amy appeared for the first time and participated in that run, and that when that April evening started, Coach and the club that he had proudly founded were, for the most part, just as they had been since the club's inception, and that when that evening was over, Coach and the club were then on a path that would see them changed completely and forever.

From this consensus, however, the accounts of that evening begin to differ and go their separate ways. Most accounts state that during Coach's announcements, Amy just magically appeared at his side. "Coach was talking," Edsel said, "and next to him was this girl no one had seen before. One moment she wasn't there and the next she was, standing right next to him and looking up at him." Bulldog said, "Coach was making his normal announcements, and I bent down to stretch, and when I looked up, this girl was standing right next to him. I had never seen her before. I figured it was her first run with the club, but I couldn't understand why she was standing right next to Coach. Coach hadn't even noticed her yet; he was still talking."

In the accounts that have Amy standing next to Coach, there is disagreement whether he noticed her while he was speaking, and among those who say he did notice her, there is further disagreement whether they spoke before the run began. "I'm telling you," Edsel said, "he saw her out of the corner of his eye. Didn't you notice when he stumbled over his words? Then right after the announcements, he turned to talk to her. Remember Slow-Mo yelled out that we should start the run? That was because Coach was so goo-goo over her that he completely forgot what he was doing."

Others, who agree that Coach saw Amy while he was speaking, don't remember him talking with her before the run. They believe that it was sometime during the run that Coach first struck up a conversation. Howie claimed, "Coach started the run, and then he checked, as he always does, to make sure nobody was running alone. That's when he saw the new girl and fell back to run with her." Howie's version had some credence, because, bringing up the rear in the runs, as he always did, he could see what was going on. There were many differences in opinion, but all the HOHAs there that evening agreed on the one thing that was the most baffling thing of all. After the run, Coach ignored the customary post-run gathering at Maxwell's and instead left with Amy.

When all the runners had completed the course and an adequate amount of time had been devoted to stretching and talking, most of the HOHAs walked casually toward the bar. Coach was always in this group, never missing a chance to have a beer and talk some more. On this Tuesday evening, Coach walked with Amy up ahead of the group, and he was oblivious to all else around him. When they reached Maxwell's, Coach and Amy just kept walking. Coach didn't even turn around, and the rest of the HOHAs stopped in front of the bar and watched in disbelief as Coach walked away. No one called after him. They were all dumbstruck, because what they were seeing just couldn't be, and those who hadn't noticed Amy before surely noticed her then. That evening, for the first time that anyone could remember, the HOHAs drank without their leader. There was the usual talk about running, but there were strange gaps in the conversation, the places in the talk that belonged to Coach and what he would have said, and the conversation was continually interrupted by speculation on what might have happened to Coach. Some guessed that Amy might be Coach's cousin or sister, just visiting town. "She's no cousin," Eck said. "Did you see the way they were looking at each other?" Ballpoint suggested that maybe Coach was already graduating Marilyn and moving on, but others argued that Coach had just enrolled Marilyn and it was much too soon for that. The consensus was that Amy was simply a new club member, perhaps injured in some way, and that Coach was just lending her a hand, but this was an uneasy consensus, because the HOHAs knew that Coach's behavior was highly unusual, and they sensed that something in HOHAdom was drastically awry.

27. A Man for All Seasons

"'WHAT IS YOUR second wish for your daughter?' the genie said to me, and I said, 'I wish that she finds true love.'"

"Thank you, Mom," Coco said. "I'm sure I will."

"Don't be so sure," Gloria said. "It's not that easy."

"It was easy for you," Coco said. "You were married twice by the time you were my age now."

"I said *true* love." Gloria smiled ruefully. "I married the wrong men, and I married too young. People would ask me how old I was when I first got married, and I'd say, 'I got born; they slapped me on the butt; and I said, 'I do.'"

Coco laughed.

"And that's what I want to talk to you about, about not marrying the first man that comes along, but holding out for the right one."

"And how do I do that?"

"Well, I'm glad you asked," Gloria said, "because I'm going to tell you another story. I never told you how Grandma Emma met her husband, did I?"

"No."

"All right then. This'll be fun," Gloria said. "Come here and sit next to me." Coco moved next to her mom. "Are you comfy?"

"Yes, Mom."

"Good." Gloria patted Coco on the hand. "Now, once upon a time, when my Grandma Emma was a girl, her daddy, my great-grandfather, Michael Dugan, moved the family to Nebraska. The early settlers often built a dugout for shelter. A dugout was a dwelling carved into the side of a low hill, with the roof and front made of poles and sod. My Great-Grandpa Mike built his family one of those dugouts, and he had Grandma and their two girls all settled in. Then one day a young man named Dexter Wheeler came passing through, looking for a place to homestead. Well, that day Dexter saw a low hill as a vantage point, rode up the grassy side of it, felt the earth give way, and suddenly found himself surrounded by the screaming Dugan family. He had ridden over the roof of their dugout, but he not only fell through the roof, he ended up falling in love and marrying Emma Dugan."

"That's romantic."

"That's one way of looking at it. Especially if you didn't know that Dexter Wheeler went from one half-baked, harebrained scheme to the next and caused Grandma Emma misery for the rest of her days.

"And why am I telling you this story? Why was Grandma Emma miserable? Because she put her feelings first. Because she married the first man who rode up on a horse."

"We live in Pittsburgh, Mom. I'm not in much danger of that."

"You know what I mean, and I wouldn't tell you the story if it didn't hold true. I married the first man that came along myself, and then the second too. I made the same mistake Grandma Emma made, but I was dumb enough to make it twice. And look where it's got me: halfway to nowhere, that's where, and without even the horses I got there on."

Gloria smiled again, but then continued thoughtfully. "It's not just fate, or a matter of luck; a man is a conscious choice that a woman makes, and you shouldn't make that choice because the man has blue eyes and a cute smile. When Dexter Wheeler fell through that roof, there were two teenage girls in that dugout: Grandma Emma and her sister, Aunt Eve. Eve was older and Dexter had his eye on her first, but Eve sized him up in short order and turned up her nose at him.

"Grandma Emma married Dexter Wheeler, but Aunt Eve waited, went on through school and soon had plenty of suitors to choose from. The man she chose was your Great-Uncle Earl. She had him court her for a year before she married him, and she stayed married to him for fifty years until she died.

"When she met Uncle Earl, she was selling pies at the church fair, and Uncle Earl spotted her and went up to her. Aunt Eve's first words to him were, 'May I help you?' and Uncle Earl replied, 'Yes, Miss, I'd like one of your smiles.' Couples often remember the first words they say to each other, and Uncle Earl remembered those first words. Fifty years later he was with Eve at her death. She suffered, and was having trouble breathing at the last, and she was scared. Her last words to him were 'Help me.' Uncle Earl understood it later, and told me about it with wonder in his voice. 'Her first words to me were, 'May I help you?' and her last words were, 'Help me!'" Uncle Earl shook his head and had tears in his eyes. 'And in between was our life together.'

"For the most part, it was a good life, too. They had their bumps in the road, like everybody, but they always loved each other. They used to tease each other all the time. They liked to travel, taking car trips all over the country, and Uncle Earl would take pictures of Eve coming out of the bathroom. They'd have slide shows when they got home, and there'd be a dozen slides of Eve coming out of some ladies room in every state they went through. Uncle Earl would say, 'We fell behind schedule again right there,' and Aunt Eve would say, 'Earl's the only man who doesn't put a single pit stop in his entire itinerary.'

"Your Great-Uncle Earl was a live wire. Aunt Eve blamed his antics on the amount of coffee he drank, and tried to get him onto decaf. He resisted it, so Eve would secretly buy the decaf kind and mix it into the regular coffee can. At first she put in too much, and Earl was getting grumpy and falling asleep in the afternoon, so she adjusted the proportions until he could stay awake all day without getting silly. 'I just kept experimenting with the mixture,' she said, 'until I got him just the way I wanted him.' Eve and Earl had a wonderful marriage, long and fun and loving.

"After Eve's death, Uncle Earl was good to Grandma Emma and me. He was with us at holidays and birthdays, and when times were really tough, he'd go with us to the grocery store to make sure we got the things we needed. He paid for it all, and he'd come behind us pushing his own cart and putting in all the things he knew we'd like to have but were too ashamed to take: canned peaches and cakes and that kind of thing. I knew he truly loved us and was doing it for us, but one day—and this is the wonderful thing—I realized he was really doing it because he still loved her. Even after she was gone, he was looking for ways to make her happy, and then even after his own death, he left all that money to us to pay for your education.

"Aunt Eve chose a husband who was strong and loyal enough to outlive her, and to be with her and take care of her at the end, and to take care of the ones she loved, even after she was gone and he was gone. Now that's stick-to-itivness. That's a family man. And that's love.

"Your Grandma Emma married Dexter for what she *thought* was love, and ended up with nothing but heartache. Two sisters, prairie girls, both as strong as tree trunks, but they had two different characters and ended up with two different types of men and two different lives. Aunt Eve picked a dependable, loving man who stood by her, and all I'm saying is that when it comes time for you to choose a man, don't do like Grandma Emma, and surely don't do like me. Do like your Aunt Eve."

"Mom, there's no man right now for me to worry about."

"*Yet,*" Gloria corrected. "There's no man *yet,* but there will be."

A young male orderly entered the room and served Gloria her lunch. When he left, Gloria said, "Did you see the way he looked at you? You took the chrome right off his bumper. You won't have a hard time finding a man. With your looks, the men will find you. Your problem will be knowing which one to choose. Some will be easy to reject, but that will just give you the false confidence to think that when you see one you like, he's the one. That's the trap. The ones you're immediately attracted to could be the worst ones for you."

"Well then, how do you know?"

"You know by taking your time, by getting to know a man real good before you give him your heart. And remember, talk is cheap; it's a man's actions that count. Your daddy charmed me right outta my panties from day one, and I married him three months after I met him. Then I had to quit work when I had you, and then he got laid off from his job. Things were tough. We had to move in with Grandma for a while, and your daddy and Grandma didn't get along. He could hardly hide his dislike for her and, well, Grandma came right out and said what she thought of him. Then he knocked me around a bit. We had the police over once, and Grandma almost clawed his eyes out. Then one day he just left. He couldn't stand up to the hard times, not for me, and not even for you. I've told you this before, but I want you to remember it now."

"I'll remember it, Mom."

"I'm not saying your daddy was all bad. He gave me you, after all, and he gave you your name. Coco Cushman. Isn't it pretty? I took my old name back after he left, but I kept his name for you. No, your daddy had his charms, but he was irresponsible. After he left, his sister came and apologized for the family. She said that your daddy had always been a trouble, and that they hadn't said anything to me because they thought maybe I could straighten him out. Isn't that something? Everybody else knew but me, and I didn't know because I didn't take the time to know.

"Get to know a man before you give him your heart. If I had to do it again, I wouldn't even sleep with a man until I'd seen him in all seasons. I'd say, 'I have to see you raking leaves, shoveling snow, holding an umbrella for me, and putting suntan lotion on my back. I have to see how you hold up in all kinds of weather. Then I'll know.' Find yourself a man that will last you a lifetime. Not just a man who is fun when the sun is shining, but a man who will stick with you through every storm.

"Promise me. Put your hand on your heart and promise me you'll do that."

"I promise, Mom."

"I'm not only going to wish that you find true love; I'm going to pray for you too," Gloria said. "I'm going to pray that you find a love that lasts a lifetime. I'm going to pray that you find a man for all seasons."

28. Biscuit

AT THE TIME Coach met Amy, he had been seeing a new girl in the club—girlfriend number 13. Her name was Marilyn, and she'd recently moved to Hoboken from Washington D.C. Marilyn had temporarily returned to D.C. to get the last of her things, and in her absence, Coach was now seeing Amy. Amy came to several runs, and after every run she and Coach would leave together. Coach began calling her "Biscuit." It surprised no one that he had given her a nickname, because he did that with almost everybody, but nobody knew why Amy was "Biscuit."

We stopped at a café after a movie for some coffee and dessert. Amy asked the waitress about one of the pies, and the waitress said it had a graham cracker crust. I told Amy that when my mum came for a visit, a waitress once had to explain to her what a graham cracker was. The waitress understood that my mum was British, and she said, "It's like a cookie, but you don't use the word 'cookie,' do you?"

"No, we don't say 'cookie,'" my mum said. "We call them biscuits."

The waitress said, "Well, if you call cookies biscuits, what do you call biscuits?"

Mum looked at her and said seriously, "We call 'em crumpets."

The waitress laughed, and then Amy laughed too. She was small and her laugh was sweet, and I told her that she was like a cookie too.

"You mean I'm a biscuit?" she said.

"Yes," I said. "You're my Biscuit."

She smiled, and her smile went right for my heart, and I called her Biscuit after that."

When anyone asked about her, Coach was touched by silence, and this was another clue that things were changing, because it was unusual for Coach to be silent about anything.

When people lack information, speculation abounds, and everyone in the club was wondering what would happen upon Marilyn's return. Coach had been wondering that himself, and despite his affection for Biscuit, when Marilyn called on her first night back, the well-worn path of habit brought him directly to her apartment. They had been enjoying the special ardor that is fueled by separation when there was a sharp and persistent knock at Marilyn's door. Coach sat bolt upright in bed and looked at the pink fluorescent clock on Marilyn's night table. It was midnight. He turned to Marilyn, who was also sitting up now. "Who could that be?"

"It's probably not my boyfriend," Marilyn said casually, but with an alarming trace of doubt.

"Your boyfriend?" Coach almost shouted. "You didn't tell me you had a boyfriend."

"You never asked me."

"Well, I think it's something a girl might mention."

"Relax. He's still down in D.C. He's not moving up here for a couple of weeks."

"Oh, I feel *so* much better," Coach said sarcastically. The knocking at the door continued. "Are you sure it's not him?"

"Yes. I talked to him this evening. I doubt he could have driven up here since then."

"You *doubt?*"

"Besides, he has a key," Marilyn said. "If it were him, he'd come right in."

"That's a comforting thought."

The knocking kept up.

"You'd better go see who it is," Marilyn said finally.

Coach got up, and put on his boxers. The knocking continued, and as he walked toward the door, he was becoming irritated. Then, in the darkness of the unfamiliar living room, he kicked a chair and let out an involuntary gasp of pain. "Bloody hell," he yelled.

When he got to the door, he looked through the peephole but could see nothing. The knocking was making the door vibrate against his face. "Who is it?" he yelled. There was no answer, just more knocking. He was pissed now and, emboldened by his anger, he grabbed an umbrella from the stand by the door. If whoever it was tried anything, he'd show them what a knock was all about.

Coach turned the deadbolt and threw open the door. It was Biscuit. She was standing there calmly with her arms at her sides. If anything, she looked tired from all the knocking. "Get your clothes on, Coach," she said.

"Biscuit?"

"Come on," she said. "You're coming with me."

"What? What are you doing here?"

"You heard me, Coach. Get dressed. We're going."

"But, Biscuit, I was in the middle of something."

She looked at the raised umbrella in his hand. "What? Singing in the rain?" she said. "I know what you were in the middle of, you twit. Now go put on your pants."

Coach was embarrassed that Biscuit had found him like this, but he was dumbfounded by the situation too. "But we've only been on one real date," he said.

Biscuit just looked at him in utter disbelief and said, "And that wasn't enough for you?" Coach said nothing. "Then you're an idiot." Coach was nonplussed and just stood there looking at her. "But you're my idiot," Biscuit said firmly, "so just put on your pants and let's go."

Biscuit was waiting for Coach downstairs, near the door of the brownstone. When he got there, she started down the steps. "Come on. Let's go for a walk," was all she said.

"Listen, Biscuit, I ..."

"Do you love her?" Biscuit broke in.

"Who?"

"Who do you think? Marilyn."

"No."

"Then why were you sleeping with her? Do you think that you're a James Bond, and that you should sleep around like some egotistical dog?"

"Well, no ..."

"We're human beings," Biscuit said. "We're better than that."

They were on Hudson, near its intersection with Sinatra Drive. Coach was still tucking in his shirt and hurrying to keep up as they turned down Sinatra toward the river. It was a crisp, cool night, and Biscuit had her coat buttoned at the collar and was wearing a cute knit cap with a pompom on top. Coach liked the way her hair came out from under the cap. She took Coach's arm as they walked. He was still flustered and embarrassed and was surprised that Biscuit was calm, despite what she had just said. Coach didn't know what to say, so he just waited.

"I'm enjoying your confusion," she said.

"If my confusion gives you pleasure, then I'm sure I can make you the happiest woman in the world."

"I have no doubt about it," Biscuit said playfully. They walked for a while in silence, and then she said seriously, "I had a rough day at work. I didn't even get home till ten." She went on to tell Coach about the project she was on and some of the problems they were having. There was a man on her work team who was undermining her authority, and she was going to have to put him in his place. When she had it all out of her system, she thanked Coach for listening.

"I wasn't any help," he said.

"You don't have to come up with answers for me. I just needed to tell you. You were the first person I wanted to call. I tried when I got home, but I just got your machine. Then I went out to get something to eat, and I ran into Edsel. You had said you were going for a beer with him and Eck, so I asked him where you were. He tried his best to cover for you, but he's too honest a person to be a decent liar."

Biscuit had maintained a steady calm in talking of her problems at work, but Coach saw a sadness come over her face now, and it hurt him to see it.

"Coach," she said softly, "I need to ask you something."

"Yes?"

"Last week. When we went out. Didn't it mean anything to you?"

"I had a nice time."

"I had a nice time too, but that's not what I mean. The entire time I was with you I felt comfortable, and yet excited too. That's an unusual pair of feelings. It's like water and fire. I just loved being with you, and when I looked at you, I knew that you were feeling the same way."

Coach *had* felt the same way, and it had confused him and scared him afterwards. If those feelings were true, they would change all that he had known, so he'd denied them and retreated to the drinking and tomcatting that had always seen him through. It was cowardly. He felt sorry that Biscuit had found him with Marilyn, and he couldn't look her in the eye. She'd not only faced those feelings, but had also had the courage to believe in them and to seek him out. He put his arms around her now and rested his chin on the top of her head. "I did feel the same way," he said softly, "and I don't understand it."

Biscuit put her arms around Coach and held him tight to her. "There are things that we're not meant to understand, but that doesn't mean that we deny them. I don't understand why I chose my profession and why I'm here, but there is a reason for everything, even if we don't understand it on the surface. When

I first saw you, and then got to know you, I understood that for me, a big part of that reason is you. I'm not afraid of the truth, Coach, whether it's easy on me or not, and that's why I came looking for you tonight."

"I'm glad you did."

"We're meant to be together, Coach."

"Hey," he said in mock surprise, "aren't I the one who's supposed to ask you to go steady?"

"I have four older brothers," Biscuit said. "I've watched them make every mistake possible with girls. One of my brothers took his girlfriend to a football game for their first anniversary," she added incredulously.

"Who was playing?" Coach said.

"There you go," Biscuit said. "That's exactly my point." Biscuit gave Coach a playful poke in the belly. "I know how dumb guys are about these things."

Coach knew that Biscuit was right, and that anything he said now on the subject of love would just sound feeble and lame. He took her by the hand and they walked some more in silence. They were on Hudson again, in the glow of the street lamps and the cover of its trees. Someone had tied the laces together on a pair of sneakers and thrown them up to the telephone wires to hang there, and now they were silhouetted against the moon. Coach pointed them out to Biscuit, and they both smiled and, arm in arm, looked up at them as if they were the most romantic sight in the world.

Their walk had brought them back to Biscuit's apartment. Coach gave Biscuit a kiss on the forehead. She looked beat. He knew that she'd had a hard day, and now an emotional night. "Are you all right?" he asked.

"I'm just tired," she said. "You should get some sleep too."

"I will."

"Are you doing the run in the morning?"

It was Saturday, and Coach ran the Saturday morning run, as long as Edsel didn't need him at the store. "Yes," he said, "I don't have to work."

"Good. I'll see you there then." She climbed the steps and Coach waited for her to get inside. She turned before closing the door and said, "Michigan and Ohio State."

"What?" Coach said.

"That was the game that my brother took his girlfriend to for their anniversary."

"Wow! Great teams," Coach said. "What was the score?"

"37 to 34. Michigan. In overtime."

"Wow! Great game," Coach said. "Your brother's girlfriend was a lucky girl."

"Yes," Biscuit said. "She was."

Coach walked home in the moonlight, and in a hazy, moonlit way, he realized that he had started the evening in bed with one girl and had ended it by kissing another girl on the forehead. And in between? What had happened? All he knew was that he felt a warmth inside him that he'd never felt before, and that even the thought of Biscuit made him smile.

To put it simply, Biscuit, as usual, was perfectly right: she and Coach were meant to be together. They felt the need to call each other first when they had to talk, and they were soon spending all their free time together. When Biscuit's cousin had to move out and Biscuit needed a roommate, Coach moved in with her, and if not officially before, they were officially then a couple.

To observers in the club—and in any club or group, most take either a keen or a passing interest in these things—it all seemed to happen quickly. One day there was just Coach, the freewheeling bachelor with the streak of conquests, and the next day there was Biscuit at his side, and the day after that—or so it seemed—there was Coach and Biscuit together. Then they went to Wisconsin to visit Biscuit's family, and when they returned, they were married.

The HOHAs soon sensed and knew, before Coach himself even sensed and knew it, that with Biscuit, Coach's luck had definitely improved, and the HOHAs also knew that, as the saying goes, it's better to be lucky than to be good. Coach and Biscuit renewed everyone's faith in the wonderful fortune of love, and for all those in the club who were alone, and who darkly feared that they might be so forever, Coach and Biscuit offered hope that someday, maybe even tomorrow, their own true love would magically appear.

29. Underdogs

AFTER COACH and Biscuit's wedding, the HOHAs noticed changes in Coach. In a surprising way, Biscuit changed Coach by making him even more like himself. Coach figured if a woman as wonderful as Biscuit was with him, he must be doing something right. She renewed his faith in his coaching, and he doubled his efforts to improve the club.

A great coach must first and foremost be a great teacher, and Coach was all of that. He worked with all the runners in the club, even the less-talented ones, understanding that each runner is different and must be guided in his own particular way. Coach considered each runner's strengths and weaknesses, character and temperament, in order to come up with suitable drills or motivations. He devised personal programs for any HOHA who wanted one, and even for some HOHAs who didn't, and it was a tribute to his pure brainpower that he kept everyone's program straight in his head. Coach often got carried away and, losing track of time, would call HOHAs late at night or early in the morning if he'd hit upon the perfect workouts for them.

Coach was tireless and, to bring out that same effort in others, he would come up with monthly mantras, such as "The greatest runners are the hardest workers," or "Discipline is the mother of habit." Coach worked with the runners every week at the Tuesday and Thursday runs, and on the long training runs on Saturdays and Sundays. In the winter and summer there were strengthening workouts on the Fourteenth Street viaduct leading up to the palisades, where Coach led groups of HOHAs up the hill and back down again, over and over, until they were ready to drop, and in the spring and fall Coach led interval workouts on the Hoboken High School track.

The Hoboken High School track, squeezed into the urban landscape near the city's center, and in keeping with Hoboken's diminutive stature, was only a 300-meter oval instead of the normal 400, but this didn't bother Coach, because it was on the track—any track—that Coach was completely in his element. Maybe that was because he believed strongly in its importance. A track is to running practice what meditation is to spiritual practice: an essential tool, a controlled environment in which to work on one's conditioning, physical and mental, and to work on one's form. The principle of track workouts is to condition oneself to faster speeds by alternating intervals of speed with intervals of rest. For example, one workout might be to run 800 meters at a fast pace, followed by 400 meters at a slow jog, and then repeat that four or five or six times. The length and pace of the intervals—both the speed interval and the rest interval—along with the number of repetitions, depends upon the conditioning of the runner and his stage of development. Week after week, the intensity of the workout should increase, until after ten or twelve weeks the runner is in racing shape.

It is a science and an art to design these workouts and their progression, and to adapt them to the needs and capabilities of each runner, so that each runner realizes the maximum benefit without crossing the line and getting burnt out or hurt. Coach had studied the pioneering coaches of the world and had synthesized their theories and training into a program of his own, and he continually tweaked that program based upon information he obtained from other running enthusiasts in Great Britain and beyond. Through this grapevine he would learn of the latest workouts of the Kenyans, Ethiopians, or great European runners, and only weeks later he would introduce modified and toned-down versions of those workouts to his HOHAs. Even the toned-down versions of some of those workouts were intense: 20 x 400 at 80 seconds with 200-meter rests, or 3 sets of 600, 400, 200 at 75 seconds on each 200 with a 400-meter rest between sets. The numbers alone could make experienced runners break into a cold sweat, because they could foresee the pain that hitting those numbers would bring.

It is on the track really that a runner practices with pain, and as Coach often said, managing pain is what racing is all about. "If two runners have equal talent and have trained equally hard, who will win the race?" Coach would ask. "The runner who is willing and able to press further into pain and stay with it longer," he would answer. Then he would lecture, "And you don't learn to do that on race day. You learn it day after day during workouts, on the road and especially on the track."

As a runner, one has to become friends with pain. One has to spend time with it, know what to expect from it, and even come to like it. Pain is one of the things that makes running unique. We spend most of our lives avoiding pain and even discomfort, but in running, and especially in racing, we bravely seek it out, challenging it and ourselves.

Because track workouts are painful, all but the most dedicated amateur competitors shy away from them, and for that reason, track workouts are best done in groups, because the group provides the moral support to approach the track in the first place and to get through the workout when it gets tough. Coach was great at setting up the workouts and in inspiring and cajoling HOHAs to the track. Once there, he would divide the HOHAs into groups based on their talent and conditioning. There would often be three or four groups running workouts at the same time, and Coach orchestrated these workouts and monitored their progress, usually while participating with one of the groups himself. He had an uncanny ability to observe everything that was going on, and after the workout would make suggestions to individual runners on their training and form.

Coach believed that perfect running form is smooth and efficient and somehow looks effortless. He stressed that runners should watch their form, run erect, use both their arms and legs in perfect harmony, and never strain. When he wanted to say all that in one phrase, he would just say "Run pretty." Coach watched the form of the runners on the track, and would ask them to adjust their stride, their arm movements, and the tension in their hands and even their face. There shouldn't be the slightest waste of energy, or the slightest loss of focus, only body and mind together in the moment, working steadfast to the finish.

If the track workouts are the study, then racing is the test, and despite Coach's dedicated and expert teaching, not all the HOHAs learned their lessons. In those cases, Coach had a corrective approach that was all his own. For example, once Slow-Mo ran a three-mile race in over eighteen minutes. That was a poor showing for him, because at that time he was capable of running that distance a good minute faster. Slow-Mo had done his cooldown when Coach strolled up to him.

"How ya feeling, Mo?" he said.

"Not bad."

"I saw you get out quick. You were right with the lead pack."

"Yeah, it felt cool running with those guys."

"What'd you do the first mile in?"

"Five flat."

"Wow," Coach said. "Flyin'. And your second mile?"

"About six," Slow-Mo said. "I couldn't hang with those guys and blew up about halfway."

"And excuse me," Coach said, "but what did you say your finishing time was?"

Slow-Mo hadn't said, and Coach, of course, had already checked the results and knew. "Eighteen and change," Slow-Mo said, with some shame.

"Now let me get this straight," Coach said. "You ran the first mile in five minutes and the second mile in six." Coach had his chin between his fingers and his thumb and was stroking it, as if he really had to concentrate to do the math. "That means you must've run the last mile in over seven minutes."

"Yeah, I was hurting pretty bad," Slow-Mo admitted.

In racing it is good practice to choose a goal pace and hold evenly to it, running each mile at the same speed. It is even better to run what are called negative splits: that is, to run each mile progressively faster.

"Five, and then six, and then seven," Coach said, with an alarming matter-of-factness. "How did that strategy work for you?"

Slow-Mo was fidgeting now, knowing that Coach was working him. "I guess I ran that first mile a little fast."

"Really?" Coach's sarcasm was heavy, and he set his expression as if Slow-Mo's words were a revelation to him.

"Yeah, I probably would have been better off taking it easier at the beginning and running even splits." Slow-Mo had just violated the cardinal rule of racing by going out too fast, and now he had said something as stupid as, "I probably shouldn't have had that bowl of chili before I went on the roller coaster."

Coach just looked at Slow-Mo with mock fascination and said, "You think so, huh?" Then he walked away, shaking his head in disgust, as if he couldn't stand the sight of Slow-Mo even one second longer.

Throughout the year, but especially during the spring and fall racing seasons, Coach looked for events in which the HOHAs could test themselves against other clubs, and if there was a local race that included a club competition, the HOHAs dutifully met in front of Snail's Pace to carpool to the event. The RORA could carry Coach and four other sweaty HOHAs—five if he had to cram them in. Bulldog and Slow-Mo and a couple of other HOHAs also had cars, and would sometimes help with the driving. Together, they formed HOHAs caravans, and with Coach and the RORA leading the way, set off to all five boroughs of New York City, and ventured to the far reaches of New Jersey. The HOHAs were happy if they could even muster a full team, and they considered it a moral victory if they could return to Hoboken having finished even one place better than last, but Coach didn't become discouraged or let the HOHAs hang their heads. He just used the latest HOHAs effort, or embarrassment, as grist for constructive criticism and even more training.

Coach's hard work was contagious, and his enthusiasm was an inspiration, and the HOHAs did improve, but the starting point had been so low that even solid improvement left the HOHAs a long way from the top. Throughout the running circles of the Northeast, they were still just the little club with the funny name, but even in their mediocrity—and sometimes outright ineptitude—they tried. Through all their trials and mishaps, they were infused with Coach's spirit and optimism, and that spirit blessed them with a warm feeling of camaraderie and underdog pride.

30. The UFO

IN LATE AUGUST of 1997 there were two separate UFO sightings in Hoboken, and HOHAs made both of them. A HOHA named Arturo made the first sighting, but being new to the club, he failed to comprehend its importance. Ballpoint made the second sighting, and Ballpoint, a HOHAs veteran who understood full well the meaning of what he saw, wasted no time in reporting the news to Coach.

Coach and a handful of HOHAs were gathered in front of Edsel's store for the Saturday morning run when Ballpoint arrived. He went directly to Coach, and before even a hello or good morning, blurted out, "Coach, you're not going to believe what I saw last night. I saw the fastest runner I've ever seen. Right here. In Hoboken."

Ballpoint then recounted how he had been running the previous evening on Sinatra Drive when another runner flew by him so fast that it had blown his cap off. "I was running hard myself," Ballpoint said, "but his speed made me feel as if I were standing still. There was just this Swoooooosh sound when he went by." Ballpoint paused to reflect and enjoy the memory. "It was like the sound of a sword fight in a Zorro movie."

"Was he wearing any team colors?" Coach asked.

"No, just a plain T-shirt, shorts."

"What did he look like?"

"Coach, like I said, he just flew by, so I couldn't get much of a look, but he was tall and had scraggly brown hair."

Ballpoint was of sound mind and was not prone to exaggeration. He was a journalist, after all, and therefore had a passing respect for the truth. Coach was excited by what he'd heard, but was weighing the news and still assessing The Point's reliability. Then Arturo chimed in. "That must have been the same guy I saw."

"You saw him too?" Coach said.

"Yeah, on Monday. After work. On Hudson Street. I wouldn't call it a Swoooooosh sound though," Arturo said. "It was more of a Wooooooohhhhh, you know, like when a train roars by. Wooooooohhhhh."

"My God," Coach said. "Swoooooosh, Wooooooohhhhh ... who gives a crap. Did you get a good look at him, Arturo?"

"No, it was like The Point said. He was just a blur. It's true about his hair though: it was scraggly and brown."

Then Coach made an announcement to all the HOHAs who were gathered. "If anybody sees that guy again, or any other exceptional runner for that matter, I want to know about it. Immediately! I don't care if it's three o'clock in the morning. And for God's sake, try to get his name and number, and if you can't do that, at least give him a HOHAs card."

Most runners seen on the streets are doing nine- or ten-minute miles. This is a slow pace, meant to provide aerobic conditioning or to shed a few pounds. These runners are casual exercisers and are often slightly overweight, wearing headphones, or talking to a partner as they put in their time on a modest fitness program. They may not even consider themselves runners and may ignore, or be surprised by, a greeting from another runner along the way.

A smaller percentage of runners are doing seven- and eight-minute miles. This is a solid pace, fast enough to demand their attention as they focus to economize their breathing and movements to its demands. These runners are athletes, at least moderately fit, and one can see from their demeanor that their training program is serious and regular. They consider themselves runners, and will acknowledge other runners as part of their small fraternity.

A tiny percentage of runners are doing six- and even five-minute miles. This is a fast pace, and these runners are fine athletes, seriously working in a speed session or tempo run on the roads. Their speed attracts attention, and onlookers stop, and even turn to watch, as they fly by. These runners may nod at another runner, but they have no opportunity for friendliness in the demands of their workout and the purity of their pursuit of speed.

Coach was friendly to the slowest runners and supportive of their efforts, but he knew they were not ripe for running, and he left them alone. Coach asked the faster runners to join the HOHAs. Runners like these form the heart of any club, and from their ranks a runner with talent might be culled and trained. But the fastest runners, rarely seen, Coach stalked and made every effort to recruit. If he saw one on the street, he would drop whatever he was doing and give chase. He had met a couple of excellent runners in this manner: one had just been in town on a visit, and the other had been affiliated and loyal to a New York club. Coach never lost hope that one day he would find and get the ace he needed.

In early September of 1997 there were two more sightings and reports of the runner that Ballpoint and Arturo had seen. Eck spotted him down by the river, again on Sinatra Drive, and described it by saying, "No, it wasn't a Wooooooohhhhh or a Swooooooosh, it was more like a GrrrrrrrrrBoom. You know, that sound a jet makes, high up in the clouds, when it breaks the sound barrier."

"GrrrrrrrrrBoom?" Coach said.

"Coach, I'm telling you," Eck said, "the guy was awesome."

Slow-Mo made the other sighting on Washington Street. "I was coming from the PATH station on my way home," Slow-Mo said, "when I noticed people stopped on the sidewalk and looking toward the street. Their heads moved quickly from side to side like people at a speedway watching a race car whip by down the straightway. Then I looked out in the street myself and saw him, and then my head did the same thing, and then he was just gone. Yeeeeeohhhhh. Like a high-pitched race car."

"The same guy?" Coach said. "Tall, brown scraggly hair?"

"Yeah."

"And you didn't follow him?" Coach admonished.

"Follow him?" Slow-Mo said. "I could barely see him."

"Yeeeeeohhhhh?" Coach said.

"Coach," Slow-Mo said. "It's all true. The guy is a frigging beast."

It's not that Coach didn't believe Ballpoint, or Arturo, or Eck, or even Slow-Mo; it's just that their descriptions were so incredible that Coach would only believe them when he saw this guy for himself. A few weeks later Coach got his chance. He was walking down Hudson Street on his way home from work when the runner appeared. He came from behind Coach going north against the one-way traffic on Hudson. He was running in the space between the parked cars and the traffic, and Coach just got a glimpse of him as he flew past between cars. He saw the tall, lean frame and the scraggly brown hair, and with that speed, how could it be anyone else. "Holy shit," Coach said aloud. Later, when recounting the story, he would add, "All I saw was a blur, legs circling like a gazelle's, and hair flying back from the rush he created, and there *was* a sound as he flew by, it's true. There was this heart-stopping Blaaaaaaam."

Coach was carrying his briefcase from work and a bag of groceries that he'd bought on his way from the train station. Once he got over the shock, he took a couple of quick steps in pursuit of the runner before he realized the hopelessness of catching him. "I couldn't have caught him if I were as naked as the day I was born," Coach would say, "and there I was loaded down like a camel."

Coach hurried home and dropped off his stuff and then went back out on the street for a while, hoping he would see the runner again, but he had no luck. He noted that he had seen the guy about 6:15 PM and inferred that he liked to get in his run right after work. Coach vowed that he would be at the place of the sighting the next day at that time and every day after that at the same time until he saw the runner again, but he worried that even that strategy—as rigorous as it was—was insufficiently determined. If Coach had had a picture of the guy, he would have put up WANTED posters, and if he'd had a badge, he would have formed a posse.

The mysterious runner was all Coach could talk about that next week, and he had all the HOHAs on the lookout for the guy. "How will we know him if we see him?" some would say.

"Well, first you'll have a sense of beauty," Coach would say, "and then you'll see perfection."

The instructions were to somehow flag him down or trail him till he stopped, get his name and number, and get the information back to Coach, but as it turned out, Coach himself would be the one to find him first.

About a week later, one evening after work, Coach had just come up the stairs from the PATH train. He was standing with other commuters waiting to cross Hudson Place when the guy came blowing by. Again Coach described it as a blur that left not only him but those around him in a state of shock. All heads turned in unison to follow what had just flashed by. Before Coach could register who it was, the runner was already well down the street. Again, there was no chance of catching him, but then Coach had a thought. The runner was heading toward the old ferry terminal. The road ended there at the plaza, which connected with Newark Street. Unless the guy intended on stopping and turning around, which was unlikely at his pace, he would continue through the plaza and return out on Newark. Coach could just run the one block over to Newark and cut him off there when he came out.

When Coach got to the intersection with Newark, he saw the guy coming out of the plaza a half block away and heading toward him. Coach stood in the crosswalk waving his arms. As the guy neared, Coach was jumping up and down and yelling, "Stop!"

The runner slowed and approached Coach at a jog. He was confused, unsure whether he should be alarmed for his own safety or prepared to lend assistance. "What's wrong?" he said.

"Who are you?" Coach said.

"Who are *you*?" the guy said.

"I'm Emmitt F. Bean, the founder, first president, and coach of the Hoboken Harriers Running Club."

The guy nodded and waited, and Coach said, "I want you to run with us."

"OK."

"That's it?" Coach said. "You mean you will?"

"Sure."

"My God," Coach said. "That's great."

"My name's Andy."

Andy held out his hand and they shook. "You're fast, Andy," Coach said. "And look at you: you're not even breathing hard. Where did you run before?"

"UCLA."

"You ran for the Bruins?"

"Yeah. A few years ago."

"Andy?" Coach thought for a moment. "Don't tell me you're Andy Bell?"

"That's me."

"My God! Andy Bell. I followed your career. You were Pac-10 All Conference your junior and senior years." Coach was shaking his head from side to side in disbelief at his luck. "What are you doing in Hoboken?"

"Working on a graduate degree at Stevens."

"And you're not running with anybody now?"

"No. Been going solo."

"And you'll run with us?" Coach asked again.

"Sure."

"Well, hot damn!" Coach was still shaking his head in disbelief. "Welcome, Andy," Coach said. "Welcome to the HOHAs."

Andy Bell was true to his word and, much to Coach's delight, ran with the HOHAs regularly. Coach worried at first that Andy would be bored with the pace of the runs. No one in the club was even close to him in talent, with the exception of Moses, but Moses was forty years older and, of course, couldn't run at Andy's pace. But Coach soon saw that Andy was willing to do his own faster-paced training on his own and use the club runs as a way to put in some easier mileage.

Coach was also pleased to see that Andy mixed in well with the other club members and made friends easily. He and Moses in particular took an immediate liking to each other. They did their cooldowns together after the group runs and they ran together at other times during the week. On their slower runs, Moses looked for abandoned junk that he could sell, and Andy helped him take it back to his place at the salvage yard. They often got takeout food and ate at Andy's apartment, and they watched rented movies, preferring science fiction, monster flicks, and the occasional western. As their friendship grew, Coach stopped worrying that Andy would leave the club. He could see that Andy would stay, if for no other reason than to hang out with Moses.

Andy and Moses' attraction ran deeper than their respect for each other as runners. Andy confided to Moses later that his mother had left him and his father when Andy was three, and that his father had killed himself a few years after that. Andy had been raised by his paternal grandmother, June, and her old friend Gen, and he missed June and Gen now, more than he liked to admit. When he met the elderly Moses, he was drawn to him as a natural substitute. Moses, for his part, missed the steady support he had enjoyed with his friend Buddy, and he welcomed the friendship of Andy, who felt like the son, or grandson, he'd never had.

They made an unusual pair, but in odd ways fit together. They were both tall and lean and had a natural quickness to their movements. They looked like versions of the same person, two generations apart.

And they had something else in common too. Moses and Andy were the only HOHAs that Coach never even tried to nickname. They were just Moses and Andy. Coach knew, and all the other HOHAs knew too, that they were already special just the way they were.

31. Bad Bob

NO SOONER had Coach become secure in Andy's loyalty to the HOHAs than another great runner—Bob Bartaleta, or Bad Bob, as he soon came to be known—appeared on the scene. Coach had had to wait and pray for years for a runner like Andy, and then hunt him down and bring him in, but Bad Bob just fell into Coach's lap. It was as if Coach had asked for oil, but also got some vinegar; as if he'd said pass the salt, but also got the pepper. Andy and Bad Bob came together like that, like good and bad.

Bob had just moved to Hoboken, and he showed up one Thursday evening for the club run. He arrived during Coach's announcements, and Coach only had time for a brief introduction before the run started. Bob was a handsome and well-groomed young man, tall and thin, but it was only his thinness that Coach noted. A great runner appears to be all lungs and legs. Appearance, then, was the first test that Coach put runners through, and Bob had passed that test.

Coach then watched a runner's form, looking for a gracefulness of motion, because all great runners make it look easy. Bob had a smooth stride, efficient and flowing, and Coach was impressed by the steadiness of his upper body.

Runners who also passed that test would have Coach's complete attention, and next he would be hoping to see one of two things: a cat-like quickness that revealed the gift of speed, or strong pacing and easy breathing that revealed the achievement of endurance. Coach watched Bob as the run progressed and was impressed by the way he quickly and effortlessly glided toward the front, where Andy was leading the group. Bob was eager to pass Andy too, and would have if he'd known the course and hadn't needed someone to lead the way. Bob glanced around, hoping someone would step forward to increase the pace, and he surged ahead a couple of times to display his desire. When no one responded, he flashed a supercilious smirk, as if to say, "Is this all this club has to offer?" and then fell back again to Andy's side. Bob could tell that Andy was a good runner, but he had no idea how good. He'd tried to draw Andy out with those early surges, and when he failed to do so, concluded that Andy had nothing to give.

Andy was deeply confident in his talent and had no need to prove it, but he had come up against runners like Bob before and knew that sooner or later it was necessary to put them in their place. A mile into that run, after Bob had made another cocky display of his speed, Andy decided to get this inevitable task out of the way. Without warning, he accelerated and opened up a ten-meter lead, and then he held back and let Bob close the gap. As soon as Bob thought that was all Andy had, Andy administered another surge dose and opened up another lead, this time holding the pace longer and forcing Bob to work harder to return to him. This left Bob breathing hard, but again confident that he had taken Andy's hardest shot. Then, before Bob could recover completely, Andy delivered a third surge that forced Bob into his final gear to close the gap again. Andy had timed this third attack perfectly, because by the time Bob caught up, he was completely out of breath, and they were now at the base of the Stevens hill.

When Andy allowed Bob to catch him for the third time at the base of the hill, it was a calculated show of mercy that was no mercy at all. At that point, Andy was a cat toying with his prey. From the corner of his eye, Andy could see that Bob's form was broken, and he could hear that Bob's breathing was labored. Andy slowed briefly as they began the climb, so that Bob could feel the steepness of the hill in his quads and could add that discomfort to the burning pain that was already in his lungs. Then without warning, Andy surged again, and this time he didn't let up. He flew up the hill without even looking back. Bob tried to respond but was physically broken by his own fatigue and mentally broken by the authority of Andy's ascent. Andy just buried Bad Bob on that hill. Bob trudged to the top alone, and when he started down the other side, he saw Andy at the bottom waiting. Andy was jogging in circles there, not only to keep himself loose, but to underline for Bob, with the amount of time he'd had to wait, the disparity in their talent. They finished the run together that night, with Bob keeping a respectful half stride behind.

This was not to say that Bob wasn't a great runner; he was, but Andy was even greater. And this was not to say that this encounter put an end to Bob's arrogance; it didn't, but from that first day onward, as runners at least, the pecking order was established, and Bob knew exactly where he stood.

That evening, after the run, Andy went off with Moses, and Coach corralled Bob and brought him to the bar. Coach bought Bob a beer and asked him about his running experience. Bob had run track and cross-country for two years at North Carolina State, posting some promising times, before injuries derailed his collegiate career. His running credentials impressed Coach and the HOHAs, and they were impressed too by how he had run that night. Bob understood that he was a celebrity among them just by having been able to go out with Andy and hang with him as long as he had.

Coach and the HOHAs bought Bob more beer, and the beer, along with all the attention and praise, soon revived Bob from the ass whipping he had just taken at the feet of Andy and returned him to his natural arrogance. After the third beer, Coach asked Bob if he wanted to join the club.

"I'll take it under consideration," Bob said haughtily.

Coach ignored Bob's tone and then outlined all the benefits of the club, from the free T-shirt to the discount at Snail's Pace. "And members get all that," Coach concluded, "for a measly five dollars annual dues."

"Dues?" Bob said. "Well then we got a problem, because I don't pay any dues."

Coach's mouth dropped open, and he and the other HOHAs just looked at Bob. They were learning for the first time that annoying and shocking people was Bob's favorite pastime.

"I haven't had this much fun since last week," Bob said. "I was entertaining a client at the Chart House, and I had too much to drink. Afterwards, I was in the parking lot and I had to take a piss. I didn't feel like going back into the restaurant, so I went between two cars and peed off the pier. The parking attendant, this high-school kid, he comes over to me and says, 'May I help you, sir?' And I said, 'Not unless you want to hold my dick for me.'"

There were some nervous chuckles, but the HOHAS were looking at Bob with expressions of discomfort and slight shock. As soon as Bob got this reaction—and he usually did, having a natural knack for it—you could just see his contentment and pleasure. Bob was feeling good now. "You should be paying me to join your little club," he said.

Coach's face dropped and Bob smiled. "Can't do that," Coach said. "That would be unfair to the other members."

Eck was in the group that night, had had a few beers himself, and was feeling magnanimous. "Let's take up a collection for Bob," he said. "Everybody throw in a buck and we'll pay Bob's dues right now." Eck and some others threw in a dollar and Eck handed the money to Coach.

"Looks like you're in," Coach said, annoyed and pleased at the same time. "Welcome to the HOHAs."

So Bob began to run regularly with the club. He loved to run, and he loved to drink beer, and the HOHAs were good for both. Bob also had a begrudging respect for Andy, and a resentment of his superiority. It was a relationship that attracted him and repelled him at the same time, and held him close to the HOHAs world. The HOHAs, for their part, got used to Bad Bob and learned to live with him. Bad Bob was like a New York City taxi driver, brash and aggressive, but consistently and unabashedly so. The HOHAs learned to expect his behavior, adjust to it, and even admire it in a perverse way.

There was another Bob in the club then, Bob Caytums. This was the HOHA whom Coach called Tums, because of his last name and because he complained about his stomach. That nickname was well established and would have been enough to distinguish between the two Bobs, but Coach saw the need, or the opportunity rather, for a more clear-cut distinction and so Coach started calling Bob Caytums "Good Bob" and Bob Bartaleta "Bad Bob." Later, when Good Bob moved out of town and there was no longer any need to distinguish between the two, Coach continued to call Bartaleta "Bad Bob," a nickname that he continually proved to deserve. Some of Coach's nicknames needed explaining through the years, especially to new members, but whenever Coach said Bad Bob, anyone who'd met Bob Bartaleta knew to whom the nickname referred and exactly what it meant.

Bad Bob always gave the HOHAs something to talk about, and he kept them on their guard, because besides his nastiness, there was also his penchant for practical jokes. One time, Bad Bob was running with Coach and a group of HOHAs on a course that took them along a short stretch of Highway 1/9, a major truck route to the west of Hoboken. Bob noticed all the trucks and fell back to the rear of the group. When none of the HOHAs was looking, and when one of the trucks was right behind the HOHAs, Bob gave the truck driver the universal hand-pumping signal to honk his horn. The driver of the eighteen-wheeler obliged, and the unexpected blast from the truck's air horn sent Coach and all the other HOHAs jumping three feet into the air. The height of that jump, its marvelous synchronicity, and the terror on the HOHAs' faces were details that Bad Bob relished and recounted at HOHAs gatherings for months to come.

Coach had talks with Bob, and tried to protect other HOHAs from him, but the prank that convinced Coach that Bob was incorrigible came at Coach's own expense. One Saturday morning in the spring, Coach and a large contingent of HOHAs, including Andy and Bad Bob, were running through a park in Weehawken, just north of Hoboken. The group had stopped at a water fountain to get a drink, and there was a flock of migrating geese nearby. One of the geese was perturbed by the HOHAs' presence and was honking loudly. Coach disliked the geese and the way that they shat all over the running paths, and so he mimicked the bird, honking back at it. The bird held its ground, perhaps protecting nearby goslings, and honked right back at Coach. Just then, with the goose focused on Coach and ready to fight, Bad Bob snuck up behind it and poked it with a stick. The goose leapt at Coach, and Coach, startled and backpedaling, fell down.

Bad Bob had followed the goose, prodding it, and the small-brained bird, confused about the identity of its assailant, and only seeing the felled Coach in front of him, attacked. It landing on Coach and pecked at him furiously. Geese are as big as turkeys, and this one was squarely on Coach's chest. Coach fought to get it off him, but the brawny bird wouldn't budge, and Coach and the goose formed a ball of flailing arms and flapping wings, screams and honks. Out of the melee came Coach's voice, half annoyed and half afraid. "Help! Somebody, help me!"

The HOHAs stood watching, paralyzed by the sight, and then Bad Bob was on the ground himself, rolling in laughter. Andy finally stepped forward and knocked the goose off Coach and chased it away. The bird took flight, and the rest of the flock, seeing it, took flight too, while Coach was still lying spreadeagled on the ground, exhausted by his battle. Unfortunately for him, when birds take to the air, they lessen their load, and so as the flock took off, they pummeled Coach with the very thing against which he had regularly railed.

"Help! Somebody, help me!" Bob mimicked from the ground.

"Fuck you, Bob," Coach said when he got to his feet. "Just fuck you!"

Bad Bob was still on the ground laughing, and Coach was a mess, covered in shit, with his hair sticking out, like a disheveled nest, in every direction. Coach did the only thing he could do in that situation—he continued the run. Andy and the rest of the HOHAs, filled with amusement and sympathy, joined him, but Bad Bob just stayed there, rolling on the ground, until he could stop laughing long enough to get up and run home.

Coach's respect for Bob as a runner was offset by his irritation with him as a person, and that tenuous balance was the mark of their relationship. To complicate matters, Bob was a salesman, and his business travel made it difficult for Coach to schedule workouts with him. When they did get together, Bad Bob questioned the training method, needed special consideration, played some practical joke, annoyed one of the other club members, or had smart-ass comments to make.

Athletes like Bad Bob are a coach's greatest challenge. Any coach can work with a cooperative athlete, but it takes a good coach to work with a troublesome one, and a great coach to work with a four-star, platinum-plated pain in the ass like Bob. Runners like Bob think they know better than you and ignore or question everything you say, and they are liable to disrupt an entire team. The challenge is to find a way to get through to them, for the sake of the team and for their own damn good. Bob Bartaleta was talented, and I figured he was worth as much trouble as I could stand.

Besides all Bob's trouble, he was a great runner, and Coach and all the HOHAs appreciated that. For a long time, the HOHAs had had a great master runner in Moses, but in their entire history they'd never had an open runner who was anything more than good. Now suddenly they had not one but two of the greatest open runners in the state and the greatest open runners the HOHAs would ever have. Andy and Bad Bob were an amazing pair, the same age, and similar in running background and style, but as different in personality as any two people could be. Coach didn't care, at least not then, that one had a halo and the other had horns. All he really cared about was that they were both as fast as hell.

32. Cross-Country

COMPETITIVE RUNNING can be divided into three categories: track, road, and cross-country. Coach, for reasons many and varied, loved them all, but just as he thought of running as the purest of sports, he thought of cross-country as the purest expression of running, and because of that, he held it most dear.

Cross-country (X-C) is beyond the elitism and glamour of track or the popularity and frills of road racing. Thousands of spectators might attend a track meet, and thousands of runners might participate in a road race, but an X-C race often attracts fewer than a hundred runners, with just a handful of their family and friends looking on. In amateur X-C racing, there are no gold, silver, and bronze medals, no souvenir T-shirts, no goodie bags, no age-group awards, no split times and water stations, no electronic scoring, no post-race party and entertainment. In X-C, even the finishing clock doesn't really matter, because the scoring is based on finishing place, not time. Runners run only against the hardships of the course, against each other, and against themselves. X-C is running stripped of everything nonessential. X-C is running for the connoisseur.

X-C is run in the autumn, when the leaves are turning and falling and the weather is growing sharp and cold. The sun is low on the horizon, casting foreshadows of the darkness to come. The faint-hearted seek flannel shirts or pajamas, hot tea or warm cocoa, and a place by the stove or fire, while avid runners seek one last fling in shorts and singlet, through the woods and fields, through fallen leaves and twigs and slush, mud, and ice. X-C is the childlike desire to keep on playing, to take one more turn, one more time at bat, even as our mother is calling us in from the waning light and the coming cold.

The Shore Athletic Club—better known as Shore A.C., or just Shore—was one of the oldest amateur running clubs in New Jersey, and every fall they hosted a series of X-C races in the parks and woods of Monmouth County, about an hour's drive south of Hoboken. Shore held these races on six consecutive Saturday mornings from late September into early November. The races started at 9:00 AM and ranged between 2.8 and 3.1 miles in distance. They were run every year at the following parks and in the listed order:

1. Thompson Park   4. Thompson Park
2. Tatum Park   5. Tatum Park
3. Huber Woods   6. Holmdel Park

Over the years, this race series had come to be revered as the New Jersey Cross-Country Championship. The series was open to individual runners, but was meant as a competition among amateur running clubs of the Northeast. Some prominent New Jersey clubs had won the championship over the years: Shore A.C. themselves, the Raritan Valley Road Runners, the Morris County Striders, the Green Pond Harriers, the Sneaker Factory, and others. Occasionally, New York clubs like the West Side Runners, the Central Park Track Club, and the New York Flyers had ventured over to New Jersey to compete for and claim the title. The series drew the strongest competition in the region, and the rules made it a difficult championship to win.

The scoring required that a team have not only depth but diversity. A team scored their top seven runners, and this seven had to include four open runners (any age, either gender), one master runner (over forty, either gender), one veteran runner (over fifty-five, either gender), and one woman runner (any age). A runner could be counted in only one of these categories in a race, and a runner was scored by his or her overall finishing place within the category (open, masters, veterans, women). The finishing places of these seven runners were then added to give the total team score. The team with the lowest total won the race and received a score of one point for the series. The second place team received a score of two points, and so on. At the end of the series, these points were added, and the team with the lowest point total won the championship.

A team had to show consistency and strength to score well in all races over six consecutive, grueling weeks, and it was most important to score well in the final race at Holmdel Park. Holmdel Park was by far the toughest course, and the score there was counted twice. This was meant to add excitement and suspense, and to reward the team that could endure the hardships of the series and still be strong at the end. In the event of an overall tie for the series, Holmdel was the tiebreaker, and the winner there was the champion. The champion team was awarded the most coveted trophy of the New Jersey running world: a foot-tall, gaudily painted, ceramic statuette of a woodland elf. "The Elf," as it was known, was meant to symbolize the no-frills toughness of the race series and the enchanted nature of the parks and woods in which the series was run.

Through the running grapevine, Coach had got wind of the Monmouth County X-C Series soon after his arrival in Hoboken, and through the years he and a handful of HOHAs had trekked down to Monmouth County to participate in some of the races. In the early years, the HOHAs couldn't even put together an entire team, never mind a team good enough to compete with, let alone win against, the older and more established clubs of the region. When they could eventually put together a team to meet the requirements, and could get them all together and down to one of the races, it was a motley assemblage that invariably finished near the bottom. Moses excelled in the veteran division, but that was all the HOHAs had to show for their efforts.

In later years, as the HOHAs grew in number and improved somewhat in quality, Coach was able to field more consistent teams, but they had never placed better than fifth in any one race, and hadn't succeeded in fielding a team in the entire series of races in a given season. Coach had never given up on his dream of someday winning the series, being the state champion, and gaining possession of the prestigious Elf, and when Andy and Bad Bob were firmly established with the club in the spring of 1998, he was quick to realize that the next fall's series could be his greatest chance.

Coach's throat went dry and his hand trembled the first time he jotted down a team roster for that series. Andy and Bad Bob would fill the first two open spots of course, and Moses would take the veteran spot. Coach was ecstatic just seeing those names at the top of the list. The third and fourth open spots would be a great drop-off in talent from Andy and Bad Bob, but there were a number of moderately talented HOHAs to be considered, and prominent among these contenders were Edsel, The Eck, and Slow-Mo. Coach penciled in their names on the roster. Being a young running club, the HOHAs were weak in the older age groups, in fact besides Moses, the only older runners the HOHAs had were Icky and Boston. Icky was 42 and could run as a master, while Boston was 56 and qualified as a veteran. Coach added their names to the roster and placed an asterisk next to them and a note, "Need a lot of work." For the woman's spot, Coach had two names in mind, Patti and Sheila. Both were former girlfriends of his, and both were decent runners. Coach had trained them himself, and according to Coach's skewed logic, they owed him a favor for all he had taught them.

That summer, Coach kept an eye out for other runners who might strengthen the team, but he felt that the runners he had, if properly motivated and trained, had a chance to win the series that fall. He prepared special training programs for everyone he had on the roster, and he worked with them individually and during special group track sessions and runs. Coach had two goals that summer: to train and condition his team, and to motivate the team to want the cross-country championship as much as he wanted it himself, that is, more than any other thing in the world.

One of the ways Coach built team spirit that summer was to schedule HOHAs participation in a number of local road races. He figured this would not only get the team used to racing, but would be a good way to work out the logistics of meeting and carpooling to the races on time. Coach got the team used to meeting early at Edsel's store on the morning of a race, checking in with him, and being assigned to one of the cars of the HOHAs who had volunteered to drive. He gave detailed written directions to the race site to each driver, in case they got separated from the group, but advised each of them to stay in the caravan of cars that was to be led by him in the RORA. Coach's system was methodical and overbearing, but it worked. By the time the summer races were over, Coach had ironed out all the glitches, and the HOHAs were used to assembling and transporting themselves to a race site early enough to warm up properly and get to the starting line on time. Coach also created a HOHAs banner that he hung up at the race sites. He wanted the banner to both promote the club and to mark a place where the HOHAs could gather before and after the races.

Besides the physical work, part of preparing runners for a big race is to instill in them an appreciation of the race's importance, and Coach had been doing that throughout the year with his pep talks and tirades. Another part of that preparation is to make the runners feel special, and honored to be part of the team, because with that honor they will feel the obligation to live up to it and perform at their best. Coach encouraged the HOHAs to wear their HOHAs T-shirt or racing singlet to each race, and in addition, Coach ordered special gold-mesh jerseys with the HOHAs insignia printed in navy blue, and awarded these special jerseys to the leading members of the racing team just before the start of each race.

Coach made a big production of gathering the team together at the HOHAs banner, giving a final inspirational talk, and then bestowing the race jerseys one by one on the runners who were expected to score for the team. Since seven runners score for a team in the X-C championship, Coach had seven of the special jerseys to honor the team's top runners. Coach wanted the jerseys to be not only an honor for the leading HOHAs runners but an incentive to other HOHAs to work harder to earn one for themselves.

By the time the first race of the X-C championship arrived, the HOHAs were the well-oiled machine that Coach had trained them to be. When they arrived at Thompson Park early on the last Saturday in September, the other clubs there thought that a new club had arrived on the scene. No one recognized the organized and punctual team of athletes that they saw standing before them now as the same HOHAs group that in past years had wandered into the park disheveled, unfit, and rushing just to make it to the start.

The other runners took notice too as the HOHAs assembled near their club banner in their uniform HOHAs shirts. They saw Coach, clipboard in hand, instructing the HOHAs about the characteristics of the course, they saw Coach distribute the honorary jerseys to the current team leaders, and they saw the HOHAs huddle together in unison to deliver a victory chant before they began their warm-up together.

Coach could sense the team's excitement as they warmed up for that first race and he was confident that he'd done everything in his power to get them ready. The weather was perfect for racing too: in the low fifties, with no wind, and a cloud cover to keep the sun from beating down on them. Coach was relieved that the weather had been fair all week and the course conditions were good, because he didn't want the other clubs to have the advantage of their experience with wet and muddy footing. He felt nervous nevertheless, because during the warm-up he'd noticed that all the other leading clubs were there, and Coach knew that they had proven themselves through the years to be well trained, tough and ready.

At 9:00 AM sharp the race director, after only a short speech to welcome the runners to the first race of the 1998 series and to wish them luck, started the race with an air horn. The course at Thompson Park started on a grass-covered path cut around and through a meadow of tall bush. Coach was in the middle of the pack of about 150 runners—a position befitting his pace—and watched as Andy and Bob went out with the front pack. At the first turn, he spotted them in the lead. The great Neville Harrington of Shore was right behind them, along with a couple of NY Flyers. He could also see Edsel, The Eck, and Moses not far back from the leaders and running well. A half mile into the race, the course left the meadow and began a hard, steep climb into the woods, after which it wove its way up and down and around through the woods before opening onto a clearing that led to a wooden bridge across a stream and then to an open field and the finish.

When Coach got in, he sought out Andy and Bad Bob and learned that they'd finished one-two, with Neville Harrington a distant third. Moses had run well too, and it would turn out that he'd won the veteran division, but Edsel, The Eck, Icky, and Patti had struggled and surrendered places and points to the other clubs.

When all the runners were in, Coach gathered the HOHAs and led them on a cooldown run over parts of the course. The HOHAs felt they had scored well, and their spirits were high. By the time they returned, the race director had posted the results on a bulletin board near the finish. Standing on tiptoes to see over the heads of all the runners crowded around the board, Coach saw the points of the top three teams and realized, with a thrill that went right up his spine, that the HOHAs had won.

1. HOHAs   57
2. Shore A.C.   63
3. NY Flyers   78

Coach got a big kiss from Biscuit and high fives and hugs from the team, and felt a sense of satisfaction that he had never experienced before. He led the caravan back to Hoboken driving the RORA, but he could have floated back in the warm bubble of pride and joy he felt that day. The HOHAs celebrated that night at Moran's, with toasts to their individual and collective performances, and only Coach and about half the team made it—bleary-eyed and exhausted— to the recovery run the next morning. The rest of Sunday was lost in a hangover, and it wasn't until Monday morning at work that Coach faced the fact that the victory, as sweet as it was, was only for week number one. There were five more weeks to go. Coach realized too that the HOHAs victory would serve as a wake-up call to the other clubs. Shore and the Flyers might have other good runners that they would call into the battle, or they might even recruit to strengthen their teams.

Coach threw himself into preparations for week two with the same vigor with which he had prepared the team during the summer. At lunch that day, he drew up a special track workout for Tuesday that would sharpen the team without tiring them for the coming race, and he made notes about special diets, exercises, and training considerations for each member of the team. He also made phone calls to team members throughout the week, checking on their training and their health. Bad Bob just laughed and hung up, but the other HOHAs listened, and with the exception of Andy and Moses and Edsel, wondered what in the world they had got themselves into.

The HOHAs won again in week two at Tatum Park, and again Shore and the NY Flyers finished second and third. They were obviously the teams to beat that year, and the margin of victory in the second race was even tighter. In week three, there was a slight reversal, with Shore edging the HOHAs for victory, despite the continued dominance of Andy, Bad Bob and Moses, and the NY Flyers slipping to fourth behind an improved Sneaker Factory team. In week four, the HOHAs won again, with Shore in second place again. In week five, those positions were again reversed, leaving the HOHAs with the narrowest possible lead, a single point, going into the final race at Holmdel. The lead itself was insignificant, because the points would be doubled at Holmdel, and the HOHAs would have to beat Shore if they were to win the series title.

33. Small but Mighty

THE INFAMOUS X-C course at Holmdel Park is a rigorous series of challenges, the first of which presents itself at the outset. The start is at the northern end of an open, grassy area about the size of a football field, and the runners line up shoulder to shoulder along the starting line facing this field. The field slopes steadily uphill and then funnels into the opening of a winding, even steeper uphill path that's only wide enough for a single runner. Runners who don't get to the opening quickly are caught in the bottleneck, forced back behind other runners, and unable to pass until they reach the top end of the path. Experienced runners know that one should ease into any run or race, but at Holmdel runners are forced to start fast to reach the opening before their competitors and, as a result, find themselves right away in oxygen debt and pain.

A runner must be fit to recover from a start like that, and the course is merciful enough to provide a flat stretch following the initial climb to allow runners to recover if they can, but most of them are still struggling when they reach the second challenge, a vast amphitheater of a field—known to local runners as "The Bowl"—around which the course circles for a half mile. The course slopes down on the east side, and the runners pick up speed to take advantage of the downslope, but just as they become breathless with the speed, they must begin the gradual climb up the other side of the amphitheater, a climb that finishes with a gruesomely steep path to the top that almost brings the runners to their knees. By then, they're almost cooked, but there's still over a mile to go. The course is flat then for a half mile, giving each runner time to listen to the heaviness of their breathing, to feel their heart pounding in their chest, and to feel sorry for themselves, and then the course drops into a steep and winding downhill trail that has runners throwing their arms out to balance themselves and to keep from flying into the surrounding trees. At the bottom, the trail flings the runner out into an open field. They can see the finish then, three hundred meters away, and are in clear view of the spectators and other runners at the finish, so they must fight to hold on and finish strong, and when they cross the finish line and are handed the numbered Popsicle stick that marks their place, they're exhausted, but relieved to have survived the crucible that is the Holmdel course.

No runner who has ever experienced Holmdel takes it lightly. Coach had analyzed the course—running it over and over again in his mind—and felt that besides overall fitness, the secret to success there was leg strength, and skill and toughness in hill running, both up and down, and had kept Holmdel in mind all during the summer as he'd trained the team. One of the HOHAs lived in a high-rise near the river, and Coach often got small groups together to run the stairs there, up and down over twenty flights. He also scheduled group training runs on the hill at Stevens and on the Fourteenth Street viaduct. He particularly liked the Stevens hill with its long climb, steep finish, and quick drop-off on the back side, and he liked how it circled around so it could be run in loops, one after the other. On the Monday evening before the championship at Holmdel, he had the team make five loops of that hill before he let them go home. After that workout, Coach was satisfied that he had done everything possible to prepare the team both physically and mentally. Now the HOHAs just had to rest to be ready for Saturday.

In the days leading up to the race, Coach, unable to rest himself, called every HOHA who wasn't on the racing team and encouraged them to come out that Saturday to provide moral support, and most of them—more than forty as it turned out—made the trip down to Holmdel that day. It was a chilly morning, a day befitting the coming of winter and the last race of the year. The dimness of the sun, the icy moisture of the air and the bold wind blowing across the starting field spoke without words, and the finality of the season added to the tension inherent in the championship race.

That morning, Coach led the HOHAs through the familiar and comforting pre-race routine that they had followed in each of the preceding weeks. The HOHAs were quiet that morning in the unspoken knowledge of what they had accomplished and of what they still had left to do.

As the runners lined up across the starting line, and looked with nervousness up the sloping field to the winding path that was the first painful challenge of the course, Edsel came up to Coach and whispered in his ear, "I just heard two Shore runners talking," he said. "Art Nolan and John Rogers aren't here. Nolan has a pulled hamstring and Rogers a bad back."

Without Nolan and Rogers, Shore's best runners behind Harrington, Shore was no competition for the HOHAs or any of the other leading teams there that day. Injuries are a part of the sport, but Coach had a sense of barriers pulled down and doors opened to him. He felt a mysterious complicity, inexplicable and fateful. The starting gun went off, and the runners bolted from the line. Coach hesitated for an instant and then joined in, running with the others up the field, his mind filled with the strange knowledge that before the race had even started, the HOHAs had already won.

Soon after the race, the series points were tabulated and posted, and the HOHAs victory was confirmed. In the modest award ceremony inside the recreational center, the race director handed Coach the Elf. Coach was surrounded by his team, exuberant with their victory, their joy undiminished by the role that fate had played. Coach held the Elf triumphantly aloft. No hockey player ever held the Stanley Cup with more pride. No actor ever smiled with more affection at his Oscar. At one point Coach, lost in his recollection of all that he had been through to achieve this goal, kissed the Elf on its tiny plaster lips, and a tear ran down Coach's unembarrassed cheek and nestled into a cranny of the Elf's gaudy, lime-green vest.

Before the spring of 1990, the HOHAs hadn't even existed, and now, only eight years later, the small but mighty HOHAs had bragging rights over the entire Northeast running world. It was everything Coach had worked for and dreamed about for so long. For weeks he glowed with satisfaction, and there was now a distinctly heightened tone of pride in Coach's voice. "I'm Emmitt F. Bean, the founder, first president, and coach of the Hoboken Harriers Running Club, the reigning New Jersey State X-C Champions."

34. Your Dream Come True

GLORIA CLOSED her eyes then, and Coco sat by her bed for a long time watching her sleep. Then she went down to the hospital cafeteria, and when she returned the nurse was there changing her mom's IV.

"I feel refreshed," Gloria said.

"That's good, Mom; you need your rest."

"I'm floating a little."

"It's the medication."

"I want to talk some more," Gloria said. "I want to tell you about my third wish for you."

"I think you should rest some more."

"No, I need to tell you this now."

Coco could hear that need in her mother's voice. Her frail hand was resting above the sheet, and Coco reached over to hold it. "OK, I'm listening, Mom."

"You're not going to like what I have to say."

"When did that ever stop you?"

Gloria smiled. "True."

"Go ahead, Mom. I'm sure you saved the best for last."

"Of course, and I said just that to the genie. I said, 'I've saved my third and most exciting wish for last. I wish that my daughter's dream comes true.'"

"And what dream is that, Mom?"

"You know what it is. You want to go to New York to be in that graduate program. You want it more than anything."

"Thank you. I'll get to it someday."

"No. Now," Gloria blurted out, surprised at the suddenness and firmness of her words. "I've been building up to this, because it's going to be hard for me to say and even harder for you to hear."

"Say it, Mom."

"You're gonna get all twisted in your shorts."

Coco braced herself for the worst, but at the same time, couldn't cope with the unknown. "Go on, Mom."

"Coconut, I want you to leave me."

"That's it? That's ridiculous. Why would I do that?"

"Because it's been a whole year since you graduated from college, and you've been hanging around all that time to be with me. You've been accepted into that program at the fashion institute, which is your dream, and you've got your student loans lined up and that money that Uncle Earl left you. Now's the time."

"I can go later. You need me now."

"No, the opportunity is now, and I need you to go. I know how it is with school. It's like everything else. The farther you get away from it, the harder it is to get back to it. Things don't stand still, and every day you wait is another day when something can happen that will send your life in a different direction. I was thinking I'd go back to school when I met your dad, and you know what happened with that."

"I can't leave you in this condition. The doctor said …"

"The doctor said a lot of things. I've been pricked and probed, rolled over and looked at, and drugged and tested until I don't have a shred of dignity left, but no matter how many tests they do, they can't know for sure what's going to happen to me. That's God's territory."

"Six months, Mom." Coco could hardly say the words, couldn't believe that she had the courage to say them. "The doctor said six months now, if you don't get a donor."

Gloria could see the hurt on her daughter's face, and she knew that every word felt like a painful good-bye. "Listen, Coconut. I'm going to tell you something I realized in all this. I'm not going to die until it's the right time for me to die. I want to be here with you for a while longer. I want to see you get your career on track, and I want to dance at your wedding. I need a miracle, but miracles don't move to anybody's timetable, and you don't put your life on hold waiting for one either.

"Leave me here to work on getting well, and go to school in New York. It's what you really want, and you won't be so far away that you can't visit, or get here if I need help right away. Go. Will you do that for me? Will you help me with this wish for you?"

Coco looked in silence at her mother. When the first tear fell down her cheek, she got up and gave her mom a hug.

"Those are my three wishes for you, Coconut. Those are the best things that a mother can wish for her child: health, true love, and your dream come true."

35. A Mile in the Winter

IN EARLY DECEMBER, following the championship, Coach ran into Harry Horton at the Hot Chocolate 10-Miler in Central Park. Harry and his Striders had come over from Brooklyn to run the race, and they had run well, as usual. Coach had read about the success of the Striders in the New York Road Runners magazine, and he had seen the names of the Striders consistently among the leaders in the race results. Coach had only seen Harry himself a handful of times since they had parted, and on those occasions, neither one had gone out of his way to talk to the other, but Coach didn't mind talking on this day, and was eager for the opportunity to work his club's X-C championship into the conversation. As it turned out, after a civil exchange of greetings, Harry himself brought it up.

"I hear your club got lucky at Holmdel," Harry said. "Shore had injuries."

Coach had already rationalized his victory over a weakened Shore and had his answer ready. "Injuries are part of the sport, Harry. If you don't train smart, you don't make it to the starting line."

"I still think it was a fluke, Bean," Harry said. "Luck can win a championship, but it takes talent to repeat." Harry spat on the ground. "I might just bring my club over there next year," he said, "and then we'll see how you hold up."

"You might as well dream while you can, Harry," Coach answered, "because if you come over to Jersey, we'll be giving you a nightmare."

Harry snickered, and to Coach's ear the sound was sinister and villainous. "We'll see about that," was all Harry said.

"Bring it on, numbnuts," Coach shot back. "We'll be there." Coach then spat on the ground himself and walked away.

That exchange had Coach cursing Harry and talking to himself for days.

"*Lucky?* He's the one who's lucky. Lucky I didn't kick his ass for him, right then and there," Coach fumed. "I'll show him lucky."

There were plenty of quality races in New York, and Coach knew that there was no compelling reason for Harry to bring his club to Jersey to run, except to rain on Coach's parade, but it would be just like Harry to do that, and Coach brooded all winter and through the spring over the prospect. Perhaps what bothered Coach more than anything was the nagging possibility that Harry was right, and that the HOHAs would have to win a second championship to prove that the first one hadn't been a fluke. The more Coach thought about it, the more he became determined to prepare his team again.

"A mile in the winter is worth two in the spring." That was one of Coach's philosophies. No matter how tough it is, the winter is when a runner not only survives, but builds up strength and lays the foundation for the coming season, and that winter, with Harry's chilling threat in the air, Coach's philosophy bore the weight of urgency. Coach was determined that the HOHAs would not rest on their laurels, but would instead build on their mileage and come into the spring stronger than ever.

Coach believed that preparation and performance were inseparable. Everyone wants to perform well; everyone wants to be a champion; but only a champion wants it strongly enough to do the work of preparation. Coach believed that freedom comes from discipline. He believed that the freedom to drop a pack of pursuers, to surge beyond an opponent, to out-kick a challenger at the finish, came from discipline, the miles of preparation, the miles of running in the toughest conditions.

The winter of 1998/99 gave Coach ample opportunity to test those beliefs, for it was brutally cold.

There's only one pleasant season for running on the East Coast, and that's the fall. The winter is cold, the spring is rainy, and the summer is hot and humid. Those who haven't lived anywhere else say it's not bad, but everybody else knows it sucks. But that attitude gets you nowhere, and as far as I was concerned, it was all good for running. The cold makes you strong, the rain keeps you cool, and the heat and humidity keep your weight down. A good runner has to be a runner in all seasons.

There were two months of subfreezing temperatures, with howling winds and gray, icy skies. The short Tuesday and Thursday runs in the dark were tough enough, but the longer runs on Saturday and Sunday, to the north of Hoboken and then back along the river, meant extended exposure to the piercing winds and frigid air. HOHAs came in from these runs with sweat frozen to their clothing and small icicles hanging from their eyebrows and hair. Coach led the HOHAs through that winter armed not only with fortitude but with a comic defiance. He wrote in the January newsletter that year:

> Eleven HOHAs completed the Saturday run on 1/19 in 9-degree weather with a windchill of minus 3. We came upon three non-HOHAs runners on the course: two lying stiff where they had fallen, and the other with his tongue frozen to a water faucet. Edsel and Andy ran the course twice that day to show their utter contempt for the cold.

36. HOHA Gothic

IN JANUARY of that winter, Edsel mentioned casually that one of his cousins, Darla, was coming over from Ireland and would be staying with him for a while. He said that she had got into some trouble at home and that his family had asked him to help her out. Coach, who was preoccupied with Harry's threat and the HOHAs training, had taken this news at face value and hadn't seen it for the warning that it really was. In fact, Coach had forgotten about it, and so was in no way prepared for what he would see one morning in February when he entered Edsel's store.

There was a storm that day, with sleet that pierced the skin like needles, and Coach rushed into the store with his head still down against it and stopped just inside the door to shake the ice from his clothes and stomp it free from his boots. When he finally looked up, he did a double take as he glimpsed Darla near the counter. He glanced around, thinking he must have entered the wrong store, but when he saw that he had not, his eyes returned disbelievingly to her.

The right side of her head was shaved and tattooed with a skull. On the left side, the hair was spiked on top and then long and black down the side and back with a blood-red streak and a single dreadlock in front. Her skin was as white as the belly of a fish, and there were rings in her eyebrows and in her lips. Her lipstick was black, and her mascara was purple and descended in painted scars below her eyes. Around her neck was a black leather collar with chrome studs and a velvet strap that hung from it like a leash. Coach could only stare. In all his life, he had never seen such an outlandish creature.

"'What the fuck you lookin' at?" she said.

She was wearing a black velvet gown, cut short and opened at the top over a leather bodice, and her arms were covered in torn nylon mesh. Her black stockings were torn, and she wore military boots with platform soles. Her bracelets were handcuffs, and on her hands were black lace gloves cut off at the fingers to reveal one ring in the form of a coffin and another bearing an iron cross. Seeing her among all the running products—the Converse stars, the Nike swatches, the Adidas stripes—was like seeing graffiti in a church, or a nose ring on a nun. One would expect to see someone like her in a tattoo parlor or head shop in the East Village, but not in a running store in Hoboken. Coach couldn't help gawking.

"'What the fuck you lookin' at?' I said."

"Excuse me?"

"You're staring at me."

"Sorry. Didn't mean to offend," Coach said. He gathered himself. "Is Edsel in?"

"He stepped out."

"You must be Darla then. Edsel's cousin?"

"Heard of me, did ya? Then you must be one of Edsel's wanker friends."

"Actually, I work here."

"Well then, I guess we'll be doing time together," she said, then added with bored disdain, "Lucky me."

Coach was still having trouble adjusting to the sight of her, let alone her nasty mouth. He'd been about to introduce himself, but thought better of it. Instead, faced with a dilemma as uninviting as "the devil or the deep blue sea," he backed quickly away from Darla and out into the raging storm. Once outside, he dared to mutter the word that he had been thinking the entire time he was inside: "Whoa!"

That evening, Coach called Edsel at home. "I had the pleasure of meeting your cousin this morning," he said, in his sweetest and most sarcastic voice.

Edsel had been anticipating Coach's reaction, but merely replied, entirely deadpan, "Oh yeah?"

"Let me ask you something, Edsel," Coach said. "Is she on her period?"

"How should I know?" Edsel said.

"You don't know?"

"No!" Edsel said, "Why should I?"

"That's great, Edsel," Coach said. "Do you know what that means? It means that I might actually have caught her on one of her *good* days."

"Come on," Edsel said. "She's not that bad."

"Not that bad? Compared to what? A black widow?"

"She's just a little different."

"Different?" Coach said. "Edsel, she's a Goth!"

"She's had a rough life," Edsel said. "Both her parents are alcoholics."

"Are they vampires too?" Coach said. "Because, I'm telling you, Edsel, I saw her in daylight, and I was still afraid of losing blood."

"Coach, she's my cousin. I didn't have a choice. I had to give her some work."

"She's going to scare away all your customers, Edsel."

"Oh, come on."

"Edsel, she scared the living shit out of me, and I work there. I was backtracking out of the store so fast that I should have had one of those backup beepers on my butt."

"It's only temporary."

"Temporary? That's what the Irish said when the British took holidays in Northern Ireland."

"Coach!"

"Excuse me, I must be in the wrong place," Coach said sarcastically, pretending to be a Snail's Pace customer. "I wanted to get a pair of running shoes, not get my nipples pierced and my bottom spanked with a leather whip."

"Oh, come on," Edsel said again.

Coach mused out loud, "What is it with the letter 'D?' It always starts something dastardly: disease, destruction, death, *Darla.*"

"It's only temporary," Edsel repeated. "Until she finds something else."

"What in hell is she going to find in Hoboken?" Coach said. "This isn't Transylvania."

"I don't know," Edsel admitted, "but she'll find *something.*"

Darla had not only tampered with Coach's dignity, she was a blatant affront to his worldview and sense of decency, and now he was cutting Edsel no slack. "What's she going to find? This is February, Edsel," Coach reminded him. "It's nine whole months until Halloween."

37. The Striders

COACH WORKED out a schedule with Edsel so that he saw Darla as little as possible, but that spring he had more important things on his mind. In March, a runner named Tom Waters—Running Water, Coach dubbed him—moved from Brooklyn to Hoboken and joined the HOHAs. Tom had run for a while for Harry Horton's Striders, and Coach worried that he might be a spy for Harry, so one night in the bar after a run, Coach saw to it that several of the HOHAs bought Tom beers, and when Tom was drunk enough, Coach began grilling him. "How long had he run with the Striders? Did he still associate with any of them in any way? Would he be willing to take a lie-detector test?" All Tom's answers were drunken ramblings, punctuated with burps, hiccups, or giggles, but the gist of them was satisfactory. Coach had saved for last, however, the most important question of all. "And what do you think," Coach said, "of Harry Horton himself?"

Tom was feeling good, and at that question, he put down his beer for emphasis. "When dealin' with Harry," he said dramatically, "you better have the word 'bullshit' in your pocket." Running Water took another superfluous drink of beer.

"What do I theeng of him?" he said rhetorically. "I theeng he's a pompous ass."

This was the A+ answer, and you could see it on Coach's face, which lit up in a big grin. Coach had put down some beers himself, and now he raised his voice above the din of the bar. "What kind of ass?" he shouted with joy.

"A pompous ass," Tom shouted back.

"Harry Horton," Coach chanted. "What kind of ass?"

"A pompous ass," Tom and several others repeated, and from that moment on, Running Water was not only accepted as a full-fledged HOHA, but became one of Coach's favorite HOHAs, Harry-haters, and running allies.

Tom was a good source of information, and over the following weeks Coach continued to ply him with questions about Harry, his team, and their plans, and everything he learned only served to increase his sense of foreboding. He learned, for example, that John Malcolm was running for the Striders now. Malcolm had run the 1500 meters at Pitt ten years before. He had been all-conference then, and was now getting into shape again and into road racing. He also learned that Harry had lured a good master runner named Don Abrams away from the West Side Runners by promising that the Striders would pay all his racing fees. Coach soon knew everything that Tom had to tell, but as time passed and Tom's information grew dated, Coach worried about what Harry and the Striders were up to now. His initial suspicion that Tom was a spy had planted a seed in Coach's mind, and now he played with the thought of doing some spying himself.

One day in late May, Coach suggested to Tom that they go over to Prospect Park in Brooklyn on a Saturday morning and do a long run there. Prospect Park was the site of many New York Road Runner races, and Coach said he wanted to get more familiar with the course there and its many hills. Tom had forgotten that he'd told Coach that the Striders did their track workouts on Saturday mornings at a high school near the park, and didn't realize until later that the trip to Brooklyn and the run itself were merely a pretext for Coach to see Harry's Striders for himself and ascertain how much of a threat they would be if they ran the X-C series that fall.

Coach and Tom drove over to Prospect Park early that Saturday and had their run. On the way back, Coach took a different route that brought them by the high school. "Look over there," Coach said nonchalantly. "There's a team working out on the track."

"That's probably the Striders," Tom said.

"Really," Coach said, feigning surprise. Then he added as casually as he could, "Let's just take a look."

Tom still didn't suspect anything, because in the short time he'd known Coach, he already understood that if Coach wasn't running himself, or talking about running, then he would consider watching somebody else running to be the next best thing, but as they approached the track, Coach's true intention became clear. Coach abruptly held out his arm to stop Tom short, and then motioned him behind a retaining wall. Then Coach took out a pair of opera glasses.

"Where'd you get those?" Tom said.

"They're Biscuit's."

Coach was already looking through them toward the track.

"What are you looking at?" Tom said.

"You were right," Coach said. "It looks like Harry and the Striders. They're just finishing their warm-up." He said this with satisfaction and relief, realizing he had timed the morning perfectly and would get to see their entire workout.

The Striders had been jogging in groups of three and four and were now gathering near the start line, talking and stretching and changing into their lighter shoes. There were about fifteen of them in total, all guys. "They've got a big squad," Coach said. It was a good turnout. Coach was lucky to get nine or ten HOHAs to the track.

When the Striders had completed their preparations, they gathered and began a final warm-up lap together. When they reached the start, they would begin their first repeat. Coach still had the opera glasses glued on the group and, without removing them, he said, "When they start, Tommy, I want you to time them."

Tom was still shocked by Coach's intention that morning, but he cleared his chronograph and got ready. As the Striders came into the home straight, their easy pace slowed momentarily as they shifted positions. In a group that large, everyone aligns himself according to the pace he thinks he'll run. Harry and his faster runners were at the front now, the slower runners behind, and they all moved in place going down the straight. Near the start, they slowed again and there were final adjustments as the runners spaced themselves for acceleration. Hands went to wrists as they prepared to start their watches, and then they were off.

Two runners were setting the pace, shoulder to shoulder around the first turn. A second group, Harry among them, was tucked in right behind. Coming out of the turn, the inside runner took a few quick strides and established himself at the front. "Look at him," Coach said in admiration. "Look how smooth. Who is it?"

"That's John Malcolm," Tom said. "The one I told you about." Malcolm was like a locomotive, powering around the track.

"And who's that with him?" Coach asked.

"That's Don Abrams," Tom said, "the master runner Harry stole from West Side."

The pace was quick, but not too quick—a sign that the first interval would be six hundred meters or more. Malcolm, followed by Abrams, Horton, and the Frieder twins, tall and gangly and identical, formed the lead group.

The Frieder twins were well known in local running circles, not only for their identical looks but also for their identical running styles and times. When you saw them running together, you wanted to rub your eyes, as if you were seeing double, and when you saw their race results in the paper, you thought they were a typographical error: Frieder, Adam and Frieder, Alan, sometimes without even a second between them. Coach took their presence in Harry's club as a personal affront to sportsmanship and human decency. He thought it unnatural, as if Harry, not satisfied with just one good runner, had taken a good runner and cloned him. Coach referred to the Frieders as the "Freaks." "And look at the goddamn Freaks," he said. "My God!"

Most of the Striders formed a second group a short distance off Malcolm and the others, and there were a couple of slower runners coming up behind. They came out of the back turn and down the front stretch, Malcolm still pacing the team with an effortless rhythm. When they reached the start, Coach said, "What's the split?"

"Seventy for Malcolm," Tom said. Tom waited until the first of the second group crossed. "Seventy-five."

They continued through a second loop, everyone holding their position. Some in the second group showed some strain, but the rest looked fine. They continued through eight hundred meters. "Two-twenty," Tom said when Malcolm finished. "Two-thirty," he said for the rest.

Coach winced. "Not bad." Coach put the opera glasses down for the first time. "They bit off a lot," he said. "Now let's see if they can chew it."

A key to a good track workout is to establish a pace that can be held throughout. The first intervals are easier, but as runners tire, the pain sets in as they try to hold the pace. The Striders regrouped, jogged out a one-loop rest, and then did a second eight-hundred-meter interval. Malcolm again floated through at two-twenty, and the second group again hit their two-thirty.

"They're gonna stick with the eight-hundreds," Coach said. "At that pace, they'll only be able to handle six."

Coach was right, and he and Tom watched as they repeated their times for four more intervals. Only a few of the weaker runners fell off the back on the last two. The rest finished steady and strong. It was an impressive workout for an amateur team, and Coach stood in silence. Only Andy and Bad Bob for the HOHAs could hang with their first group, and the HOHAs had nowhere near their depth. "Not bad is right," Tom said.

"Malcolm looked great," Coach admitted. "And Abrams too. They run pretty."

"Malcolm's just a stud," Tom said in admiration.

"And the Freaks look as good as ever," Coach said.

"Harry didn't look too shabby either," Tom said, and as soon as he'd said it, wished he hadn't. Coach went white, and Tom realized that in complimenting Harry's running, he might as well have punched Coach in the gut. Then Tom learned something about Coach, and other HOHAs learned it too when Tom repeated the story to them later. They learned, if they hadn't already known it or had ever doubted it, that there was not an ounce of give-up in Coach.

Coach mulled it all over—what he had just seen and what Tom had just said—and then he smiled.

"What you thinkin', Coach?" Tom said.

"I'm thinking about our next track workout," Coach said. "I'm thinking that we have our work cut out for us." Then he put his hand on Tom's shoulder and smiled again. "And I'm thinking about how sweet it will be to beat the living crap out of a team like that."

38. Back to Basics

ONE OF THE MANY adages of athletics is that if you want to improve your performance, you should go back to the basic building blocks of your sport, or the fundamentals, as they are sometimes called. Doing all the little things right will result in better overall performance. In baseball, for example, that means the practice of such basics as turning the double play, hitting the cutoff man, and advancing a runner from first to second. In football it means the practice of proper blocking stances, tackling positions, and handoff techniques. In running, the basics are all about proper form. The idea is to have every body part moving correctly and the entire body working in unison for maximum energy efficiency.

Coach had worked the HOHAs through the winter to keep up their mileage for increased strength and endurance and now, in the spring, with the cross-country season just months away, it was time to get back to basics and ensure that the HOHAs were getting the most out of their conditioning. Coach would keep an eye on his runners during the weekly runs and advise them when he saw a flaw in their form or an opportunity for improvement, and he also had some group drills that he put the team through. One of those drills he called "The Potato Chip Run," and the purpose of this drill was relaxation.

When you watch professional sprinters, you notice that the muscles in their cheeks are bouncing up and down. They have learned that even the effort required to hold their mouth closed takes precious energy that is better directed toward their movement down the track. You may also notice that their hands are relaxed, not clenched in fists. Again, the effort and tension of even making a fist is a drain of energy, and detracts from their goal.

We often think that in making an effort, we must show signs of that effort, when really the best thing is to relax and let go. Grimaces and clenched fists are the outward signs of trying. We are not trying to run hard; we are running hard. There is no need for acting. There is no need for show.

Coach devised "The Potato Chip Run" to practice proper movement of the arms and relaxation of the hands, and that spring he arrived at one of the HOHAs Tuesday-night runs with a bag of potato chips and gave two chips to each runner. "Hold your hands loosely, the thumb and forefinger holding the potato chip gently, so as not to break it," Coach said. "Now when you move your hands, move them in a piston-like motion from your hip straight forward, as if you were drawing a gun from a holster and shooting it."

"I'm confused," Bad Bob said. "Are we holding a potato chip or shooting a gun?"

Bob was wearing a look of mock seriousness and puzzlement, and Coach said, "You're holding a potato chip, smart ass."

"Oh."

Bad Bob had taken the cheap shot, and Coach was used to it, although sometimes he still wanted to wring Bob's neck, but on this occasion he checked his anger and said, "Bob makes a good point. If we're moving our arms as if we're drawing a gun, then we can think of the potato chip as the trigger." Coach looked patiently at Bad Bob and made his point. "And it's best to squeeze the trigger gently."

The HOHAs ran the Tuesday course that evening holding their potato chips, or gently squeezing the trigger if you will, and it was a decent drill, making them conscious of their arm movements and their hands. When they got in, Coach went from runner to runner, like a general inspecting his troops, to check if the chips were broken. He had just finished the inspection, and was giving additional pointers on arm movement, when Howie came in. Howie had taken his customary shortcuts, but as usual was still the last HOHA to finish.

"Terminator!" Coach said. "Good job. Now let's see your potato chips."

Howie put his hands behind his back.

"Where are they?" Coach said.

"I ate them," Howie admitted.

Bad Bob laughed.

"I got hungry."

"Hungry?" Bob said. "Before the run, I saw you coming out of Marie's bakery with a smile on your face."

"What did you have, Howie?" Coach asked.

"Just jelly donuts."

Bob laughed again. Just then, a foghorn sounded from the Hudson River, and Bob exclaimed in mock shock, "Howie! Excuse yourself."

"Cut it out, Bob," Coach said, and then said to Howie, "You promised you'd give up junk food."

"I ate them for medicinal purposes," Howie explained.

"What are you talking about?" Bob said.

"I'm taking diet pills," Howie said. "My doctor said I should take them on a full stomach."

"That makes absolutely no sense at all," Bob said.

"Leave Howie alone, Bob," Coach said.

"High carbohydrates," Howie said.

"Oh yeah!" Bob said, as if now enlightened, "I've heard of that. That's the Dozen-Donut Diet. Eat six donuts, take a diet pill, and eat six more donuts."

"Bob!"

Despite Howie's lapses, he'd been making slow progress, but ever since he'd joined the HOHAs, his parents had been worried about what they viewed as his abnormal concern with exercise and diet. They'd seen him come home tired, sweaty even, and had watched in shock as he turned down dessert and shrank to a relatively emaciated two hundred and forty pounds. They'd held family meetings and begged Howie to stop the insanity. Why couldn't their son just relax and eat normally like the rest of their family?

When Donna finally dumped him and Howie buried his sorrow in a binge of pastry, it had been Coach who'd intervened again to get him back on track. Although Howie was by far the least natural athlete among the HOHAs and by far the least promising, Coach spent more time with him than with anyone else. The Moochs thought Coach was brainwashing Howie, and had on several occasions accused Coach of running a cult. Coach thought this was absurd, but the last thing he wanted now was more phone calls from Mr. and Mrs. Mooch complaining that cult members were harassing their son.

"Hey, Howie," Bob said. "Can I have the number of your doctor?"

"Goddamn it, Bob," Coach said.

"What for?" Howie said suspiciously.

"I need a prescription," Bob said.

"Cut it out, Bob," Coach said.

"For what?" Howie said.

"I want a prescription," Bob said, "for an apple fritter."

39. Destiny

ANDY OFTEN got in his extra mileage before the group runs, and on Tuesdays he usually did a five mile out-and-back to Jersey City and timed it so that he'd be at the YMCA by eight o'clock, in time for any club announcements and some socializing before the start. On one Tuesday that spring, Andy was running late. He'd received a phone call just before heading out the door, and then a neighbor had stopped to talk with him while he was stretching in front of his apartment. He'd failed to make up for these delays with a stronger pace in Jersey City, and by 8:05 was back in Hoboken but still a half mile from the Y, running north on Hudson, a one-way, southbound street that parallels Washington.

He'd made a habit of running against the traffic, a safe practice that allowed him to watch oncoming cars. Parked cars lined both sides of Hudson, and Andy ran to the left, along the driver's side of the cars parked there. He'd been steadily picking up the pace to make up time and was running at a clip just over five minutes per mile, enjoying the speed, his focus, and the warmth it brought him on the cool, damp evening. It had rained earlier, and now the water on the road reflected the glow of the street lamps, and he pretended he was running from lamp to lamp as if they were safe spots in a childhood game. In this playfulness of speed, and warmth, and light, he hummed along, in tight quarters against the traffic, hugging close to the parked cars, and was alongside the driver's door of a van when suddenly a guy stepped out into the street from the back of the van and pivoted quickly, ready to walk along the van to the driver's door. Andy saw him step out, saw him turn, but with no time to stop or change course, ran straight into him, his left shoulder slamming into the guy's forehead.

The blow was violent, and yet strangely beautiful, and sent the guy flying through the air and onto the pavement. He landed flat on his back a good six feet from the point of impact. It happened in an instant, but seemed to pass in slow motion. It wasn't until the guy braced his arms and raised his upper body from the ground that the normal speed of events returned. The guy shook his head in a cartoonish way, as if shaking away the stars he was seeing.

Andy stayed standing, his forward motion neutralized rather than negated by the blow, a sharp pain now shooting through his shoulder. He watched the guy shaking his head and could now see blood streaming from his nose. He was trying to get up, and Andy stepped forward to give him a hand.

"Are you OK?" Andy said, as soon as the guy was upright.

The guy was stunned, and couldn't talk, but was trying to get himself, bodily at first, back to normal. At least he was standing now, and could see straight. He saw the blood from his nose, and responded to that as much as to Andy's question. "I bleeding," he said, in a neutral tone, touched with some surprise.

Andy wanted to give him a handkerchief, but realized that, of course, he didn't have one. "Do you have a tissue or anything?" he said.

"In my van," the guy said. He cupped his nose with one hand and took some keys from his pocket with the other, which was trembling. Andy took the keys from him and opened the van door. "Under the seat," the guy said. Andy found a rag and handed it to him.

"What's your name?" Andy said.

"Chuck."

Chuck was Chinese, in his mid-twenties, and small. Andy noted his size, and realized why his shoulder had struck Chuck's forehead, and why Chuck had flown so far. If Chuck had been bigger, they would have knocked heads, and the result would have been worse than a sore shoulder and a bloody nose. "Are you OK, Chuck?" Andy put a hand on Chuck's shoulder. "I'm sorry I hit you. I didn't see you until it was too late."

"Is Chuck's nose broke?" Chuck asked. Chuck held the rag away from his nose so that Andy could take a look. Beneath all the blood, there was a distinct bump on Chuck's nose.

"I can't tell for sure," Andy said. "It could be."

"Oh, my goodness!" Chuck exclaimed.

"Take it easy, Chuck." Andy gripped Chuck's shoulder to brace him. "A doctor can fix it."

"The laundry!" Chuck exclaimed again.

"What?"

"The laundry! I making special delivery. We promise customer right away. Miss needs to catch a plane!"

Chuck was suddenly a whirlwind of action. He stumbled to the back of the van and opened the doors and returned with plastic-covered hangers of clothes and a paper-wrapped bundle. He held them at arm's length, away from his bleeding nose. "Take," he ordered. "You need to deliver. Chuck still bleeding."

"What?"

"You need to deliver. Address 422, #3. It's on ticket. Go. Quickly, quickly. Chuck wait here."

"Chuck, I don't know ..."

"Don't be a idiot." Chuck was still holding the rag to his nose, the nose Andy had probably broken, and his eyes were wide with urgency. "Go. Go quick."

Of course Andy was willing to help, but he was startled by the sudden turn of events. One moment he'd been running down the street, and the next thing he knew he'd had a fierce collision, met Chuck, and was now delivering laundry. His mind couldn't quite catch up. From the sidewalk, Andy looked back and saw Chuck, one hand holding the rag to his nose and the other hand urgently waving him on.

Hudson Street was blocks of brownstones, and the van was parked in front of 422. Andy headed up the sidewalk steps and pushed the button for #3. A young woman's voice came over the intercom: "Yes?"

"Laundry delivery," Andy said. He was surprised by the naturalness with which he made the announcement.

The woman buzzed Andy in without a word, and he climbed to the third floor, wearing his running gear, still sweaty from the run, shoulder red and hot with pain from the collision, and carrying the plastic-covered blouses and skirts and the paper bundle. When he got to the third floor, he tucked the bundle under his sore arm and knocked on the door.

It was the apartment of Coco Cushman, and Andy was not at all prepared for the shock he received when Coco opened the door. The collision with Chuck had rocked him, set him back on his heels, and now the sight of Coco, before he had been able to fully collect himself, almost brought him to his knees. She had olive eyes and black hair, cut in straight bangs across her forehead, and she looked like Cleopatra, Andy thought, or at least what Cleopatra had looked like in the movies. Her beauty, and the instant attraction he felt toward her, was like the second blow in a staggering one-two combination.

When Andy failed to speak, Coco looked him over. She, for her part, was also surprised, surprised that the delivery man wasn't Chinese—the laundry was obviously a family business—and surprised that a delivery man would be in running attire. This second fact, along with the young man's humorous diffidence, made her smile. She looked back and forth, from the laundry to him, waiting with growing amusement for him to get it together.

What could he say to a girl so beautiful? He saw her smiling and waiting for him, and finally said, "I'm not who you think I am."

"Well then," she said playfully and with a little laugh, "who are you?"

"I mean, I'm not really the laundry guy."

"You're not?"

"No. I was running. I was hurrying to my running club, and I accidently ran him over. He's downstairs bleeding."

"Oh my God! Is he hurt badly?"

"No. It's just his nose. It could be broken though. I should get back to him." Andy said this, but he didn't move. It was hard for him to take his eyes off her. He couldn't feel his shoulder anymore, but his mouth was dry, and he felt completely numb.

Coco, for her part, thought Andy was cute, and polite, and charmingly shy. She waited for him to say something, but when he didn't, she said, "Oh. Wait." She reached into her coat, which was hanging inside the door, and found some money. She handed Andy two dollars.

"What's this?"

"Your tip."

"No. You don't need to do that."

"I need to get to the airport," she said. "And you had better see to your friend."

"My friend?" Andy said. "Oh, Chuck. Right."

Coco gave him a sympathetic nod, smiled, and started to close the door. Then she stopped, thinking of the sudden free fall that had brought him to her apartment. "Just one question," she said. "Where'd you leave your horse?"

"What?"

"Never mind," she said. With that, she slowly shut the door. Standing just inside the door she smiled and then mouthed the words "I'm not who you think I am," and "Well then, who are you?" On the other side of that closed door, still standing there, Andy understood, with a clearness that shocked him, that everything leading up to this moment, his entire life as he had known it, had been just a necessary prelude to delivering him here.

When Andy got back downstairs, he found Chuck sitting on the curb near the van in the glow of one of the street lamps. He still had the rag to his nose, but the bleeding had almost stopped. Andy handed Chuck the two dollars.

"What that?" said Chuck.

"The tip."

"No way," Chuck said, waving off the money. "You saved the day."

Andy sat down next to Chuck on the curb. "Are you OK, Chuck?"

"Yeah. I think Chuck able to get up in minute." When Andy didn't respond, Chuck looked at him and saw him deep in thought. "What's matter with you?"

"I just met the most beautiful girl in the world."

The earnestness and dreaminess in Andy's voice brought Chuck out of his own fog. "Poor you," Chuck said. "I only got smacked in nose."

"She smiled at me."

"Oh no!" Chuck looked at Andy with concern. "Are *you* gonna be OK?"

"She looks like a model, Chuck, and she has the sweetest smile." Chuck looked at Andy with even more concern. "When I was looking at her," Andy continued, "I could hardly talk."

"Did you feel like somebody punch you in the gut?" Chuck said.

"Yeah, how did you know?"

"That how Chuck felt when Chuck first see Nancy Chong."

"Who's Nancy Chong?"

"The girl who broke Chuck's heart."

"You were in love?"

"Yes. Chuck in love with her, take her to dinner, buy her flowers, buy her chocolate. Chuck make complete ass out of himself. Chuck take Nancy out two times. The whole time Chuck thinking how wonderful she is and how Chuck don't deserve her. Then one night Chuck walking by her house and see her in the car with another guy. Chuck can't believe it, so Chuck hide in the bushes and watch what she do. Rose bushes sticking Chuck in the butt."

"You hid in the bushes?"

"Yes. Of course," Chuck said. "Don't be a idiot."

"Well, what happened?"

"They kiss. Tongue kissing. Windows get foggy and Chuck go nuts. Chuck jump out of bushes yelling and run to car. Chuck try to get in, but they hurry up lock doors. Chuck dive on hood, yelling through windshield window. 'Nancy,' Chuck yell."

"Oh, man."

"Chuck scare guy shitless. The guy panic and drive away. Chuck fall off hood and run down the street yelling after them, 'Nancy, Nancy, I love you,' like complete idiot. Chuck wish he had camera to take picture of himself. Chuck call it 'Picture of Idiot.'" Chuck paused and concluded, "That's what women do to men."

"Sorry, Chuck."

"Next morning flowers and box chocolate were on floor in front of laundry. Nancy dump Chuck."

"Were you really in love with her?"

"If you mean was Chuck miserable whole time Chuck know her, then answer is yes."

"Sorry."

"She ate half the box."

"What?"

"She ate half the box chocolates. She only leave pieces with nuts." Chuck pondered the significance of that. "One piece with nuts have bite out of it." Chuck then pulled the rag from his nose. Both his eyes were swelling. He was still wobbly, but he was the one most able to get to his feet, and he helped Andy get up too. He grabbed both of Andy's arms and held him firmly. "Get hold of yourself," he said. "Get a grip."

"I miss her."

"You just saw her two minute ago."

"I know it's weird, but I already miss her."

"Call 9-1-1," Chuck said. "Need ambulance."

"You hurt that bad, Chuck?"

"No," Chuck said. "Ambulance for you. You basket case."

Andy shook his head to clear the daze he felt. "I'll be all right."

Chuck pulled the rag away from his nose again and saw that the bleeding had stopped. "Chuck need to make another delivery," he said. "You need ride, Andy?"

"No, I can make it."

"You look like crap."

"Coming from you, that says a lot," Andy said.

"Chuck just saying."

"I'll be fine," Andy said. He was trying to convince himself as much as Chuck.

"Call Chuck tomorrow." Chuck handed Andy a business card. "Chan Laundry."

Andy walked home then. He would have been late for the HOHAs run anyway, but he'd forgotten all about it. Now, he sat in his apartment in a daze. He thought about how beautiful Coco was, and was filled with an inexplicable longing that made his heart ache. Everything had changed, and suddenly nothing mattered—his running, the institute, his entire life—if he couldn't be with her. He looked at his crumby apartment and at his sweaty, dirty self. "Why would she ever want to be with me?" he thought. All of his grandmother's admonitions flooded in upon him, and he wished with despair that he had made more of himself, if only just to impress her. He threw himself back on the bed and lay there staring at the ceiling and feeling lovesick, and then he remembered Chuck's last words to him before Chuck pulled away in the van. "Andy got to know one thing," Chuck had said to his new friend. "Women put on earth for one purpose, one purpose only: make men miserable."

40. Yahtzee!

JUNE HAD put a small chicken, along with some carrots and celery, salt and pepper, in the Crock-Pot that morning, and she'd added a dash of Worcestershire sauce to the tablespoon of water, just the way Gen liked it, and it was all tender and juicy now. The top of the Crock-Pot was beaded with the juice, and steam slipped from around the edges of the top and rocked it with a gentle clacking sound, filling the kitchen with a satisfying aroma. Preparation and patience, June thought, are always rewarded.

Gen and June were at the kitchen table playing Yahtzee, a favorite dice game of theirs. Each player has three rolls of the dice per turn, and the object is to get different combinations of the dice to score points. There are five die, and the highest score is to get all five with the same number, which is called a Yahtzee. A Yahtzee is rare, and the player who gets one usually wins the game. June had had three sixes on her first roll and one more on her second. In her last roll, with the last die, all she needed was another six. "Boxcar," she said. June raised the cup and then stopped to pray. "Good God, give me a six."

"God," Gen countered, "don't listen to her."

June shook the dice cup three times, the way she always did, and was about to roll when she suddenly stopped. A pensive look came over her face, and she looked out past Gen toward the schoolyard across the street.

"What's wrong, June?"

"Gen, do you remember that time when you had that premonition that your brother Weaver had been killed in the war and then the telegram arrived that night?" Gen nodded, too reflective to speak. "Well, I just had a premonition now."

"God," Gen said. "Who died?"

"Nobody. I just had a feeling about Andy."

"What happened?"

"He's met a girl."

"Thank God for miracles," Gen said.

"He's troubled by it though," June said. "It's his trouble I feel."

"Let's call him," Gen said. She reached across the table and put the phone in front of June.

"What time is it there?"

Gen looked at her watch. "It's six o'clock here, so that means it's nine o'clock there."

"What day is it?"

"Tuesday," Gen said. "The same day it is here."

"I guess he might be home." Her feelings had left June unsure and hesitant.

"If he's not, we'll just leave a message," Gen said. "This is urgent, June."

June dialed Andy's apartment in Hoboken. Andy was still lying on his bed, lost in worry over the events of that evening. The phone startled him, and he answered on the first ring. "Hello."

"Andy, this is your grandma."

"Is anything wrong, Grandma?"

"That's what I was going to ask you."

"I'm OK."

"You don't sound it." Andy was silent. "Andy, are you in trouble? Is something going on?"

Normally, Andy would have made every effort to evade questions like these, but he *was* in trouble—a trouble he hadn't experienced before, and couldn't fathom—and he felt the need to talk it out. The words just poured from him. "I met a girl," he said. He then told his grandma about his collision with Chuck and all that had followed.

June put her fingertips over the speaker and, nodding to Gen, said, "There's a girl."

"What's her name?" June said to Andy.

"I don't even know," Andy said, with as much desperation as could be packed into so short an utterance.

"What's the matter?"

"I'm in love with her, Grandma. I loved her the minute I saw her."

"That's good, Andy."

"She doesn't even know I'm alive."

"You met her, didn't you?"

"It was an accident."

"There are no accidents," June said.

"Yeah," Andy said blankly.

"What are you going to do?" June said. There was no answer, and June covered the phone again and said to Gen, "He doesn't know what to do."

"Tell him to behave himself," Gen said.

"Just be yourself," June said to Andy. "Ask her out. Get to know her. Take it slow."

"I guess," Andy said. What his grandma said sounded logical, but Andy was sick with love, and he wondered if he could even last until he saw her again.

"We'll pray for you, Andy."

"Thanks, Grandma."

"You call us if anything happens."

"Yeah, sure."

June hung up the phone. "Andy's in love," she said.

"Does he got it bad, June?"

"Gen, the boy doesn't know if he's in heaven or hell."

"Oh, my!" Gen said. "I still remember how my toes tingled the first time Joseph kissed me out behind the barn. I didn't know what planet I was on, and didn't care, either."

"Well, Andy's still on planet Earth. At least that's what my telephone bill says."

"Do his toes tingle?" Gen said.

"He didn't say anything about his toes, but he's got it bad."

"I was beginning to think that Andy would never find a girl," Gen said.

"Every pot has its top," June said.

"What's her name?" Gen said.

"He doesn't even know."

"God have mercy," Gen said. "What are we going to do?"

"We've got some praying to do," June said. June took a pen and wrote "Andy's Girlfriend" on a piece of paper and pinned it next to Andy's picture on the corkboard of the shrine. The two old ladies knelt down to pray.

June prayed, "God, in your ever-loving mercy for those confused, please bless Andy and the girl he loves."

Gen prayed, "God, don't let Andy blow it."

When they'd finished with their prayers, they returned to the kitchen. "Let's finish our game and eat," Gen said. "It's your roll, June."

June shook the cup three times again, and thought about Andy and his newfound love. She was concerned for him, but at the same time she felt as if a weight had been lifted from her. She rolled, and out tumbled the die in a beautiful six. "Yahtzee!" she yelled.

"Damn it," Gen yelled, almost at the same time. "Why be good when you can be lucky."

June heard the lid of the Crock-Pot jiggling with the steam, and smelled the wonderful aroma again. She stepped across the kitchen to turn it off and lifted the lid, letting some of the steam rise to warm her. There was nothing as comforting as a meal well planned and prepared, she thought. She looked back toward Gen. "Luck has nothing to do with it," she said.

41. The Cardinal Sin

THE NEXT EVENING, after his run, Andy went over to the Chan laundry to see if Chuck was all right. A middle-aged Chinese woman was behind the counter, and when the cowbells on the door chimed, she looked up from her paperwork and saw Andy in his running clothes.

"You Andy?" she said. "The guy broke Chuck's nose?"

"Was it broken?"

"Like cheap chopstick."

"Yes, I'm the guy. I'm sorry."

"I'm Chuck's mom."

"Nice to meet you, Mrs. Chan. I'm sorry about Chuck."

"How's your shoulder?"

"It still hurts, a little stiff. I'll be OK."

"I bet it hurt," Mrs. Chan said. "Chuck head hard as a rock. Fact, I think it is rock. Ha-ha-ha-ha-ha." Mrs. Chan reached under the counter and brought out a small jar with a colorful label. "This Tiger Balm," she said. "You rub it on shoulder every night." She handed the jar to Andy.

"Thank you. Is Chuck OK?"

"Chuck gonna live. Chuck has two black eyes, and his nose looks like door knob. Doctor says he'll be right when swelling goes down. Chuck proud. He thinks he looks like fighter. Ha-ha-ha-ha-ha. That a good one."

"Is Chuck here?"

"He doing deliveries." The phone rang then, and Mrs. Chan picked up the receiver and covered the mouthpiece with her hand. "Come tomorrow for dinner. Six-thirty. We live upstairs. I tell you about your girlfriend."

"Thank you." Andy nodded shyly and wondered how much Chuck had told his mom.

"Good," Mrs. Chan said. "I tell Muhammad Ali that you coming. Ha-ha-ha-ha-ha."

Mrs. Chan spoke in Chinese to the caller as Andy backed toward the door. When he opened the door, the cowbells chimed again, catching Mrs. Chan's attention. "Don't forget Tiger Balm," she said, then winked at Andy and laughed again. He backed out the door, holding his jar of Tiger Balm and watching Chuck Chan's mom on the phone. She was smiling, and her head was tilted back in yet another lovely chorus of 'ha-ha-has.' She stopped her conversation again and yelled after him, "Tiger Balm for your shoulder. Ha-ha-ha-ha-ha. Even Chinese have nothing that soothe heart."

Andy thought it was nice of Mrs. Chan to invite him to dinner. He thought about bringing a bottle of wine, but didn't know if the Chans drank, so he decided on flowers, and bought a mixed bouquet at an outdoor stand on Washington Street on his way over the next evening. Mrs. Chan blushed when he gave them to her, and then led Andy into the kitchen and introduced him to Mr. Chan, who was wearing a "Kiss the Cook" apron, and to Chuck's twelve-year-old sister, Patty, who gave Andy a coy smile, which Mrs. Chan saw. "Patty, don't get excited," she said, "Andy already in love. Ha-ha-ha-ha-ha."

"Mom, please!" Patty said.

"How your shoulder, Andy?" Mr. Chan asked.

"It's better today. Thank you. That Tiger Balm helped, Mrs. Chan."

"Good. Tiger Balm couldn't help Chuck's face though," Mrs. Chan said. "He a mess. He in his room. I go get him." She turned at the kitchen door and said to Andy, "Do you want to know a secret about Chuck?"

"Mom!" Patty said.

"I guess," said Andy.

"His real name is Charlie. Get it? Charlie Chan. But all the kids at school tease him, so we call him Chuck." With that, she went down the hallway, calling, "Charlie! Charlie Chan! Ha-ha-ha-ha-ha."

Chuck's face *was* a mess. Both his eyes were black and his nose was swollen. "Chuck don't know if breathe through it or honk it," he said. He ushered Andy into the living room where they could talk alone until dinner was ready.

"You going to be OK, Chuck?"

"You betcha. Sure. Big piece of cake," he said, dismissing Andy's concern. "What about you. You meet that girl yet?"

"No. No, of course not," Andy said. "How could I meet her?"

"You go to her door and ask her out."

"I can't do that."

"Why not? You bashful?"

"No, I'm not *bashful*. It would be too weird. It would be like stalking or something. Besides, she was leaving on a trip. Remember? The rush delivery?"

"What's her name?"

"I don't know."

"You didn't even get name?"

"I was in running shorts. You were bleeding downstairs. It wasn't exactly the right time to ..."

"Her name is Coco Cushman," Mrs. Chan said from the doorway.

"How you know that, Mom?"

"She called this morning to ask about you. She felt bad that you got hurt delivering her clothes. She had to leave quick to visit her mother."

"Did she ask about Andy?"

"No. Sorry." Mrs. Chan smiled sympathetically at Andy. "She very beautiful. I see, Andy, why you a goner. She *hot*! Ha-ha-ha-ha-ha."

"Coco," Andy said aloud, trying out the name.

"She a fashion student," Mrs. Chan said. "She make her own clothes. Size six. And she show me a dress she made for her mom."

"Mom," Chuck exclaimed, "isn't that confidential information?"

"Don't be a idiot," Mrs. Chan said. "I'm laundry lady, not doctor."

"Oh," Chuck said. Chuck's wheels were turning and he could see his mom's point. "OK, then," he said. "What else you got?"

"I find out more next time Coco come in, but I know she a sweet person, because she good to her mother." Mrs. Chan made a face at Chuck. "What you gonna do, Chuck, when I get old and can't take care of you no more?"

"Chuck gonna go to Bahamas. Be a cabana boy," Chuck said. "But first Chuck gonna put you in a home."

"Ha-ha-ha-ha-ha."

"Chuck already make you reservation."

"Ha-ha-ha-ha-ha."

"Chuck can't babysit. Chuck gonna be a playboy."

"What about you, Andy?" Mrs. Chan said. "You a playboy or a good boy?"

Andy knew he wasn't a playboy, but he couldn't bring himself to say that he was a good boy either.

"He's a good boy, Mom," Chuck said. "Like me."

"If you so good, why girls call the police on you."

"Only one girl, Mom."

"Why can't you get girlfriend then?" Mrs. Chan said.

"Chuck told you. Chuck give up on girls."

"Maybe you like boys better. Ha-ha-ha-ha-ha. Maybe that the story."

"Are you kidding Chuck?" Chuck said.

"Just checking," Mrs. Chan said.

"Mind own business," Chuck said.

"If you can't find a good girl," Mrs. Chan said, "you should go to call girl."

"You want Chuck go to call girl?"

"It's better than go to jail."

"Chuck didn't go to jail, Mom."

"Chuck had close call," Mrs. Chan said to Andy. She held a thumb and forefinger about a half inch apart and said, "This close to slammer."

"Well, Chuck still don't need call girl." Chuck paused for emphasis and then announced, "Two things Chuck don't pay for: water and *that*."

Mrs. Chan laughed, and then spoke to Andy. "Chuck spend lot of money though on chocolate and flowers."

Chuck laughed too. "Chuck admit," he said, "it easier get free glass of water."

At dinner that night Mrs. Chan asked Andy about his family, and he told them about his grandmother and her friend in California. Mrs. Chan said Andy was welcome to have dinner with them any time, and she invited him over for the next Friday night. Then Mr. Chan asked Andy about his running, and he talked briefly about his high school and college career. Chuck said that he wanted to run, but didn't know how to start. Andy offered to help him, and they agreed to meet in front of the laundry the next morning. When Andy arrived, Chuck was waiting outside wearing basketball shoes, Bermuda shorts, a Harvard sweatshirt and some wraparound shades.

"You look cool, Chuck," Andy said.

"Do I?" Chuck said eagerly.

"Yeah, we'll get you some real running gear later on, but you're cool for now."

"How many miles we gonna do?"

"Let's not think about the mileage yet. Look at your shoes."

"What wrong with them?"

"The laces are touching the ground, for one thing, and you need to double knot them."

"Why?"

"So they won't come untied while you're running. Running will work them loose. That happened to me in my first high-school race, and it was a drag. Better to get in the habit of double knotting them, and you won't have that problem."

Chuck took care of his shoes.

"All right, let's go," Andy said, and started walking down the sidewalk.

"Why we walking?" Chuck said.

"We're warming up."

"But Chuck walk all the time."

"It's Sunday morning. You got out of bed, you had a cup of coffee, you watched the news on TV, and now you just want to start right in running?"

"Chuck had milk and watched cartoons."

"My point is, Chuck, that you need to warm up. We'll walk for a while, and then we'll do some light stretching, and then we'll run a little."

"OK, you the boss."

"Running looks easy," Andy said, "but there's more to it than you would think. The most important thing for a beginner to understand is that you have to start slow. And I mean S.L.O.W. You're going to be using muscles that don't even know they're alive. You have to take it easy at first. Otherwise, you'll quit or get hurt."

"Andy, you the boss."

Andy thought about Coco again. Ever since he'd met her, he couldn't get her out of his mind. After a while he said, "Last night, when your mom said that you almost went to jail, what was that about?"

"That about Nancy Chong."

"The girl who dumped you?"

"Yes, the girl who broke Chuck's heart."

"What happened with the police?"

"They almost arrest Chuck."

"I know. But why?"

"Chuck brought the flowers and chocolate back to Nancy, and Nancy called police."

"Why did she do that?"

"Maybe 'cause it four o'clock in morning, and maybe 'cause Chuck drank bottle wine, and maybe 'cause Chuck banging on the door."

"Why did you go over there in the middle of the night?"

"Because of boobs."

Andy laughed.

"Nancy have beautiful boobs," Chuck said, his voice full of admiration. "She wears tight top and nipples poke out like candies. Chuck dream about those nipples. In Chuck's dream Nancy say, 'Come here, Chuck, and have some candy.' Chuck woke up and couldn't breathe. If Chuck don't get some candy, Chuck going to die."

"So you went right over and banged on her door."

"First Chuck knocked. Then Chuck banged."

"And the police came."

"Police came. Nancy come out wearing tight T-shirt. Police see Nancy and know why Chuck crazy. Police drive Chuck home. Say if Chuck go near Nancy again, they arrest Chuck."

Chuck was pouting and Andy laughed again.

"You laugh," Chuck said, "but Chuck see you after Coco, and you a mess from day one."

Andy wanted to change the subject, and stopped walking. "Our muscles are warm now," he said. "Come on. Now we can stretch." Andy put his palms to a brick wall and leaned forward. "Do like me, Chuck, and keep your heels to the ground. Lean forward gently. This will stretch your calves."

"Chuck don't feel nothing."

"Move away from the wall more, and keep your heels down."

Chuck tried it. "Ouch," he said.

"That's good."

"Chuck say 'Ouch,' and you say, 'That good.'"

"You don't want to hurt yourself, but you should feel the stretch."

"OK."

"We'll just stretch a few minutes more, and then we'll walk home."

"You mean Chuck not going to run at all?"

"Chuck, we just walked fast for ten minutes, and you're already breathing hard."

"That 'cause Chuck can only use mouth; Chuck nose don't work."

"All the more reason. And remember what I said about taking it slow at first. You're going to have sore muscles tomorrow just from this stretching alone. Starting too fast is the cardinal sin of running, especially in a race."

"OK Andy, you the boss."

"With Nancy, was that the first time you were in love?"

"Yes, first time," Chuck said. Then he stuck a finger in the air and said, "No. Correction. First time *and last time* Chuck in love."

"Was it that bad?"

"Let's see. Chuck lose ten pound, because Chuck can't eat, can't sleep. Mama say Chuck look like Chinese noodle. Chuck got no money, because Chuck spend all money on Nancy, and Chuck almost go to jail, because Chuck go out of Chuck's mind. Otherwise, love great!"

"Take it easy."

"What about you, Andy? You in love before?"

"No. I never went out with any girl long enough for that, I guess. As soon as they tried to change me or control me, I'd just leave. Why do women do that? Did Nancy try to make you jump through hoops?"

"You kidding Chuck? Nancy Chong the Queen of Hoops. Chuck ready to jump, too. But Nancy say, "No. Wait, Chuck. Let me set hoops on fire first. Like Nancy have whip and Chuck in circus."

"You're over her, aren't you?"

"Nancy like malaria; never over it."

"Well, then just stay away from her."

"That a problem."

"Why?"

"Chuck and Nancy have same friends, and they getting married this summer. Chuck in wedding party, and Nancy in wedding party too."

"So, just keep your distance."

"That a problem."

"Why?"

"There will be dancing."

"So?"

"You not see Nancy Chong dance. Nancy butt move like blender, and boobs bounce up down up down. Hypnotize Chuck."

"Just don't let her get to you."

"Chuck have no choice. Nancy make Chuck heart beat like bongo." Chuck sighed. "Chuck afraid Chuck go ballistic."

Something occurred to Andy. "Hmm," he said.

"What you thinking, Andy?"

"I just remembered this health show I watched on TV last week."

"What about it?"

"They said the heart itself is a muscle."

"Yeah, so?"

"Well, it just occurred to me," Andy said. "Maybe the heart has to warm up too."

42. Age-Group Birthday

IN THE LATE spring of 1999, Coach got a consulting job with a company in the City to work on their Y2K project. In the infancy of computing, the early programmers had saved what was then precious computer memory by only coding the last two digits of the year. With the advent of year two thousand, those dates would roll over from 99 to 00, and events that were to be in the future would now appear to be in the past. This would bollix up entire software networks and all the crucial systems they ran. The work to prevent this had been going on for years, but as the rollover approached, corporations were growing increasingly nervous and were calling in the top computer geeks to ward off possible disaster.

Coach was working long hours during the week, and on weekends too, but he didn't miss a HOHAs run or neglect his duties as the HOHAs' leader. Despite the importance of his Y2K work, he never lost focus on what he saw as his most important work of all: to prepare the HOHAs for their fateful meeting with the horrendous Harry Horton and his nefarious Striders. This around-the-clock work contributed to the bleary-eyed tiredness in which Coach lived the events of the rest of that year.

Our lives are always changing, but sometimes there is a quickening of events or a milestone that draws our attention to that change. Everyone felt the importance of the millennium and of that turning of the clock, but perhaps Coach, working against it daily, felt it more than anyone else. He sensed and feared the end of something and the beginning of something new.

Much of competitive running is a battle not just against other runners and one's own weaknesses, but against the race clock and even against time itself. Runners feel their bodies every day and feel the subtle changes that come to them. They struggle to improve their performance, even as they are growing older and losing their ability to improve, but running might be the only sport where there is a built-in advantage to getting older. Runners compete in age groups, and are judged and rewarded based on how they do in their own group. When a runner turns forty, or forty-five, or fifty, for example, he or she enters a new five-year age group and has the advantage of being the youngest in that group. Coach called these milestones "age-group birthdays," and liked to celebrate whenever a HOHA had one. Often, the celebration would be just a toast at the bar, or a congratulatory mention in the HOHAs newsletter, but when Moses turned seventy in June of 1999, Coach, in addition to all the other things he had going on, took the time to throw a party.

Moses' birthday fell on a Tuesday, and for the Tuesday run that week, Coach had Ben at Counter-Fit Printing produce racing bibs with the number 70 on them that all the HOHAs would wear. Over forty HOHAs showed up for the run that night, and Coach kept the pace slow so they could all run together. Most of the HOHAs had grandfathers about Moses' age, and everyone felt how special it was to be running with him that night, while Moses himself rose to the occasion. A mark of an older runner is a certain stiffness in the upper body and in the stride, and over the last few years that stiffness had crept its way into Moses' once-flawless form, but that night it seemed as if the years were stripped away, and Moses glided through the course like a youngster.

As a HOHA, Moses had dominated the 60–64 and 65–69 age groups throughout the region, and now at seventy, he was entering an age group where most men were happy to be walking, let alone running the times that Moses could still run. Running with Moses every week, and watching him keep pace with runners half his age, it was easy to forget how old he was. If you looked at him closely, you could see his age, of course, but being there at the weekly runs, in all kinds of weather, set him apart from what you expected of a person that old. And he gave no one the impression that he should be treated differently because of his talent or because of his age. That's how special he was.

Andy and Moses usually did a cooldown together after the run, and Coach had Andy come up with a pretext to bring Moses back to Moran's bar afterwards for the surprise party. Coach had enlisted Duane to collect Buddy and bring him to Hoboken, and they were there with all the other HOHAs when Andy and Moses arrived. Everything went as planned, and Moses was surprised, especially by the presence of Duane and Buddy. The party itself was great. There was food and drink and two ice cream cakes that Howie had brought. Coach made a laudatory speech about Moses' accomplishments, and Moses blew out the seventy candles. Everyone had a good time, except perhaps Buddy, who was ill at ease, especially with Coach. Later in the evening, Coach and Moses had some time alone to talk, and Coach expressed his concern. "I don't think Buddy likes me much," Coach said.

"Why do you say that?"

"Because every time I try to talk to him, he grumbles and walks away."

"Don't take it personally, Coach," Moses said. "That's just Buddy. He believes that I had to leave Newark, but when you get right down to it, he blames you for taking me away. We were together a long time."

"How did you meet?"

"I met Buddy after my Gladys passed. She'd been sick for years, and we didn't have enough insurance and fell behind. Then the outfit I was working for moved their plant overseas. Nobody wants to hire a middle-aged man, and when my unemployment ran out, I lost the house. I started drinking, and things got foggy then. It's strange how fast it happens. The next thing I knew I was in a soup line, not knowing where I was going next. Buddy saw me and took me under his wing."

"That explains a lot, I guess."

"I couldn't believe it when I saw him here," Moses said. "I can't believe Duane got him to come out."

"Of course he came. He's your best friend."

"Yeah, but Buddy doesn't like to leave home."

"Has he ever been to Hoboken before?"

"Just the once, right after I moved here," Moses said. "He wanted to see what you showed me on our first run together down by the river."

"You mean our beautiful view of New York?"

"Oh no," Moses said, as if Coach had said something out of the question. "Buddy wouldn't care nothing about that. He came to see that hundred-seat toilet that the college kids built. When I told him about it, he didn't believe me at first, and when he finally did believe me, he wanted to get on the first train over here to see it himself. He looked at it from every angle, shaking his head. 'A hundred-seat crapper,' he kept saying. 'So that's what the college kids are up to these days.' He said, 'When I was a kid, we were satisfied just to knock over an outhouse. I guess that's progress.' As soon as he'd seen enough, he wanted to get on the next train home."

"Well, it was great of him to come tonight."

"Buddy told me tonight that anyone who makes it to seventy in this world should have a party."

"How old is Buddy?"

"He just turned sixty-eight. He says he's just a kid."

"Did you celebrate his birthday?"

"Yes, we went to the International House of Pancakes. IHOP. They put whip cream on the pancakes there and bring you all the coffee you can drink. A bottomless cup, they call it. Buddy kept asking the girl for refills, and she said, 'Sweetheart, how many cups of coffee can you drink?' and Buddy said, 'Sugar cup, I just turned sixty-eight, and I just might drink my age.' I don't know if Buddy drank that many, but he drank a lot, and he ate two stacks of pancakes, too. Buddy told me it was the best birthday he ever had."

"That's nice," Coach said.

"Are you OK, Coach?" Moses said. "You look real tired."

"I guess I've been working too hard," Coach said. "You know, that Y2K thing I told you about."

"Remember to heed your own advice," Moses said. "You have to pace yourself."

"I will, Moses. Thanks. This Y2K thing is important, though." Coach paused, and smiled at his thought. "Y2K is going to be an age-group birthday for the whole human race."

"A new start?"

"Yes, a new start for us all."

"Thank you, Coach," Moses said.

"For what?"

"Thank you for the special run and for the party. Having Buddy and Andy and you and the whole gang come out for me, that's special." Moses gave Coach a hug. "Buddy's not the only one who had a great birthday this year," he said. "This is the best birthday I've ever had too."

43. Siren Song

CHUCK HAD joined the HOHAs, and under the instruction of Andy and Coach showed some potential as a runner, and quickly became a HOHAs regular and favorite. He high fived everybody before the runs and could hardly contain his enthusiasm, which was his weakness, really. Full of it, he'd take the lead at group runs, like the baton twirler in a band, arms and legs strutting in exaggerated excitement, and then, soon exhausted, fall back to run proudly with Andy and Bad Bob, then back some more to run with Edsel and The Eck, then Slow Mo and Running Water, Moses and Coach, then farther still to run with Pinky and Ballpoint, before finally fading to the rear of the pack, breathing hard and finishing the run at a walk, just ahead of the slowest women and Howie.

Andy continued to have Friday-night dinners with the Chan family, and Chuck and Andy continued to discuss their problems with women. Chuck had nightly dreams about Nancy Chong that he had to get off his chest. These were wild dreams in which Chuck often had supernatural power or wealth or fame, which somehow failed to impress and capture the infinitely desirable and elusive Nancy. Andy did his best to interpret those dreams for Chuck and to advise him on how to get over her, but all the while, time had not healed Andy's own heartache for Coco. He had altered his daily commutes and running routes to pass by her apartment in the hope of seeing her, but so far he'd been unlucky. Now Andy had decided to accept Chuck's advice and take the initiative to meet Coco again. He'd asked Chuck if he could make the next laundry delivery to her, and he'd rehearsed some ways of turning that delivery into a request for a date. One evening, just before one of the HOHAs Tuesday runs, he was going over the simple details of this plan with Chuck. Andy had his back to the rest of the group that were gathered for the run, and he said to Chuck, "So next time you have a delivery for her, just give me a heads up and I'll meet you in front of her apartment."

In the middle of that sentence, Chuck's eyes widened as he looked past Andy toward the rest of the HOHAs. "That not be necessary," Chuck said.

"What are you talking about?"

"Look who here," Chuck said.

Andy turned then and saw Coco talking to Coach. Coach had given her an application form, and she was filling it out.

"That's Coco!" Andy said in disbelief.

"You right, Sherlock," Chuck said.

"Look at her!" Andy was mesmerized anew by her beauty. It was a warm evening in late spring, and Coco was wearing only shorts and a halter top. Her limbs were long and slender and beautifully shaped. She had the body of a model and the face of a cover girl. Her hair had been tied back when Andy had first seen her, but now, dark and silken, it flowed halfway down her back. "And look at that hair," Andy said.

"What you waiting for?" Chuck said. "Go talk to her."

"What?"

"Go on."

Chuck gave Andy a push on the back, and Andy made his way over to Coco. She had just handed the application back to Coach when Andy walked up. "Hi," he said to her. "Do you remember me?"

"Oh, hi," Coco said. "Yes, of course. You're the guy who's not who I think you are."

"I'm Andy."

"I'm Coco. Nice to meet you."

"I didn't know you were a runner," Andy said.

"I'm not. But I promised my mom that I would exercise, and when you told me about the running club, I thought I'd give it a try."

"That's great," Andy said. "You picked the perfect evening."

Coach made the club announcements then, and Andy stood self-consciously next to Coco until he'd finished. When Coach started the run, Andy, relinquishing his regular position at the head of the group, fell in next to Coco. When the group settled out, and Boston saw Andy running near the back of the pack, he said, "Hey, Andy, what are you doing back here, slumming?"

"You don't have to wait for me," Coco said.

"It's OK," Andy said. "I ran hard earlier today. This feels good."

Andy ran with Coco the whole way, at a pace that was nothing more than a jog for him, and he gave her pointers on her running along the way. Coco asked about Chuck, and Andy told her that he too had joined the club and was there that evening. When they got to Stevens Institute, Andy mentioned that he was going to school there, and he pointed out the buildings where he took his classes. He in turn learned that Coco was taking classes in the City. There wasn't much time to get to know each other, and in Andy's mind the entire run passed in a blur, but he was thrilled that they had met, and pleased that the conversation had gone well. After the run, he was just about to ask Coco to join him and the others for a drink when Bad Bob came up to them.

Bob had arrived for the run just as it was starting, and hadn't noticed Andy. He'd been surprised to find himself alone at the front, and had assumed that Andy wasn't there, but seeing Andy after the run with a gorgeous girl, he quickly put the pieces together. Now, Bob was like a kid who sees that his brother has a new toy and immediately wants to play with it. Bob was cocky in his good looks, had the confident demeanor of a salesman, and quickly took control of the conversation. He soon had Coco smiling and laughing, and commanded the majority of her attention. Coco declined their offers for an after-run drink, saying she had to get home, and both Andy and Bob offered to walk with her.

Coach noticed the three of them talking, and also noticed when his two best runners, instead of doing the extra mileage that they normally put in after the group run, or joining the group for a beer, just walked away, one on either side of this new girl, Bad Bob talking glibly and gesturing expansively, and Andy quiet, hangdog, just tagging along.

A great coach is like a policeman, in that he is always on duty and watching out for trouble. He keeps an eye on his athletes, both on and off the field, and notices the little things that indicate how they are doing. Coach could tell how Howie was doing with his diet by the puffiness in his cheeks, or how a runner was doing with a leg injury by how they favored it when they walked. Coach watched all his runners, but as all coaches will, he kept a closer eye on his stars. He checked regularly on Moses to ensure he was healthy and doing well. If Andy was quiet and calm, then Coach knew he was fine. If Bad Bob was cocky and sarcastic, Coach knew he was all right too. With the arrival of Coco, however, Coach soon saw in the behavior of both Andy and Bad Bob that there was trouble on the course.

They had both asked Coco out on dates, and Coco had gone out with each of them. There were the customary dinners and movies, chocolates and flowers, and Coco kept it casual and didn't favor either one, but both Andy and Bob feared the success of the other, and were jealous of even a perceived advantage. Competition for the same woman can destroy even the best of friendships, and Andy and Bad Bob hadn't even become close to being friends. Bob's respect for Andy was a jealous one, and Andy's tolerance of Bob was predicated on Andy's own superiority as a runner. Their relationship had been nothing more than civil, but now, their competition for Coco quickly destroyed that civility.

Andy regularly dropped Bob on the runs, and Bob, his pride hurt, ran alone. Bob, in turn, intensified his courtship of Coco, and in that race, seemed to drop Andy to a second place of his own. As the warmth of spring turned into the heat of summer, the HOHAs looked on as the tension between Andy and Bob rose along with the temperature. Not since the days of Coach's own love affairs had the HOHAs enjoyed a soap opera as juicy as this one.

Coach was watching too, and viewed Coco's influence as alarming. He countered his alarm with humor and, pretending he couldn't pronounce Coco's name, referred to her as CooCoo instead, but his focus remained on Andy and Bob's running. If anything, Coach had to admit, the competition between them had improved their times, but although the immediate results were good, Coach knew that the emotions were too high. Solid running should be built on meticulous training, and emotion is a waste of energy that eventually exacts its toll. Their performance was a flame burning hot and out of control, and Coach knew that performance like that couldn't last. His greatest concern, however, was that one of them would eventually win the headbutting contest for Coco, and the other would then leave the club.

44. Pillow Talk

BEFORE GOING to sleep, Coach and Biscuit ended each evening with their pillow talk. It was an idea that Biscuit had had for sharing their thoughts with each other at the end of the day. Biscuit usually talked about her family, or about ideas for decorating the apartment, or about places that she and Coach could go together. Coach, for his part, talked about the club. One Saturday night that summer, Coach talked again about Andy and Bob's competition over that new girl, CooCoo.

"Don't worry about it," Biscuit advised. "Let nature run its course."

Coach didn't like it, but he could see the wisdom of a hands-off approach, and at the same time he was pleased with Andy and Bob's performance in the tune-up races that year. In general, Coach was pleased with the progress the entire racing team was making with their training program, and with the preparations for the X-C championship. "You're right," he said, hearing in Biscuit's words his own thoughts. "I've got the team right on schedule to peak for the fall," he concluded. "Everything is under control."

Just then, the phone rang.

Looking back, it almost seems that it rang on cue, because the call was the first recognizable event in what was to become a series of events that were beyond Coach's control, and that would seal the fates of both Coach and the HOHAs.

It was late for a call, and Coach and Biscuit looked at each other in the darkness, waiting for the rings to register their persistence and importance. The phone was on the nightstand on Coach's side of the bed, and he rolled over to pick it up.

"Yes, this is Coach." ... "He's where?" ... "Yes. Sure. I'll come get him." ... "OK, put him on." ... "Chuck, what happened?" ... "Slow down." ... "Uh-huh." ... "What?" ... "OK, take it easy." ... "I'll be right there."

Biscuit had been listening, and as soon as Coach put down the receiver, she said, "Who was that?"

"Chuck," Coach said. "He's in jail."

"For what?"

"For being in love."

"What?"

"That's what he said. He said, 'Chuck guilty of love. Love in the first degree.'"

"That's it?"

"He said something about being hypnotized, wanting some candy. You know how hard Chuck is to understand."

"What are you going to do?"

"I'm going over to bail him out. The sergeant said they'll release him into my custody. Then I'll take him home."

Coach got up and got dressed, and then went through his dresser and stacked a pile of clothes on the bed.

"What are you doing?" Biscuit said.

"Getting some clothes for Chuck."

"Why?"

"Because evidently, when the police arrested him, Chuck was completely naked."

It was dawn when Coach returned home and slipped back into bed. Biscuit rolled over and put her arm around him. "What happened?"

"Chuck's in love with this girl named Nancy, and evidently they got in a fight. They were at a wedding, and Chuck drank two bottles of champagne and got naked in a fountain. When the police tried to grab him, he climbed a tree. They had to call the fire department to get him down."

"Is he OK?"

"No. He's a wreck. He was crying and mumbling about dirty dancing. I took him over to the Malibu Diner and got some food and coffee into him. Then I brought him to the laundry."

"Why didn't he call his parents?"

"That's what I asked. He said, 'You crazy? Mama laugh head off.' Evidently he was too embarrassed to call them, and he didn't want to call Andy either, because he'd promised Andy that he'd stay out of trouble. 'Chuck promise Andy Chuck be cool.'" Coach sighed. "Poor Chuck's a mess."

"He's in love."

"We're in love too, but I don't get naked in a fountain."

"There are different kinds of love. Our love was like a gentle fog. We walked into it, and it just enveloped us, softly. We were lost too, but it was quiet and cozy, and we were together. Chuck's love is like a thunderstorm, violent and out of control."

"You make love sound like a weather report," Coach said.

"Well, love is a force of nature," Biscuit said. "Some loves are a bright spring day, others a stormy winter night."

Coach was pensive, and after a moment he said, "I'm worried about Andy and Bad Bob."

"Why?"

"They're not themselves. Andy is grumpy, and Bad Bob is trying to be nice. CooCoo's got them acting all gaga."

"I've never seen such a beautiful young woman," Biscuit said.

"Do you think they're in love with her?"

"I don't know."

"If they were, what kind of love would that be?"

"I think she'd hit Andy and Bob hard. That love would be like lightning."

"Can love kill?"

"Oh yes. But I don't mean literally, like lightning. It's a love that strikes you and shocks you to the core. It's beautiful, but it's completely overpowering. It's the most dangerous type of love, just as it's the most dangerous type of weather."

"Well, I don't care what type of weather it is," Coach said. "Andy and Bob are great runners, and great runners can run through anything."

"We'll see."

"What do you mean, 'We'll see?'"

"Let's sleep," Biscuit said.

Coach turned out the light and lay in the darkness. "Poor Chuck," he said. "What a mess."

"Chuck will be all right," Biscuit said. "Go to sleep now."

Maybe Chuck will be all right, Coach thought, but what about Andy and Bob. Coach wasn't going to wait and see. He wasn't the type to leave anything to chance, not if he thought he could do something about it, and he certainly wasn't going to leave the well-being of his best runners in the hands of a girl who had just started with the club. No, we won't *see* about anything, Coach decided. Coach was going to do things the way he always did them; his way. Lightning or no lightning, Coach was going to fly his kite with a key.

45. HOs vs. HAs

IN THE WEEK following Chuck's skinny-dip in the fountain and climb up the tree, Andy consoled and counseled him and tried to help him get over Nancy Chong. These talks made him realize that he had to resolve his own problems with Coco. For one thing, she kept him at a polite distance on their dates, and then there was the disconcerting competition between himself and Bad Bob. That Thursday, Bad Bob was on a business trip and couldn't make the HOHAs run, and Andy saw this as an opportunity to talk with Coco alone. When the group was splitting up, Andy fell in beside her and offered to walk her home. "Your running's coming around," he said.

"I still have to cut the course way short to finish with everyone else. I probably only did three miles tonight."

"That's all right," Andy said encouragingly. "Little by little." He hesitated. He was unsure of himself with her. "I was wondering," he said, "if you're free one evening next week, maybe we can see a movie."

For her part, Coco had been becoming uncomfortable in her friendships with Andy and Bob. She liked them both in their own ways, but she knew that she would soon have to decide between them. She had taken to heart her mother's advice to her, and wanted her decision to be based on which of them really cared for her more, and felt that now was the time to find out about Andy. She stopped and turned to him. "Andy," she said, "I'm really busy with school next week, but if you have some time, maybe you could do me a favor."

"Sure," Andy said. "Anything." He figured she needed help with some small errand, and he would be glad for any excuse to spend time with her. "What is it?"

"There's a lady. She lived in my neighborhood when I was growing up, and she was kind to me. She's alone now and can't get out. I'd like you to visit her."

"You want me to visit an old neighborhood friend?"

"Yes. It would mean a lot to her. Will you do that for me?"

"I guess. Sure."

"Good. She lives in Pittsburgh."

"Pittsburgh!" Andy couldn't conceal his shock. "That must be a day's drive from here."

"Yes."

"But I have school."

"Not on the weekend."

"Coco, you want me to spend the weekend driving to Pittsburgh, visiting your friend, and driving back?"

"You could fly," Coco said casually, "if you wanted."

"Just fly to Pittsburgh? To visit someone I don't even know?"

"I see."

"What do you mean, 'I see?'"

"You said you'd do anything for me, but I guess that doesn't include going out of your way."

"I thought you meant a small favor, not taking the entire weekend. I have things to do, Coco."

"Like running?"

"Among other things."

"And those things are more important than doing something for me, no matter how much it means to me."

"Coco, you're being unreasonable."

"Yes. I guess I am." Coco's agreement was without a trace of apology, and the cool calmness of it was worse for Andy than any argument would have been. They had reached the steps of Coco's place. "Look," she said, with a devastating perkiness. "You've walked me home. Good night then." With that, Coco turned and jogged up the steps and into the building.

"Coco," Andy called after her, but she didn't turn. "Great, Andy," he said to himself. "That went really well."

The next day at school, Andy continued to think about his disagreement with Coco, and couldn't understand why she was being unreasonable. He kept reinforcing in his mind the righteousness of his own position, but that wasn't enough for him, and he sought support from his friends. At the student lounge, he told a couple of the guys about Coco's request, concluding, "Is that nuts, or what?"

"That's whacked, man," one of them said. "You hardly know her."

"Some girls just want to make you jump through hoops," the other said. "It's a power thing."

Both agreed that Andy had been right in turning Coco down. Andy hadn't told them how beautiful Coco was, and what a spell she had on him. His own conviction and the agreement of the guys still left him unsatisfied, however, and like a dog chewing on a bone, the more he thought about it, the less satisfaction he got. Andy felt he needed to get a woman's opinion, and the woman he wanted to talk to was Biscuit. People took their troubles to her, and as she listened and commented, they somehow felt better or refreshed. Biscuit listened between the lines. She listened for the hope or fear that made the person want to talk in the first place, and her response was to those feelings rather than to the details of the story itself. People felt that she really heard them. It was a gift she had, and Andy needed that gift now.

Andy was going out with Coach and some of the HOHAs that evening for a beer, and so he stopped by Coach's apartment early on the chance that he would get a few minutes to talk with Biscuit alone. He was in luck, because when he got there, she told him that Coach had just called and was running late. Biscuit sensed Andy's worry, and sat down with him to talk.

"How's Chuck doing?" Biscuit said.

"He's got a bad cold, from being in the fountain and then up in the tree, but otherwise he's holding up." Andy hesitated, and Biscuit waited. "Biscuit, can I get your opinion on something?" Andy said. "In confidence?"

"Sure, Andy."

"Do you know Coco, the new girl who's running with us?"

"Yes. She's beautiful, and she seems nice."

"Oh, she is," Andy said. "I met her before she joined the club." Andy told Biscuit the story of his first meeting with Coco, and how he'd felt about her from that moment on. "We went out a couple of times," he continued, "and the other night I asked her out again." Andy then told Biscuit the details of the exchange with Coco, and even as he shaded the account in his own defense, Biscuit heard his doubt and his strong attraction to the girl. "I don't know what to do now," he concluded.

"Why do you think she would ask you to do such a thing?"

"That's what I don't know," he said. "Maybe it's a power thing."

"But you're attracted to her, and yet you wouldn't be attracted to someone like that."

"No. I guess not."

"And she's attracted to you."

"How do you know that?"

"She came and joined the club, didn't she?" Biscuit said. "Knowing you would be there."

"I guess you're right."

"She came to you, and now she wants you to do something for her. It must be important to her."

"You're right," Andy said. He was shaking his head.

"And now you wish you'd agreed to make that trip for her. You wish you'd trusted her."

"Yes."

"Then go. Call her right now and tell her you'll go."

"It just seems crazy."

"You like her. Trust her, then. Trust that she has a good reason. You don't want to just go to a movie with her; you want to get to know her. If you make this trip, I'll bet that you'll learn a lot."

"I still think it's crazy."

Biscuit heard the stubbornness and resistance in Andy's voice, and tried another approach. "Coach once told me that the greatest quality of a good runner is his obsessiveness, his need to go out day after day, mile after mile, and do the work needed to improve. That same obsessiveness is a runner's greatest weakness, too. That kind of runner is often unwilling to back off his schedule or routine, even when it will cause him injury or degrade his performance. Coach said he's seen many good runners just run themselves into the ground.

"I thought how true that is for all of us. Often our weakness and our strength are bound together. Coach said that all good runners are obsessive, but that great runners are intelligent too. They know that their obsessiveness is just a tool, and that sometimes that tool is not appropriate and must be set aside. They take a day off. They take a step back in order to take two steps forward. They know how to adapt. They don't allow their strength to be their weakness."

Just then, they both heard the key in the door, and Coach entered the room. "Hey, Andy," he said, and then gave Biscuit a kiss on the cheek. "You been making time with my girl?"

"No, just getting some advice."

"Andy and I and some of the other guys are going for a pint," he said to Biscuit. "Do you want to come?"

"Not tonight. And Andy might have something else to do," Biscuit said. "Isn't that right, Andy?"

Before Andy could answer, Coach broke in. "Ah, no, not you too. I just saw Bad Bob at the train station, and he said he had to make an unexpected trip to Pittsburgh."

"Pittsburgh?" Andy exclaimed. "What for?"

"Just said he had to do a favor for a friend."

Andy felt sick, like someone who had just missed his train and was watching it pull out of the station. He looked over at Biscuit.

"Sorry, Andy," she said.

"What's up?" Coach said. "What do you have to do, Andy?"

"Nothing now," Andy said in a dejected tone, and then with the little enthusiasm he could muster, he added, "Let's go have a beer."

That evening, Coach learned the full extent of Andy's trouble with Coco, and learned that Coco had been testing Andy and Bob. Coach had already begun to see the first signs of wear and tear in their running. At the Cranford Five-Miler the week before, Bob's time was 30 seconds off what Coach had expected it to be, and when Coach asked him about it after the race, Bob said he hadn't been sleeping well. Andy's performance was also weaker than Coach expected. He'd won the race, but had failed to completely drop two of the top local runners that he normally would have left in the dust. Coach understood why now, and he was hot to confront Coco the next time he saw her.

Coco came to the Saturday morning run, and Coach immediately pulled her aside. "This is a *running* club," he said. "If you want to mess around, go join the ski club. All they have are parties and outings where they sit around in a hot tub. There are plenty of guys there."

"What are you talking about?" Coco said.

"I'm telling you that this is a running club. Period. And I want you to stop messing around with my runners."

"You mean Andy and Bob."

"Just back off."

Coco laughed. She had heard of Coach's own romantic involvements in the past. "And you didn't date any of the girls in this club?"

This caught Coach short, but he rallied. "That's exactly what I'm talking about. Gossip. That's not what this club is about either."

"You hit on every pretty girl who came along."

"I've been friendly with several of the female members, yes," Coach admitted. "And I made each of them a better runner."

"Yes, taught them to run for their lives, more like it."

"Don't mess with my runners."

"*Your* runners?"

"I want to clue you into some stuff," Coach said. "Andy and Bob are the fastest runners the HOHAs have, and I've worked hard to build our racing team. I'm not going to stand by and let you screw it up." Coach put his hands on his hips. "If you don't stop molesting my runners, I'll revoke your club membership."

Coco was speechless, and after a moment Coach took her silence for acquiescence and walked away. He felt self-righteous, but only mildly satisfied, sensing correctly that the problem was far from over.

That night, during his pillow talk with Biscuit, he told her what had happened, and when Biscuit objected, he justified his actions by insisting that Coco—or CooCoo, as he still called her—was breaking up his racing team. In recent weeks, what Coach thought of as Coco's sabotage had reminded him of John Lennon's wife, the woman accused of breaking up the Beatles, and that night, trying to express his frustration with her, and feeling that his current nickname for her didn't suffice, he struggled to find the perfect name with which to describe her, and then finally hit upon it: "Coco ... that ... that ... that ... Yoko!"

46. Ice Cream

COCO HAD been stunned, as many were at first, by Coach's effrontery, and she was unable to respond immediately. She had given him a piece of her mind all right, but it was only a small piece, and it wasn't until later that she thought of the many things she should have said. What did he mean by *"my* runners," and how dare he say that "I'll clue you in on some stuff," and my God, just who in the hell does he think he is?

Coco had recounted their entire exchange, and decided to go over to Coach's apartment the next morning to tell him off. On the way, she rehearsed the cutting words she had for him. She stomped up the steps, rang the bell with determination, and was ready to let Coach have it when Biscuit opened the door. Coco hadn't met Biscuit, but had heard a lot about her, and was struck now by how small she was. How could such a great spirit come in so small a package? How was it possible?

> *There was a great woman marathoner about that time. Her name was Tegla Loroupe. She was less than five feet tall and weighed only eighty-five pounds. She won the New York City Marathon twice, and when she crossed its windswept bridges, the wind would lift her into the air.*
>
> *The source of her strength and spirit was a mystery. Where did it come from? How could she be so strong? You witnessed that strength and spirit and just knew that she was blessed by God. And that same blessing lived in Biscuit.*

"Biscuit?" Coco said.

"Yes."

"I'm Coco, from the running club."

"Yes, I know. I've been hoping to meet you."

"I'm sorry for just dropping by, but I need to talk with Emmitt."

"He's at work today."

"On a Sunday?"

"He's a Y2K consultant. It was an emergency. Something about the end of the world as we know it."

"I didn't know his power reached that far."

"Oh, yes. Coach fights enemies and evil on many fronts." Coco's smile was faint, and she didn't move. She was now wondering—as many before her also had—how such a sweet person could be with such a lunatic. Biscuit, for her part, sensed Coco's need to talk, and understood, of course, why she was there. "Please. Come in," she said.

Biscuit and Coach's apartment, like their relationship, was an odd and enchanting contrast in styles, and Coco only needed a moment inside to take that in. Above the sofa was an art print by Cézanne, while above the chair was a poster of Roger Bannister breaking the four-minute mile. On the end table was a vase with roses, while near the door there was a pile of dirty sneakers. The lamp shade in the corner was an exquisite Victorian fabric, while the light switch on the wall was a picture of Bill Clinton, with the switch knob serving as his nose.

As soon as Coco entered the apartment, she noticed a peculiar smell coming from the kitchen. It was an unpleasant combination of odors that reminded her of medicine and detergent. She didn't want to be rude, but was too curious not to ask, "What's that smell?"

Biscuit lifted her nose and breathed in the air. "Oh," she said, "that's a sports drink Coach is working on. It's called Coach-Aid. I'm so used to it I don't even smell it anymore." Biscuit lifted her nose and breathed in again. "That batch needs some work." She laughed. "May I get you something to drink?" She laughed again. "No Coach-Aid, I promise."

"No. Thank you," Coco said. "I'm fine."

And Coco *was* fine now. Just a few moments with Biscuit had calmed her. There was a peaceful space around Biscuit, and everyone who came within that space felt their tension drain away. To the same degree, Biscuit absorbed Coco's tension and transformed it into her own concern. They sat together on the sofa, and Biscuit placed her hand gently on Coco's knee. "What is it?"

Coco still had the same thoughts about Coach, but now the meaning was different. She saw the humor in Coach's audaciousness, and in her own reaction to it. How could one be upset with Biscuit there? She gave Biscuit a self-deprecating smile before she spoke. "I guess I came over to tell your husband off. He's been horrible to me."

"What did he do now?"

"I guess he didn't do anything. It was just talk, really. He told me to stay away from his runners. He meant Bob and Andy. They both like me, and he thinks I'm messing with their heads."

"Are you?"

"Maybe I am. I've been testing them, to understand their feelings for me. I have them both upset."

"Tell me what you think about them."

"Well, I like them both, but I don't know which one is right for me. They're both handsome, but they have such different personalities. Bob is outgoing and confident, even brash, and Andy is quiet and reserved, almost defensive. He doesn't trust me, and I don't know if I can trust in him."

"And you trust Bob?"

"He's done everything I've asked of him, without hesitation. The only thing I dislike is his sarcasm and his practical jokes, but maybe he'll grow out of that. I think he's a diamond in the rough."

"I think he's a golf ball in the rough," Biscuit said. "Coach has told me about him, about some of the pranks he's pulled and things he's said. Even Coach only just puts up with him because he's a great runner and helps the team."

"But he's kind and generous with his time," Coco said. "He even went to Pittsburgh to visit my mom when I asked him to."

"And what did your mom say about him?"

"She said she wouldn't make up my mind for me, that I had to do that myself, but I think that Bob going all the way to Pittsburgh for me says a lot about his character."

"Coco," Biscuit said, in a tone that was meant to slap her to her senses. "What does Bob do for a living?"

"He's a salesman."

"Exactly. He's a salesman. He sells people on things, and he travels all over the East Coast doing it. Coach is always worried about Bob missing a workout or a race because of his travel. So do you think it was any big deal for Bob to hop on a plane to Pittsburgh? It was just another day at the office for him," Biscuit said. "He was just closing another deal."

"I didn't think about it that way."

"Is he really generous, or is he just willing to do what it takes to get what he wants? Words can lie, but actions can lie too. And even if he is sincere, is he the right guy for you?" Biscuit added.

"I don't know. I'm more attracted to Andy, but he's emotionally distant. I know he really likes me; I can see it in his eyes. But he won't let go of something. He won't open himself up. And yet he's jealous of Bob. They can't stand the sight of each other now."

"You've got them butting horns, and Coach is trying to get them ready for cross-country. That's why Coach is upset."

"You call him Coach?"

"He wants me to. He *prefers* it." Biscuit smiled. "He says I can call him Emmitt in private, if I want to, but that in front of other people, especially HOHAs, he would prefer that I call him Coach."

Coco laughed. "And you do it?"

"It's a small thing," Biscuit said. "And I love him."

"How did you know? How did you know that you loved him?"

"Well, my family's from the Midwest, but I was inexplicably drawn to the East Coast. I couldn't explain it, but that was my first clue that something was happening, so I was paying attention, trying to understand "why here?" and when I came to Hoboken, one of the first things I saw was one of Coach's flyers for the club. It said that the HOHAs was the premier running club of the East Coast. That amused me, the word 'premier.' And when I came to my first run, I saw Coach showing another runner how to tie his shoelaces. I mean he was actually down on his knees tying the guy's shoes and instructing him on the proper procedure. He was completely absorbed in it. As if how a runner tied his shoes really mattered. Then he stood up, and I saw those nerdy glasses and his goofy grin. I just knew then why I had come east, moved into Hoboken, and joined the HOHAs. It was to be with him."

"That's amazing."

"You'll know too. You just need to pay attention to the signs. You need to listen."

"I just wish that Emmitt would stay out of it. Why can't he mind his own business? He's like a fanatic. Why does he even care?"

Biscuit didn't mind hearing Coco complain about Coach, because the things she was complaining about were the things she loved about him the most: his care, his commitment, his passion.

"Do you know what he said to me once?" Biscuit said. "We'd only gone out a few times, and we were down by the river on a moonlit night. Coach was unusually quiet, and I was thinking that he'd fallen silent because he was thinking about us and was feeling the romance of the moment. I said, 'What are you thinking?' and he said, 'About the future.' I'm thinking that it's about *our* future, together, and I said, 'What about the future?' and he said, 'The future is polypropylene.'"

"What's polypropylene?"

"That's what I said, and Coach spent the next twenty minutes telling me all about it. It's this new synthetic material that wicks the sweat away from your skin. It keeps a runner drier and cooler, so he can achieve ultimate performance."

"How romantic."

"Yes, and all that time I was imagining that the future was love and marriage."

"Or even solar energy. Or genetic cloning."

"But no. It's polypropylene, and I didn't have a clue."

"It *wicks* the sweat?" Coco said with a smile.

"Yes, it wicks it away, which allows a runner to stay cooler and expend his energy on the running process instead of the cooling process. Coach had tears in his eyes."

"You've got a live one."

"Don't I?"

"Men!"

"They'll drive you nuts if you let them. At my sorority, we had a tradition that whenever a girl met a new guy, she would buy a quart of her favorite ice cream and keep it in the freezer, and whenever the guy did something stupid or thoughtless, instead of getting all crazy, she would just go to the freezer and have a spoonful of her ice cream. Our freezer was full of quarts of ice cream with the names of guys on them."

"So that's the secret. Just buy a quart of ice cream whenever you go out with a guy?"

"No, as soon as you first *meet* a guy that you like. One girl, Christine, went through an entire quart before this guy even got around to asking her out." Biscuit thought for a moment. "Christine went through a lot of ice cream, but she didn't hold the record though."

"Who held the record?"

"Darlene, a freshman, went through fifteen quarts of Vanilla Fudge before she finally broke up with her boyfriend. She decided he was such an idiot that she was getting fat."

"How many quarts did you go through with Coach?"

"Well, I had three spoonfuls when I learned that the future was polypropylene, but I was still on the first quart by the time he proposed."

"When did he propose to you?"

"Three weeks after we met."

"Oh my God!"

"Yes, it happened fast."

"I think that's the best," Coco said. "My mom told me to be careful though. She told me to find a man who would be there for me in good times and bad."

"That's great advice."

"But is it possible to find someone who's perfect?"

"I doubt it. But we don't fall in love with perfection. We fall in love with a person's weaknesses and vulnerabilities. Their needs provide a place for us to get inside. They're cracks that we can fill."

"My mom said that some men get married simply because they can't take care of themselves; they don't so much need a wife as a live-in maid."

"That's true too," Biscuit said. "We don't want a man that's too cracked."

They both laughed.

"I feel better already," Coco said.

"Good," Biscuit said. "Just take your time, and don't let Coach push you around. He doesn't dislike you really. It's just that the cross-country championship is his world."

Coco noticed the ceramic statuette of the Elf on the coffee table. "Is that the famous Elf that Emmitt is always talking about, the Holy Grail of running?"

"Yes, we're the proud parents."

"My God, to hear Emmitt talk you'd think it was the Heisman Trophy or the Stanley Cup." Coco laughed. "It's just a lawn ornament. It should be on someone's grass, along with a fake windmill and some plastic ducks."

Biscuit laughed too. It was a delighted laugh of agreement that contained a trace of nervous shock. Biscuit had watched Coach fondle and pamper the Elf almost as long as she had known him. He gazed at it in admiration and moved it about the room, from mantle to bookcase to coffee table, to give it the perfect place and the most accentuating light. In watching him, she herself had come to view it as a valuable possession and now, hearing Coco call it a lawn ornament was like hearing the kid say that the emperor had no clothes.

"It's the ugliest thing I've ever seen," Coco said.

Biscuit laughed again. "Don't let Coach hear you say that."

"Yeah, well," Coco said. She reached over and picked up the Elf from the coffee table. She looked at its chalky outlines and its garish colors, truly seeing the Elf for the cartoonish creation it was. "It's still the ugliest statue I've ever seen."

"There is one worse," Biscuit said, and told Coco about the pink ceramic cat at her sorority, the one called Pussy, and all the trips it had made.

Coco laughed.

"We had so much fun with it," Biscuit said.

"Where's Pussy now?"

"The last I heard, Pussy made it onto the Great Wall of China."

"What fun!" Coco said. She put the Elf back on the coffee table and bobbled it a bit.

"Be careful," Biscuit said. "If anything happened to the Elf, Coach would go out of his mind."

"He would?"

"Are you kidding me?"

Coco, with exaggerated care, placed the Elf down. "Sending a statue on a trip," she mused aloud. "What a great idea."

Coco had arrived feeling angry, but when she left, she had a new way of looking at things, and saw the opportunity for fun. At the door, Biscuit smiled and said to her, "Don't forget to buy a quart of ice cream."

"I'll need two quarts," Coco said. She thought for a moment and then laughed. "I'll get Rocky Road for Andy and Chunky Monkey for Bob."

47. Party of Two

COCO'S CHAT with Biscuit had put Bad Bob's behavior in perspective, and now she had decided to have a serious talk with him. She was bothered by Bob's practical jokes, and by the immaturity of his humor, and she wanted to see if he could clean up his act for her. They were meeting for dinner the following evening, and Coco thought that would be a good opportunity to discuss it.

When they got to the restaurant, there was a considerable crowd at the door. "It looks like it might take a while," Bob said. "Shall we wait?"

"Yes. Let's wait," Coco said. "Anyway, we need to talk."

"I'll just get our name on the list," Bob said.

Bob went up to the hostess and left his name while Coco held the last two seats in the crowded waiting room. "It'll just be a few minutes," Bob said when he returned. "I told the girl that I have diabetes and need to eat right away."

"That's exactly what I wanted to talk with you about," Coco said. "Everything is just a game or a joke to you."

"I'm just having fun."

"Yes, but did you ever notice that your fun is always at the expense of others?"

"No it's not."

"Remember at the movies last week. The guy in front of us had a hooded jacket, and you poured your leftover popcorn into his hood."

"It was a harmless joke."

"You're not a boy anymore, Bob. You should grow out of that." Coco looked at Bob intently. "You're not serious enough for me," she said. "I think that for you, even love is just a game."

"Coco, I do love you and I can change. I swear. Just give me a chance. I promise: no more jokes, no more goofing around. I've never met anyone like you. I just need time to adjust."

"Bob, one more smart-aleck comment, one more practical joke, and I've had it."

"That's it," Bob said. "I'm a changed man."

"Do you promise?"

"On all that I hold sacred," Bob said.

"I mean it," Coco said. "Consider yourself on probation. One more silly prank and we're done for good."

"You're looking at Mr. Serious," Bob said.

Coco looked doubtful, but she said, "OK."

Bob looked anxious then, as if he'd just remembered something. "Let me check on the wait," he said.

Bob was just getting up when the hostess stepped from the podium into the waiting area. All eyes turned expectantly to her and then to Bob as she looked directly at him and paused nervously. She looked at her clipboard to read the next name. She wanted everyone to see that she was reading the name, and not just making it up. The look on her face was an odd mixture of embarrassment and determined duty. Bob himself had an unusual expression that was a mix of boyish anticipation and manly regret. Everyone was waiting. The hostess took one last look at the clipboard and then again at Bob, and then in a firm voice she announced into the mike on her lapel that carried through the speakers positioned in all corners of the waiting room, "Mr. and Mrs. Harry Buns, party of two."

48. Matchmaking

NOT ONE of the HOHAs was surprised when Coco dumped Bad Bob. She was an intelligent girl, and was bound to come to her senses sooner or later. It was Bob's reaction to being dumped that took the HOHAs by surprise. Everyone had thought that he would just brush it off and move on. He was too self-absorbed to take it personally, too vain to think that there was anything more to his rejection than Coco's own bad judgment. But to the contrary, and to the amazement of every HOHA who'd been keeping an eye on the affair, Bob went down, and went down hard.

Nobody had thought that Bad Bob had a heart, until it became obvious that it was broken. He appeared at one HOHAs run with a dozen roses, and he got down on one knee and asked Coco to marry him. This was just the type of juvenile gesture that Coco disliked, and she tossed the roses into the crowd of onlooking HOHAs, throwing them over her shoulder as if they were a bouquet thrown by a bride who wouldn't be a bride at a wedding that was not to be.

Bad Bob went through days of reclusion, and his mood soon affected his running. His poor performances in a couple of races increased Coach's concern, and he talked with Bob, but as good as he was as a coach for running, he was a poor coach for love. His advice was full of clichés about getting back on the horse, fish in the sea, and even dogs having their day. In the entirely predictable stages of loss, Bad Bob had already passed from sad to sullen, and his response to Coach was equally predictable. "Who the fuck do you think you are?" he yelled one time, "Miss Fucking Lonely Hearts?"

Coach complained to Biscuit. "Everything was going great," he said. "I had the team right on track, and now there's this."

"Now there's what?" Biscuit said.

"Love," Coach said. "Andy lovesick and Bad Bob brokenhearted. Everything I've worked for could go down the tubes, and talk is getting me nowhere. I've got to do something."

"Just let nature run its course," Biscuit advised again. "Besides, what are you going to do?"

Coach already had a plan. He said, "You know how firemen sometimes need to use fire to fight fire?"

"Yeah," Biscuit said doubtfully.

"Well, I've got to fight love with love."

"What do you mean?"

"I've got to do the almost impossible," Coach said, relishing the challenge. "I've got to find another girl for Bad Bob."

Once the initial excitement over his fight-love-with-love strategy had worn off, and Coach had fended off the objections and ignored the warnings of Biscuit, he was left with the problem of just how to find a girlfriend for someone as difficult as Bob. Coach decided to wage an all-out onslaught on love. As he put it, he would attack by air, by land, and by sea. He used his own money to enroll Bad Bob—without Bob's knowledge or consent—in several dating services, and he placed personal ads in the local newspapers, on the bulletin boards of businesses, and even in the PennySaver. All of Coach's ads were variations on the same theme.

Successful SM seeks SF for romance, marriage, children, and eternal love. Love to cuddle and take long walks holding hands.

Coach knew that the real Bob wouldn't cooperate, and that in his pissy mood would scare away any decent girl that Coach would find for him, so he decided to screen the girls himself and to sell the most likely of them on Bob's good qualities and hidden potential.

Coach had a picture of Bob from one of the HOHAs parties, and the picture of the young, handsome Bob, along with Coach's description of Bob's successful career, love of wholesome activities, and unique sense of humor, made Bob sound like a real catch. Coach had cast a wide net, and soon had a long list of girls who were eager to meet him. He reviewed the candidates, looking for girls who would be pretty enough to get Bob's attention and yet simple enough to overlook Bob's obvious drawbacks. From the list, Coach culled his "finalists" and arranged a series of introductory "dates."

The dates were to be at Maxwell's, and Coach set them up in one-hour blocks, on the Saturday and Sunday afternoons of three consecutive weekends. He had twenty-seven candidates in all, and drew a strange confidence from the knowledge that only one of them had to be right. The scary part of this confidence was Coach's willingness to accept that the other twenty-six dates could go bad.

Coach reserved his own table at Maxwell's, and on that first Saturday, with the profiles of the candidates for that day in hand, asked the headwaiter to direct any young woman asking for Bob to him.

All of these dates played out differently, of course, but most of them went something like this …

The headwaiter would escort the girl to Coach's table, and there would be initial confusion on the girl's part as Coach rose to greet her. Coach was a good-looking guy, but he wasn't nearly as handsome as Bad Bob, and was far from what Bob's picture had led the girls to expect. The girl would invariably comment that Bob didn't look much like his picture.

"We'll get to that shortly," Coach would say.

Coach would have the waiter attend to the girl's order, and then he would begin the interview. "Tell me a little about yourself."

The girl would be surprised by Coach's approach, but would comply. Coach would listen patiently at first, but when he'd heard enough—usually at about the time the girl's food or drink was served—he would abruptly interject, "What do you think about running?"

"Excuse me?"

"Running. The sport. What do you think about it?"

"It's good exercise, I guess. I don't run myself."

"Of course you don't," Coach would say dismissively, "but if you had a boyfriend who was a runner, would you interfere with his practice of the sport?"

"No."

"There will be races every weekend," Coach warned.

"What are you talking about?"

"Bob, the guy I'm fixing you up with, he's a runner; he'll need some quality time for training and racing."

"Do you mean that I'm not here on a date with you? That you asked me here in order to set me up with one of your friends?"

"Oh, he's not my friend, he's one of my runners."

"Who are you, anyway?"

"I'm Emmitt F. Bean, the founder, first president, and coach of the Hoboken Harriers Running Club."

"What's that got to do with anything?"

"This guy, Bob, he's in my running club, and I'm finding a girlfriend for him."

"What are you, his pimp?"

"I'm no such thing."

"Then why doesn't he get his own dates?"

"Are you going to be difficult?"

"I'm going to be however I damn well please to be."

"Well then, I'm going to have to disqualify you," Coach would say, and would then actually cross the girl's name off the list he had and write a single adjective to describe her: impudent, abrasive, unrealistic, or temperamental.

The girls would invariably become alarmed at the preposterousness of this. One girl said, "I want you to know that I told two different friends that I was meeting you here this afternoon."

"That's clever," Coach said, "but you shouldn't be proud of your dating skills."

"Why not?"

"Because it's a sign of failure."

"What are you talking about now?"

Then Coach, with the logic and insensitivity of the computer nerd that he was, would say, "Being wise at dating is like being the career home-run leader of the minor leagues." Coach would raise his eyebrows, waiting for the girl to acknowledge his point, before underlining that point himself. "And you're supposed to move up from the minors, not be a star there."

That was the point at which Coach would get slapped with a purse, or have a drink thrown in his face. The busboys got to where as soon as they heard a broken plate or glass or any other sign of disturbance they would immediately head to Coach's table. Coach was invariably baffled by this turn of events, and would hold out a HOHAs business card to the girl. "In case you have a change of heart," he'd say.

"You're out of your fucking mind," the girl would yell, and then everyone in the restaurant would be looking at them.

Coach, usually annoyed as well by this point, would add fuel to the flame. "Do you like skinny men?" he'd say.

"What?"

"Runners are skinny," Coach would say. "Do skinny men make you hot?"

Then there would be more yelling and often an overturned chair as the girl rushed away. Coach was on the verge of being banned from Maxwell's before he finally, albeit reluctantly, abandoned his plan.

49. In My Sleep

AFTER THEIR runs together, as part of his cooldown, Andy often walked with Moses back to the salvage yard, and would help Moses carry any of the junk he had spotted and retrieved along the way. One night in late August, they were carrying two folding lawn chairs that Moses had dug from a sidewalk dumpster. They were a few blocks from the salvage yard when Moses heard something and put out a hand to stop Andy. "Did you hear that?"

It was a cloudy, moonless night, and they were a long way from the nearest street lamp. Andy looked for the sound first, saw nothing, and then listened in the darkness. "I don't hear anything, Moses," he said.

"It came from over here." Moses was already moving into the deeper darkness of an empty lot nearby. Andy followed, and out of the darkness, near the brick wall of the building that bordered the lot, a face turned toward them. It was a man's face, strangely white, as if it reflected light from an unknown source. "He's dead," the man said. As he said it, he turned his face away, and the light from it illuminated another man, lying lifeless at his feet.

Moses stepped forward, unafraid, and knelt next to the dead man. "He's still warm," Moses said. "Are you sure?"

"Oh yes," the man said. "I'm quite sure."

"We should call the police," Andy said.

"I'll see to that." The man held his hand out to Andy, and Andy shook it. Then he held his hand out to Moses, and Moses shook it too. He said to Moses. "A terrible way to go, isn't it? Alone, on the street."

Moses was still huddled near the dead man, looking down at him. He was a street person: stubbled beard, Goodwill clothes, unkempt hair. Moses had seen fallen bums before, men and women. He'd seen them frozen stiff, and he'd seen them ripe and bloated. All those dead lay on the landscape of Moses' mind. He knew the bodies weren't everything, merely something left behind, and he imagined the wings that had taken their true selves away. The bodies, however, still filled him with dread. To the man's question, Moses replied simply, "Yes."

"Can you think of a worse way to die?"

Moses had given this question nights of thought over the years, and his answer came readily. "I wouldn't want to die in a storm at sea, sinking to the dark bottom, and I wouldn't want to be lost and freezing in the woods. That would be a lonely and slow way to go. And I wouldn't want to die by knife, feeling my own blood on my skin, or by suffocation."

The corners of the man's lips turned up, just slightly, as if he found Moses' fears amusing. "Yes, I see," he said. "And just how is it you would like to die, Moses?"

Moses was about to answer when Andy grabbed at his arm and pulled him away. "Let's go," he said. He hurried Moses from the lot, keeping his hand on Moses' arm until they were a good block away. Andy had looked back only once and had seen the man's illuminated face watching and smiling at them. "That man," Andy said. "Do you know him?"

"No, I never saw him before."

"Then how did he know your name?"

"I don't know."

"Did you feel how cold his hand was?"

"No," Moses said, "it felt all right to me."

"The whole time we were there," Andy said, "that guy was giving me the creeps. I felt cold. It was like a bad dream."

Andy was indeed shivering now, and was unsteady on his feet. Moses unfolded the chair he was carrying and set it down on the sidewalk. Then he took Andy's chair from him and set it down next to his own.

"Let's sit down for a moment," Moses said.

They would have made an odd sight, if anyone had been around to see them, a young man and an old man, sitting in lawn chairs on the sidewalk in the darkness of the night.

Moses looked with concern at his young friend and said, "When I was a boy, and I had a bad dream, my mama told me that the best way to forget about it was to go right back to sleep and have a good dream right over the top of it. You've had good dreams, haven't you, Andy?"

"Sure."

"Do you remember any of them?"

"Yes," Andy said. "There was one dream that I had over and over again when I was a boy. It was the first sign I had that I would be a runner."

"Tell me that dream, Andy."

"I would dream that I was running down the street and that with each stride I was going farther and higher, until eventually I was soaring above the ground. I wasn't flying, and I was glad that I wasn't. I was running. It was all in slow motion and under my control. With each stride, I would touch down lightly and then soar again. People saw me and looked on in wonder. Gravity itself couldn't hold me; nothing could keep me down. In that dream, when I looked down from above, all my problems looked small. I wasn't afraid at all."

"That's a great dream, Andy."

"I had it a lot after my mom left, and then after my dad died, and then occasionally afterwards. Then it stopped, and I haven't dreamt it in years."

"Maybe that's because you're living it," Moses said. "You've achieved a lot with your running, Andy."

"No, Moses," Andy said. "I've never come close to the way I felt in that dream."

"You will."

"Did you know that Coco stopped seeing Bad Bob?"

Moses wasn't one to gossip, or to even pay attention to it, but even he knew that. He nodded.

"I thought that would clear the way for me, but Coco is still keeping me at a distance."

"We don't win when others fail," Moses said. "We only win when we don't fail our self."

"But I don't know how to win her heart."

"Yes you do," Moses said.

Andy said nothing, and Moses went on. "Coach had something to say about that. He told me that when I did my training runs, I had to visualize the race. I had to see myself racing well and finishing strong. He said that in the race, I would fulfill my vision." Moses paused. "I've tried it," he added, "and it works."

"Yes, I know it does," Andy said. "I do it in my training too."

All the great ones do it. They see it and practice it, before it even happens. In practice, they make it so real that their adrenaline surges, and they practice controlling that too. Before the race has started, they've already run it.

"Buddy says the same thing in his own way. He says we have to dream things before they can happen."

"I know."

"Then you know what to do then."

"Yes."

"Coach and Buddy are the smartest guys I've ever known," Moses said. Then he chuckled. "Maybe that's why they can't get along. Can you picture them spending a day together, Andy? Both of them talking and neither one of them listening?"

Andy could picture it, and laughed.

"You see," Moses said, "it helps to think of a good dream."

"You're right," Andy said. "Thank you."

"We'll thank my mama for that one."

They got up then, picked up their chairs, and walked on in silence until they got to the salvage yard. Andy handed his chair to Moses, and they said good night. Andy was still pensive, and had taken only a few steps toward home before he stopped and turned back toward Moses. "Moses," he said, "how *would* you like to die?"

Moses had his answer to this question too, and said softly and without hesitation, "While I'm dreaming. In my sleep."

HOHAs *in* Love

DREAMS

The clock is the last thing taken down at a race.
After the last runner or walker comes in, the race staff
dismantle it and take it from the finish line.
It's a sad thing to watch, the aftermath of an event.
It's like staying in your seat after a play and watching
the stage crew take down the scenery. Lost is the
illusion of something real. Dismantled, packed away,
all signs removed, it's as if your race—your play, your
life even—never happened. It's as if it were all a dream.

HOHAs *in* Love

50. Made in Heaven

"I TOLD you so," Biscuit said.

All the girls that Coach had interviewed for Bad Bob were absolutely terrible as far as Coach was concerned, but at the same time, he had to admit, they were entirely too good for Bob. "It's Bob's shitty character," Coach lamented. "I didn't have anything to work with."

Coach was pacing back and forth across the living room while Biscuit sat on the couch. "I couldn't just let the girls meet him right off, could I, without preparing them first?"

"I told you to just stay out of it."

Coach mused, "Coco is terrible herself, but compared with Bad Bob she's an angel. I'm surprised that Bob lasted as long as he did with her."

"Just stay out of it," Biscuit repeated.

"As much as I want to get Bad Bob back on his feet," Coach persisted, "there's no girl nasty enough to deserve him."

Then, as if this episode of Coach's life were a Saturday-morning cartoon and a light bulb had suddenly come on above his head, a look of wondrous enlightenment appeared on his face. "Darla!"

"Oh no!" Biscuit said. "You wouldn't."

Darla! All brilliant ideas are beautiful in their simplicity, and Coach only wondered then why he hadn't thought of it before. There was such poetic justice in it, too. No two human beings could deserve each other more, or be better matched in their nastiness. If they had been around at the time of the great flood, Coach thought, Noah would have marched them together onto the Ark.

"Oh yes," Coach said. "I would."

Now the only thing left to do was to get the two lovebirds to meet and mate, but that too would be a problem. Coach had worked out a schedule with Edsel so that he rarely had to work with Darla, and outside of the store, he had been lucky enough never to have run into her. He didn't know Darla's haunts and habits, nor did he want to know them, and as for Bad Bob, he'd never set foot in Edsel's store, because that was where Coach encouraged the HOHAs to meet, and Bob was too contrary to do what anyone, especially Coach, wanted him to do. But it is in the nature of human thought that one far-fetched notion is often accompanied by another, and Coach immediately hit upon a far-fetched plan to bring the two together.

Coach told Bob that he had been working on a new track program for him, a cutting-edge series of workouts used by the Kenyans, perfect for Bob's running strengths. He told Bob that he was sure these workouts would catapult Bob's running to a new level. Bob was skeptical, so Coach played on his ego and his competitiveness with Andy. He lied and said that Andy had asked for the program himself, but that he had told Andy that he didn't have the natural endurance for a program as rigorous as this one. The ploy worked, and Bob was immediately interested. Coach told him that if he stopped by Snail's Pace early on Saturday morning, he could pick up the training program then. Coach knew that Darla would be there to stock a new shipment that had come in and that Edsel wouldn't be in until after ten. When Bob arrived, Coach figured he would make an excuse to leave the two of them alone, and then he would just let nature do its nasty work.

That Saturday morning, Bob arrived at Snail's Pace right on schedule. While he and Coach were talking, Darla ignored Bob, treating him with the same haughty air of disdain that she dispensed to all customers, and with the double dose that she saved for anyone who appeared to know Coach. Coach watched Bob's reaction carefully. Bob was a handsome guy, not used to being ignored by any girl, and Coach could see that he was assessing the challenge.

Darla was wearing a leather bodice that revealed an ample cleavage, and although Coach didn't like to give her credit for anything, even he had to admit that she looked good. Bob eyed her from head to toe, taking in not only her fiery attitude but every part of her sensuous body. When Darla passed close by, Coach took the opportunity to introduce them. Then he told Bob that he would go get his track program from the back room. When Bob squared off toward Darla, Coach ducked behind one of the shoe racks, from where he could watch and hear everything that was said.

"So, you're from Dublin," Bob said. "I like Irish beer. Does that mean we have something in common?"

Coach braced himself for the firestorm.

"Yeah, we're both in a bloody running store," Darla said. "But I have to work here. What's your excuse?"

Bob looked around and saw that Coach had disappeared. "I'm the best runner in the state of New Jersey," he said. "One of the best in the nation."

Behind the shoeboxes, Coach was shaking his head at Bob's unbelievable ego.

"Oh, you're such an amazing catch then," Darla said.

"Exactly," Bob said. "But you don't have to worry about that, because you're not my type."

"And what type is that?" Darla said. "Gullible?"

"No, I prefer a girl who can see and hear, and you're obviously blind to beauty and deaf to charm."

"Well, now there's a crock," she said.

"Maybe I'm the answer to your prayers."

"Yeah, maybe that's it," Darla said. "Or maybe you're a little prick looking for a jerk."

Bob laughed and, without hesitation, advanced. "I bet if you'd smile, you might even be pretty."

Things weren't going well by Coach's assessment, but it was a good sign that Darla was still even talking to Bob. Her reply, although rude, lacked her normal tone of hostility. "What do you do when you're not running around like a dolt?" she said.

Bob belched.

Coach closed his eyes. He couldn't look. Who knew how Darla would react to that. Her response was a giggle, and Coach opened his eyes again. She was still standing in front of Bob, her body language was receptive, and Bob was smiling. Coach now understood Bob's tack. A girl like Darla couldn't be chatted up in any polite and conventional way; she had to be grossed out and amused.

"I'm a male model," Bob said.

Darla laughed, and the faintest smile snuck onto her face. Coach was encouraged now. Darla never talked to anyone for this long. And she never smiled.

"What do you model?" she said.

"Underwear."

Darla laughed again, louder this time, and her smile stayed longer. Coach had to admit that she was pretty when she smiled. Her smile was charming in its unpracticed awkwardness.

"Bikini briefs," Bob added.

"Oh yeah," she said. "Can I see one of your ads?"

"You can see the real thing," Bob said. "I'll give you a private session. I might even take you out on a date."

"A date?" Darla said. "Is that what you call it? You just want to take me to dinner and then get into my panties."

Darla waited for Bob's response, and Bob flashed his nasty grin. "Who said anything about dinner?" he said.

Darla couldn't hide her pleasure and that uncharacteristic smile slipped across her face again. It was plain that she liked Bob, and that she was already halfway charmed. "You really know how to wow a girl, don't you?" she said.

"But I'll tell you what," Bob said magnanimously. "I *will* make you breakfast in the morning. How do you like your eggs?"

That pretty smile of Darla's snuck back again, and without missing a beat, she stared at him and said, "Unfertilized."

Coach was telling all this to Biscuit later, and he repeated, "I swear to God, she looked right at him and said, 'Unfertilized.'"

"And what did Bob say to that?"

"He didn't say anything for a while. He had this look on his face of half surprise and half admiration, as if he'd finally met his match. It was perfect. I couldn't have hoped for more. I was standing behind the shoeboxes and I had this epiphany: 'There is perfect balance. For every Darla, there's a Bad Bob. God does have a plan.'"

"And that would make you one of God's helpers?"

"I guess you could say that, yes."

Biscuit rolled her eyes.

"But I can't rest with my success," Coach said. "I still have more of God's work to do."

The attraction between Bad Bob and Darla took root, and there was an immediate improvement in Bob's disposition and racing. All the HOHAs, except Coach, were surprised by this turn of events. For Coach, it was just another testament to the infallible holy trinity of planning, preparation, and performance. Coach was emboldened by his initial success in the field of love, and figured if he could match up an A-1 jerk-off like Bad Bob with the most god-awful female that God had ever inflicted upon the Earth, then nothing, but nothing, was beyond his matchmaking skills, and smoothing the path of love for a nice guy like Andy should be a jog in the park.

51. The Elf

BY JULY, Coach was already worn out by all his Y2K work and his evening and weekend training of the HOHAs. To the casual onlooker, he may have seemed like the same old crazy Coach, but the HOHAs who knew him well saw the signs of his stress. Some of his mannerisms had become nervous tics, and his passions had crept their way up the scale to the point of obsessions. Throughout that summer and into the fall, he brought the Elf to club meetings. He thought of it as an inspiration to the team, and as the symbol of the HOHAs' greatest victory. At the July club meeting, while he talked about the team training and upcoming races, he twice held the Elf aloft, as proof of what the HOHAs had achieved and would achieve again.

Coach was also showing lapses in judgment. He thought so highly of Andy as a runner and as a person that it was inconceivable to him that any problem between him and Coco could be anything but Coco's fault. He concluded that if he was to smooth the path of love for them and get Andy back to a healthy state of mind, all he needed to do was have another talk with Coco, and so at the conclusion of the meeting, Coach, Elf in hand, took Coco aside to do just that.

"I'm sorry things didn't work out between you and Bad Bob," he said. "I know I wasn't encouraging, but I don't see how you can blame me for what happened." Coach acted as if their previous conversation had been only a small misunderstanding, and that Coco would accept his sincerity. "But as far as you and Andy are concerned, I want you to know that I won't stand in your way." Coach held the Elf up and forward slightly, as if he were anointing her with it. "You have my blessing."

Coco was almost struck speechless by what she had just heard. She thought then of her conversation with Biscuit, of how much she liked her, and of how it would be best to call upon her sense of humor. "That's what I live for," she said.

Coach, seeing that as highly likely, didn't come close to picking up on her sarcasm, and carried right on. "Andy's a great person, and one of the greatest runners I've ever seen," he said. "You're a lucky girl."

"Don't I know it."

"But he needs to keep his primary focus on his training now," Coach said. "I hope you'll understand that. If you're going to be his girlfriend, you should support him completely in his running."

"Oh, I will."

"Great," Coach said. "I'm glad we had this talk."

Coco shone a beatific and grateful smile on Coach. "Oh," she said, "so am I."

Andy walked Coco home from the meeting that night, and she told him about her encounter with Coach. She also told him about his previous lecture to her.

"You're kidding."

"Nope. It seems I'm a lucky girl, because you're a perfect guy."

Andy had been anxious to apologize to Coco, and he saw this as his opportunity. "I've been thinking about what you asked me to do before. I know that it was important to you, and I should have done it for you. I wish that I had."

"That's good," Coco said, "because I have something else that I want you to do for me now."

"What is it?"

"I want you to kidnap Coach's Elf."

Andy laughed. "That would hit Coach where it hurts the most."

"He deserves it," Coco said. "He's been completely over the top with that goofy Elf and his pep talks."

"What do you want me to do with it?"

Coco thought for a moment and then smiled. Biscuit's story about Pussy had first given her the idea, and she'd liked how the girls took pictures of Pussy and brought them back to the sorority. "Well, Mr. Bell," she said, speaking as if she were delivering critical instructions, "your mission, should you choose to accept it, is to free the Elf, take a picture of it in front of the Liberty Bell, and bring the picture back to me."

"Is that all?"

"And don't tell Coach anything about it."

"Why didn't you have Bob do this?" Andy said. There was a trace of hurt and resentment in his voice.

"Because I just thought of it," Coco said evenly. "And because I want *you* to do it. Besides," Coco laughed at the thought, "Bob would be the first person that Coach would suspect."

"That's true."

"So, will you do it for me?"

"Consider it done."

"You won't have any trouble getting the thing?"

"No. I know where he keeps it."

"In a secret underground vault, surrounded by votive candles?"

"How'd you know?"

"A wild guess," Coco said. "Thank you, Andy."

"You're welcome."

"Don't you want to know why?"

"Only if you want to tell me."

"Well, I want you to be true to your word, and I want to know that I can depend on you," she said. "And I want to teach Coach a lesson."

"It'll be fun to play a joke on him."

They'd reached the steps to Coco's apartment. "It'll be perfect," she said. Coco raised her hand, and Andy gave her a high five. "So I'll see you when you get back from Philadelphia?"

"Yes," Andy said and smiled. "When I bring you the broomstick of the Wicked Witch of the East."

Whenever Coach went out for a run, he hid his apartment key on a ledge above a window in the foyer of his building. Andy had seen him put the key there when they'd gone on runs together, so he didn't expect much trouble in abducting the Elf. He simply waited until the next evening, when both Coach and Biscuit were at the HOHAs run, and got into the apartment and out again in no time, carrying the Elf in an old grocery bag.

Andy had no car, and had thought of taking the train to Philadelphia, but then he decided to ask Chuck to take him. He'd swear Chuck to secrecy, and then they'd have some fun and make a day of it. Chuck was up for it, and said they could take the laundry van.

"That's perfect, Chuck. You wouldn't happen to have a camera, would you?"

"My mom has one of those Polaroid ones."

"Can you bring it?"

"Chuck have to bring everything?" Chuck said in mock vexation.

"I'm going to pay for the gas," Andy said. "And I'll buy you lunch."

"Anything Chuck wants?"

"Anything you want."

"Chuck like steak."

"Then steak it is."

"All right!" Chuck said. "Philly cheese steak." He nodded his heady comically, as if he were getting a sweet deal.

Andy had never been to Philadelphia, but Chuck knew his way around. They went to the Liberty Bell right off and got the picture out of the way. The picture was good; well, as good as you could expect of an elf and a bell, at least.

Chuck had to sit on the ground and hold the Elf up above his head so that Andy could get both the Elf and the Bell in the picture. Chuck's hand could be seen beneath the Elf, but the important point was that it was definitely *the* HOHAs Elf in front of *the* Liberty Bell.

After they'd had lunch, Chuck took Andy to see the spot where Sylvester Stallone had run up the steps and raised his arms in triumph in *Rocky*. His footprints were carved into the granite at the top of the steps, with "Rocky" carved above them. Andy and Chuck took pictures of each other standing in those footprints with their arms raised in celebration of their own success. That evening, when they got back to Hoboken, Andy called Coco and told her the deed was done.

"Fantastic," Coco said.

Andy felt fantastic too. He felt like Rocky. It was as if he'd passed a test for Coco, and was now in the clear. Then Coco said, "If you come over tomorrow, I'll give you your next assignment."

Coco laughed when she saw the picture. "It's perfect," she said. "I'm going to put it in his mailbox tonight."

"He'll pee in his pants."

"God," Coco said, "I'd love to see his face."

"Are we going to give the Elf back to him?"

"Eventually," Coco said. Then she laughed again. "Maybe."

"What do you want me to do now?"

"I'd still like you to visit my friend in Pittsburgh."

"You sent Bob there, didn't you?"

"Yes, I did," Coco said. "Now I'd like you to go. Will you?"

Andy had thought a lot about Moses' advice, and he'd visualized himself happy together with Coco. He'd also thought a lot about what Biscuit had said about trusting Coco and getting to know her. Biscuit had been right. He'd opened himself up and let things happen, and he'd learned right off that Coco had an offbeat sense of humor and the spunk to stand up to Coach, and in doing what Coco had asked him to do, he'd ended up having a great day with Chuck, and now felt closer to Coco than he had ever felt before. Now Coco was looking at him in a frank and questioning way, and this time his answer was immediate and without doubt. "Yes."

52. Enemies

COACH AND BISCUIT met over in the City after work and came home together on the PATH. Coach checked the mail when they got home, and immediately noticed an unusual envelope. It was addressed to him, and each letter had been individually cut from a magazine and pasted in place, as if it were a ransom note. There was no return address. When he opened it, he found a Polaroid of the Elf with another hand-cut and pasted caption that read, "Let Freedom Ring." Coach didn't know what to think. "Biscuit, come take a look at this," he called. "Somebody sent me a picture of the Elf." When he handed Biscuit the picture, he said, "What's that in the background?"

"That's the Liberty Bell."

"How can you tell?"

"Well, it's a big bell," Biscuit said. "And it has a crack in it."

"Why would anyone send me this?"

As soon as Biscuit saw the picture, she understood what had happened. "I guess someone is telling you something," she said.

"That the Elf was once at the Liberty Bell?"

"Or that the Elf has been set free," Biscuit said. "And that they have it now."

"What?" Coach said with alarm. He ran directly to the living room and looked on the coffee table for the Elf. "It's gone!"

"Somebody's playing a practical joke."

"Who?" Coach said. "Who would do that?"

"One of your enemies."

"I don't have any enemies."

"OK, not enemies. But there are plenty of people who would enjoy playing a joke on you, don't you think?"

"Why?"

"Why? Because hardly a day goes by that you don't argue with someone.

Have you noticed that? Not everyone is as passionate as you are, and not everyone appreciates your opinions."

"Who have I argued with since you've known me?" Coach said. "Go ahead. I dare you to name one."

"OK. There are the neighbors. Remember? The ones you screamed at to turn down their music, because you had a race the next morning. And there's Mr. Pansen at the high school. You know, the middle-aged gentleman you called Mr. Pant-load when he insisted that you guys get off the track at closing time. There's Darla at the store. Although I doubt Darla would bother stealing your Elf. She would go right to clawing your eyes out. And there are at least three HOHAs women that I know of who haven't quite recovered from how you treated them. Oh, and what about that lady at the supermarket you shouted at last week who wouldn't take your discount coupon for a PowerBar, just because it was a measly three weeks past its expiration date. And of course, there's Bob," Biscuit concluded. "Hardly a week goes by that you don't have words with him."

Coach had been making dismissive faces throughout Biscuit's litany—not believing that any of the people she mentioned could harbor any real ill will toward him, despite any imagined slights—but when Biscuit said Bob's name, his face lit up like a slot machine on a jackpot, and he rang out, "That's it. It's that friggin' Bob."

"How do you know?"

"Because it's a dirty trick," Coach said. "And it's just the kind of dirty trick Bob would pull, too." Coach shook his head in disgust. "And after all I've done for him."

"Don't you think you're jumping to conclusions?"

Coach looked at the picture again. "Whose hand does that look like, holding up the Elf?"

"I don't know," Biscuit said. "It's a hand. It could be anybody."

"Man or woman?"

Biscuit looked closer at the picture. "It looks like a man's hand."

"Aha!" Coach said.

"What do you mean, 'Aha'?" Biscuit said. "That only narrows it down to half the human race."

"It narrows it down to Bad Bob is who it narrows it down to."

Coach called Bob immediately and accused him of stealing the Elf.

"I didn't touch that butt-ugly Elf," Bob said, "but I wish to God I had. Whoever did it was a genius. They couldn't have got to you more if they'd have cut off your nuts."

"Excuse me," Coach said, "but did you just use the word 'butt' in referring to the trophy of the New Jersey State X-C Championship?"

Coach heard Bob laugh, and then say to someone who was with him, "Somebody stole Emmitt's Elf." Then he heard that person laugh, although the laugh was more of a cackle, and he knew it belonged to Darla. Coach hung up the phone and said to Biscuit, "Bob didn't do it."

"How can you be so sure?"

"Because the sick bastard loved the idea and was only sorry that he hadn't thought of it himself, and if he had done it, he wouldn't have been able to resist the temptation to gloat."

"Well then, who do you think did it?"

"I don't know. You have any other ideas?"

Biscuit had been holding the name of Harry Horton in reserve. She knew it was the name that would most capture Coach's imagination, and divert him from Coco's trail. "Well," Biscuit said, "I guess there's always Harry."

"That's it!" Coach said. "Of course. Why didn't I think of it? It's that dickhead Harry Horton."

"I didn't say it was Harry," Biscuit said. "I just meant that he's a possibility."

"No. You nailed it. It was Harry. That son of a bitch!"

"Coach," Biscuit said soothingly, "my point was that it could be any number of people."

"No. No. Only Harry has a motive."

"What motive?"

"Envy."

"Envy of what?"

"He wants the Cross-Country Championship, and he doesn't have the team or the guts to win it himself, and the only way he can get any satisfaction is by stealing the trophy from me."

Biscuit shook her head resignedly and then turned and, with a small smile, returned to the kitchen. Coach then called Harry and accused him of the theft.

"You're out of your mind, Bean," Harry said. "Besides, if I wanted an Elf, I'd just bring my team over to Jersey this fall and win one of my own."

"But you don't have the guts to do that, do you, Horton? So you had to steal mine."

"That settles it, Bean," Harry said. "I'm bringing my team over there this fall, and we're going to kick your HOHA ass around every cross-country course in the state."

There was some cursing then, and the connection was terminated. Coach paced the apartment, examining the situation and looking for a bright side. What his feverish mind saw was that Harry had just unwittingly handed him the ammunition he needed to rally his team. The State Champion Hoboken Harriers would not stand for insults from any upstart, wannabe team from Brooklyn. The HOHAs *would* repeat. There *would* be a second Elf. And that second victory, at the expense of Harry and the Striders, would be the sweetest one of all.

53. On Track

FEW THINGS are as soothing as a trip on a train. There is the steady onward hum of it, and there is the comfort of being on track and losing our fear of losing our way. We wish we were on track through our life, unable to go wrong, making steady progress to where we are destined to be. And perhaps we are. We are guided in life by the things we want and do not get, and by the things we get before we even know we need them. That guidance can be a gentle touch or a sharp slap. It may come in a casual encounter or in a momentous meeting. We may get glimpses of it, but most often, like the tracks on which a train runs, we take our guidance for granted.

Andy took a red-eye out of Penn Station that would have him in Pittsburgh on Saturday morning. He'd had a long day at school and a long run, and by the time he got on the train that night, he was exhausted. He thought he'd be able to sleep, but the strangeness of the train, and its unfamiliar rumbling as it tunneled out of New York and westward through the darkness, left him restless.

The woman in the seat across from him had turned on her reading lamp and, in its insular glow, was paging through a movie magazine. She was a big, buxom woman, maybe sixty, adorned in rainbow colors and exotic jewelry. She had gold necklaces with pendants of the moon, the sun, and the stars. One of the necklaces had a charm with her name on it, "Leona." Her hair was elaborate, red and orange, and her lips and cheeks were made up to match. Andy guessed she was a former actress or showgirl, and thought that there was little her eyes hadn't seen.

She could feel Andy watching her from the darkness, and she put down her magazine. "Where you going, sweetheart?" she said, in a voice that was husky and sensual. Andy could have said "Pittsburgh," but from her tone, he understood that she didn't mean a place, and found himself saying, "I met this girl."

"Hmm-hmm," was all Leona said.

He then told her about the night he'd first seen Coco. While he spoke, she murmured, "hmm-hmm, hmm-hmm," as if coaxing out of him every heartache he'd ever known, and he felt that if he could tell her everything, she would have every answer he could want. Then he told her about Coco's request that he travel to see her friend in Pittsburgh. "And that's where I'm going," he concluded.

"Hmm-hmm."

"I really don't know what I'm doing," Andy admitted.

"Do you want to be with your girl?"

"I've never wanted anything more in my life."

"She's testing you," Leona said. "You know that, don't you?"

"Yes," Andy said. "She wants to see if I'm true to my word."

"Hmm-hmm. And she wants to see if you'll be there for her later too."

"Yes."

"When you're with Coco's friend, imagine you're with Coco thirty years from now. Be that attentive and that kind. Don't just look at her—see her. See how it is she's beautiful, and tell her that you see. Don't just hear her—listen to her. When she tells you the sky is gray, what does she want you to know? Don't just go there—be there. What is it like for her, and how can you make it better? She's there, and if you're really there too, she won't be alone. She'll feel that you're with her, and whatever she feels, Coco will feel it too. Coco will feel your care. Believe that she wouldn't send you to this woman if their hearts weren't close."

Andy didn't know what to say. What could one say to that? He felt the train again now, rumbling on through the darkness, purposeful, strong, and steady. He looked out the window into the darkness and, unseeing, could sense the world passing by. He thought out loud, "It's nice being on the train."

"The Lord blesses us in mysterious ways." Leona reached up and turned off the reading lamp, and they were together in the blackness. "Thank the Lord."

There was the smooth rumbling of the train, and Andy, resting in the knowledge that he was on his way, and soothed by the comfort of Leona's words, drifted off to sleep. His sleep was deep and dark, as restful as he had ever had, and he didn't awaken until the tracks had delivered on their promise and the train rolled into Pittsburgh early on that Saturday morning. He shook himself out of the fog of that sleep, looked at the empty seat across from him, and wondered if Leona had only been a dream.

Andy remembered everything that Leona had said, or that his dream of Leona had told him, and his visit with Coco's mother went well, although he never suspected that she was Coco's mother, and Gloria, true to her word to Coco, didn't let on. She "put him to work," as she called it, having him help her trim back some bushes along her side yard and plant some geraniums. They had iced tea afterwards and talked on the porch. The two of them got along easily, and when it came time for Andy to leave, although nothing exciting had happened, they both felt that it had been a great day.

The message that Coco got from her mom was positive too. Gloria, who believed in the adage, "If you don't have anything good to say about someone, it's best not to say anything at all," had had nothing to say about Bob. But about Andy, although she again said that she had no intention of influencing Coco's decision, and although she was circumspect in providing details of their day together, she bordered on effusive in saying that she saw Andy as "a nice young man."

After his experiences with the Elf in Philadelphia and the visit with Gloria in Pittsburgh, Andy was excited by the closeness he felt to Coco. It was a feeling he sometimes had on training runs and in races, when he suddenly felt strong, invincible, and able to run forever.

Competitive running is a mental battle more than anything else, and that battle is to keep the mind focused and calm. Runners must avoid negative thoughts and doubts of any kind, but they must avoid exuberance too. There may be points in the race where a runner feels strong, and there is the temptation then to be bold. A rush of adrenaline accompanies those temptations and brings with it a heady feeling.

In his running, Andy knew to deny these excitements, because he'd learned the hard way that they cost more than they were worth, but Andy's excitement about Coco was new to him, and he got carried away in it. He opened up to her about his childhood and his fears, and about how his grandmother had sent him here. In doing that, he assumed an intimacy that she hadn't yet granted him, and made her uneasy with his attention. When she backed away, he felt confused, and then hurt, and then resentful. He felt that he'd earned her affection, and yet she still kept him at a distance, as if still appraising him. He fell back into his groove of distrust, and Coco, sensing his stubbornness and resistance, once again doubted him.

Exuberance exacts a price, however, and later, when things get tough again—and they always do—the runner is depressed by his folly and the energy it has wasted. The experienced runner learns that it is best to deny excitements of any kind and to keep working calmly and steadily to the finish.

Andy and Coco settled into an estrangement. Then, when the summer sessions were over at school, Coco returned to Pittsburgh to be with her mom, and the distance between her and Andy precluded any casual chance they had to get together. Coco devoted herself to her mother, while Andy found solace in his running, and in hanging out with Chuck and Moses. Both Andy and Coco wondered what had gone wrong. They felt lost, not knowing where to go or how to get there. Saddened and bewildered, they felt that their lives together had somehow gone off track.

54. Mile 20

MOSES ALWAYS attended the Tuesday and Thursday night runs without fail, but he wasn't at the first Tuesday run in September. Coach held up the run for a few minutes past the grace period to wait for him. Andy wasn't there either, and Coach thought that maybe he and Moses were putting in some extra miles together and were running late. Coach was unconcerned at the time, but the next day he called Andy and learned that Andy hadn't seen Moses either.

Wednesday was Moses' day off at the car wash, and he usually spent the day with Buddy. "Maybe he went out to Newark early this week," Andy said to Coach. "He's been talking a lot about Buddy lately."

"Yeah, but it's not like him to miss a run."

"You're right," Andy said. "I better stop by the car wash and see what they know."

After classes that day, Andy went right over to the car wash. There were a few cars lined up and one of the kids was brushing at the hubcaps of the first car in the line. "You seen Moses?" he said to the kid.

"Day off."

"I know, but have you seen him around?"

The kid just shrugged. Andy worked his way through the puddles and slop to McDougal's office. Andy had heard about McDougal's charming ways, so he got right to the point. "Moses is missing," he said. "Was he at work yesterday?"

"Yeah."

"Did he say anything about going anywhere?"

"Do I look like his mother?"

There were a few tattered business cards on McDougal's desk, and Andy took one in case he had to call the next day. "If you see Moses, will you tell him Andy's looking for him?"

"I'll be delighted," McDougal said. "And if *you* see the old man, tell him I'm not running a fucking old-age home." McDougal ground his green cigar into the filth of an ashtray. "If he's not at work tomorrow, he's fired."

Andy hadn't seen Moses since Sunday, but at least now he knew that Moses was accounted for through Tuesday afternoon. Maybe he had gone out to Newark Tuesday after work and was back in his apartment by now.

In the time that Andy had known Moses, he hadn't been inside the apartment once. He'd helped Moses carry a lot of junk back to the place, but Moses had never invited him in. A wooden staircase was the only access to the apartment, and now Andy took the creaky steps up to the small landing at the door. The door was metal, painted with only a gray primer. It was hollow, and made a drum-like echo as Andy knocked. Andy listened for any sound inside, but could hear nothing. He tried the door, but it was locked. There was a single window above the staircase, but because it was without curtains and facing south, Moses had it covered with aluminum foil to block out the sun. In any case, the window was closed, and it was out of reach from the landing. Andy looked down the alley in both directions, but no one was around. He called out, "Moses. Moses, are you there?" There was no reply. Andy went back down the stairs and looked up at the apartment again. Moses must still be in Newark, he thought. I'll just call the car wash tomorrow to make sure he made it in.

Andy called the car wash the next morning and got McDougal on the line. "This is Moses' friend, Andy," he said. "Is Moses at work?"

"No, and I'm shorthanded," McDougal yelled. "If you see the old man, tell him to fuck himself," and then hung up.

Andy was worried now, and called Coach at work. "Moses wasn't home yesterday," he said, "and he didn't show up for work today."

Coach thought for a moment. "I'm going to call Duane and see what he knows."

Duane told Coach that he hadn't seen Moses since they'd run together the week before. Coach called Andy back with the news. "Let's wait till the run tonight," Coach said to Andy. "If Moses doesn't show up then, we'll know something is wrong."

Andy was buried in work that afternoon and couldn't get out of the computer lab until 7:00, so he had to hurry to get to the run on time. Moses was normally one of the first to arrive, but to Andy's dismay, he wasn't there. When Coach arrived a couple of minutes later, he and Andy canvassed the other runners, asking if they'd seen Moses in the last couple of days, but no one had. When it was time for Coach to start the run, Andy headed over to Moses' place again.

Again, Andy got no answer at Moses' door, and there was still no sign of him. Andy met Coach at the finish of the run, and they agreed they should get Augie to open the apartment. Augie lived just a block from the salvage yard, and he'd just finished dinner when Coach and Andy arrived. They explained the situation, and Augie recollected that he hadn't seen Moses since late Tuesday afternoon. He'd been leaving the yard for the day, and Moses was just getting home from his shift at the car wash. He said that they'd exchanged hellos and that the only unusual thing he noticed was that Moses was moving slowly. "Dragging butt," Augie called it. Augie agreed to go with them to the apartment and open it up.

It was dark when they got there, with just one street lamp at the corner of the alley, and in its stark light, Augie pounded on the door. "Moses," he yelled. "You there?" When there was no answer, he pulled at a spool of keys on his belt, somehow identified the correct one, and opened the door, but it only opened a foot before something obstructed it. Augie leaned into it with his shoulder, but it would move no farther. He reached inside and flipped on a light switch, and a dim glow emanated from somewhere deep in the room. "I can't see much," he said, "but there's a shitload of junk in there."

Augie stepped back, and Andy peered into the room. In the dim light, he could see stuff piled from floor to ceiling. Andy remembered all the things he had seen Moses collect and drag home: tires, clothing, furniture, lamps, electronics, and junk of every kind. He had thought that Moses went over the stuff later, saving some but discarding or selling the rest, but he now realized that Moses must have kept most, if not all, of it.

Augie had gone down to the office to get his flashlight, and now he used it to get a better look. "Good God," he said when he'd seen enough.

"It looks like you got to get on your hands and knees and crawl through a tunnel."

Augie was too big to squeeze through the door, and Coach couldn't fit through either. Andy, if he exhaled, could just squeeze past, so he took the flashlight from Augie and went in. There was a solid wall of stuff in front of his face. Slowly bending his knees, he lowered himself to the level of the tunnel that Augie had spotted, knee-high off the ground and about two feet in diameter. He aimed the flashlight into it. The base of the tunnel was covered in pieces of carpet and newspaper, and the sides and top were a web of the junk that formed the bridgework of the passage. It was hot and stuffy, and Andy began to sweat. He yelled out to Augie and Coach, "I'm gonna take a look."

"Be careful, Andy," Coach said.

Andy wanted nothing less than to explore that maze of junk, but Moses might be inside and in need of his help. He put his hands onto the base at the entrance to the tunnel and tested its strength. It seemed to support his weight. He ducked his head down, extended the flashlight into the darkness and crawled inside, moving slowly forward on his elbows and knees. About three feet in, the tunnel turned sharply to the right, and Andy's left arm sank into a hole in the flooring. This triggered a collapse, and a wooden pallet came down about a foot ahead of him, completely blocking the passage.

Andy was overcome with the dread he thought a miner must feel after a mine collapse, and slowly backed his way out, and with relief squeezed through the door and back to the fresh air of the landing. He told Augie and Coach what he had seen, and what had happened. "I can't go in there," he concluded.

"Course you can't," Augie said. "We got to call the police."

Augie went down to his office again and called the police out to the yard. A patrol car arrived within a few minutes, and Augie explained to the officer about Moses being missing and showed him the situation with the apartment. The officer said that it was not uncommon for some elderly people to build barricades like this to protect themselves and their property, and they often created obstacles and booby traps to keep people out. He said that the county had a special squad that had the equipment and experience to go in safely.

"We're going to have to get them in here," he said, and then went down to his patrol car to make the call.

Augie told Coach and Andy that they could wait at his house, but Coach wanted to go home to tell Biscuit what was happening, so Andy told him he'd call him when they knew more. Andy then went home himself to change out of his running gear before returning to Augie's.

It was an hour before the county squad arrived, three of them. They took a look at the apartment, and then asked Augie and Andy about Moses. Did Moses have any weapons, explosives, chemicals? Then they questioned Augie about the layout of the apartment. They decided to cut through the wall and remove the door and its framing, and then they would begin to remove the junk piece by piece, working their way through the apartment.

They called for a dumpster to be placed below the landing, set up some lighting and put on protective clothing. In the strange glow of the night lights, and in their bulky silver suits, they looked like astronauts. Andy was astounded that there were men like these whose job it was to go in and dig out people from their homes, astounded that there were enough people that needed to be dug out. He and Augie watched for a while, and then went back to Augie's house to wait.

Later, Augie went to bed, while Andy fell asleep on the couch, until he was woken the next morning when one of the squad arrived to deliver the news. Andy answered the door still groggy with sleep, and when he saw the man still wearing his astronaut suit, for a moment he felt like he was in a Sci-Fi movie, but the man's words, like the nasty buzz of an alarm clock, quickly jolted Andy back to reality.

"We found your friend deep in the living unit, lying in a narrow bed space he'd made for himself." The man paused as Augie came up alongside Andy. "In these cases, there has usually been a heart attack or stroke, and the person was unable to get themselves help." Augie put his arm around Andy's shoulder. "It appears that your friend died just last night." The man looked from Augie to Andy and added, "If it's any consolation to you, it appears that your friend died peacefully. In his sleep."

55. Last Run

ANDY FELT weak in the legs and had to sit down, and Augie, seeing how shook-up Andy was, got him a glass of water. "Are you going to be OK, Andy?"

"I'll need some time, Augie."

"You take all the time you want. Just take your time," Augie said. "I'm gonna have to get over to the yard now though and open up for the crew."

"I'll just sit here a while before I go," Andy said. "But I have to tell Coach, and it's better that I do it in person."

Andy waited a few minutes after Augie left before he got up. He reminded himself to breathe deeply, the way he did when he was running, and felt steadier then. He made it over to Coach's apartment. Biscuit had already left for work, and Coach answered the door. Coach only had to take one look at Andy to know the news. They talked for a while, and then Coach called in sick, then called in for Andy too.

Coach and Andy spent all morning and most of the afternoon at the morgue and the county administrative offices arranging for Moses' burial. When they'd finished, they realized they hadn't eaten all day, and went over to the Malibu Diner. Coach was talkative as usual, but his talk that day was a nervous chatter, as if he were afraid of the silence that would descend when he stopped. He reminisced about how he'd first met Moses, how Moses had joined the club, and about all his accomplishments. "I want to have a tribute for Moses," Coach said, "and I want it to be about his running."

"That's a good idea," Andy said.

"I'm going to talk to Biscuit, and to Edsel, and we'll come up with a plan," Coach said. "Then I'll call all the HOHAs and everyone else that Moses knew."

The thought of the tribute lifted their spirits for a moment, until Andy said, "I'll have to go out to Newark and tell Buddy."

Andy and Coach sat in silence, their spirits dampened again, as they thought of how hard Buddy would take the news. Then Coach said, almost as an afterthought, and to deliver them from that mood, "One of us should go over to the car wash and let McDougal know."

"That would be me," Andy said. "I'll take care of that."

Andy was in shock, but he wouldn't realize that until later. The plan for Moses' tribute and his knowledge of all those who would attend had filled Andy with a warm pride, and an appreciation of those who'd loved Moses, and now these feelings set McDougal in sharp contrast, and as Andy walked over to the car wash, he remembered all the times when McDougal hadn't allowed Moses to adjust his schedule to attend running events, and he remembered the extended shifts he'd made Moses work when someone else didn't show. He thought of McDougal's ugly scowl, and of his threats and disregard for Moses' well-being, his anxiety over the last couple of days fuelling his resentment toward McDougal, and by the time he got to the car wash, he was full of frustrated anger.

The same kid he'd seen the day before was washing hubcaps outside. Andy marched up to him. "Is McDougal in there?" he demanded.

"Yeah."

Andy grabbed the bucket of dirty water at the kid's feet and went inside. McDougal was at his desk. "I got a message for you," Andy said. McDougal stared back in surprise. "You're not fucking firing anybody," Andy said. "Moses quits. And here's his resignation." Andy then flung the slop from the bucket across the desk and all over McDougal. "You need a bath, you rotten piece of shit."

With that Andy turned and left, his heart racing with hot-blooded satisfaction, but that feeling, as it cooled, revealed the sadness at its core, and Andy had a harrowing glimpse then of loneliness and despair. Suddenly, he felt weak again, but again he steadied himself, in the same way he steadied himself in his running, and turned his focus from the pain he was feeling to what he still had left to do, which was to convey the news to Moses' best friend.

Andy had been to visit Buddy twice with Moses, but this time he would go to Newark alone. The afternoon was hot, and the shade under the bridge where Buddy still lived was a relief from the sun. Andy blocked out many things that day, but he remembered that heat, and calling up to Buddy in the darkness, and seeing Buddy's face when he received the news. He would always remember that look of pain, and what he learned from it. He learned that sometimes, we only know our own strength when we witness the vulnerability of others.

Moses' funeral was held two days later. It was the simplest of burials, paid for by the county, but Coach had arranged for a priest to be there for the blessings and the prayers. Coach wore a suit, which looked strange on him, but stranger still was the look of loss and bewilderment he wore. With his enthusiasm and energy gone, he seemed to be a different person. Now, it was as if he were having his first sobering realization that our life and our dreams aren't wholly of our own making. Standing right next to Coach, with her arm in his, was Biscuit. There were tears in her eyes, but she was like a rock, supporting him, and one could feel the strength of their togetherness. Buddy had gravitated toward Biscuit, sensing that strength, and stood at her other side wearing a look of cantankerous defiance that couldn't mask his childlike pain.

Besides Coach and Biscuit and Buddy, there was Andy and Augie and Duane, and two of the old guys from the car wash, Freddy and Enrico. Slow-Mo, Bulldog, Howie, and Chuck made it too. Sheila was there, representing the girls of the club, and she brought a bouquet of flowers. Edsel had Darla watch the store so that he could be there, and that was it. The rest of the HOHAs, the ones not as close to Moses, couldn't take time off work, but they'd all promised to attend the tribute that evening.

The tribute was scheduled for 7:00 at the Hoboken High School track. Everyone who'd attended the funeral was there, and all the rest of the HOHAs made it as promised, and even a few former HOHAs, whom Coach had called, had come in from out of town. He took a count, and there were just short of seventy people in all. Coach had everyone gather on the infield of the track, near the starting line. He'd set up a table there, and on it were all the trophies and plaques and ribbons that Moses had won in races and brought to Coach to keep. Coach stood in front of that table and asked everyone to sit while he said a few words. First he introduced and welcomed the non-HOHAs who were there, and then he paused a moment to quiet everyone and indicate that the tribute would now begin.

"We are here this evening to honor a great man. Moses was a great man, not great in riches or worldly accomplishment, but great in a more important way: great in spirit, and great as an inspiration to all of us who had the honor to know him.

"We all know what Moses accomplished as a runner. Beside me here are the many trophies that he won. There could have been many more, but Moses often ran races without a number, because he didn't have the money for the entry fee or, more likely, because he had given his money to someone more in need.

"Moses' accomplishments as a runner are a testament not only to his talent, but to his hard work and to the energy and youthful enthusiasm he brought to everything he did.

"Moses was a no-frills guy, a hardworking guy who, in addition to his job at the car wash, picked up jobs bagging groceries and working on Christmas tree lots, and yet Moses always made time to attend the club runs, to help with the club charity events, and to give advice on running and on life to any of us who asked. Moses was a great runner, but more than that, he was a great friend. Tonight, we are gathered here to pay tribute to our fellow runner and dear friend.

"In all the years I spent with Moses, and in all the ways he impressed me and inspired me as an athlete and as a person, there is one memory of him that stands foremost in my mind. When runners brought the Olympic torch through Hoboken on its way to Atlanta, the route went down Observers Highway, right past the car wash where Moses worked. Moses was sixty-seven years old at the time, and he'd just finished an eight-hour shift washing cars, and yet when he saw the torch, he was so excited that he ran with that procession for five miles, just out of enthusiasm and pride.

"Moses told me afterwards that his run alongside the Olympic torch was one of the greatest moments of his life. Moses embodied the spirit of the Olympics, the indomitable spirit of man to fight though hardship, to strive toward excellence, and to act with honor, but more than anything else, Moses embodied the Olympic pureness of heart and the friendship that brings people together in sport.

"Tonight, as our tribute to Moses, we are going to carry a torch, Moses' Olympic torch, around the track seventy times, in honor of Moses' seventy years with us. I think that it is a loving tribute, and it will give us time to be together, to pray, and to reflect on how much Moses meant to each of us. Each of us will take a turn, and then pass the torch on to the next of Moses' friends.

"We were all Moses' friends, and two of us here were as close as any friends could be. I am speaking of our Andy, who ran with Moses more than any of us did and was his close companion over the last two years, and I am speaking of Moses' oldest and dearest friend, his friend from Newark, Buddy, who is with us here tonight. I'd like to ask Andy to carry the torch first, and I'd like to ask Buddy to do the honor of carrying the torch last, on the anchor leg, the leg that brings the torch home.

"Edsel." Coach looked toward Edsel, who rose and brought the torch over to Coach. Edsel had fashioned a realistic facsimile of the Olympic torch out of papier-mâché, and had installed a light inside it that illuminated some red paper at the top, giving the appearance of a fire-like glow. Coach took the torch and stepped out onto the track, then nodded to Andy, who joined him. Coach handed the torch to Andy, who took it solemnly, and the two of them stood there on the track looking at each other, sharing a quiet moment. Then, without a word, Andy held the torch aloft, turned and ran. Everyone broke into a spontaneous burst of applause and watched as the red glow circled the track.

When Andy came back around, Coach yelled out "One!" to begin the count, and Andy handed the torch to Bulldog, which produced more applause as the torch started the circle again. As each torchbearer left the track, Coach gave them one of Moses' trophies to keep as a remembrance of him, and so it went as, one after the other, HOHAs and friends took their turns. Each time a runner completed a loop, everyone shouted out the number and applauded the next runner on their way. Freddy and Enrico walked their loops, receiving even more applause as they set off. There was silence as the torch circled while, as Coach had suggested, everyone reflected and prayed. It was in one of those silences, as his turn approached, that Buddy came over to Andy, who was stationed on the infield. "I can't make it, Andy," he said.

"You can walk it, Buddy," Andy said, "just like Freddy and Enrico did."

"It's not that," he said. He glanced out at the far reaches of the track, and then looked down, as if slightly ashamed. "It just looks lonely out there."

There had been summer light when the tribute began, but it was dark now. Andy looked into the distance and saw the glowing torch moving alone through the darkness, like a falling star in the far reaches of the night. Its journey was lonely, and Andy knew how Buddy felt. "We're not alone, Buddy," he said. "We have each other." He put his arm around Buddy's shoulders. "I'll tell you what. All of us will walk the last loop with you. We'll do it together."

Andy went over and spoke with Coach, and when the last HOHA began the penultimate loop, Coach motioned everyone silently onto the track. He positioned Buddy in the center to receive the torch, and when Buddy took it, he held it proudly and raised it high. With a charming earnestness, he led everyone slowly around the final loop.

> Buddy walked a steady pace, but in the stretch, with no more than fifty meters to go, he walked faster and then faster still as he brought the torch in. I didn't think of it until later, but that is just the way that Moses ran. He always picked up the pace toward the finish. My grandma would say he "smells the barn." An old carriage horse, after a hard day out, will, surprisingly, increase the pace at the end. It knows its work is almost done, it "smells the barn," and hurries then to complete the journey and reach the comfort of home. It's a great quality in a runner too, and of all the runners I ever coached, no one, not even Andy Bell, had a greater desire than Moses had to make his way home.

At the finish, everyone stood together in a circle on the track, and Coach concluded the tribute. In silence, he held aloft the torch that represented Moses' life and the journey he had taken. He held it there a moment and then, still in silence, he reached up and turned out the light.

56. Honorary HOHA

COACH HAD arranged for a gathering at Moran's after the tribute. There was to be a buffet and beer and wine. Everybody walked together in that direction now, but Andy noticed Buddy lagging behind hesitantly, and fell back to join him. "Hey, Buddy," he said softly, "come with us and have a drink."

"Is that guy who calls himself 'Coach' gonna be there?"

"Yeah, sure."

"What's his real name, anyway?"

"Emmitt Bean."

"God, what a handle!"

"Emmitt F. Bean, actually," Andy said. "He includes his middle initial."

"What's the 'F' stand for?"

"I don't know, Buddy. He doesn't say."

"I could take a guess."

Andy chuckled. "Coach is OK."

"God, he's got a handle like that and he's bashful about the 'F.' He's one whacked out son of a bitch." Buddy shook his head. "You know what he said to me today? He said I was an honorary HOHA. I don't even know what a goddamn HOHA is. I don't understand half the goddamn things he says."

"He was just saying that you're a friend of ours, of the running club, and that you're always welcome with us."

"Why didn't he just say that then? Like somebody normal." Buddy shook his head in disgust. "That Coach is one crazy bastard."

Andy had heard Coach called lots of things, but he hadn't heard it put quite like that before.

"I've seen some flipped out bastards too," Buddy went on, "living on the street, talking nonsense to themselves and to anybody else who'll listen. I knew one bum who thought he was Bill Clinton, as if that was somebody you'd want to be. All I'm saying is that I've seen about all the crazy there is to see, but I've never seen anybody who has a leg up on that Coach. The only good thing about that crazy bastard is Biscuit. She's something special."

"Yes, she is."

"Did you ever notice that?"

"What?"

"That the only thing that saves some men is the woman they got with them. I guess that's God takin' care of the feebleminded."

"But Moses loved him too," Andy said.

"I know he did. That's the only reason I give that dope the time of day and don't just kick him in the nuts—because Moses saw something in him. Of course, Moses never saw another bum or dumb animal that he didn't try to help."

Buddy shuddered. They were standing next to a street lamp, and Buddy reached out to grab the pole to steady himself.

"Come on, Buddy," Andy said. "Come have a beer with us, something to eat."

"I don't think so, Andy." Buddy looked unsteady and was shaking a bit. He looked at the trophy that Coach had given him. It was a statue of a runner, and with one finger, Buddy absentmindedly caressed its head. "You go ahead without me."

"Come on. It will do you good."

"No, no, no, no, no, Andy. I ... I should go home."

Buddy was fighting back tears and shaking more now. Andy reached out and held his drooping shoulder. "Come on."

Buddy straightened himself then and toughened his face, fighting back the sadness and the fear. "Do you know how many years I carried that no-good bum?" he said. "When I let him under the bridge, he didn't have a rag to blow his nose. If it wasn't for me, he'd've starved long ago."

"Yeah."

"God knows my life will be easier now."

Andy understood Buddy's tack. "Yeah, don't I know it," Andy said. "He didn't know half as much about running as he thought he did."

"He didn't know nothin'," Buddy corrected. "But that didn't keep him from whistlin' like Meadowlark Lemon every morning. What's worse than somebody who's happy first thing in the morning? And he couldn't carry a tune worth a good goddamn. But that didn't stop him, and I had to live next door to him all those years."

"We're good to be rid of him," Andy said.

"And did you ever eat with him? You'd've thought God never invented a fork. If Moses could eat it with his hands, he would. I seen him eat a whole plate of spaghetti once, sucking it up one noodle at a time."

"A complete slob."

"You got that right," Buddy agreed. "And didn't he have a big head, ever since he got that glamour job."

"Glamour job?"

"At the car wash. Are you kidding me? A ten-minute break twice a day, and a paycheck every Friday. Sometimes he even got tips. That job was cushy, with a capital 'C.'"

"I had my own opportunities, but I put my life on hold for him. Who would've took care of him if it weren't for me? He wouldn't've lasted a minute. Then he got too important for his old friend, after all I done for him. And did he ever appreciate it? No!"

Andy knew that of all the love Moses had given, he'd loved Buddy more than he'd loved anyone else, and Buddy knew it too.

"Well, come on, Buddy, let's go have that drink."

"No. You go on. I got important things to do, and I wasted enough time already."

"Will you come visit, Buddy?"

"Yeah, sure, right. Now go on."

"All right then," Andy said. "Take care." Andy put his hand on Buddy's shoulder, and then he walked away. When he got to the end of the block, he turned to see if Buddy had gone, but he was still there, leaning with one hand on the street lamp, the other hand to his face, silhouetted in the glow of the lamp, his body shaking with tears.

57. The Series

THE SUDDEN LOSS of Moses had been a shock to all the HOHAs who, being for the most part young, had little experience with death and its various ways, but the loss hit hardest on Andy and Coach, who each handled their grief in the way that suited them best, or perhaps in the only way they could. Andy, who was on the quiet side, became quieter still, while Coach, who needed to talk as much as he needed to breathe, found himself delivering speeches, the theme of most of which was, "We have to win for Moses."

There is a tradition in sport that the game must go on, and a belief that the fallen teammate would have wanted it that way. It's a good belief, because when it comes right down to it, what else is one going to do? Coach reminded everyone of Moses' love of the HOHAs, and said that he saw it as his duty, as leader of the HOHAs racing team, to move the HOHAs forward. He had black armbands made up for the HOHAs to wear in competition, intensified the HOHAs training regimen, and declared that the HOHAs would not only participate in that year's X-C series, but would win the championship for Moses and dedicate the victory to his immortal memory.

These were noble sentiments, but the outcome, even in Coach's determined and optimistic mind, was less than assured. Without Moses, the HOHAs team was sorely weakened, and Harry Horton, true to his word—or threat, as Coach saw it—came over from Brooklyn with his Striders that year to run the series. The Striders were a powerful team and, fueled by Harry's dislike of Coach, which he had somehow transmitted to all the other Striders, they came to the series with a desire for victory equal to the HOHAs' own.

The competition itself lived up to the anticipation and desire that both teams had brought to it. The first five races of the series were a seesaw battle, with the Striders claiming narrow victories in weeks one, three, and five, and the HOHAs narrowly taking weeks two and four. Shore was a close third in all the races, and was poised to take second place should either the Striders or the HOHAs falter.

John Malcolm of the Striders was an animal in the races, with his long legs and muscular torso churning like a tiger on the prowl. He was scary strong, and just chewed up the race courses. Andy, with all his talent, had all he could handle to hold him off. In the fifth race at Tatum Park, Malcolm put on a late charge that forced Andy to sprint the last two hundred meters to get the win. Not far behind them in all the races, Bad Bob was having his own battles with the Frieder twins. Bob was a great climber and could gain a margin on the hills, but the twins would work together on the flats and downhills to reel him back. He couldn't tell them apart, and felt as if he were fighting off two men in one, but he held them off in all but the fifth race at Huber Woods, where Bob somehow managed to finish in the eyelash that habitually separated the twins.

Edsel finished third for the HOHAs in the Open division of each of the races, and so the Striders, with Malcolm and the Frieder twins already in, gained points there. Harry Horton was the fourth man for the Striders, and easily finished in front of Eck in every race. The Striders gained more points in the Master division, where Don Abrams finished well ahead of Icky. In the Veteran division, Boston held his own with the Striders runner, so that was a wash, but the HOHAs gained the points back on the distaff side, where either Patti or Sheila consistently finished ahead of the Strider women.

Coach himself, without ever figuring in the scoring, nevertheless ran inspired races. Driven by his own excitement and his desire to minimize the margin between himself and Harry, he ran personal records on each of the courses and was an inspiration to all the HOHAs running in the middle of the pack. All in all, everyone was running in top form, and after five races, there were no injuries to tarnish the results or the prospects for the final race. As in the previous year, the standings couldn't be tighter, and it would all come down to Holmdel Park, where the points would be doubled and the winner would claim the championship.

There was a picture taken of Coach after that fifth race, when the results had just come in, and in that picture his normal expression of confidence had been replaced by an unmistakable look of concern. Coach had the club as a whole as ready as it could be, but the result the following week would hinge on the performances of his two stars, and the behavior and well-being of both of them was, to Coach's finely tuned sensibility, not quite right.

There was now an added cockiness to Bob since he'd taken up with Darla, but there were sometimes scratches on his face, hickey-like marks on his neck, and bruises on his arms. Once, he explained that he'd fallen into a rose bush, and another time he said that he'd been scratched by Darla's cat, but Coach, and the rest of the HOHAs, suspected rough sex and a volatile chemistry. Watching Darla, who was always clad in black leather, chains, and spikes, Coach and the HOHAs knew that the Frieder twins, as troublesome as they were, were the least of Bob's problems. Coach thought of having a talk with Bob to make sure he was all right, but then thought better of it, remembering past experiences, and decided it was best to just leave him be.

Coach was more concerned about Andy, who had been listless during the series, racing more out of habit than inspiration. At this level of competition, it was unusual for any runner—even a runner as good as John Malcolm—to stay with him. "What happened out there today?" Coach asked him after the fifth race. "I heard that Malcolm almost got you at the wire."

"I guess I was distracted."

"Distracted?" Coach said incredulously, as if it were impossible for anything to distract one from something as important as the race. "Distracted about what?"

"Coco, I guess," Andy said. "I called her twice this week, and she didn't answer, and then she didn't show up today. I guess I just had her on my mind."

"Just stay focused on your racing," Coach said. "It will take your mind off any troubles you're having."

"Yeah."

"We just need one more win, Andy," Coach said. "Just one more week."

"OK."

"This is the state championship we're talking about, Andy." Coach lowered his voice then, and said with seriousness, "And we vowed to win this one for Moses."

"I'll take care of Malcolm next week," Andy said.

"Do you promise?"

"I promise."

"Good."

"Good," Coach repeated to himself after Andy had walked away, but truth be known, Coach's talk with Andy, and even the promise he'd extracted from him, had left him feeling somehow less than easy.

58. A Nutcase

ON THE RAINY Wednesday morning prior to that fifth race of the series, two police officers—Angelo and Alice were their names—sat in their patrol car in lower Manhattan having their daily coffee and pastry. They had been partners for three years, and while they liked each other, they knew each other's weaknesses all too well. Alice teased Angelo about being uptight and too much of a control freak, while Angelo never missed a chance to tease Alice about her flakiness. Angelo often had to take Alice by her house after they'd started their shift because she'd forgotten something. It had happened that very morning, and when Angelo asked Alice what she'd forgotten this time, she said, "I forgot my gun."

It would be a long time before he let her live that down. "Hey, Alice, did you forget your bullets too?"

Despite the fun he was having at her expense, Alice could tell that Angelo wasn't quite himself that morning, and that something was on his mind. She could usually help him with his troubles, but she invariably had to coax him into talking. Today, she started by saying, "The doctor is in."

"What?"

"I know something's bothering you," Alice said. "We better talk about it now, or you'll be grumpy all day long."

"Nothing's bothering me."

"I saw you roll your eyes. You're having one of your imaginary conversations, and whoever you're talking to said something you think is stupid."

"I am not."

Alice rolled her eyes, mimicking him.

"Is it Tina?" Tina was Angelo's wife, and they usually fought about Tina's mother, or about Tina's shopping. "Did she buy something expensive again?"

"No."

"Then what is it?"

"This time it's what she *wants* to buy."

"What?"

"A house."

"And what's wrong with that?"

"We can't afford it."

"Well, you just get a mortgage like everybody else."

"That's just step one. Then she'll want to have a baby."

"So?"

"I'm not ready for that," Angelo said. "It's always about what she wants."

"It's not for her; it's for both of you."

"But I'm not ready yet."

"You will be. It's what you're going to want too, but you just don't know it yet."

"You're saying she knows what I want before I do."

"She's a woman," Alice said. "A woman is always one step ahead of a man."

"That's ridiculous," Angelo said. "And from a woman who forgot her gun that was sitting right next to her hair dryer." He rolled his eyes again and said mockingly. "One step ahead!"

Alice laughed. "Maybe two."

In 1999, Coco was among the first to have a cell phone. She wasn't usually a purchaser of the latest things, but she got it so that her mother, if in need of help, could reach her at any time. The cell phone was as big as a shoe.

Coco was in lower Manhattan early on that rainy Wednesday morning. There was a fashion shoot downtown, and she had a class assignment to report on it. The sidewalks were still cool with the early morning rain, the workday rush was just starting, and Coco was walking toward the shoot on Wall Street when her cell phone rang. Besides her mother, only a few of her friends had the number, and she couldn't imagine any of them calling her at this hour. She was crossing Broadway at the time, and she stopped in the middle of the crosswalk, juggling her umbrella, and dug in her purse for the phone.

Angelo and Alice, from their patrol car nearby, noticed Coco in the middle of the intersection. "What's she doing?" Angelo said to his partner.

"Looking for something in her purse," Alice said.

"In the middle of the street?"

"That does appear to be her location," Alice said.

Coco had pulled the phone from the purse. "What's that?" Angelo said. "Is that a gun?"

"No, you fool. That's a phone."

The traffic had started, and Coco was now caught in the center, with cars and trucks passing close by her in both directions. "Jesus," Angelo said. "Is she nuts?"

Gloria's doctor had called, and when Coco recognized his voice, she blurted, "Is Mom OK?"

"We have your mother in the hospital," Dr. Spencer said. "She's had a collapse."

"Oh my God!"

"She's in intensive care. I don't want to alarm you. I'm confident that we can stabilize her, but it would be a good idea for you to come."

"Yes, yes, of course. I'll get the first flight I can."

When Coco ended the call, the light had changed, and she made it to the curb to hail a taxi, but it's tough getting a taxi in Manhattan in the rain, and Coco was having no luck. Meanwhile, the police officers were still watching her from down the block. "She was walking downtown," Angelo said, "and now she's trying to get a taxi uptown."

"That does appear to be the case," Alice said.

"She must be a nutcase."

"No, I think there's a problem." They watched a while longer as Coco, in obvious desperation, tried to flag down a cab or any other car she could stop. "Let's take a closer look," Alice said.

Angelo drove slowly toward Coco's location. Although her behavior was suspect, and they were watching her closely, the officers were nevertheless shocked when, just as they were nearing her, she spotted them and suddenly jumped out in front of their car, causing Angelo to jam on the brakes. The cream puff he was eating plastered his face, and Coco, waving her arms, ran around to his side of the car.

"Are you nuts?" the officer said.

"My mom's in the hospital," Coco cried. "I need to get to Newark airport as soon as possible."

"Does this look like a taxi, miss?" Angelo said.

"Get in," Alice said. She motioned to the other side of the car. "Over here."

Coco ran around and got in the backseat behind Alice. Angelo looked at Alice in disbelief. "We can't take her to Newark, you know."

"Of course not, you fool. We'll take her to the taxi stand at Fulton." Then Alice turned to Coco. "It's going to be all right, baby."

They drove her to the taxi stand, and Coco tried to give Angelo a ten-dollar bill. "You *are* nuts," he said. "Get outta here."

Alice got out with Coco and spoke with the taxi driver. When she returned, she said to Angelo, "Turn on the siren."

"What?"

"Turn on the siren. We're escorting them to the Holland Tunnel."

Coco hardly knew what was happening as her driver, following the patrol car with its lights flashing and siren wailing, raced through the streets of lower Manhattan. As the taxi passed out of the rain and into the tunnel, Coco turned to see Alice waving to her, and Coco waved back. When she turned again, she was inside the tunnel, and felt as if she were passing into another life. The meaning of all that could happen now flooded in upon her, and she fell back across the seat and cried all the tears of her fear.

Angelo had returned to their original location, and now he noticed one of the regular bums going through a trash can. "Look, Alice," he said. "There's Motown looking for his breakfast. Maybe you want we should drive him somewhere. To the Ritz maybe." He shook his head at what a soft touch Alice was. "I still say she was a nutcase."

"The dearest person in the world to her is in the hospital," Alice said. "She's only thinking with her heart. She's not a nutcase." Alice reached over and wiped a trace of whip cream off of Angelo's chin. "She's a woman."

That day was a nightmare for Coco: the wait at the airport, the flight itself, the second taxi, all the time spent worrying about her mom and not knowing how she was. When she finally got to the hospital, she learned that her mom was still in intensive care, but in a stable condition and sleeping. Dr. Spencer told her that everything would be OK for now, that this had been only a warning, albeit a serious one.

Dr. Spencer released Gloria from the hospital the next morning, and by Saturday she was back to her old self. Once again, despite Coco's protests, she insisted that Coco return to school.

59. In Mysterious Ways

COCO GOT back to Hoboken late on Saturday night, and the next afternoon she went to see Biscuit. She needed to spend some time within that halo of peace that Biscuit offered. When Biscuit saw Coco, she gave her a hug. "I haven't seen you all week," Biscuit said. "And we missed you at the race yesterday."

"I just got back from visiting my mom," Coco said. That was exactly what she wanted to talk to Biscuit about, but she felt guilty introducing her own problems, so she started by asking how Biscuit and Coach had been.

"I'm doing all right," Biscuit said. "And Coach pretends to be all right, and won't admit that he isn't. He misses Moses." Biscuit reflected for a moment and then said, as if in argument, "Of course, he's not all right. People occupy a place in our lives, and when they're gone, there are empty places in our heart where they've been."

"And how's Andy doing?"

"He's even worse off than Coach," Biscuit said, "although we don't see as much of him as we used to. He only comes to about half the club runs now. He hangs out mostly with Chuck. Chuck told me that Andy studies a lot now, and runs a lot of miles."

"Oh."

"That's the thing with guys," Biscuit said. "When they're really down, they don't acknowledge it. They throw themselves into their work and hobbies, and think that if they ignore their problems, they'll go away. Both Coach and Andy are obsessed with the cross-country championship, and the final race is this coming Saturday. Coach is at work right now, but I talk with him and get him to work through his feelings. All Andy has now is Chuck." Biscuit stopped and smiled at Coco. "I love Chuck, but I wouldn't want him as my advisor."

Coco gave a small but preoccupied smile. Biscuit excused herself then, saying she had to go to the bathroom, but when she got down the hall, she ducked into the bedroom and called Andy. Biscuit thought that this was an ideal time to bring Coco and Andy back together. When Andy answered, she asked if he could lend Coach a quick hand to move a piece of furniture, and Andy said he would come right over. Back in the living room, she found Coco holding one of Moses' trophies.

"I'm sorry I missed Moses' funeral and tribute," Coco said. "I was in Pittsburgh with my mom." She placed the trophy back on the coffee table. "It's amazing what he accomplished," Coco said. "But to be strong, and then to die suddenly," she thought aloud."

"Moses had a hard life," Biscuit said, "and it took its toll on him."

"I'm worried about my mom," Coco said. Biscuit sat down next to her on the couch. "She just had renal failure. If she doesn't get a transplant soon, she's going to be gone too." Coco started to cry, and Biscuit put her arm around her. "I can't be a donor for her," Coco said. "I'm not a match, and there's nothing I can do. It's such a hopeless feeling."

Biscuit got Coco some tissues, and Coco told Biscuit about her mom, about how brave she'd been, and about how she insisted that Coco keep following her own dream. Biscuit just listened through it all. When Coco got it all out, she felt relieved. "Thank you for listening," she said.

"I tell Coach that the only way to calm our fears and solve our problems is to let others in," Biscuit said.

"Thank you."

"Let me know if there's anything I can do."

"I will. Thank you," Coco said. "I should get going now. I just invited myself over, and I've taken a lot of your time."

"It's all right." Biscuit looked at her watch. "Stay longer. I'll make us some tea."

"No, thank you. I should go."

Before Biscuit could delay her any longer, Coco got up and moved to the door, but just then, the bell rang. Biscuit opened the door to reveal Andy standing there.

"Andy?" Biscuit said, as if surprised to see him. "Did you come to see Coach?" Andy looked dumbfounded of course, having been called over by Biscuit just a little while ago, and Biscuit didn't wait for a reply. "He's working today." Biscuit nudged Coco toward the door. "And Coco was just leaving." Andy and Coco nodded toward each other and just stood there awkwardly, as Biscuit forged on. "Coach will be home this evening," she said to Andy. "Why don't you come back then?" And then to Coco, "Thanks for stopping by." She gave Coco a hug. "It was great to see you." With that, she closed the door on both of them.

Coco and Andy turned and walked down the steps together in silence, then headed down the sidewalk. They'd walked a few houses down the block before they stopped.

"How are you doing, Andy?"

"I've been great."

"Really?"

"Sure," Andy said. "And how are you?"

"If you're great," Coco said, "then I guess I'm great too."

Andy heard the hurt in her voice. "Coco, you know I don't mean it that way. The last couple of months have been hard, and you know that I miss you. I don't even understand what happened between us."

"What happened is that we're not right for each other."

"Coco, that's not true."

"You don't trust me, Andy," Coco said. "You don't really trust anyone."

"Coco."

"Do you remember how you told me about your grandmother and how she used her savings to send you here?"

"Yes."

"Do you realize that she wasn't just sending you to school? She was sending you out into the world, so that you could find your own way."

Andy was silent.

"Your grandmother sent you here to set you free of your past, to get you clear of everything that happened with your mom and dad, and my mother is helping me avoid what happened to her and the life she had. They love us and are trying to give us a chance." Coco paused to let what she'd said sink in. "Do you understand that? Do you even appreciate what's being done for you?"

"Of course I do."

"Then why are you holding on to that past?"

"I'm not. I'm here, aren't I?"

"Yes, and you brought that cloud over your head with you. And once again, you've surrounded yourself with people who think everything is fine with you, because you're such a great runner. Then you can feel proud of yourself and pretend that you're fine too."

"Coco, I've changed."

"No. You haven't. You're still holding on to the same fears and resentments. You're full of doubts and suspicion, and that's why you can't come out of that safe shell of yours and open yourself up to the love and the needs of others."

"That's not true."

"Then let me ask you something," Coco said. "You know my neighbor? Gloria? The one you went to visit?"

"Yes, of course."

"She's not feeling well now, and she could use some company," Coco said. "I'm wondering if you'd visit her again."

"Sure. I could do that."

"How about this coming Saturday?" Coco said pointedly.

Andy paused. "Coco, I can't this Saturday. It's the final race of the cross-country championship."

"What if I told you it was more important to me than any championship," Coco said. "Would you do it then?"

"But, Coco, I made a promise," Andy said. "I promised Coach. It's the state championship."

"The state championship?" Coco said. "I guess you can call it that. Or you could call it 'a run in the park.' The point is that there are matters of love, and of life and death, and *your* priority is another run through the woods."

"Life and death?" Andy said. "Coco, what are you talking about?"

"You have no real interest in me, do you?" Coco said. "No interest in the problems I'm facing." Coco threw up her hands in frustration. "Your grandmother was right about you," Coco said. "You're stubborn. Impossibly stubborn."

Coco turned and walked away, and Andy called after her, "Coco, do you know how much I love you?"

Coco stopped, turned, and called back, "Yes, Andy, I do," she said. "Evidently not enough."

When Coco left, Andy returned to Coach and Biscuit's apartment.

"Did you call me over just because Coco was here?"

"Of course," Biscuit said. "I wanted you guys to talk again. How did it go?"

Andy told her about the argument, and how Coco had asked him to go to Pittsburgh to visit her neighbor again, and how angry she'd become when he said he couldn't.

Biscuit had kept Coco's confidence, but now that she'd pulled Andy back into the affair, she felt an obligation to tell him the truth. She told him the whole story then: that the neighbor, Gloria, was really Coco's mother, and that she was going to die if she didn't get help.

Andy listened to it all and then said, "Oh my God. Why didn't she just tell me that?"

"Because it's difficult for her to talk about it, and because she wanted to see if you would trust in her without knowing everything."

"But she's being irrational," Andy said. "What can I do? Going to Pittsburgh again isn't going to solve the problem."

"Just be patient with her," Biscuit said. "That's all you can do right now. Just be supportive and understanding."

Andy left Biscuit's house more troubled than before. How could he be supportive and understanding when Coco wouldn't let him close to her? And what was completely baffling to him was why she somehow blamed him for everything that was happening.

Andy went out with Chuck that evening for a few beers, but he was still troubled when he got home late that night, and decided to go for a run to clear his mind. When he'd run with Moses late at night, they'd run slowly and talked, leaving him relaxed, but running alone that night, in an agitated state, Andy ran longer and harder than he should have, and instead of leaving him relaxed, the run left him restless and wired, and it was 3:00 AM when, completely exhausted, he finally slept.

Then it happened. He had the old dream, the dream he hadn't had since he was a boy. He was running, and with each step he took he soared higher into the air. People were watching, looking at him in awe. Moses was there, and Coach saw him too. Once he warmed up, he crossed America in three strides. He stepped down on Hawaii the way one would jump onto a stone to cross a pond, and then he was in Japan. It was easy running across Asia, and Europe was a jog. He touched down in Greenland, and two more strides brought him back. He did a quick loop to the North Pole as a cooldown, and then he came home.

When Andy awoke in the morning, he felt completely rested and refreshed. He lay in bed thinking about the dream, and tears filled his eyes. He didn't know why the dream had come to him again, but he accepted it from the world as a sign of grace, and as a blessed gift. The dream told him that he was on the right course, and that he only had to keep moving forward. Since his boyhood, running, and his talent for it, had been his solace. Coco was wrong in saying it was a place of refuge. He knew that running was a deep well from which he drew strength. His running was a meditation that grounded him, that brought him to the center of himself. Coco said he was just stubborn, but she was wrong again. It's not stubborn to hold a course in the right direction. Despite all that Coco had said, Andy knew in his heart that it was running that gave him all the answers he would ever need.

60. A Good GM

COACH HAD been obsessing about the state of his team, and all the things that could go wrong. What if Andy couldn't keep his head on straight and hold off John Malcolm? What if Bad Bob couldn't handle Darla and keep the Frieder freaks at bay? What if someone got injured before the race? And what if

Harry—as he had done before—recruited another top runner? There were just too many unknowns.

Coach knew that sometimes teaching athletes and motivating them just isn't enough. Sometimes training rigorously doesn't get it done. Sometimes even an invention as great as Coach-Aid won't put your team over the top. Sometimes, even with all that, doubt remains and victory is less than assured. That's why a coach also needs to be a good general manager. A good GM goes out and gets the athlete he needs to ensure victory for his team. In baseball, it could mean trading for a relief pitcher late in the season to shore up your bullpen for the pennant drive. In football, it could mean carrying a solid backup quarterback in case your starter goes down. And in running, it could mean calling in a ringer to fill a gap on your squad.

The championship race would be too close for comfort, and that was too close for Coach. He felt he had to make a move; he had to improve the odds. In high school or college, a runner has to attend the school in order to run for the team, and there are other restrictive rules, but in amateur club running, things are simpler. Any runner can join a club and compete for it, as long as that runner hasn't run for a competing club that year. Coach just had to recruit a great runner, and as a good GM, he had that ace up his sleeve.

Philip Barlow was his name. Coach had run with him at school, and Philip had gone on to run at the university and was now running for a club in Manchester. Philip was the fastest runner that Coach had ever known, all legs and lungs and a gorgeous stride, with guts and a kick-ass competitive drive to boot, but as far as Coach was concerned right now, the best thing about Philip was that he owed Coach a favor, big time. How had Philip put it? Oh, yes, it was like this: "I won't forget this, man. If there's ever anything I can do for you—anything—just ask."

"Oh, I'll ask all right," Coach thought, and Coach knew there was no way that Philip could say no. Coach had practically saved Philip's brother's life. His brother, Perry, had been busted for possession of cocaine, and Coach had lent Philip ten thousand pounds for his bail. Coach had the money from an inheritance from his grandmother, and none of their other friends could have come up with it. What Coach didn't know at the time, and Philip suspected, was that Perry would jump bail. Perry had double-crossed some unsavory characters, and knew that if he did jail time, they would get to him. It had taken

Philip three years to pay Coach back, and it was during that time that he often repeated his thanks to Coach and his pledge to return the favor.

Coach had been happy to help Philip out. He was a friend, after all, and Coach was awestruck by his talent as a runner, but a favor is a favor, and Coach was not above calling in the debt. He dialed Philip's number with the confidence of a gambler holding a royal flush, and Philip answered. There was no mistaking his raspy snarl of a voice. "Is this Philip Barlow?" Coach said. "The Philip Barlow who buried Ian Ruggle on King's Hill on his way to running a fucking *unbelievable* 14:42. The Philip Barlow who dueled with John "The Hammer" Hamilton for two miles on the bloody toughest course in all of England, and then out-kicked him to win the Manchester championship."

"Emmitt?" Philip said. "Emmitt Bean? The Emmitt fucking Bean with the two left feet. The Emmitt Bean who made his entire team look faster just by running with them." Philip laughed at the thought. "Hey, Bean, remember when you tried to hang with us on that trial run through Gloucester, and we handed you your butt?"

Coach did remember. It was on that very run, led by Philip, that Coach finally realized he would never make it as a runner himself. Indeed, Coach had Philip to thank for awakening him to his true calling as a coach. Coach and Philip spent a few minutes bringing each other up to date with their lives and the news of old teammates before the question of just why Coach had called began to fill the air. "So what's up, man?" Philip asked, finally laying it out.

Coach answered the question with a not-so-subtle one of his own. "How's your brother doing?"

Philip knew then that Coach was cashing in his chip. He was relieved in a way, because he wanted to even the score, but he was edgy too, because he had no idea what Coach wanted. "Perry's clean and lying low," he said. "Listen, I still owe you for that, man. Is there anything I can do for you now?"

"No, Philip. You don't owe me anything, dude." It wouldn't hurt to be magnanimous, Coach thought; there was no way out for Philip. Coach paused, and then added, as if it were an afterthought, "You *could* do me a favor though, if you have some time." Coach laid out the situation with the X-C championship, with Horrible Harry and the Striders, and with the state of his team. "If you could hop over and run with us, we'd have the Striders by the balls."

"What day did you say you were racing?"

Coach told him.

"I want us to be square, man."

"Run this one for me, Philip, and we'll be as square as Prince Charles."

"All right then," Philip said. "I'll call you when I have my flight."

When Coach rang off, he shot both arms up in victory and did an involuntary jig around the room, then penciled in Philip's name at the top of the roster. Just seeing his name there, relegating a runner as great as Andy to the second spot, made Coach's heart soar. Coach couldn't contain himself, and he called Edsel right away to share the news. What a dream team! The race was a week off, and it was already all but over, and the sweetest thing of all, Coach thought, was that that wanker Harry, the Freaks, and the whole bloody Strider team didn't even know it.

61. If You Need a Hand

AT 5:00 AM on the morning of the big race, while Coach and the HOHAs and Hoboken slept, Coco's cell phone rang on her bedside table. Coco grabbed at it, and when she heard her mother's voice, she blurted out, "Mom, what happened?"

"I'm in the hospital," Gloria said. "There's a donor."

Gloria and Coco had been told, and often reminded, that a donor could become available at any time, from an auto accident or from any other sudden death, that time was essential, and that they had to be prepared. These thoughts came to Coco now, and she felt the gravity of death and the magnitude of this moment. She could only gasp at the news.

"It's OK, Coconut," Gloria said. "It's the gift we've hoped and prayed for."

Coco collected herself then. "When is the operation?"

"In an hour."

"In an hour?" Coco exclaimed. "I can't get there by then."

"Of course you can't," Gloria said. "It's OK. There's no need for you to be here during the operation, but can you be here when I come out?"

"Yes, yes, of course. I'll get the first flight."

"It's a miracle, Coconut," Gloria said. "I'm getting a second chance."

"Mom, I'm happy, but I'm scared for you."

"Don't be scared. This is a blessing."

"Does Dr. Spencer think that everything looks good?"

"He thinks it's a perfect match. He said, 'All systems are go.'"

"I love you, Mom."

"I love you too, Coconut. I'll see you soon. They have me medicated, and I should rest now."

"Yes. Yes. You rest now," Coco said. "I'll be there as soon as I can."

Coco was able to get the first flight out of Newark, and was at the hospital by ten o'clock. Gloria had just come out of surgery, and the nurse told Coco that the doctor would speak with her soon. It was only a few minutes before Dr. Spencer came out, but to Coco it seemed like hours. He was still in his surgery scrubs, and she could read nothing from his face as he crossed the room.

"Miss Cushman," he said. "Great news. The surgery went perfectly, and your mother is doing fine."

"Oh, thank heaven," Coco said. "And thank you, doctor."

"We'll be cautiously optimistic. We should see a rapid improvement in your mother's health."

"Thank you."

"You won't be able to see your mother for about an hour, but you can see the donor now."

"The donor?" Coco said. "You mean the donor wasn't deceased?"

"No. Your mother had a voluntary donor." Dr. Spencer was surprised that Coco didn't know. "She didn't tell you?"

"No. Mom just called to tell me about the surgery. I assumed a donor had just become available."

"Well then, I'll let them tell you all about that."

A nurse showed Coco to the room, and she entered quietly. There was only one bed, and the curtain was drawn to screen it from the door. She stepped around the curtain to the foot of the bed. The room was white, and the bedding was white, and her eyes were immediately drawn to the wild splotch of color on the bedside table. Her first thought was of a bouquet of flowers, but she now saw that it was the Monmouth Elf. When that surprise had registered, she looked at the person lying in the bed. He was pale, and it took her a moment to realize that it was Andy. Coco stepped around the bed and up to him. His eyes were half open, and he saw her now.

Andy was clearly weak, and said nothing, but raised his forearm and held his hand open to her. She pressed her palm to his, supporting it with her other hand. "Andy," she said.

Andy swallowed, and struggled to turn his head toward her. "How's your mom doing?" he said.

"I can't see her yet, but Dr. Spencer says she's doing fine."

"She's a great lady."

"Andy, why didn't you tell me?"

"I had to do it for your mom, and for you," he said. "I was afraid you'd try to stop me."

"You're the most generous person in the world."

"If you need a hand, I have two: one for me, and one for you." He tried to smile, but the pain stopped him short.

"That's sweet. Did you make it up?"

"It's a rhyme that my grandma used to recite to me when I was growing up. Especially when I was in trouble. It's been on my mind lately."

"I'm so grateful. Whatever made you do it?"

"Moses, I guess. I was young when my mom left and my dad died, and I didn't know them well. Moses was the first person I really loved and then lost. When I felt that pain, and when I saw Buddy's pain too, I understood what it means to lose someone. Then, when Biscuit told me about your mom, I understood what you were facing, and I didn't want you to feel that."

"Thank you, Andy."

"Don't forget to thank the Elf." Andy's smile broke through this time, and he tilted his head toward the Elf. "It brought us luck." Coco looked over at the goofy Elf on the nightstand and smiled through her tears. "I know you don't care much for Coach, but he helped me too. When I ran in college, I learned to visualize the races and how strong I would run. Coach and Moses reminded me recently about the importance of envisioning what you want the most."

Andy's words had tired him, and now his eyes closed softly. When they opened again, he continued his thought. "And I visualized us together."

Andy looked right at Coco now, his eyes filled with love. Coco raised her hand and kissed Andy's palm, and then gently lowered his hand to the bed and tucked it under the coverlet.

"And I visualized myself finding my way into your heart," he said. Now Andy's exhaustion overcame him, and he fell asleep.

Coco looked down at the calm beauty of his face, and tears ran down her cheeks. "You're already there, Andy," she said. "You're already there."

Coco watched over Andy while he slept until the nurse came in and told her she could see her mother now. Gloria was sleeping too when Coco entered her room, so Coco sat down in the chair next to the bed. A couple of minutes later, she heard her mom say her name.

"Yes, Mom, it's me. I'm here."

"Coco, you're here."

"How do you feel, Mom?"

"I'm feeling no pain now, but I guess that's the drugs. I might hurt later."

"Dr. Spencer said the surgery went perfectly and that you're going to be feeling better soon."

"I'm glad that you're here."

"I love you, Mom." Coco gave her mother a kiss on the forehead. "I just saw Andy. Why didn't you tell me?"

"How's he doing?"

"He's tired, but the nurse says he's doing fine."

"I've been worried about him," Gloria said. "Dr. Spencer said it's more difficult for the donor; they were well, and are not used to being ill."

"Mom, why didn't you tell me?"

"Andy asked me not to tell you, and I didn't want to worry you. If you'd known that the operation was scheduled, you'd have worried."

Coco could see that her mom was exhausted, and her reply was soft and loving, rather than argumentative. "You still should have told me, Mom."

Gloria reflected for a moment before replying. "You know, they make you sign release forms, acknowledging that you might not make it. I was lying on my back looking up at the nurses, and I was thinking that it might be the last time I saw anyone in this world. When they wheel you into the ICU, you see the sign for the morgue right next to it, and all that's separating them is a set of swinging doors, and you put your head back and think, 'Oh, my God! Here I go!' What gave me courage was knowing that my angel had gone in there before me, and he didn't even have to. He took that risk for me. Maybe I should have told you. I don't know. It was a miracle, Coconut, and I don't know the rules for miracles."

62. The Big Dance

EARLY ON THE MORNING of the championship race—or the big dance, as Coach had been calling it—Coach got a call of his own. It was Edsel. "I might not be able to make the race," he said.

"What?"

"I called over to the store and nobody answered. Darla's not there. There was no answer at her apartment either."

"She knows she has to open when we have a race," Coach said indignantly.

"That shipment came in yesterday afternoon," Edsel continued, "and she was supposed to be at the store stocking it. If she doesn't show, I'll have to do it myself before I can open the store."

"She'd better show."

"I'm going over to the store now to see what's going on," Edsel said. "I'll call you from there."

When Edsel got to the store, there was no Darla, and the shipment she was supposed to be stocking was still piled up in the middle of the store. Edsel was still shaking his head at the sight when he noticed a note on the cash register. It was from Darla. He took a moment to let the message sink in, and then called Coach. "I've got good news and bad news," he said.

"You bastard," Coach said. "What is it?"

"The good news is that we won't have to put up with Darla anymore. She's eloped."

"What do you mean 'eloped'?"

"What do you think I mean? She's run off to get married."

"Who in the hell would marry her?" was Coach's immediate reaction.

Before Coach could put two and two together, Edsel dropped the other shoe. "That's the bad news," he said. "She's eloped with Bad Bob."

This was a punch in the gut, and Coach felt his stomach heave up to his throat as the news registered. The loss of Bob would be a severe blow to the HOHAs' chances in the championship. Coach was rarely at a loss for words, but this news left him speechless.

There was a prolonged silence, until Edsel finally said, "Coach?"

"I guess that means Bob won't be at the race," Coach said.

"People don't run races on their honeymoons," Edsel said.

It was a testament to Coach's tenacity that he didn't give up, even then, still holding to one glimmer of hope. "Did she say where they were going?" he asked.

"Does it matter?"

Coach was hoping that they'd just run off to Jersey City or Queens, and that he might still rescue Bob that morning.

"Where, Edsel?" he demanded.

"Las Vegas."

That last hope was now extinguished, and the irony of Coach's own fatal matchmaking dawned on him then. Coach scrambled to salvage something. "You can still make the race, Edsel," Coach said. "You'll just open later, and I'll help you."

"Coach, don't you remember?" Edsel said. "We advertised a sale today. I've got to shelf this shipment and open on time."

Coach now understood the maliciousness of Darla's timing and the nefariousness of her plan. Fortunately, Edsel had spared Coach the antagonizing postscript to Darla's note: "PS: tell Coach I said 'Hi'!" He knew that it would only have incensed him, and Edsel himself was already pissed enough for the both of them. "We're screwed," Edsel said.

Coach was running the situation through his mind. Darla had abducted Bad Bob and abandoned her job, and because of that, he'd lost not only Bob, but now Edsel as well. She'd deprived him of his number two and three runners on the most important race day in HOHAs history. She might as well have punched him below the belt. Coach felt as if he were being pummeled in a fight, and his only thought was to keep his hands up and stay on his feet.

"Coach?" Edsel said again, then waited, but Coach still didn't respond. Finally, Edsel yelled into the phone, "Coach, what are you thinking?"

Coach refocused and was suddenly back again, re-energized and impassioned by Darla's attack. He would have to replace Edsel with The Eck. The team would lose some time there, but maybe not too many points. And he still had Philip Barlow and Andy Bell, and if that wasn't a one-two knockout punch, he didn't know what was. With a steely determination that meant a round had been lost but the fight was not yet over, Coach said, "That bitch!"

Philip Barlow had flown in to town the previous afternoon and had spent the night at Coach and Biscuit's apartment. He was with them when they arrived at Edsel's store for the gathering before the race. Coach had recruited all the HOHAs who weren't racing to come out and provide moral support, and there was a large turnout at the store. The news about Bad Bob and Darla had everyone talking. Coach himself got caught up in several exchanges about them, and this, along with the introductions of Philip, kept him from his customary headcounts and the organization of the rides. Because of this, it wasn't until Coach got down to the race site that he realized he hadn't seen Andy all morning.

Coach asked around and found that no one, not even Chuck, had seen him. Chuck, as it turned out, hadn't even spoken with Andy in the last few days. Then Coach thought that maybe Andy had somehow come down alone and had gone out on his own warm-up run, and he sent several HOHAs out on the trails to look for him. Then, when those searches came up empty, Coach went out on a search of his own. He saw Harry and the Striders, Shore, the Sneaker Factory, and all the other clubs, who were out in force, but nowhere could he find Andy. Coach was growing frantic as the race start approached. He asked around again, and again got the same answers. Finally, with less than twenty minutes to go before the race, he had no choice but to gather the team for the pep talk and the distribution of the jerseys.

Coach looked beat. He'd been working hard, and the shocks of that morning brought the fatigue to his face. Mixed with that fatigue was his realization that now, the HOHAs had no chance. Even with Philip Barlow, the HOHAs couldn't overcome the loss of Andy and Bad Bob, and Edsel too, but Coach was such a positive force that, out of habit alone, he held to hope. He kept looking over the heads of his assembled team for the appearance of Andy, and gathered his remaining energy and started his final pep talk with his customary enthusiasm.

"Today we are going up against the Brooklyn Striders, Shore, Sneaker Factory, Fleet Feet, and all the other top teams in the region. This run is for the New Jersey State X-C Championship, and I want to remind everybody that we are the defending champions here. This great title belongs to us. We are the champions, until somebody has the juice to take it away from us."

All the HOHAs applauded.

"A team is a championship team when every runner on that team is a champion. We don't have to worry about the competition. We just have to know that when we cross the finish line, we have given everything we have. If each one of us is a champion today, we will go home knowing that the HOHAs are champions too."

The HOHAs applauded again.

"Now, let's name our squad," Coach said boldly.

Coach was ready to pass out the racing jerseys, and all the HOHAs knew that for this race it would be different. With the team leaders gone, there were question marks and a couple of jerseys up for grabs.

"First, I want to thank my old running buddy Philip Barlow for coming over from England to run for us today," Coach said. "Philip is an old friend and a great runner, and he's going to tear up this course and lead us to victory." There was applause for Philip. "Philip, the number one jersey goes to you."

Coach then handed out jerseys, as expected, to Patti, Icky, and Boston. He was down then to the three remaining jerseys for the open runners, and the first one, also as expected, went to The Eck. Then Coach stopped. He looked over his shoulder once more, in the hope that Andy had arrived, but there was no Andy, and Coach knew then that no matter who he gave the last two jerseys to, they would be unable to help the HOHAs win. Coach looked out over his team, scanning their faces, returning to them over and over, in the way someone hungry returns to an empty refrigerator time and again, knowing there is nothing there, but refusing to believe it.

At that point, the Striders passed by, doing their final warm-up. Coach saw John Malcolm, in all his glory, the Frieder twins, Don Abrams, and Harry himself and the rest of his impressive squad. Coach watched them pass in silence. It was then that he really knew, finally admitted to himself, that the HOHAs didn't have a chance.

Biscuit was standing to his right, and Coach looked over to her and rested his eyes on her for a while. There was always energy between them, and anyone could see it that day. Their eyes were locked, and then Coach's eyes softened. In his eyes then, there was surrender, and an epiphany. When Coach looked away from Biscuit, he looked out at the rest of the HOHAs and smiled.

The captains picked the teams before the game, and the other boys lined up in front of them. They picked the best players first, of course, and it got lonely on the line, hoping your turn would come. Even if you were the last one picked, you were alone no longer, troubled no more, as you were welcomed into the warm huddle of your team.

Given the tensions of that day, the smile that came from Coach was unexpected. It was a smile full of mischievousness and glee, and all the HOHAs could feel that Coach was going to do something special. There was a picnic table next to him, and he jumped up and stood on top of it, as if he had something important to say. Then he took the sixth jersey and held it high. "The next jersey goes to our newest HOHA and our most improved," he said. He found Chuck in the group and smiled at him. "Chucky, come on up here."

Everyone was shocked, but none so much as Chuck himself. All year long, as he'd learned the basics of running, he'd heard Coach weaving the legend of this championship and this race, and now Coach had chosen him to wear one of the golden jerseys and represent the team. All those around him were slapping him on the back, but even this didn't shake him from his shock. Finally, Coach got down from the table and brought the jersey to Chuck and gave him a hug.

Chuck's selection created heightened attention among the HOHAs, because if Coach had selected Chuck, then any one of them could be next. Coach had returned to the table and was now holding up the seventh jersey for everyone to see. "When I founded this club almost ten years ago," he said, "I had to run the first runs alone before the first HOHA appeared. That HOHA has been with the club ever since, and he's here today." Coach was looking to the center of the group now, and the veteran HOHAs, who knew the club history, were looking there too. "Today, we're going to honor that runner," Coach said. "So the seventh and last jersey goes to the first HOHA." Coach grinned and looked at Howie. "Howie, this one's for you." Howie had been eating a bagel and still had it to his mouth when Coach brought the jersey to him. Coach just slipped the jersey over Howie's head, bagel and all. Everyone was applauding, but they were also thinking, "Howie has never even finished a HOHAs club run, let alone a race, let alone five kilometers of the toughest cross-country terrain on the East Coast." But everybody was also thinking, "I guess it's OK, if Coach thinks it is."

Right up until race time, all Coach was really thinking was "Where is Andy?" He didn't stop scanning the crowd, hoping that Andy would miraculously appear. Even as the race director instructed the runners to take the starting line, Coach was taking one last look around, and when the race director gave the final instructions and sounded the air horn to start the race, Coach held out hope that Andy had somehow snuck onto the line unseen and was in the race.

63. Bringing It Home

THE RIGOROUS Holmdel course commands attention, and despite Coach's preoccupation with Andy, he had to focus himself on his racing, the immediate demands of the uphill start and the other challenges of the course. Coach fought his way through the start and was two-thirds of the way back in the pack and breathing heavily when he approached the amphitheater, which, with its half-mile loop around a sloping, open field, provided Coach with his first view of the leaders. Philip Barlow was already completing the loop, with a good hundred-yard lead on the following runners. Coach saw him, like a man among boys, running easily, as if toying with his competition and the course itself. This gave Coach a brief moment of hope, until he forced his eyes to draw back from the mesmerizing sight of Barlow to the pack of runners behind him. There wasn't a single HOHA, but there were five Striders. First was Malcolm, flailing somewhat, bereft of his normal grace, shocked that there was already someone else so far out in front. Ten yards back from Malcolm were the Frieder twins, running in such unison that despite Coach's familiarity with them, he had to remind himself again that he wasn't seeing double. Behind the twins were Don Abrams and Harry Horton himself. Harry was a hundred yards from Coach, but even from that distance, Coach thought he saw Harry's trademark smirk and gloating satisfaction. Coach watched Harry for a while before he let his eyes drift back to the next group of runners, hoping in vain that he would see a gaining throng of HOHAs, but he saw only Shore and Sneaker Factory runners, with only one HOHA, The Eck, struggling amongst them. Only then did Coach know, and finally admit to himself, that it was over.

The Holmdel course is tough enough when you have hope for victory, but it is even tougher when a quarter of the way through, you know that the race is lost, and yet Coach kept on running. He fought his way around the amphitheater and raced on through the flats in the middle of the course. Some of the slower HOHAs had packed around him then, and despite his own fatigue, he encouraged them on. Coach watched his form and worked through the last legs of the course, taking some satisfaction in finishing with a band of his HOHAs around him.

There is exhilaration at the finish of any race, no matter how poorly a runner or his team has performed, and Coach joined the other HOHAs in that satisfying moment, before the reality of their loss sank in. He congratulated and thanked Philip Barlow, and then joined Biscuit, who was waiting for him near the finish.

"Philip ran great," Coach said, "but the Striders really kicked our butts."

"It's OK," Biscuit said.

"I hope Andy's OK," Coach said with concern. "It's not like him not to show."

"I think he had something really important to do," Biscuit said. The way she said it, and the look she gave Coach, made him understand.

There was some loud cheering then, and applause, and Coach and Biscuit turned to see that Chuck was coming in. All the HOHAs had lined the homestretch, and were cheering him on. Chuck was in a group of slower Shore and Sneaker Factory women and, bolstered by the cheers of the HOHAs, was pumping his arms and sprinting with all he had to beat them to the line. He was shoulder to shoulder with the fastest of them all the way to the finish, and he leaned forward at the line like a sprinter to get the win. The HOHAs gathered around him in congratulations.

"Tough running," one of the HOHAs said.

"Big slice of cake," Chuck said.

"You looked great, Chuck."

"Chuck busted a move," Chuck said.

Chuck and his entourage were moving past Coach and Biscuit now, and Coach said, "Way to run, Chuck."

Chuck was beaming with pride and basking in the attention. He raised his arms in Rocky-like victory. "Hey, Coach," he said, "Chuck gonna go pro."

A few stragglers had come in after Chuck, but the excitement of Chuck's finish had seemed to mark the end of the race. Chuck and the rest of the HOHAs were leaving the field when they heard the first scream from the top of the steep hill that leads down to the finish.

From the upper plateau of the course, there is that sudden drop-off to a steep and winding downhill trail through the woods that leads to the open field of the homestretch. The trail is a treacherous and exhilarating piece of running. Even experienced runners must focus on the sharp drops and turns and work to avoid flying off the course and into the trees. By the time Howie reached this portion of the course, he was already past that point in a run where he would normally have stopped and just walked it in, but throughout the race, he'd been conscious of the gold jersey he was wearing, and had felt pride as he passed spectators along the way, because the jersey told them that he was running for a team. Of course he was slow, but he was clearly part of a team, and perhaps they saw him as a good runner just having a bad day. He thought of the gratitude he'd felt when Coach had given him the jersey. He knew how much this race meant to Coach, and he was inspired by the faith that Coach had in him. All of that had kept him going. Then he saw the ledge, and the drop-off to the downhill, and although he didn't fully understand how harrowing a piece of running this trail would be, he knew it would be far beyond his ability and experience. Howie looked down again at the gold jersey, swallowed hard, and took that first irretrievable step over the edge, whereupon his weight propelled him like a runaway truck down the grapevine of the trail. Within moments, Howie was a passenger in his own out-of-control body, and all he could do was hold on for dear life and scream.

Slow-Mo had been at the bottom of the trail cheering the last runners and had just started back across the field toward the finish line when he heard Howie's first scream from above. He ran back to the trailhead and peered up into the shadows. He could see little through the woods, but could hear Howie's screaming getting closer. The screams were half fear and half exhilaration, like the screams that come from riders on a roller coaster. Slow-Mo peered up the hill toward the screams and caught a glimpse of the familiar gold HOHAs jersey. He was mesmerized by the sight of Howie moving fast, by Howie's flailing arms and bouncing blubber and, as Howie got closer, by the super-size combo of terror and excitement that he could see on Howie's face. Then Slow-Mo realized with alarm that he was standing in the middle of the trail, and that Howie was barreling inexorably toward him. Slow-Mo ran out onto the field to get out of the way, and then shouted to the crowd at the finish, "It's Howie!" He raised his arms in disbelief, and shouted again, "Howie's coming in!"

Slow-Mo's shouts captured the crowd's attention, and all the HOHAs came to a stop, shocked by the news that Howie was still running the course. Several of the HOHAs then ran out toward Slow-Mo to see for themselves. One by one, they peered up the trail into the woods, saw the big gold blur coming fast, heard the screams getting louder and closer and, like Slow-Mo before them, retreated to the safety of the field where they formed a corridor at the base of the trail and waited. Now the screams grew more frantic as Howie came through the final drop-offs and hairpin turns that would slingshot him from the woods. When he eventually emerged, his arms were extended like wings in a desperate attempt to balance himself and slow himself down.

At this point in the course, the finishing banner is in sight, beckoning from across a pleasingly flat stretch of open grass. Howie was now feeling a flush of pride in surviving his descent, and was enjoying the unfamiliar sense of speed that the downhill and his own body mass had given him. He heard the cheers of his fellow HOHAs as he emerged from the woods, and saw them lined up for him, waving him home. Then he saw the crowd at the finish too, and heard their applause. All eyes were upon him, this moment was his, and he would rise to it. "Use your arms," Coach would say. "Watch your form." Howie straightened his shoulders, raised his chin, and pumped his arms. The HOHAs looked on and struggled to believe what they were seeing: Howie was gaining speed. He was not only going to finish, he was going to finish strong.

Howie's legs felt like rubber, his breathing was heavy and his chest was gripped in a vice of pain, and he realized that all the past discomfort of his jogging and walking were nothing compared with this. He'd brought himself to a new level of effort and commitment and, for the first time, understood its reward. He could see the finish, and he felt the pride of knowing he was doing all that he could do.

"Visualize your performance," Coach would say. "See yourself succeed." Howie projected himself toward the finish and saw himself triumphantly crossing the line. Then he lowered his chin and took one stride after another to bring himself to where he had seen himself to be. In all his pain, his mind screamed at him to stop, but he beat those thoughts away. There would be no quitting now. He could hear the cheering, and could see the HOHAs waving him on. It was all a blur of noise and excitement, and his heart pounded wildly, and then, somehow, unbelievably, he was there.

The HOHAs surrounded him and held him steady until he could catch his breath. Then they tried to lift him onto their shoulders, but there were groans and then laughs as they gave up the attempt. Instead, they broke into a boisterous and exuberant chant of "Howieeee! Howieeee! Howieeee!"

When Howie saw Coach looking on, he yelled over the noise, "Coach, I did it! I finished!"

Coach yelled back just one word: "Terminator!"

As the HOHAs left the field in triumphant defeat, Harry Horton came up to Coach, who introduced him to Biscuit. "Congratulations," Coach said.

"Your club ran strong."

"And your team had some injuries, I take it."

"Injuries," Coach repeated. "Yeah, I guess you could call them that."

"That's too bad."

"No, that's just the way it is, Harry," Coach said. All that had happened in the last year came together in one thought, and Coach remembered and repeated his own words to Harry the year before. "Injuries are part of the game."

When Harry left, Biscuit said, "What injuries?"

"I don't know," Coach said. "Broken hearts, I guess."

"It's funny," Biscuit said. "Harry didn't have the horns and pitchfork I thought he'd have."

"No, but he's still a wanker," Coach said. "Although I guess he got the best of me today."

Biscuit knew more than anyone how much this race had meant to Coach, and how disappointed he was. "Did you see Howie's face?" she said. "I've never seen him so happy." She put her hand on Coach's back and rubbed it up and down. "You did that, you know."

"Yeah, I guess."

"And Chuck. Two months ago he was in despair, and now he's 'going pro.' You did that, too."

"Yeah, Chuck's coming along."

Biscuit looked back to see the race staff taking down the finishing banner and the clock, and she and Coach stopped, alone on the field, and watched. "It's odd," Biscuit said. "Time only exists while we're counting it. When we take away the clock, all that came before is gone, and there's just right now." The leaves on the trees were red and gold, and the autumnal sun cast long shadows across the field. Biscuit slipped her arm into Coach's and leaned against him. "And right now is wonderful, isn't it?"

"Yes, it is."

They stood there for the longest time, together, side by side, and then Biscuit put her head against Coach's chest and gave him a hug. "Come on," she said. "Let's go home."

64. Y2K

WHEN THE RACE staff took down the clock that day, with Coach and Biscuit quietly looking on, they were really taking down the clock on a whole decade of history. Nobody knew it then though, and it wasn't until some looked back on that day from a distance that it became clear that that day marked the end of an era.

Time hints at the beginning of things before they really begin: a rooster crows before the sun rises. And time foreshadows the end of things before they really end: a mother calls her children home before the sun sets. Coach and Biscuit did go home that day, but it wasn't the same home they'd left that morning, and the HOHAs ran the following Tuesday and Thursday, but those runs weren't the same as the runs that had come before. The small changes that had been occurring all along now subtly and seamlessly shifted into place. Coach had sensed this shift coming, and had been fighting against it for months, fighting it before he really knew what he was fighting against, before he knew that he was fighting against even himself, against the changes not only outside himself but also inside his own mind and heart.

Time accompanies change with a heightened activity that marks the change itself, and at the same time distracts from it. The pace of life picked up then. There was the anticipation of the holiday season, and the celebrations to mark the year 2000. If it were any consolation to Coach, he didn't have time to dwell on his loss to Harry. After the race series, he worked almost around the clock, deep in the final leg of the Y2K preparations, and because of Coach and other computer whizzes like him, at the stroke of midnight and the dawn of the new millennium, our systems didn't crash, and the Earth didn't turn into a pumpkin. In reality, the Y2K celebrations turned out to be the greatest party the world had ever thrown. From continent to continent, from city to city—like sports fans rising up in a continuous wave around a stadium—there was a wave of fireworks and popping champagne corks and dancing through the night that circled the globe. This wave could be seen from outer space, and heard from there too. One could imagine the neighbors, the Venusians and Martians, calling the galactic police and asking them to make the Earthlings quiet it down. In the end, the celebrations finally gave way to yet another sunrise and quiet morning, and the eternal question of what to do with the coming day.

Coach faced that day with his usual optimism, seeing not the loss but the opportunity. He called it a new beginning, and said that the HOHAs could chart personal records from that day forward. Coach was already looking forward to the spring racing season, and to sweet revenge over Harry that next fall. He exhorted the HOHAs through their training that winter, not knowing yet that this would be his last season with the club. In early spring, Biscuit got a job offer in Boston, and knew, in that mysterious way she had of knowing, that it was time to go.

> *Life often presents us with a choice: to move forward or to stay put. Biscuit said that that's no choice at all, but just an illusion, because if we resist a calling and think we can keep things the same, we're left to watch everything change around us. Biscuit said that we eventually have to move on, so it is better to step boldly forward.*

That spring brought sadness as Coach and his HOHAs acknowledged the progression of time and the passing of a part of their lives that they had pretended would never end. All times are lost, of course, but some are more remembered, and Coach didn't let that time go quietly. He organized a party and a send-off run in early May to coincide with the HOHAs' 10th anniversary. Many former HOHAs came in from out of town, and all the local HOHAs were there. The party was at Coach and Biscuit's apartment on a Saturday night, and the run was the next morning. The party went late into the night, and the HOHAs were bleary-eyed the next day, but they ran the Tuesday course together as a team and then gathered in Sinatra Park down by the river for a picnic. It was a nostalgic day, and many lingered through the afternoon, not wanting to let go, but eventually everyone said their good-byes and, just like that, it was over.

65. Welcome to Hoboken

THE CUCKOO CLOCK sounded in the living room of Elysian Fields, startling Britney and Jeanie and Uncle Bill, bringing them back into the present moment, as if from a long sleep.

"When they take away the clock," Uncle Bill said, "you look back and say, 'Where did it all go?' It's as if it were all a dream."

"But it wasn't a dream, Uncle Bill," Jeanie said. "It did happen."

"I guess it did," Uncle Bill said, "because there's something that proves that it did. Girls, if you remember, at the beginning of the story I told you there was a sign at the entrance of Hoboken that said, 'Welcome to Hoboken—Birth Place of Baseball and Frank Sinatra.'

"Well, early on the morning of the HOHAs' 10th anniversary, the day before Coach and Biscuit were to leave for Boston, Coach called me and asked me to come over. He said he needed help with something, but he wouldn't tell me what it was. You know by now how he liked to be dramatic. When I got there, he came out of the house with a backpack and a flat cardboard package. He wouldn't tell me what he had, and he wouldn't tell me where we were going, but we walked toward the north of town. When we got to that sign at the entrance to Hoboken, he stopped. He took two bottles of beer out of the backpack and gave me one. He said he wanted to make a toast.

"'To the Hoboken Harriers,' he said. 'Ten years old today, one time a champion, and officially an established club for the practice of the great art of running. Today, I declare your right to stand with your forbearers and declare you worthy to do honor to the fine town from which you received your name.'

"He touched his beer bottle to mine, and we drank. It was too early to be drinking beer, but that's what made the beer taste great: the early morning, and the silly speech, and the two of us together on the side of the road."

"'Would you like to add anything, Bill?'" he said.

"'Just that I'm gonna miss you, Coach. It was great running with you these years.'

"'Rubbish,' he said. 'Declare your feelings for the HOHAs.'

"'To the HOHAs,' I said, holding up my beer again, 'the greatest running club in New Jersey.'

"'Not in America?'

"'The greatest running club in America.'

"'Not in the world?'

"'The greatest running club in the world.'

"'That's more like it.' He slapped me on the back and we both took another swig of beer. 'Now that the speeches are over,' he said, 'we can proceed with the dedication.'

"Coach opened the cardboard package and took out a metal plate, a couple of feet high by about three feet wide. There was something printed on it, but Coach had it turned toward himself so that I couldn't read it. He motioned toward the signpost and said, 'Read the sign, and put some gusto into it.'

"I read loudly and with enthusiasm:

'*Welcome To*
Hoboken
Birth Place Of
Baseball & Frank Sinatra'

"'Keep reading,' Coach said. Now he turned the plate that he was holding toward me so that I could read from it, and I kept reading in the same voice:

'*and home of the*
Hoboken Harriers'

"Coach's addition to the sign, in both lettering and color, matched the rest.

"'That's cool,' I said. 'How did you make it?'

"'I asked Ben at Counter-Fit Printing to make it for us. Didn't he do a great job?'

"'Perfect.'

"'Come on. Help me put it up.'

"Coach had brought the tools and hardware we needed to attach our sign to the posts, and we fixed it securely below the original sign. We then stood back to get a good look at it.

"'It looks great,' I said.

"We clinked our beer bottles and took another swig.

"'It is great, isn't it?' Coach said.

"'You did it, Coach.'

"'I can go now,' Coach said. There were tears in his eyes and a discernible mix of sadness and pride in his voice. 'My work here is done.'"

66. An Old Photo

"WHAT HAPPENED to all the HOHAs?" Britney asked.

"After Coach and Biscuit left, the HOHAs were in denial for a while, holding on to the possibility that they would return, but that was just a bandage to make the separation easier. Then there was a period where the HOHAs pretended they were better off without Coach and all his craziness, but that was just a bandage too. Eventually, as time went on and news of Coach and Biscuit's successes in Boston came in, it became clear that they wouldn't be back, and the HOHAs were left to do the one thing that they had always done, and that Coach had taught them was most important: they kept running together.

"And they're still together now," Bill said, "and going strong. Coach still gets the newsletter and a request, as the founding father, to attend some special event now and then. There have been different presidents, of course, and whole generations of HOHAs have come and gone, but they still run every Tuesday and Thursday evenings on the same courses that Coach laid out. I ran with them for several years after Coach left, but it was never the same for me without him and Biscuit. Some of the old regulars stayed on for a while too, and new runners came and went, and there were more love affairs, and squabbles too. When I left, I calculated that the HOHAs, as a club, had already produced fifteen marriages, eighteen children, one divorce, and three restraining orders."

Britney laughed. "Who had the restraining orders?"

"The first one belonged to Chuck. After the incident at the wedding, Nancy decided to take revenge by driving poor Chuck crazy. Even in the courtroom that day, she was wearing a skimpy halter top that made even the judge's throat go dry. The judge couldn't very well order Nancy to wear a bra, although I think the thought crossed his mind, so he had no choice but to slap a restraining order on poor Chuck."

"And the other two?"

"Well, the divorce and the other two restraining orders belonged to Bad Bob and Darla. Darla was a bad influence on Bob. She got him staying out late, going to clubs and doing drugs, and his running went to hell. Running was the only good thing that Bob had going for him and, deep down, he probably knew that. Then the fighting escalated, and Bob would show up at runs with claw marks and bruises all over him. The two of them eventually ended up in court. I was in the courtroom that day too, and they had to have two bailiffs, one assigned to Bad Bob and the other to Darla, just to keep those two from tearing each other apart.

"The Judge didn't like what he saw and, not wanting to have blood on his hands, he issued the restraining orders. He said it was the first *double* restraining order he'd ever had to impose, where not just one party but both parties were legally ordered to keep away from the other. He set the restraining distance at a half mile, and with Hoboken being a mile-square city, you could see how tough that made it for them. They both eventually moved away. Nobody knows where Bad Bob went. Some corner of hell, I suppose. Darla went back to Ireland I think, if it would have her."

"And Andy and Coco?" Britney asked. "Did they get married?"

"They surely did. They married in Our Lady of Grace church in Hoboken. June and Gen came in from California, Gloria from Pennsylvania, and all the HOHAs were there. Chuck was the best man. Coach and Biscuit came in from Boston too, and Biscuit was maid of honor. It was quite a day."

"What happened to them then?"

"They stayed in Hoboken until they finished school, so in love with each other that it just made you sick to watch them. Then they moved out to California to be near June and Gen. We heard from them for a while but eventually lost touch. I guess they were just meant to be with us for a while, but they played a big part in our lives. As Biscuit once said, 'Nothing's an accident, least of all our friends.'"

"And Coach and Biscuit?" Britney asked.

"They stayed in the Boston area, and both had successful careers, Coach as a high-school teacher and coach, and Biscuit as a marriage counselor. Coach coached cross-country and track, for both the boys' and the girls' teams. His teams won lots of championships, and he was respected throughout the Northeast. His dedication and devotion to the sport spanned six decades. Biscuit was successful in her own right. She had a busy therapy practice and published a couple of popular books on relationships, but when Biscuit was with Coach, she made herself smaller out of deference to him. She stepped into the shadow and gave him the spotlight.

Biscuit never asked me to choose between running and her, but if she had, I would have given up running. She was everything that running was to me anyway: poetry and perfection. When I was with her, I felt the peace that came after the best of runs. When I was with her, I felt at home. With her, I was always at the finish line.

"Did they have any children?"

"Yes. Thousands. Every kid that Coach had on his teams was part of their family. Even a lot of the kids that were in his computer science and math classes ended up on his cross-country and track teams. He made students into runners and runners into better students. If a kid was having a problem in school, he would tutor them, and Biscuit would help them with personal and family problems. And if a kid didn't have money for a pair of running shoes, Coach would buy them out of his own pocket, or he and Biscuit would organize some event to raise money for the teams. They were always having the kids over for barbecues and gatherings at the house. The kids just loved them.

"Coach still gets letters from some of them. 'Dear Coach,' they start. 'I still remember that hill workout you made us do in the rain,' or 'I thought yesterday about what you told us to do when things got tough.' He taught them lessons that would last a lifetime, and they wanted him to know it, and Coach was enough of a kid himself to remember to make it fun. He just spoke their language."

"What happened to them?" Britney asked. "Coach and Biscuit?"

"Well, Biscuit passed on a few years ago ...

> *She knew to come and find me, before I knew I had to be found.*
> *She knew we were in love, before I could admit it. And she knew we*
> *were leaving Hoboken, before I knew it was time to go. She always*
> *knew things first and prepared the way, so when she told me that she*
> *was dying, I didn't take it hard. I just thought, "OK then, I guess I'll*
> *be along shortly."*

... and Coach has Alzheimer's disease. Before Biscuit died, she asked me if I would take care of him for her."

With a dawning suspicion, Britney said, "Where is Coach now?"

Bill looked over at Jeanie, and Jeanie answered her friend. "That's Coach right there in the wheelchair."

Britney looked at the old man who had been sitting across from them during the entire story and hadn't said a word. She noted his size then, and his nerdy glasses. "That's Coach?" she said. "Oh my God!"

"Yes, this is Coach," Bill said. He reached over and patted Coach on the shoulder and then held the shoulder with a firm affection. "The one and only."

Britney looked questioningly at Bill. "But you've been calling him Diz, and Louise called him Mr. Dizzy when she brought him in."

"Dizzy is a nickname that Biscuit gave him after he retired," Bill said. "Before he got real sick, he was having dizzy spells. You know how Coach liked to give people names, so Biscuit thought she'd give him one too. It made him laugh and helped him through."

"He doesn't look the way I pictured him," Britney said. Bill had told his story as if it had happened yesterday. The passage of time suddenly struck her. "Oh my God," she repeated. "Can he hear us?"

"I think so, but I don't think he understands. He doesn't talk anymore, and he doesn't respond. Sometimes he mumbles in his sleep, but nobody can make it out. When Biscuit died, I got Coach in here to live with me. I talk to him every day, and when the weather's good, I take him around the neighborhood for some fresh air. We call it our run. I guess we do OK."

"You should see Coach's room," Jeanie said. "Uncle Bill put up pictures and trophies from Coach's teams."

"Jeanie," Bill said, "why don't you go get that picture of the HOHAs that I like the best. We'll show Britney the gang."

Jeanie went down the hall and soon returned with a large color photo in a wooden frame. The photo showed about forty HOHAs standing in three rows on the steps in Sinatra Park, all wearing their HOHAs T-shirts. Bill got up and sat down between the two girls so that he could describe the photo to Britney.

"This picture was taken on the occasion of the HOHAs' 10th anniversary, in May of 2000, just before Coach and Biscuit left for Boston."

"Oh my God," Britney said. "This is so totally twisted."

"When I look at an old photo," Bill said, "what surprises me is people's hair. The haircuts look wrong, and that's the clue that other things are different too, that it was a different time. But this was the gang then."

"Which one is Coach?" Britney asked.

"That's him there in the center with the glasses."

"Wow." Britney looked from the picture over to Coach and then back to the picture again.

"Look at that grin," Bill said. "Coach was a happy man that day."

Besides the day I met Biscuit, and the day we married, that day was the happiest day of my life. I was proud to have all the HOHAs, my team, around me.

"And is that Biscuit next to him?"

"Yes. That's her."

"She was cute. And look how small she was next to Coach."

"Small in size only," Bill said.

Jeanie pointed to a girl in the third row. "Guess who that is."

"She's gorgeous," Britney said. "That must be Coco."

"And that's Andy next to her," Jeanie said. "Look at that smile."

"And where are Bad Bob and Darla?"

"Darla's not in this picture," Bill said, "but that's Bob there."

"Look at that smirk on his face."

"Yes, that's Bad Bob, all right," Bill said. "And there's Edsel and Slow-Mo and Bulldog and Chuck."

"And where are you, Uncle Bill?"

"That's me, standing next to Coach, on the other side from Biscuit."

"You were his best friend, weren't you?"

"No. That job was Biscuit's, but Coach had lots of friends, and I was one of them. Coach and I were about the same speed: slow. So we ran a lot of miles together."

"You were handsome, Uncle Bill," Jeanie said. Then she added, "How come you never married?"

Just then, the cuckoo clock sounded four o'clock. "Didn't you girls say you had to leave at four? You'd better be getting along."

"You didn't answer my question, Uncle Bill."

"I don't want to talk about my life today. That's a whole other story. But what about you?" Bill said to Britney. "Did this story help you at all?"

"Yes it did. Thank you. It made me realize that I need more time to think, and I think I'm going to take a trip. I need to get away for a while."

"That's wise. It's good to take your time," Bill said. "And if you're going to take a trip, then I've got something for you." This time, Bill got up and went to Coach's room. When he returned, he had something in his hand.

"It's the Elf," Britney exclaimed. Then she laughed. "Coco was right. It is ugly, and it's all beat up."

"It is a bit the worse for wear," Bill admitted. "After I left Hoboken, I had to travel a lot on business, and Biscuit gave the Elf to me and told me to send them pictures of the Elf from different places. It was our joke, and a fun way to stay in touch. Then other HOHAs took it out. It's been all over the world over the years. We have one picture of the Elf in front of the Taj Mahal.

"If you go on a trip, Britney, I want you to take it with you. Biscuit said it brings good luck. You just need to send me and Dizzy a picture."

"I will, Uncle Bill."

There was a pause, and Jeanie said, "We should get going now, Uncle Bill."

"Thanks again for telling us the story," Britney said. "Jeanie was right. It's the best love story ever."

"You're welcome. You come again, and we'll tell you another story. I've got more, you know."

The girls both gave Bill and Coach a kiss, and then Bill walked them to the car.

When Bill returned, he straightened the blanket over Diz's knees and sat down again on the couch. "The girls liked our story, Diz," he said. "Let's rest a while now. I feel as if I lived it all over again."

67. The Pure Land

BUDDY AWOKE in a sweat, lifted the flap on his cardboard box and looked out into the eerie stillness of the Newark night. It was just before dawn, and Buddy had been awakened by a dream. He had dreamt that he was riding a horse hell-bent across the plains. He was riding toward the orange setting sun, riding to keep pace with it and be in the light forever. His faith was so strong that it burned on its own, as if it were a part of the sun itself, longing to be home. Buddy knew that a horse in a dream means dominance, and because he was riding it, and riding passionately, it meant that he would capture his desire.

Buddy got up and went over to Moses' old place. He'd kept Moses' refrigerator box just the way Moses had left it, except that he had Moses' trophies in there now. Andy had brought the ones that were left over from the tribute, because Coach had thought that Buddy should have them. In the box with the trophies had been a certificate, framed and with a golden seal and some Latin motto and everything, that Coach had made up specially for Buddy. It stated that Buddy was hereby declared an Honorary HOHA, on this day of our Lord such and such, and was thereby entitled to all rights and privileges thereof, and other such nonsense. The crazy bastard.

Buddy had kept the certificate though, and had placed it in with the trophies, along with a picture of Moses and some newspaper clippings about him. It was a shrine of sorts, Buddy knew, and whenever he was thinking of Moses and feeling low, he would go in there and sit, and he'd talk over the events of his day, pretending that Moses was there with him, listening and understanding. Sometimes he'd get talking along so good that he'd forget it was pretend, and he'd ask Moses a question. "What do you think, Mose'?"

The silence was always a shock, and that morning the silence made Buddy so sad that he feared his own sadness, the sinking feeling he had, and the bottomless depth of it. Then Buddy heard Moses' voice, like a hand reaching out to him. He heard Moses say something that he'd said before. He said, "When I get worried, I go out and walk it off and leave my troubles behind."

"Yes, Moses, yes," he heard himself say, "I'm listening. I'm listening." Buddy got out onto the street and walked. He didn't even know where he was going. He'd just walk, the way he was told. He was doing his best to shake off the sadness, and that was all he could do. Then he was standing at a street corner, waiting to cross. Life puts a cloud over you sometimes, he thought, and you wonder if you'll ever see the light. As he stood there, a patrol car passed slowly by in front of him. The officer riding shotgun was a young woman, and she turned and looked at him and held a steady smile on him as she passed by. It was a big smile, meant just for him, and it said, "I love you, and everything will be all right." That smile filled Buddy with warmth, and he stood there transfixed. He knew that he'd just seen an angel, and that her smile was a message from God. He felt a burden lifted from him, and took a deep breath. That one smile was all he needed to keep him going, and it reminded him of the last woman who'd ever smiled at him.

Buddy went back to the bridge and got his best clothes and took them to the Laundromat and washed them. Then he went over to the YMCA to take a shower and dress. He sure felt better, and thought he looked good, but he decided to go to the neighborhood pharmacy to apply the finishing touches. He snuck a squirt of hair gel on the Male Grooming aisle and slicked back his hair, but one of the clerks spotted him and started following him from aisle to aisle. Buddy wanted a spritz of cologne, and examined the prices on several bottles as if he were considering buying one, then took a free spritz from a fancy sampler bottle called "Obsession." The clerk was watching him suspiciously, and Buddy sniffed at the air, pretending not to like what he smelled. He put the bottle down with feigned disappointment, and then hurried from the store with the clerk on his heels.

He headed straight to the grocery store, and when he got there he looked through the front windows. He could see Geena working at her register. There was a gum-ball machine in front of the store, and Buddy bent down to see his reflection in it. He put some spit to his fingertips and slicked back his hair some more. Buddy now had the endearing appearance of someone who had taken his best shot at looking good and hadn't quite succeeded, but he was pleased with what he saw. He practiced his smile and saw his jack-o-lantern grin reflected in a pattern as wild as the gum balls themselves. Just then, Geena looked out the window and smiled back at him. One smile today had saved his life, he thought, and a second smile was telling him what to do with it. Then Geena brushed back her own hair, prettying herself for him, or at least trying to. When Buddy saw that signal, he waved to her and marched into the store with an equestrian confidence. He remembered Moses teasing him about Geena, and that lit him up with a smile of his own. He marched to the produce department, grabbed a pineapple, and headed for Geena's register, laughing out loud. "Yes, Moses, yes," he said. "I'm listening, and I'm gonna get me a juicy smooch and a Jell-O cuddle from my old girl." When he got to Geena's register, she looked at him as if they had barely been apart. She smiled again and said, "Where you been, baby?"

"I thought I'd died and gone to heaven," Dexter Wheeler would later say. "The last thing I remembered was riding my horse up onto that rise, and then it all went black. I had not only fallen into the ground, but my horse had kicked me in the head, and when I came to, all I could see was big puffy clouds in the sky and two angels with the prettiest faces I'd ever seen just a lookin' down at me.

"I heard the blonde angel say, 'He's easy on the eyes.' I kinda came to then, and when they seen that I wasn't dead, the blonde angel smiled and the red-headed angel turned up her nose and looked away."

Coach came up the stairs of the train station and into Hoboken carrying all that he owned in two worn carpet bags. It was late March, and he was met by a numbing wind and a glaring sun. He put the bags to the sidewalk, as if laying down a burden at the end of a road. Then he took two steps forward, as if all that he owned was to be left behind. He planted his hands in his overcoat pockets and looked north down the street and into his future. His eyes were clear and his gaze was steadfast, and down that street he envisioned as much of that future as any man can imagine or is allowed to see. Coach saw not what Hoboken had been—he didn't care—or even what it was—that mattered just as little—but only what he would make it to be.

When Howie told his parents that Coach was leaving Hoboken, Mr. and Mrs. Mooch had a box of chocolates and a glass of wine to celebrate. "Thank God Almighty," Mrs. Mooch said. "We're free at last." Howie had to admit that he felt some relief himself. It had been tough trying to live up to Coach's standards, but deep down Howie knew Coach was right in insisting that exercise and diet went hand in hand. And Howie was going to keep trying, he really was. And tomorrow he would start a new diet, he really would. He just needed a jelly donut now to hold him over until then, but it was better that none of the other HOHAs saw him coming out of Marie's Bakery. Howie stuck his head out the door and looked both ways down the street. The coast was clear. The bells jingled on the door as Howie left the shop, but no one had heard. Howie walked with relief down the street. At the corner, he saw The Eck, Slow-Mo, and Ballpoint out for a run. He waved to them, and they waved back. Then they laughed. Howie smiled back at them hesitantly, not sure why they were laughing, not realizing that his entire mouth was covered with powdered sugar.

On weekdays, Gen and June knew the time of day by the sounds from the schoolyard across the street. The beginning and end of the recesses and the lunch periods were marked with a schoolyard buzzer. The younger grades had their breaks first, followed by the older grades. Even they, mere children, were marked by age and taking their turn.

The children's chatter, the bouncing balls, and the teachers' whistles filled the house with a music that, year after year, through generations of children, didn't change. It was a rhythm and pulse as common as the Earth's orbit and as regular as the waxing and waning of the tides, but it was the music and motion of the dance that mesmerized Gen and June, and all those who listened and watched, and held them entranced.

The children rolled on and off the playground like waves to the shore. On warm days, the heat glimmered off the asphalt and the children appeared to be inside it, as if part of a mirage. There wasn't much to see, but it was hard to stop watching it. There were tiny variations, but even that was part of the pattern. On stormy days, seagulls soared over the playground, while on clear days the sun beat down, but that too repeated, year after year, and the children never got older, and the old people watching them never got younger.

Gen and June watched from the kitchen window across the street, through the chain-link fence of the schoolyard, continuing to watch their favorites long after Andy had left the school, and they looked forward now to the day when Andy and Coco's little boy would start in kindergarten there.

Andy and Coco, along with little Moses, had been by just the day before for a visit, and now the two old ladies had a new picture of Moses on their prayer board.

"Have you ever seen a cuter baby?" Gen said. "He's got Coco's eyes and Andy's hands."

"He's cute all right," June agreed. "And a fart in a mitten."

"Did you see the way Coco waited on Andy?" Gen said. "As if he were the king himself."

Gen was looking on the floor for the final piece of the puzzle they were making, and June was smiling, letting her look, all the while having that final piece tucked away safely in her lap.

"Oh yes," June said. "I saw."

"I can't find it anywhere, June," Gen said. "Maybe it's lost."

"Oh, here it is," June said finally, acting surprised. "It must have fallen into my lap."

"Oh, yeah," Gen said skeptically. "That must have been what happened."

Then June, with a mischievous smile, put the final piece of the puzzle in place.

Whenever their games of cards or Yahtzee were over, or their puzzle was done, Gen and June would continue watching the children, and would often fall asleep to the sound of the children playing, until the schoolyard buzzer would alarm one of them, who would poke the other and say, "Wake up."

"Wake up, Mr. Bill." Bill heard Louise's voice and the last note of the cuckoo. "It's five o'clock."

Bill appeared from the fog of his slumber. "Where are the girls?"

"Don't you remember? You saw them off an hour ago, and you and Mr. Dizzy dozed off and have been sleeping since."

"What time did you say it was?"

"It's five o'clock. I woke you because we'll be having dinner soon. You should wash up, and get Mr. Dizzy ready too."

Sometimes when Bill awoke, he would still be dreaming. This had frightened him at first, because he had no control over it, but now it didn't seem to matter, because his waking life seemed like a dream too.

"I didn't just dream that the girls were here?"

"No," Louise said, and then laughed. "You OK, Mr. Bill."

"Thank you, Louise."

"You were a perfect host. The girls loved your story, and they sure left here with more on their minds than they came in with."

68. In Another Lifetime

IF EACH DAY is a flower, the afternoon is full bloom. As the girls left Elysian Fields that afternoon, bathed in the rich light and succulent warmth of that day, they felt the satisfying fulfillment of that moment, and Britney felt swelling within herself the possibility of all that could be. There was no need for regret or excited anticipation, and the girls both reflected, in uncharacteristic silence, on the story they had heard.

The leather of the car seats was warm, and the plastic of the dashboard radiated waves of light and heat. Jeanie, with only a small smile to acknowledge the joke, placed the Elf next to her in the seat belt as they started off. The breeze from the open windows was warm but refreshing as they drove. They'd only gone a few blocks when Britney suddenly slammed on the brakes and broke their silence. "Oh my God!" she exclaimed.

The car jolted to a stop, and Jeanie grabbed at the Elf to keep it from flying to the floor. She looked over at Britney, who was staring straight ahead, lost in thought. "What happened?"

"I just can't believe the depth of his love," Britney said.

"I know," Jeanie agreed. "Andy was a dream."

"I don't mean Andy," Britney said.

"Then who do you mean?" Jeanie said. "Coach?"

"No."

Jeanie thought for a moment. "Buddy?"

"No," Britney said, slightly exasperated, "I'm talking about your uncle." There was a tone of wonder in her voice. "He's taking care of Coach."

"Oh yeah," Jeanie said, "he really loves Coach."

"No," Britney said, emphatically, "he really *likes* Coach, but he *loves* Biscuit."

"What are you talking about?"

"Don't you see? Didn't you see his eyes? Didn't you hear his voice whenever he talked about her? Why do you think your uncle never married? Why did he stay close to Coach and Biscuit all those years?" Britney waited, but Jeanie was silent. "He never married because he was in love with her, and he stayed close in case she ever needed him. He's been completely devoted to her. Now he's watching out for Coach, and that's helping her still, even after she's gone. It's all for her. All of it." Britney understood the meaning of her words only as she spoke them. "Oh my God!" she said. "That is true love."

Britney's words revealed to Jeanie one of those truths a person knows but doesn't see. Jeanie bit on her upper lip with a dawning concern. "I never thought about Uncle Bill like that."

"I didn't pick up on it either until you asked him why he'd never married, and he suddenly became speechless. That's not like your uncle. My mom says that people reveal most by what they don't say."

They were at an intersection, and now Britney made a sudden and determined u-turn, causing Jeanie to grab hold of the Elf again, and headed in the opposite direction. "What are you doing?" Jeanie said. "Where are you going?"

"Do you remember how Biscuit said that there are different kinds of love, just as there are different kinds of weather?"

"Yes."

"Well, I want my love to be like today, like a summer day, full of warmth and richness. Scott doesn't understand that, and he probably never will. I don't need time to think about anything. I'm taking his stuff back to him right now. I'm holding out for something better."

"You're going to dump him?" Jeanie said. "But he's so cute."

"So is a teddy bear. But can you count on it when things get tough?"

"Maybe he'll come around."

"Yes. Maybe," Britney said. "But that will be in another lifetime." Britney looked at Jeanie. "And it will definitely be with another girl."

"What are you going to say to him?"

"I don't know. That there's a fork in the road. That our separate destinies call. Something stupid like that." Britney sighed. "No. Why bother. He just doesn't get it. He doesn't love me, and he doesn't even know what love is. I'll just lay out the facts for him: that I'm going to a wedding and that he's going to be the first 's' in 'sucks.'"

69. Won't That Be Sweet!

AFTER DINNER, Bill wheeled Coach back to the day room, and then took the photo of the HOHAs from the coffee table and looked at it again. The haircuts *were* funny, he thought. It was another time. He looked at Coach in the photo and then again at Coach sitting in his wheelchair. Coach had lived an outdoor life, and his skin was weathered from the seasons. The wrinkles on his face were the map of his life. Coach had never been a great runner, but boy had he loved to run.

Bill then realized that Coach hadn't been outside all day. He got up and straightened the cover on Coach's lap. "Let's go out for a run," he said. "We'll go once around the block."

> *My brother was a fine runner, small and quick, and he got me loving the sport as a boy. He'd make a game of it. Our grandma had a sink in the garage next to her washer, and my brother would plug the drain and turn the tap on and see if he could run around the block before the sink overflowed.*

Bill wheeled Coach to the front door and called to Louise in the kitchen, "Louise, I'm taking Dizzy out for a run now. We'll be back shortly."

"Don't be too long, Mr. Bill," Louise said. "It will be dark soon."

My brother could do it, and he wanted me to try. "Go fast," he'd yell, "or Grandma will pitch a fit!"

"We'll stay out as long as we want," Bill whispered to Coach.

When they got outside, the evening sun was still warm. "This run will do me good, Diz," he said. "I'm tight from my PR this morning."

Never focus on yourself and how you feel—good or bad. Focus on the things you can control—your breathing, your form.

"I gave Jeanie that hill workout of yours, Diz, and she liked it." Bill laughed. "She's tight herself, though."

The hills make you work, but they make you strong. If you work the hills in practice, it will be second nature in a race. Use your arms. They're not just along for the ride. And lean forward slightly and shorten your stride. Keep working through the crest, and then work the downhill. You don't coast just because things are going easy. Constant effort. Through all the ups and all the downs, focus and hold your form.

"Tomorrow I may do that tough course, the one that winds up around the reservoir."

Every course will come at you as it will. Just take it as it comes, tough or easy, with a steady effort and a steadfast will.

They started down the block through the day's last light. The light filtered through the trees and cast intricate shadows on the sidewalk. It had travelled far to reach and warm them. Bill felt its final warmth now, and picked up the pace, the way Coach would like it.

"Run fast," my brother said to me, "and don't even think of stopping."

Nothing is more satisfying to an exhausted racer than the first sight of the finish line. When Bill came around the block, he could see Elysian Fields in the distance, and said with pleasure, "Dizzy, I can see it. I see the finish."

Don't run to the finish line; run through it. As if you're not tired, as if you own the course, as if you want even more.

Bill tightened his grip on the handles of the wheelchair and looked down at his hands. The veins and bones stood up under the skin like the gnarly roots of an old tree. Whose hands were they? Could they really be his? Bill put one of those hands on Coach's shoulder.

"Yesterday, it took us twenty minutes to get around the block," Bill said, "and today we'll set a new record." Bill laughed. "That will make two PRs in one day."

Totally twisted.

"Hold on, Dizzy. Here we go." Bill gave Coach's shoulder a squeeze and then picked up the pace some more. He kept his eyes focused on the finish line and the fading sun. "We'll be home soon," he said. "And oh, won't that be sweet!"

THE FINISH